PAPER Cuts

*To Andie
All The Best
L.J. Sealey*

L.J. SEALEY

PAPER CUTS

Copyright © 2022 L.J. Sealey

ISBN: 9798430128869

First edition published in 2022

The moral right of the author has been asserted

This is a work of fiction. Names, characters, businesses, places, events and incidents are either the products of the author's imagination or used in a fictitious manner. Any resemblance to actual persons, living or dead, business establishments or actual events is purely coincidental.

All rights reserved. Except for the use in any review, the reproduction or utilization of this work in whole or in part in any form by any electronic, mechanical or other means is forbidden without the express permission of the author. Your support of the author's rights is appreciated.

What People Are Saying About L.J. Sealey

"L.J. Sealey has such a knack for writing. She has delivered yet another page turner. Her writing captures just the right amount of suspense and intrigue and her descriptions leave you so sure of everything you can picture it perfectly in your mind." – Sarah's Book Corner Blog

Of her paranormal romance books:
"Highly recommended for anyone who loves paranormal romance — this is how it should ALWAYS be written." – Hazel Butler Author
"L.J. Sealey has fantastic story telling skills." – Reese's Reviews

ACKNOWLEDGEMENTS
For you mum..

AUTHOR'S NOTE:
This book contains sensitive content that may be triggering to some readers. Domestic abuse is talked about in a small part of the book, but does not play out on page.
Written in British English.

Prologue

There was blood everywhere.

Smudges up the wall in a number of places. A trailing hand print just above the handle of the door that led to the kitchen. The grey rug was ruined; too much on it to clean.

The mess? Anyone could be forgiven for thinking the place had been ransacked by a group of thugs.

He knew better.

There was only one explanation.

A fight had taken place in the dingy front room, and as he stood there, frozen, ignoring the broken ornaments, the chair that was on its side over by the window, and numerous other things that contributed to the carnage, the trembling began to travel through him, like a delayed shockwave taking over his entire body. Somehow, as his eyes tried to comprehend what they were seeing, he found himself walking towards the sofa where the woman lay, her body splayed out over the faux brown leather in a weirdly contorted way. Arm above her head, her face tilted up to the ceiling. Her body faced away from him while one leg had dropped off the edge, foot at a strange angle on the floor. Her eyes were vacant, staring lifelessly at what they'd paused on as she'd taken her final breath. Her neck was deep red where the hands that had no doubt ended her life had been. He was numb, like he wasn't standing there in his own body.

No thoughts. No feelings. It was the strangest thing.

It wasn't until his knees hit the floor that he realised he'd collapsed. And when he took her delicate, blood-soaked hand in his that was when he lost it. In a rush, he felt everything, his body, his heartbreak, inconceivable pain. It hit him all at once. He cried out in agony, his throat stinging from the sheer force of it, unable to comprehend what had happened. The woman he loved with everything he had. His world.

She was gone.

No longer living.

He'd lost her in the most brutal way and there wasn't a damn thing he could do to change that fact. No amount of pain and anguish would change anything. No matter how loud he cried with grief, he couldn't undo it. He couldn't rewind time. He couldn't bring her back.

She was gone.

His world had shattered into tiny little specs of dust. He was broken.

Still, the loss alone wouldn't be what changed his life and his future. The moment things went even more wrong for him, wasn't when, in his grief-stricken state, he saw the hilt of a knife sticking out from under the sofa. No. It was when, without thinking, he picked it up to see it drenched in her blood, holding it in his hand as he knelt over her, too shocked to move. The echoing voices didn't register straight away, and what followed happened so quickly it was hard to accept it as reality.

Rough hands grabbed his shoulders and dragged him up from the floor. He held onto her hand for as long as he could, knowing the moment he let go she would disappear forever; he knew he would never see her again.

The separation happened when his arms were wrenched around his back.

"No!" he heard himself cry. "Let me stay with her."

Something cold and hard slammed around his wrists, and then words were said beside his ear.

"You have the right to remain silent..."

He didn't hear them. Not really. It was hard to hear anything above the rage that was now coursing through his blood.

Vaguely aware of being led from the room, images of the past shot through his mind like someone was hitting the forward control on a slide projector, fast. The shouting, the backhands, the bruises, all of which had gotten more frequent, the violence intensifying, leading up to this moment.

His world had ended the moment he'd walked into the room he was being led from in cuffs. Grabbing hold of the inferno raging through him with both hands, he knew there was only one reason for living now; the only thing that would get him through.

He'd make damn sure that bastard paid for what he'd done.

Chapter One

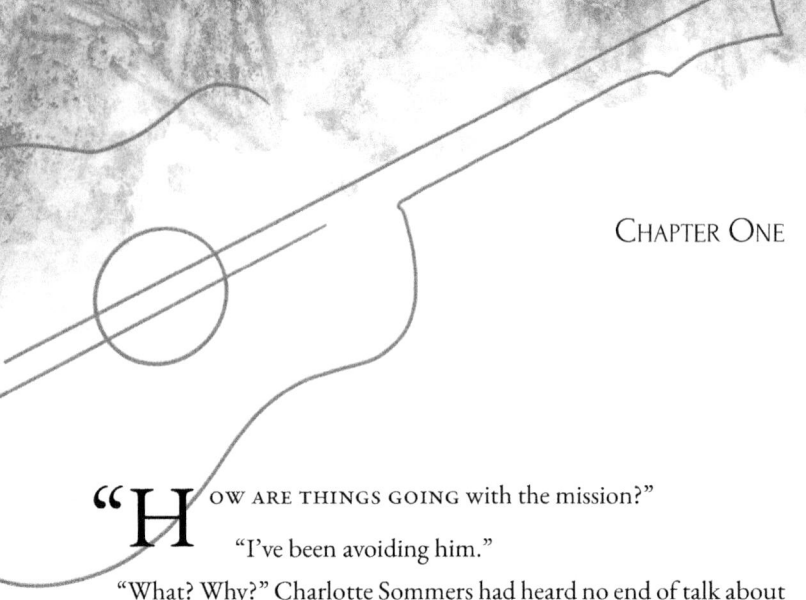

"How are things going with the mission?"

"I've been avoiding him."

"What? Why?" Charlotte Sommers had heard no end of talk about Nathan from her best friend over the last few weeks. She'd chased and chased the guy, not that he'd ever known it because the woman had been too shy to actually chase the guy so she'd mostly done it from afar, until eventually Charlie had to make an intervention and introduce them in a casual way in the canteen at uni. At first Nathan had looked at Charlie stupid, and rightly so seeing as she'd never spoken to him before, and had accosted him on his way from his lunch break. Since the introduction, Cara and Nathan had said hi to each other in passing, and had even had a short conversation, which Charlie was sure she knew every word of by now. "I thought you were making progress."

"Maybe because I. . ." When Cara paused, Charlie thought they'd been disconnected and glanced at her phone screen. "I'm coming now," she heard her friend say when she put it back to her ear. It was distant, as though Cara had pulled the phone away from her mouth to talk to someone else.

Charlie pressed. "Because what?"

Cara's volume had dropped to almost a whisper when she started talking again. "I practically threw myself at him at Full Circle on Friday night. That's because." Back to a normal level again. "I'm aborting the mission for a little bit. I'm also giving up drinking. And clubbing. And also showing my face in public."

When Charlie laughed out loud at her best friend, the four other people waiting in line for orders at Hot Wok noodle bar turned to look. Her cheeks heated as she gave them a tight lipped smile before lowering her voice. "Sure you are, Car. I'll give it until Thursday at the latest."

"Well I'll get to prove you wrong Thursday night at open mic night. I'll be on soft drinks only. You wait."

At that Charlie winced but her lack of response alerted Cara to the impending refusal. "No way," her best friend said, her voice straining like she was fighting to keep her volume down. Charlie glanced at the clock above the counter in the takeaway. Cara would be at one of her evening classes. "Don't you dare. You're not about to tell me you're not coming are you?"

"Number sixty five!" the guy behind the counter called out.

Charlie lifted her hand for her order and made her way to the counter. "Yep. I am about to tell you exactly that. And besides, you just said you weren't showing your face in public again."

"Char! You know I'm not serious about that. This will be the third week in a row."

"I know. I'm sorry. It's just... Randall is kicking my arse with this dissertation. He's got all of us on a tight schedule with it." The disappointed sigh her friend let out made Charlie's stomach tighten. For the last few weeks she'd barely left her apartment outside of classes, and felt guilty about letting Cara down again. Her excuses were genuine though. She really did have to finish her work by the end of the week. The end of term was almost in sight. Soon she would have finished year two of her studies in psychology. She just needed to get through a few more nights of study and then she'd be able to breathe a little.

At least until next week. "I'm almost done. I promise I'll be at the next one."

"I'm holding you to it, Char. Don't let me down again. Shit! Gotta go. Harper's clocked me. Text you later."

Smiling, Charlie knew her friend was about to get a hard time from her lecturer. Harper was one of the worst for discipline. So Cara kept telling her.

Armed with her meal for one, she headed down the street in the direction of the train station, readying herself for yet another evening in front of her laptop. Three stops later and she hurried from the train, scooped up in the crowd as people from all walks of life rushed up the steps to street level, as if they were all late for dinner, most of them heading home. It was still pretty busy on public transport at six p.m. in Hertfordshire. Although she hated the busy trains and stations, Charlie preferred going home at this time. She hated having evening classes because she didn't drive so the train was her only affordable form of transport. Always looking over her shoulder, she felt unnerved when she travelled home later in the evening, particularly in the winter months when it was dark for her whole journey.

Out on the street, the sun was now disappearing behind the clouds and there was a damp feel of condensation in the air as the temperature dropped—British springtime at its best. Cold in the mornings so you put more layers on, only to lose them one by one over the course of the day, and then need them again later on. She'd left her jacket in her locker back at uni. Now she was regretting it.

Before she knew it, she was home, rounding the corner into her street, heading to the last building tucked away in the corner where her first-floor flat was. Crossing the street, she approached the main door to the building and frowned, not at the motorbike she'd seen parked out the front plenty of times, but at the pair of navy overall-covered legs that were twisted around the back wheel. She struggled to get a look at the guy who was working on the bike as she walked past, trying not to look too obvious. His head was nowhere in sight, but she did hear a sharp curse before the clink of something metal hit the concrete.

Unlocking the door, she looked over her shoulder once more just as he sat up, but still all she saw was the top of his head. At least now she knew her new neighbour's hair was dark brown before walking inside. That's all she did know about him since he'd moved in a couple of months ago. Up two flights of stairs and along the hall, Charlie desperately wished she lived at number four instead of all the way to the end at number six. Her feet were throbbing, and she couldn't wait to get in a hot bath.

Half an hour later, Charlie was submerged in deep, hot water covered with a mountain of bubbles listening to Jason Mraz on her portable speaker. It was well deserved after the tough day—no, tough fortnight—she'd had. At least at this point in her studies she felt good about herself for a change. It felt like all her hard work was beginning to pay off. It was good to feel confident for a change.

Her eyes were closed and she was drifting in and out of consciousness, lulled by the soft music and the relaxing scent of her rose and peony bath water when over by the sink her phone rang.

Ignore it, she told herself, wanting to stay put for a little while longer. The water was still a nice temperature and it was the first time in weeks she'd managed to clear her mind. Whoever it was could leave a message or call back if it was important. When it eventually stopped, she sunk down a little further, getting back into the zen-like state where she planned on staying for at least another thirty minutes.

Then it rang for a second time.

Shit.

That meant someone really did want to get hold of her. Had to be. She was never this popular. Cara maybe? Calling to beg her to go out for a drink because she'd already fallen off the teetotal wagon. Or maybe it was her mum, which meant she shouldn't really ignore it any longer. Perhaps there was something wrong back home.

Admitting defeat, Charlie got out of the bath, the cold air hitting her wet skin like she'd stepped outside, her teeth almost rattling. That bloody boiler. She needed to call the landlord about the crappy thing. It kept switching off at random times. Grabbing a towel, she wrapped it around her body, tucking the corner in under her armpit, and reached for her phone. When the screen lit up she froze. What the hell? She swiped to unlock the phone, barely trusting her eyes, and noticed her hands were trembling which this time, wasn't from the cold air in the room.

Dale.

Why had he called her? Twice?

Holding her breath she pressed the little *i* icon next to his number, scrolled down the page and hit *block contact* as quickly as her trembling fingers would allow.

Pacing the small, damp room, Charlie tried with everything she had to keep her mind from going back to the past she'd long moved on from. After he'd done such a good job of taking over her mind, it had been hard to leave Dale behind even though she'd travelled almost two hundred miles away from him. Years it had taken her to stop having nightmares about the man she'd almost married when she was twenty two years old. Charlie thought it was done; the darkness of her past had slowly become faint shadows and eventually they'd left her—mostly.

Until now.

With just two missed calls, every memory, every feeling… it all came back, hitting her unexpectedly with the force of a hurricane.

Could it be a coincidence? What if someone else now had his phone? Perhaps he'd sold it to someone and she'd received a wrong number call. The moment she thought it she knew it was wishful thinking. It was him without a doubt. Her gut was telling her as much.

Why the hell was her ex, the reason she'd left Warrington for good almost two and a half years ago, trying to get in touch with her now?

Chapter Two

Running around like a blue-arse fly was doing nothing for Charlie's pre-exam nerves as she threw everything she needed into her uni bag. Her phone alarm just had to pick today to throw a wobbly and now she was leaving fifteen minutes late. Throwing the silk scarf her mum had given her as a going-away present around her neck, she grabbed her coat off the hook in the hall and did a one-eighty by the front door of her flat, scanning every surface to make sure there was nothing else she needed. Then she took a moment to gather her breath, and out she went into the hallway, pulling her front door closed behind her—

There he was.

The new guy who had moved into the flat down the hall was coming out of his door. He closed it behind him and walked away in the same direction she was just about to head, a leather jacket under his arm and a motorbike helmet in his hand. Going into work, no doubt. It was a guess of course. Charlie had never spoken to the guy; she'd never actually seen him either. Not properly anyway. Yesterday was the first time she'd seen any part of him that wasn't hidden under clothing. Thanks to the navy blue hoodie he always wore, she had no idea what he looked like under the hood that was always pulled over his head while he kept his face down. But he was tall and his hoodie was tight enough to see that his shoulders were wide. He looked like he kept himself in shape. Thrown off by seeing him, Charlie paused for a moment, pretending she was looking for something in her bag as she let the stranger get a little further ahead.

And then he did something she hadn't seen him do before: he slowed a little and lifted his head for a second, as though he'd sensed she was behind him. Then it was back to his regularly scheduled programming, head lowering again as he disappeared through the door that led to the stairwell.

Now Charlie sped up. She was inappropriately desperate to get a glimpse of the guy's face. Well, he was her neighbour. Didn't she have a right to know who she lived by? His evasive behaviour only piqued her curiosity all the more. Not to the point of obsession though. She wasn't *that* kind of woman. At least that's what she tried to convince herself as she rushed towards the door to the stairs.

A door opened to her left and she squeezed her eyes shut, as if that was how she engaged her super power of invisibility. If only. As expected, Mrs. Hughes from number four called out her name.

"Oh, Charlotte. You're up and out early today."

Bloody hell. Charlie being Charlie, she was too polite not to stop and say hello to the cheerful old lady with the light blue plastic curlers in her hair.

"Hi, Mrs. Hughes. I have an exam this morning. Sorry, I can't stop. I—"

"I have some apples from my daughter's garden for you. Hold on and I'll get them."

The small lady with the grey hair and oversized glasses disappeared back inside before Charlie could protest. *Shit.*

Pulling out her phone from the front zip in her bag, she scrolled through to the Uber app, annoyed with herself for being so polite.

Only, it wasn't so much from having to get alternative transport into uni—*he'd* evaded her again.

Charlie couldn't help wondering why the guy was so shifty. Why he always had that hood up. Maybe he was just really shy. Or maybe his face was badly scarred or something. Suddenly the Phantom popped into her head with his white mask. She shook it out just as quickly. Her name wasn't Cara. This was her friend's kind of thinking; always the one with the wild imagination.

Maybe it was because she'd thought of nothing else other than statistics and data for so long, that she'd become so intent on discovering the identity of the man down the hall. Maybe she just needed to get out more. *Whatever*. As Charlie stood waiting for Mrs. Hughes, she knew she wasn't going to rest until she'd seen his face.

Mission on.

"How much longer do I have to see that look on your face for?"

Cara paused in the motion of taking a drink from her glass. "What look?"

"You know damn well what look. I can easily walk out that door and get a taxi home."

"Okay, okay. I'll stop now." The smug smile on her friend's face suggested otherwise. "Just as soon as you thank me for forcing your hand."

Had the choice really been Charlie's? The nine missed calls and four answer-phone messages begging her to go out had finally driven her mad to the point of agreeing just so she could give her phone's battery a rest.

So now they were sitting at a tall table to the side of the stage at The Gifted Crow, a pub just off campus that she didn't go to all that often, which was crazy really; she'd always liked the warm, friendly atmosphere of the contemporary, gastro-style pub. She loved the decor mostly. In the main part of the pub, the wood and brick was homely and inviting. Where they were now—in the large open room at the back that had the stage for the performers—was more music oriented. The décor was mostly grey and white with rustic wooden beams across the black ceiling. She loved the black and white images of British recording artists that covered the walls in large black frames. Their open mic nights on a Thursday night were legendary. There were even some rumours that a few famous artists had started their careers off playing here.

Truth was, it was probably the most relaxed Charlie had felt in months, so she stepped up, giving her friend what she wanted. "Fine. I'm glad you *forced* me to come out tonight."

Cara nudged her arm. "See. It wasn't hard was it?"

Charlie rolled her eyes. The woman was relentless when she wanted to be, but it was one of the reasons why they were such good friends. Their personalities were complete opposites of each other. Cara, with her wild, black curly hair and brown skin that always seemed to glow, was a firework in a dark, dreary alleyway—an explosion of personality and colour that lit up the space around her. Whereas Charlie was happy to melt into the shadows to watch from afar, happy for no one to notice her. The perfect pairing, even though, after they'd first met, it had taken a little time for Charlie to get used to the woman and her persistent ways. She had a feeling her first year at uni would have been far different had Cara not claimed her as a best friend pretty much from the off.

And she knew about Charlie's past—her reason for leaving Warrington.

Why then, had Charlie not mentioned the missed call from Dale?

"So, the new guy. Have you seen him yet?"

It had been a regular topic of interest since Charlie had mentioned he'd moved in down the hall. But she had as much information for Cara as she'd had the last time her friend had asked. "I know he has brown hair. Other than that, still only the back of him."

Cara's eyebrow rose. "And?"

"And what?"

"How does he look from the back? Did you check out his arse?"

"Cara! No. For all we know he's an old man." Not likely with those wide shoulders.

Her friend laughed. "I'd have still looked."

"Well, I'm not you." Then Charlie smiled. "I'm pretty sure he isn't an old man though. The way he holds himself, the way he walks, he looks strong."

Leaning in, Cara rested her chin on her upturned hand. "I'm listening."

"Looks like he maybe works out. I don't know. I can just tell he isn't an oldie. But I think maybe he's lying low or something."

Her friend's perfectly shaped eyebrows dipped. "Yeah. Actually, you're probably best not knowing, Char. He could be an ex con. Or maybe some kind of weirdo or psycho." Charlie could see the cogs turning as her friend took a sip of her drink, then her brown eyes widened. "What if he's running from the police? He could be hiding some dark secret.

"Cara!"

"I'm just saying if he's that shifty, best staying away."

And now she was thinking the same thing. "Thanks a lot Cara. You certainly know how to ruin—"

The audience ignited into whistles and applause, cutting her off as the MC, aka the manager of the pub, took to the stage and welcomed everyone as he always liked to do. He introduced the first act, a trio: drummer, singer guitarist, and bassist. It wasn't Charlie's kind of music, but the singer had a pleasant voice so they settled back, no point in trying to talk over the volume, enjoying the folk style songs.

A little later, during the solo male singer with an acoustic, Charlie was hiding her yawns. At least she thought she was.

"Hey! Looks like someone could do with another drink," Cara said as she slid off her stool.

"No. I'm fine. It's the drink that's making me sleepy." And the fact she wasn't sleeping properly because of her stupid ex.

"What? I can't hear you." Pointing to her ear, Cara walked away, and ten minutes later was back with another round, raspberry cider for Charlie and vodka and coke for herself, accompanied by a tray of shots.

"No, Cara. I am not doing shots with you." She looked at the tray. There were eight. "Seriously? Were you afraid they were going to sell out or something? I'll be on my arse drinking that lot."

"Only two are for you." And just as she said it, Jason and Selena joined them, bringing two more stools over.

"Hi!" Selena said as she sat down opposite Cara. Jas's recent girlfriend was all smiles and politeness with her neat chin-length, blonde bob, and her skinny jeans and blazer. It was a surprise because Jas usually went for the loud, skirts-up-to-their-arses, I-love-myself-far-too-much kind of women. His dark hair and good looks always seemed to attract dolly birds with no personalities. Cara and Jas were already friends when Charlie met them. And the three of them were now pretty close. This was the first time she'd seen Jas in an actual relationship, and even though Charlie barely knew Selena she liked her, and was glad he'd finally got his head out of his arse and tried staying for once.

"Hey Char," he said as he sat down and passed the shots around, two each, one was green and the other. . . well, it didn't look very inviting. That was the one Jas held up. "This one first. Right. After three." He held up his little glass.

"Wait. What is it?" Charlie had played this guessing game before and the outcome was never good. She eyed the cloudy red liquid suspiciously.

"Why spoil the fun?" he said with a cheeky smile, and then started his countdown. "One. . ."

Ah well. Charlie threw hers back along with everyone else. Then she coughed. And coughed again. "Shit. . . Jas!" Reaching for her cider, she chugged some down to calm the fire on her tongue and in the back of her throat. Thankfully, she wasn't the only one coughing. They all did, but she was definitely coming off the worst.

"Shit. I asked for the milder version," Jas said, laughing and coughing at the same time.

Why did she do it? She knew never to trust him.

Cara was the first to get over the hit. "Eew, Jas. What the hell was in that?"

"It was a Hot Shot: Tequila and Tabasco with a squeeze of lime. It was supposed to be the mild one." He laughed again. "Lucky I chose that over the hot."

"Yeah, thanks, Jas." Cara was still panting a little. "We're all indebted to you for only setting our tongues half on fire."

The next band started up and Cara soon forgot her fiery mouth when she started to wolf whistle as loud as she could. The band was pretty rocky and Charlie didn't know how much longer she could stay—too loud for her delicate ears. Her studies were so hard she wasn't used to the nights out anymore.

They did the same with the next shot, only this time it was quite pleasant tasting, like watermelon with a hint of lime. It was that one that started to make Charlie's head tingle a little.

"How'd your exam go this morning?" Jas asked, leaning in so he could talk by her ear. Soon after they'd become friends, Charlie had nearly had a thing with Jason. They'd kissed once, but she hadn't felt right about it. She couldn't deny he was boyfriend material, just not for her. Charlie liked his friendship too much and they'd talked and agreed to keep things as they were. Ever since then he acted more like a protective brother.

"Okay, I think. It was harder than I thought it would be, but I think I did enough."

"I know you did enough, Char. No one has put more into this second year than you."

She smiled. "Thanks." That's because she'd needed the distraction more this year for some reason. Cara had called her a hermit God knows how many times because all she did was study. And Charlie did feel bad for not being as present as she should have been and missing the parties and festivals.

A vibration on her lap alerted her to her phone ringing. She reached into her small handbag and when she saw the time and the unknown number, she frowned. Who would be calling her at eleven at night?

"You okay?"

Glancing up at Jas, his brown eyes full of concern, she slid down from her stool. "Yeah," waving her phone, "just going to answer this."

Heading through the crowd, by the time she got outside the call had stopped. Looking at the number, she was contemplating calling back when it started to ring again. This time she answered straight away. "Hello?"

The line was quiet for a minute and then...

"Charlie?"

The hand shaking was so instant she almost dropped the phone. But somehow Charlie managed to keep hold of it and hang up as quickly as she could. There was no mistaking the voice on the other end. She hadn't heard it for a long time and it still made her feel the same as it always did, regressing her back to a time she'd tried to forget. Heart racing, she was shaking inside. What the hell? He'd called on another number. There was a heavy dread in the pit of her stomach and she quickly did the same thing as last time, blocking the number. Staring down at the screen, Charlie felt instant panic rising. A cold sweat washed over her entire body.

Shit.

Breathe, Char.

But she couldn't. No matter how hard she tried, the panic was going nowhere. Why was this happening now? Finally, she'd started to move on—no longer looking over her shoulder, or worried every time there was a knock on her flat door.

"Are you okay, Miss?"

One of the doormen came into view and she straightened, feigning a smile. "Uh, yes I'm fine. Thanks." Putting her phone back in her bag, she rushed back inside. The night was well and truly over for her now. Glancing over her shoulder, she got a creeping sensation like icy fingers crawling up her spine. God, she was right back where she'd started: imagining him watching her from the shadows, thinking he'd followed her hundreds of miles.

Struggling to hold it together through the crush of bodies that had now filled every inch of the pub, the music getting louder the closer she got to the stage, the sensory overload almost taking her to her knees, Charlie finally made it to the table where her friends were enjoying the band with more drinks in front of them. Cara was wolf whistling again, and when Charlie pulled on her arm she turned around, the smile instantly disappearing from her face.

Clearly, Charlie hadn't done very well pulling herself together in the time it took to return to them.

"What's wrong?" Nothing ever got past her.

Her tone prompted Jas and Selina to look over too.

Taking a breath, she did her best to right the mood. "Oh, nothing. Was just going to tell you I'm leaving. I've got a headache and I really need my bed."

"Oh no, Char. You sure?" The fact that Cara didn't press confirmed her friend's sixth sense had kicked in. She knew there was something wrong, Charlie could see it in her eyes, but wouldn't say in front of the others. "How are you getting home?"

"I'll get a taxi. I'm going to order it and wait outside."

Jas leaned in and said something in Selina's ear and his girlfriend nodded. "I'll drop you back."

"Oh no, Jas. You stay and enjoy the bands. I'm really okay getting an Uber. Besides, are you even okay to drive?"

He picked up his glass. "I'm on coke now. Only had one and a shot. And I know you're capable of getting a taxi, but you don't need to." Like he'd made her mind up for her, Jas got up and put his jacket on. "It'll save you waiting and I don't charge. Why argue?"

"You sure?" She looked over at Selena who gave her a sweet smile.

"We have plenty of drinks," she said.

When Charlie looked at Cara, she had that I'll-phone-you-when-I-get-home-so-you-can-tell-me-exactly-what's-going-on look on her face. She gave her friend a quick hug, knowing it was a conversation she could no longer avoid. "See you tomorrow," she said, trying to put her off.

"Speak to you in a bit."

No point in arguing; she was going to call anyway. Nodding, Charlie left as quickly as she could, relieved that she was getting a lift with Jas and not having to look over her shoulder while she waited for a taxi. Also on the plus side, Jas wouldn't pry.

Thankful to be back, after Jas had waited for her to get safely in the building, Charlie stood at the bottom of the stairs while she tried to catch her breath. This was ridiculous. She'd been away from her hometown for two and half years, had settled in Hatfield quite quickly and felt comfortable. How could *he* have this effect on her from so far away and after all this time? Not only was Charlie all discombobulated at the sudden disruption of the normal life she'd finally started to live, but she was also angry at herself for letting him rattle her. She was supposed to be made of sterner stuff now. It seemed all that *what doesn't kill you* crap was just that: crap, because apparently it hadn't made her stronger. She only felt that way because she'd run away from the threat instead of facing it head on.

There had been no other choice though.

Marching up the stairs to her floor, Charlie was still shaking as she fumbled for her keys. She'd also drunk more than she'd planned, which wasn't helping her nerves. Perhaps she'll feel differently in the morning without the fuzzy head. She pushed through the door to her floor and headed down the hall. It took her a moment to realise she could hear music coming from New Guy's flat and she slowed her steps as she approached. It was acoustic music, softly played, chilled, accompanying a low, rich singing voice. She'd never heard the song before, but it wasn't as if she listened to much music nowadays. All she did was study, and music had always been a distraction when she was trying to concentrate so she never put any on.

That song, though, sultry and yet melancholy—the voice, rich and husky—something about it resonated deep within her. Mesmerised, Charlie wanted to pitch-up right there on the floor outside the man's door and just listen.

But no... Her feet started moving when she realised she was acting weird outside someone else's flat. Imagine if New Guy opened the door and there she stood in some dreamy haze.

It was the shots. She knew it was a mistake drinking them after the bottles of cider. She wasn't used to it at all anymore.

Time for bed. If she could get to sleep, that is. Dale was firmly in the forefront of her mind and she knew it was going to disrupt the sleep she needed. When she got into her flat, she put the chain on the door and left the lamp on in the hall before heading straight to bed, reassuring herself he couldn't get to her anymore. She was away from it all. Her life was much better now.

It would all feel better in the morning.

Chapter Three

Every step Charlie took down the stairs pounded through her head, the echoes of her shoes slapping the linoleum driving her insane. She hadn't even had that much to drink last night and yet she was rocking a bloody hangover. Great. She'd definitely turned into a lightweight. Honestly, a few ciders and a couple of shots—even that god-awful one that Jas had made her drink—was no reason to feel the way she did this morning. Her head definitely disagreed. When she got to the foyer downstairs, it was the first time she'd looked outside and it was pissing it down. Good old British weather. There was nothing like getting drenched before she'd even started her day.

Stepping up to the rows of metal boxes that were next to the main entrance door, Charlie opened her mailbox with the key and there were three letters inside. She flicked through them. Mobile phone bill, one from the faculty department, and... She paused at the third. It was for flat four and addressed to a Mr. J. Sure. The postman must have put it in her box by mistake. Holding it, Charlie stared at it, finding herself in a bit of a quandary. It was easy enough to pop it in his box, after all, it was the one right below hers, but why would she miss an opportunity when it presented itself?

Making her way back upstairs, Charlie swallowed down the nerves that were taking hold. Was she finally going to meet her neighbour? There was excitement just resting beyond. Then the conversation she'd had with Cara made her pause at the door to her floor. What if he was a weirdo or psycho? Or what if he was just an asshole? Well, then at least she would know and could get on with her life instead of acting like a spy in a James Bond movie.

Having not had much of a life at all since she'd started university, she was losing the plot, gripping onto some crazy idea that she needed to know who some guy was because it was the only interesting thing to happen in her life in years.

God, she was sad.

And this obsession just highlighted how much so.

Locking away the total embarrassment she felt at her life so she could address it later, Charlie pushed through the door and strode down the hall to the first door on her left, finding herself, for the second time, staring at the tarnished brass number five that was eye level on the stranger's flat door.

About to knock, Charlie paused with her fist in the air when she heard a muted voice talking on the other side of the door.

"You didn't turn up yesterday. What's the excuse this time?"

Holding her breath, she tried not to listen, but couldn't blank his voice out enough. It was deep with a little husk, and he sounded on edge. Maybe she should walk away. Come back later.

"Well what choice do I have? If you don't let me see him then—"

A pause.

"No. No, I'm not." He'd lowered his voice and now she could only just hear him. He sounded strange, like he was straining to keep his composure. *"I'm sorry. I didn't mean it to sound that way. I'm just. . . Wednesday next week. Yeah. See you then."*

It went quiet and Charlie looked down at the letter as she was hit with a sudden onset of shame at her school-girl behaviour. Cursing herself for losing the nerve, she bent down and slid it under his door and left as quickly as she could. It looked like the universe was trying to tell her something. Maybe it was even a warning. But these things only piqued her interest even more. The universe should know that too.

Like she said, she was losing her shit.

Back downstairs, Charlie replayed his voice in her mind, deep, mainly smooth with a slight gravel, trying to imagine what he might look like.

Who are you J. Sure?

She'd find out at some point. That was for sure.

Though, whether that was a mistake or not, she'd know soon enough.

Chapter Four

Cursing as he glanced at the clock on the table in the hall, Jake threw on the leather jacket over his navy hoodie. He was leaving for work later than planned this morning, but as long as his bike started ok, he should still get in early so he could do a bit of maintenance on the engine before he was on the clock. It was ambitious though. The weather was still pretty cold for the time of year and was wreaking havoc on his Triumph bobber's engine. It was old, it caused him more hassle than anything at the moment, but the bike was the only thing he'd enjoyed for a long time. Grabbing his backpack, Jake put his tub of beef sandwiches inside along with his phone, checking the wireless headphones were still in there. He chucked it over his shoulder, grabbed his helmet and gloves, and left.

Thankfully, after some coughing and spluttering on startup, he got to the garage where he worked without a hitch, pulling into his usual parking spot next to the office cabin that also doubled as the break room. Because he was early, he had time to make a coffee, a rare occurrence, before he looked at his bike. Jake was barely on time most mornings so the look on Sam's face when he walked through the cabin door was expected. His eyebrows almost met his thinning hairline.

"You wet the bed or somethin'?"

Jake gave his boss a smile as he walked over to the vending machine. The coffee tasted like piss, but he put extra sugar in and welcomed the caffeine hit regardless. He needed it more that morning, hoping it would stave off his tired, stuffy head.

"So what brings you in so early," Sam asked, looking down at his paperwork with his glasses at the end of his nose. "Turned over a new leaf finally?"

"I need to change the plugs on the bike; easier to do it here."

"Well, as soon as you're done you might as well get started on this MOT. Whatever work needs doing, Holland needs it ready by tomorrow."

Jake reached over and took the job slip that Sam was holding out to him. "Sure."

"Then there's an Audi A4 that needs new brake pads all around."

With Sam looking at him as if he had something else to say, Jake took another sip of coffee then poured the rest down the sink, deciding the shit wasn't worth the small talk. "Best get to it then." He gave the old guy a nod as he headed out.

"Make sure you put a note in for those plugs."

"Will do."

"Oh, and Jake?"

Yep. He knew something was coming. Jake stopped in the doorway. "Yeah?"

"I got sidetracked yesterday and forgot to mention it, but a man phoned here for you around four. You were in the pit struggling with that exhaust so I figured I'd take a message."

Jake turned to Sam, his body stiff. "What did he say?"

"Not much. Asked if a Jake Sure worked here, and when I asked who was calling, the ignorant bastard just hung up."

Inhaling the strange feeling that lit off in his chest, Jake gave a shrug, masking his unease. "I'm sure whoever it was will call back if it's important."

Sam nodded but his eyes narrowed. "Everything okay, Jake?"

"Shouldn't it be?"

In the silence that followed, he could see the cogs turning in Sam's eyes. There had always been some kind of weird tension between them. His boss was one of the few people who knew where he'd come from. The guy had given him a chance when he'd taken him on and Jake would always appreciate that. Even so, Jake suspected the guy didn't like how he kept himself to himself. Wasn't like he gave a shit. Jake had no reason to be anything other than a loner. It was easier that way.

"Better get these plugs done before I run out of time. If he calls back let me know."

Closing the office door behind him, Jake's mind went into overdrive, searching for a reason someone might call him at work. He didn't know anyone around the area besides a few people and they were only a need-to-know situation. Since moving to Hatfield he'd kept his head low. When you pretty much hated your own company why would you force it on anyone else? Only three people had his number, and one was his boss.

It was necessary to keep his contacts small. No one else needed to know about his past and that's the way he needed it to stay.

Someone asking for him by name at his work place was a huge worry. The only possibility was impossible. Nonetheless, Jake couldn't shake the damming ache in the pit of his stomach.

It couldn't be *him*. He wouldn't have the nerve. After Jake had spent the best part of a year searching for that arsehole, it had been pretty clear the waster had either fled the country, or with a bit of luck, met a nasty and fitting end where no one would ever find his rotting corpse.

Wishful thinking.

Jake couldn't allow his mind to go there. Not after everything that had happened. After months of dead ends and false leads, travelling around the country hoping that one day his wish would come true, Jake had started to think he should give up on the revenge he'd never get to take. He hadn't worked this hard to move on just to let that bastard back in his head.

Even so, there was always something telling Jake that sooner or later the little bit of normality he'd finally found was going to be disrupted.

Part of him wanted it to be. After all he'd been through, the hatred for that man still simmered under the surface, and if Jake was presented with a chance to get to him, he'd take it.

In a heartbeat.

Chapter Five

IT HAD DEFINITELY BEEN a day.

Charlie'd had about enough by the time she left her last class. After running in the rain to the station, the downpour had stopped the moment she got on the train—obviously. Typical now she was soaked right through to her underwear again. To top it all off, the train was packed. Nowhere to sit and she was wedged up against a rather large man with questionable hygiene. So she hung on to the overhead strap and tried to zone everything and everyone out for the two stops before hers.

Over the past week Charlie had done nothing but study hard, to the point where she couldn't think of anything else. It was draining. Her final exams were so close. At least she was heading down the home straight; it wouldn't be too much longer until she could relax and put this whole year behind her. Plus she'd promised Cara as soon as term was over that they'd go away for a few days to celebrate; preferably somewhere away from the city and all things to do with human behaviour or cognitive anything. Thank God she had that to look forward to after handing in her dissertation. In the meantime, though, as she rounded the corner into the estate where she lived, Charlie's head was spinning with all the uni stuff and now the added stress of *him* calling her again. It was getting too much. Plenty to keep her awake most nights. She just couldn't seem to switch off. You would think she didn't have enough room for something else in her mind. But ever since seeing that letter in her post box this morning, she hadn't stopped wondering about it amongst everything else. *Who are you J. Sure?*

As if she had time for anything else right now.

Her head was too full, which was probably why she didn't hear anyone approaching from behind until it was too late.

"Oi! You live 'round here?"

Feet shuffled around her. Her heart jumped into her mouth, Charlie paused and looked around at the four young lads who, for some reason, had decided she was the one they wanted to start trouble with tonight.

Fantastic! A fitting end to an already shitty day.

"Well?"

Thinking fast, she looked the one who'd spoken in the eye, trying to show him she wasn't intimidated when really her heart was pounding so hard she was surprised he didn't hear it. He was about an inch or two taller than she was, shaved head with a scar above his left eye. His ratty features made more sinister by the creepy smile he was wearing. "My boyfriend does, in that building right there. Front flat," she said, hoping it would be enough to make them think twice.

When she went to walk past, he shifted in front of her, blocking her path. She drew up short.

"I've seen you around here before. Ain't seen you with a boyfriend though."

"Hey lady," another one said. This one shorter and rounder with scraggly hair that stopped just below his ears. "You got any spare cash? Only, we missed our lift home and none of us got money for the train."

Aware that they'd now circled her, panic set in. Since Charlie had moved into the area she'd never really felt unsafe. Yes, she'd seen small groups of young lads hanging around, but none of them had ever paid her any attention. Until tonight. The streets were always pretty quiet around here at this time. The building where her flat was situated was set a few streets back from the main road, but it wasn't a bad area.

The fact it was quiet didn't bode well for her right now though. Rush hour had passed and most people would be settled in front of their TVs by now. Her eyes darted past the youths, searching for anyone who could help, but there was no one else around.

Shit. This was bad.

What did she do? She had about twenty quid in her purse along with a credit and a debit card. She could give them that but doubted it would appease them. Besides, she got the feeling they weren't doing this for money; she was shit out of luck either way.

Straightening her shoulders, Charlie pushed past the tallest one. "You need to leave me alone." But as she went to walk past him, he grabbed her arm and her bag.

"What would be the fun in that?"

There was laughter as the strap on her bag snapped in her struggle to get away. It fell to the floor, ejecting most of the contents. The lad that dived for it ignored the text books going straight for her purse. Meanwhile, her tormentor tightened his grip on her arm to the point where she cried out. Dear God, she wasn't going to get away from them. Her mind went into overdrive. What would they do to her? Did she have something in her coat pocket she could use as a weapon. Oh God. Her parents were never going to see her again. Had she told them she loved them lately?

"Look, you've got my purse. Now just go." She tried to yank her arm away but his hand was like a vice. Trying to think past her pounding heart, the only thing she could come up with was to knee him in the balls, but he was facing slightly away so she didn't have a good aim.

"How much is in there?" The guy who was manhandling her asked.

"A twenty, couple of cards." Another one was rifling through her bag. "No phone though."

Her captor pulled her closer. "Pocket?"

Charlie kept the fear from her face as she looked at him, staying quiet while she waited for her chance, but he got too close when he went to check her pockets.

"Get the hell off me or I'll—"

"Hey! Let her go."

She had no idea who the voice belonged to, but when Ratty looked up in surprise she was presented with the opportunity she'd been waiting for. Her knee hit the prick right on target and the gargled sound he made was satisfying.

That male voice called out again, this time sounding pretty close. "What the fuck's going on?"

Chapter Six

It wasn't speed or power that Jake craved. There was nothing more soothing than the deep throated roar of the Triumph's engine. It was music to his ears. The pipes had been cut to give that extra growl and as Jake let it fly down the motorway, the cold, damp spring air trying its best to penetrate the clothing that was rustling in the wind, he could feel all the day's tension evaporating.

As hard as he'd tried, the phone call hadn't left his mind. Although he doubted it would be one of the Morgans, Jake had called their number in case for some reason they'd been unable to get him on his mobile, but he'd got no answer. No surprise there. There was no one else it could possibly be and it had irked him all day. Whoever it was hadn't called back. They might never call back, and where would that leave him? With a case of paranoia that had already started to set in.

Zoning everything out except the sound and feel of his motorbike, Jake enjoyed the ride, imagining being somewhere else: the panoramic roads through the Venetian Alps, or around the mountains of Norway with breathtaking views of the Fjords. He'd never been to either of those places but he'd always planned to. Had his heart set on visiting as many places as he could, riding solo on his motorbike. That was before, though. Now it was nothing more than a dream, one so far beyond his reach that even his passion had faded. Still, he always imagined.

As Jake approached his exit off the motorway, he was tempted to keep going, to ride until he ran out of petrol. It was something he hadn't done in a long time, let the bike just take him, but he was starving and what was the point really. After the busy day he'd had, and the stress on top of his workload, he was ready to kick back on the sofa with a few cans of lager. That was about the extent of adventure for him nowadays.

He never usually rode home this late and was surprised at how busy the roads still were. No way he'd expected to be in slow-moving traffic at half eight at night but he guessed that was one of the drawbacks of living in a busy town and working late. It wasn't because he had to. Going home to his dark and dingy flat wasn't all that appealing, so he'd stayed late to finish some jobs, and Sam had left him the keys to lock up. Luckily he'd picked up a ready meal from the supermarket when he'd popped in earlier to get some new t-shirts for work. Processed food saves the day yet again.

When he finally got moving again, he noticed something wrong with the bike. It wasn't pulling right. He was literally three minutes from his street when the damn thing spluttered and the engine cut right out.

Shit. He'd just changed the plugs this morning. That should have sorted the problem. Turning the key to the off position, Jake realised what the issue probably was and wanted to kick his own arse. He turned the ignition back on and a glance at the fuel gauge confirmed it. Empty. His head had been so pickled all day he'd forgotten to fuel up.

Jake removed his helmet and secured it on the back of the seat, and got to pushing the damn thing, which wasn't easy considering the weight. Thank God he'd only conked out right before he turned into the estate where he lived so he wasn't too far away. At least it had stopped raining.

Working up a sweat, he was thinking about leaving the thing there until he got some fuel in the morning when voices drifted over on the wind. He'd turned off the main road, and the street that led to his was a lot quieter so he picked up on male laughter coming from up ahead. Moving a little further, a group of lads came into view though it was hard to make them out in the darker part of the street where they were. Then a woman's voice put him on high alert because she definitely wasn't laughing along with them. It sounded like she'd cried out. As he got closer enough to see her there was no doubt in his mind that she was in distress. It was a split second for his brain to realise what was going on and that was when he left his bike on its stand, rushing over.

There was a struggle. One of the lads had hold of the blonde woman's arm as the rest of them laughed and taunted. There was four of them altogether. None of them looked tough, at least not to him. To a lone female though. . . Yeah, it made them dead tough. Jake was all fired up as he made his way towards them, rage burning hot in his veins. Without even thinking how dangerous the situation could be—any of the lads could have a knife—all he cared about was getting the woman away from the scumbag and his little cronies. He removed his bike jacket so it didn't hinder his movements should things turn ugly.

The woman called for her attacker to let go of her, prompting Jake to move faster when he heard the fear in her voice. The handle on her bag snapped in her struggle to get away. She didn't manage it. But that was about to change.

"Hey. Let her go." Jake charged over to the gang just as the woman stuck a boot into her assailant's crotch. "What the fuck's going on?"

Charlie's attacker bent over choking back the pain she'd inflicted on him and suddenly she was free. Before she even had chance to blink, a large body came into view and as Ratty looked up, the new guy punched him hard in the face. He fell backwards, eyes wide and watering as he stumbled, only just catching his footing while he held his hand over his bleeding nose. Then he turned and ran, the rest of the gang following as quickly, leaving her stuff scattered on the ground. Leaning over, holding her stomach as it ached with nausea all of a sudden, Charlie could barely get her breath.

"Hey. You okay?" A warm hand pressed against her shoulder and Charlie looked up to a dark-haired man, his handsome face full of concern. His hand stayed where it was as she rested her hands on her thighs, then he removed it once he saw that she was steady. "Did they hurt you?"

It took her a moment to answer while she crouched down to gather up her things. Oh, hey, they'd been kind enough to leave her purse but when she looked inside the money and the cards were gone. The stranger helped her put her notebooks and pens back where they belonged.

Her wrist was burning from the lad's grip; thankfully that was all. "Um, no. I'm okay." Her hand went to her forehead as she went to get up and realised she was shaking, her heart erratic in her chest. The stranger helped her stand, holding her forearms gently as he guided her up, a thick leather jacket draped over his arm.

"Have you seen those lads around here before?" She noticed he was looking at his phone as he dialled a number and then his eyes went back over to the green where the gang had disappeared into the shadows. He was tall, maybe six feet or close to it. In the dim overhead street lighting it was hard to see the true colour of his eyes beyond the midnight sky they appeared to be. But why was she wondering about that right now? When he put his phone up to his ear he looked at her with a harsh frown and she remembered he'd asked a question.

"No I don't think so. I mean, I've seen lads hanging around the area before but I don't think I recognised any of them."

His hand went to her shoulder again as he spoke into his phone, as if on instinct. "Yeah, police please."

"Oh, no—" She tried to protest.

"Hello? I need to report an assault..."

It was the last thing Charlie wanted. Her day had been far too long already without having to wait for an officer to come over, which could take hours. All she wanted was to run a hot bath and put the whole twenty-four hours behind her, but it seemed her saviour had other plans for the rest of her evening.

"You live around here?" Charlie hadn't realised he'd finished talking to the officer until she looked up to see him waiting for an answer from her, the phone away from his ear.

She nodded, still trying to get her anxiety under control. "The flats in the corner of Holland Park, just over there."

His eyebrows went up briefly and his head lifted a little, but he didn't say anything. "Sorry?" He spoke into the phone again. "Uh, yeah sure. Hang on." The harshness disappeared from his features as he quickly removed his hand from her shoulder like he'd only just realised it was still on there. He held the phone out to her. "They want to talk to you. Is that okay?"

Reluctantly, Charlie nodded and took the man's phone. She recounted everything she could about the boys and told the officer she didn't think they were around any longer so there was probably no point in pursuing it, and that all she wanted to do was go home. It didn't work. The woman told her she'd send a car over to the area to see if they could find the gang from the brief description Charlie had given, and they'd call in to take a proper statement. Great. Not exactly how she'd planned her evening, or what little of it she had left anyway.

After she finished giving her details she ended the call. Handing the phone back to the stranger, she noticed he was looking at her with a strange expression on his good-looking face as he placed the phone back in his jeans pocket. For a moment, Charlie couldn't look away, noticing his jaw was tense.

"So we live in the same building."

Charlie paused. They did? He wasn't familiar. In fact, she was certain she'd never seen him before. He didn't exactly have a face she'd forget. Perhaps he lived on one of the upper floors.

"We do?"

"What floor?" they said together. Only Charlie smiled. Then they both said, "First," at the same time again.

Her floor? But there were only three—

That was when her brain switched back on and she noticed the navy hoodie he was wearing, the leather jacket on his arm. She glanced down at his worn, grey jeans, then his heavy, black boots. Then her eyes moved past him and she saw a motorbike parked by the kerb a little further down the road.

J. Sure.

It was him.

After all this time of trying to see his face, to meet or get a glance of him out in the hall, almost to the point of stalking the guy, here he was standing right in front of her after swooping in and saving her from a gang of arseholes. And it was a good job she'd already had the wind knocked out of her because. . . Wow. Her neighbour was gorgeous. When she looked at him again it was with even more interest now. His deep brown hair was all choppy and tussled, obviously from a helmet. Short stubble highlighted a strong jaw line and lips that were full, but set tight. Dark brows were pulled down, one slightly lower than the other, over intense eyes that were almost navy in the light—eyes that she noticed had narrowed on her.

"I should. . ." He twisted and pointed over his shoulder. "Are you sure you're okay?" he asked when he turned back to her.

"I'm honestly fine. My bag took the worst of it." She held it up by the body, the broken strap hanging limp.

"I can walk with you if you give me a sec. My bike's just back there." She glanced at the bike again, totally recognising it as it stood at the other end of the street resting on its stand under the street light. "I was pushing it back when I saw what was going on." He must have seen the question in her eyes. "Ran out of fuel."

"No honestly. It's two-hundred yards away. I think I'll be safe enough now. Go get your bike." As he backed away he glanced at her like he was unsure whether to leave and it made Charlie's chest fill with something unfamiliar that she would probably question later. She tried to give him a reassuring smile. "I'm fine. And thank you." He nodded and walked away. Then she called out to him. "Hey. What's your name?" It would be nice to know what the J was for.

Pausing without looking back, she wondered why he dropped his head before answering so quietly she only just about caught what he said, "Jake." Then he headed off in the direction of his bike.

Jake. Jake Sure.

He hadn't asked for hers, but Charlie hoped that now they had finally met, this wouldn't be their only interaction.

Walking towards home, she smiled and couldn't help thinking: *isn't it funny how life can knock you on your arse one minute, then give you a pretty big boon the next.*

Chapter Seven

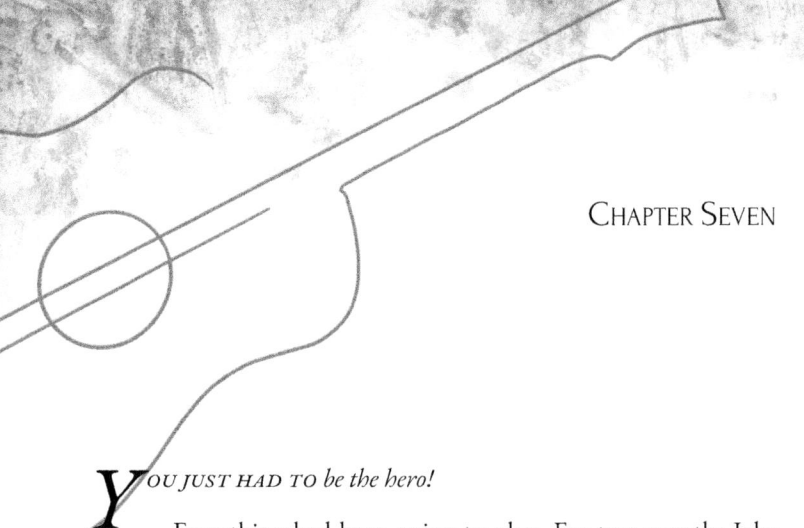

You just had to be the hero!

Everything had been going to plan. For two months Jake had been right where he wanted to be: alone. In the time since he'd moved to Hatfield from Selby, he'd successfully avoided most social interactions outside of what he had to. He'd kept his head down, avoided any and all unnecessary complications and was starting to feel like Hatfield was a place he could stay; somewhere he could get on with rebuilding his life exactly how he wanted without events of the past getting in his way.

Finally, after an unhealthy obsession with revenge had almost destroyed him mentally, Jake had started to believe he could move on.

Alone.

Now, though, in the week since he'd stepped in to help his neighbour, she'd successfully spoken to him three times in the hall outside his flat. Granted, it was little more than a quick "hey", but it was enough to mean that he was no longer anonymous.

Shit! Why hadn't he just hung back and called the police? Had there really been any need for him to step in and play the hero? A few youths thinking they were being clever, that's all it probably was. They'd have taken her money and run. But as he thought back to the look in that one lad's eyes—the biggest of the group, and the mouthiest, the one whose nose he'd happily split open—it was that look that had got him bolting over there. Jake had seen it before. Too many times. He knew exactly what was behind those eyes so he'd acted purely on instinct.

Now the woman seemed to think she'd made a friend. Going by the effort she made to say hi every time their paths crossed. Only they weren't friends, and would never be. He didn't want any friends.

Moving on, leaving his past where it was, didn't mean forgetting everything he'd been through. He wasn't kidding himself into thinking he could get over any of it. His fight had to end only because the revenge he sought was out of reach. His shitty life had shown him he was meant to be alone and he planned on staying that way.

All Jake could do was hope that the gratitude his neighbour felt towards him would eventually fade. In the meantime he would do what he could to help turn her attention away from him. At least he was getting some idea of her daily schedule so he could try to avoid her. Hopefully she'd soon get the hint he wasn't a friendly guy and move on.

Swinging the backpack off his shoulder, Jake crouched down in front of the fire that was burning steadily in the fire pit he'd made. He'd spotted this place on one of his rides and had visited the forest a few times since. Now, after leaving his bike parked up in the visitor's car park, he was some distance from the path the walkers used, quite deep into the forest where the trees were pretty dense and the undergrowth was difficult to traverse. Of course, he'd only had the moonlight to guide his way and even though he doubted anyone would be out walking their dog this late, he wanted to be sure he was well out of the way—lost in the wild.

The flickering orange light from the small fire he'd built, tried to chase away the darkness beyond. Warmed by the flames, Jake opened his pack, reached inside, and started to pull the contents out. Reluctantly at first, he threw the small pile of paper onto the fire, watching as the flames quickly devoured them, little wisps of embers rising up and disappearing. The next lot was mainly newspaper clippings and he paused at the picture of the man on the top one. Taking in a breath, he continued, throwing them ones on too, not allowing the anger that he'd worked so hard at controlling to take a hold. The contents he'd stuffed into his bag he'd kept hold of for too long.

This needed to happen. If Jake was going to have any chance at moving on, he had to start by letting go of the things he'd used to obsess over him. The clippings and the printed reports were the first step. Of course, throwing paper on a fire was the easy part. Mentally, it wasn't going to be so easy. How does your mind let go of the things that still hurt so much?

One thing at a time, he told himself.

There was no rush. If Jake had learned anything over the past three years, he knew he was a dab hand at patience.

When he was done and the backpack was empty, Jake picked up a stick and poked at the fire, moving the charred piles of paper around to make sure they were finished off properly. He was content to stay there for a while longer, so he put his bag under his arse and sat down, knees up with his arms resting on them. As he stared into the fire, enjoying the heat, his eyes were mesmerised by the dancing flames. There was something about naked flames; they captured your gaze like they were enticing you in. And in the centre of them he saw a vision. His thoughts in that moment were unwelcome. Why was he thinking of her? As if the reason he was in these woods wasn't enough to occupy his mind, she'd waltzed right in there like nothing else mattered enough in that moment.

He was damned if he could shove her out of there.

Annoyance. That's what it must be. He was angry with the situation that had arisen from his act of heroism and his mind was stewing over it enough to bring her into it. He'd first seen her two days after the attack as he'd been leaving for work. She'd called out "hello" to him as he'd sat on his bike fastening his helmet ready to go. Jake had tried not to notice her, but when he'd looked up she'd already walked past and his gaze had landed on her, lowering down her body, checking her out as she'd walked away. That was the first time he'd been ignorant to her. The memory must have manifested right now because he knew he needed to fix the problem he'd caused.

Yeah. That was it.

So what did the colour of her hair have to do with it? She could have been anyone, with any hair colour, and he'd be just as annoyed with how things had changed in the week since the attack.

And yet. . . why had he noticed how silky it had looked. And why was he trying to remember the colour of her eyes?

Fucking hell.

Like he needed a woman in his life.

Or anyone for that matter.

The only person he did want in his life he barely saw, and that wasn't for the want of trying. But even he wasn't enough to sway Jake's thoughts away from his neighbour.

He needed to get a grip.

Yeah. Time to go, Jake.

When he got to his feet, he grabbed his bag and got the bottle of water out. He poured it on the fire, smoke hissing out as he doused the flames. Then his mind shifted to the money. Reaching into the back pocket of his jeans, he pulled out the mini statement he'd got from the cash machine earlier. It had been a shock to see his balance. Last time he'd looked at his finances he was down to his last forty quid, which had to last him until his next wages went in at the end of the month. Of course, that was besides all the inheritance money sitting in his other account that he hated even thinking about.

As he looked at all the zeroes, he was hit by a myriad of emotions. The money was certainly bitter sweet, leaning far closer to the bitter. This amount alone was a lot of money for someone like him to turn his nose up at; it would pay for all the travelling he'd once dreamed of and more. But still, he wouldn't touch it. Couldn't touch it. Not with the knowledge of how he'd acquired it. It wasn't just eight months of his life he'd lost back then. Not to mention it was an evil coincidence that the money had come around the same time he'd started to think he could move on.

The feelings it brought forth risked setting him back.

Screwing up the bit of paper, Jake threw it onto the remains of the fire. If the money hadn't been digital, he'd have thrown it all on there too. He got his phone out of his inside pocket, turned the torch on, and headed back through the forest to his bike.

By the time he got back to the car park, Jake felt a little better. He'd been anxious about getting rid of the stuff, but in the end, with things the way they were, there was no reason to keep any of it anymore. This was the start of the moving on process he never thought he'd have the strength to do. It had been almost three years and while the pain of his past hadn't lessened, the anger he'd held onto so tightly had. Of course, he'd been forced to let go of that when the cause of it had fled the country.

Closing his eyes, Jake inhaled a deep breath, giving himself a minute. To his relief the anger that threatened to seep through quickly went away. See. . . he'd finally got a grip of his emotions. Now he controlled them, not the other way around. Finally, he was moving forward.

All he had to do now was make a certain woman turn her attentions elsewhere.

Chapter Eight

For the first time since she could remember, Charlie had a spring in her step as she headed up the stairs. Yes, she could barely feel her toes after she'd covered most of the campus in the latter half of the day because her last two classes had been as far away as they could possibly be. And of course she was tired after walking home from the train station after yet another long day. But today she'd finally handed in her assignment. That meant nothing could put a dampener on how relieved and proud of herself she was after working so bloody hard. End of term was edging closer. God, she couldn't wait.

In the meantime she'd settle for a nice relaxing weekend, her first since the start of the uni year. Maybe she'd treat herself and get Chinese food delivered. She had an unopened bottle of wine at home that was calling her.

Almost there, she thought to herself, wishing she lived in a building that had a lift. Just as she reached the door to her floor, it swung open, knocking her off balance, causing her bag to fall off her arm and hit the floor. Luckily she didn't follow it, managing to stay on her feet even as someone rushed past her. Charlie got a quick look at the man who had almost ploughed her down though his face was a little obscured from the black cap he wore. She saw he had pitted skin around his cheeks and jaw, silvery stubble suggested he was an older man. From what she could see he didn't look familiar. Before she had chance to call him out on his lack of manners, he was already down the first flight of stairs. Not a single word said. It was like he hadn't even seen her.

Yeah, thanks for the apology. "Rude bastard," she snapped as she bent to pick her things up. Luckily, most of her work stuff had stayed inside the bag this time, and thankfully the strap hadn't broken like on the last one. She grabbed her keys and kept them in her hand, then spotted her lip balm that had rolled over to the other side of the stairwell. Charlie wondered where the man had come from in such a rush. There were only three flats on her floor, same as the bottom and the upper two floors, and she'd never seen him at Mrs. Hughes's place. Maybe he'd come from Jake's.

Well, it was none of her business anyway.

She made her way down the hall, purposely slowing by Jake's. On light feet, she was getting ready to listen to see if she could hear that nice music again when she saw his door was open.

Charlie carried on casually. Trying to act like she wasn't being the crazy stalker lady she'd turned into, made worse since he'd stepped in and helped her and she'd seen how good looking he was. The guy had made it pretty clear since then that he wasn't in the friend-zone territory, hard as she'd tried. And Charlie had been as friendly as someone could be without being creepy. Still, Jake had barely acknowledged her the few times they'd crossed paths. He'd continued to wear his hood up, head still down, barely giving her a nod.

Glancing quickly as she went to walk past, she was surprised how wide open the door was, especially when there was no sign of him inside. Maybe he hadn't realised he'd left it open. Pausing, Charlie told herself she didn't need to knock. He was probably grabbing something before he went out and would appear any minute. So she waited, still staying where she was so that she could get to walking again casually when he made an appearance.

Still no sign of him.

Edging closer, Charlie couldn't hear anyone moving inside. Was he even home? Hesitating, she tried to tell herself to go home and forget it, but her arm moved defiantly. Right before she knocked, she heard a door opening somewhere inside, and Jake walked right into view at the end of his hallway. Wearing nothing but a towel wrapped low around his waist, he was facing away so she got a nice view of his back. And yep. . . As she suspected, he did workout. It was hard not to look at how lean and muscled it was, a deep groove down his spine. Shit. Her eyes wouldn't move away from him, and she was just standing there like a fool.

Just go, Charlie.

But wait. If he'd just got out of the shower why was his door wide open?

Before he turned around and caught her gawping, Charlie knocked twice.

Jake turned abruptly and when her breath caught, she tried to mask her reaction with a casual smile, but she knew her eyes were very probably giving her away as they dropped well below his face. *Shit. Christ.* The front was even better. His body was solid muscle all over, wide shoulders, more abs than she'd ever seen in real life before. Her gaze drank him in for a second. Until the sound of his bare footsteps padding towards her made her realise he was moving towards her and she was staring at his body. She internally berated herself. Returning her gaze to his face, she felt her cheeks heat when she met his intense eyes, and forced hers to stay there.

"Hey." He looked at her with a deep frown. "What's going on?"

With his hair wet and tussled that way, Charlie was having a hard time concentrating, but she mentally kicked herself and went to explain until she noticed the suspicious look he was throwing her way. "Why is my door wide open?"

Annnd isn't that as good as a cold shower.

"I can't answer that, but it is the reason I knocked. I've just got back and when I was walking past I saw the thing open and wondered if you knew." Her eyes made one last journey down his body and back up to his face again. "Clearly not."

Charlie knew she'd said all that with a sharp edge to her voice, but honestly. . . What? Did he think she'd just wandered into his flat?

Ignoring the confusion on Jake's face as he checked around the lock, she decided she'd done her neighbourly duty and began to walk away. She'd taken two steps when. . .

"Hey. Uh, thanks."

"You're welcome," she threw over her shoulder, wanting nothing more than to get home and have that glass of wine. Or maybe now she'd have two. Not to mention she was starving. "It's Charlie, by the way." Not that he'd asked. But she was sick of being called *hey*.

"Charlie?"

Pausing, she turned to see him half in, half out of his flat and she made sure to only look him in the eyes this time. So what he had a gorgeous body that she wanted to stare at, his attitude certainly wasn't as attractive.

"Thanks," he said with a hint of a smile that made her chest warm a little. Ok, so how was she supposed to stay mad when he looked like that? Smiling back at him, she gave him a nod then carried on up the hall.

A moment later she heard his door close.

So Jake Sure wasn't as cold as he tried to make out.

Chapter Nine

Inside her flat, she dropped her bag by the door and took her coat off, hanging it on one of the hooks on the wall, and headed straight for the kitchen. It was so good to be home. Although small, Charlie loved her flat. As soon as she'd moved in she'd decorated to make it feel more like her. Warm beige and white in all the rooms with contrasting soft furnishings, she'd themed it on the Scandinavian style that was popular right now. A few throws, cream and black cushions, and some fake plants dotted about made it cosy. Her bookshelves behind the sofa were crammed with all her favourite books, the bottom shelf reserved for uni stuff. She lit some candles, turned the lighting low, and was ready to chill for the rest of the evening.

In the kitchen—with the light-wood cabinets, and black, speckled worktop—she'd tried to contrast it with the rest of her decor, with more plants, also fake, because who had time to keep foliage alive?

Just as she started pouring a glass of wine her phone began to vibrate in her pocket. It was Cara. She answered, taking her glass and heading into the living room.

"Hey. You home?" her friend asked the minute the call connected.

"Got in five minutes ago. Literally just sat down to take my shoes off."

"Well, buzz me in. I'm downstairs."

It wasn't often Cara turned up without calling or texting first. In fact, Charlie couldn't remember her doing it at all. Hopefully there was nothing wrong; she wasn't sure how much more drama she could take.

After a few minutes there was a knock at the door. Charlie opened it and got a wine bottle held in front of her face.

"Surprise!"

Cara wasn't on her own. Jas and Selina were also there. Jas was holding takeaway bags and she was hit with a delicious smell of food that made her stomach grumble. He held one up. "Chinese?"

"Guys? What's going on?" Charlie moved out of the way and gestured for them to come in. And no, she absolutely did not glance down the hall towards Jake's before she went in and shut the door. She was losing her bloody mind.

"We thought, after all your hard work, you deserve a treat. Chinese and wine." Cara took control as everyone else removed their coats. "You lot sit."

"Oh my God, you are awesome. I was literally just thinking of ordering Chinese."

Her best friend gave her a wide grin. "We know you, babes," she said before proceeding to ransack Charlie's kitchen. "Where the hell have the plates gone?"

"Bottom left. I had a clean out a couple of weeks back and moved everything." Squeezing past Cara, Charlie reached up and got the wine glasses from out of the top cupboard. "Everyone wanting glasses?"

"Just a normal one for me," Jas said from over on the sofa. "I'm designated driver tonight."

After the food was put out and they'd piled around the coffee table, they chatted about everything and anything, laughed themselves into indigestion, and as Charlie took another drink of wine, she couldn't help feeling blessed to have such great friends in her life. She'd really needed this. Her second uni year had been so much harder than the first. Caught up in assignments and studies, she'd barely had five minutes to spare for herself never mind her friends. The year had gone by in a blur and she couldn't believe it was almost over. There would be lots more of this over the summer; Charlie would make sure of it.

Just as Cara started to gather the plates, placing them on top of each other ready to do what Cara always did and take over the clean up, Charlie's stomach sank a little as she prepared to tell them what had happened last week. She had a feeling there were going to be safety precautions and rules set out in her future, which was exactly what she didn't want. Her friends were fiercely protective of each other, and Charlie didn't want them thinking her neighbourhood was dangerous. It was the first time anything like that had ever happened.

She'd felt bad about not mentioning it, but with the pressure she'd had to finish her dissertation, she couldn't let it affect her work. So she'd tried her best to put it out of her mind until she'd handed her work in. Now that she had, she couldn't keep it from them any longer.

"Cara, leave that for now. Sit. I need to tell you guys something."

Her friend paused mid stand and instantly dropped back down to the sofa, placing the pile of plates down. She wasn't backward in coming forward, none of them were, which is why they were looking at her with oh-so-serious expressions. Even Selina who she barely knew.

"I don't like the way your voice was just then." Cara looked prepared for the worst. "I knew something wasn't right. What's happened?"

As her audience waited, Charlie took in a deep breath. "So. . . let me tell you about last Friday."

After explaining everything about the group of lads, it felt pretty good to off load it. Charlie hadn't realised how much it had shaken her until now. She'd barely had time to really think about what could have happened if Jake hadn't showed up when he did, but talking about it now brought forward everything she'd feared, the worst being the image of that prick's face while he'd gripped onto her arm. How she'd managed to push it all out for so long she didn't know, and now she was actually feeling a little shaky again. Still, she tried her best to hide it.

"Shit, Charlie. Why the hell didn't you tell us?" Jas looked like he was about to burst from anger.

"I can't believe you kept that from me." Cara looked about ready to cry.

"Are you okay?" Selina asked, and she surprised Charlie by reaching over and placing her hand on her arm.

Bloody hell. This wasn't helping her shakes.

"Look, honestly. I'm fine. And Cara, I didn't mention it because I had to knuckle down and get my dissertation finished. I didn't want the stress of it all to impact on my work. I've worked too bloody hard for a group of idiot juvies to ruin it." Glancing around at them all she lightened her expression. "But I'm okay."

Jas got up and walked over to the breakfast bar that separated the kitchen from the lounge. "What have the police done about it? Did they get them?"

"No. They came here and took my statement. I got a phone call from the same officer on Tuesday. They'd had no luck. But she promised they would keep trying." Charlie hadn't expected anything else really. Those lads knew she'd report it so they were probably laying low."

"You can't walk from the station on your own after dark anymore, Char." The worry on Cara's face made her feel like shit. "God knows what could have happened if you hadn't had help."

It wasn't even possible. She didn't have a car and couldn't afford taxis all the time. "I'll be fine. I'll get one of those alarm thingies."

"You need a spray. Or a fucking bat."

"Jas! Pepper spray is illegal. It isn't going to do me any good getting arrested for possession of an illegal weapon." This was the reason she hadn't mentioned it until now. Getting up from the beanbag she'd been sitting on, Charlie took the plates from in front of Cara, needing to do something before her anxiety spiked. She had to let her friends go through the emotions they so rightly felt. But all Charlie wanted was a nice night with alcohol and laughter, not this tension that was hanging in the air now.

"It's such bullshit." Jas turned to her. "How are you supposed to protect yourself?"

"Jas, what's the point in getting angry about something we have no control over. I'll get a taxi in future if I have late classes. Okay?"

He put his hand on the back of his neck and took a breath, seeming to calm down as he looked at Selina. She gave him a melancholy smile. "I don't know what I'd do if anything like that happened to you," he told his girlfriend as he sat back down next to her. "I'm already out of my mind with worry whenever I can't take you home and you have to get the bus late."

As Charlie looked at the couple, she felt a warm glow in her chest accompanied by a slight feeling of envy. She'd honestly never seen Jason like that with any of his past girlfriends. It was nice. And she wondered what it would be like to have someone look at her the way he looked at Selina.

When she'd finished putting the dishes in hot soapy water in the sink, she went back to join them, plonking herself down on the saggy beanbag.

"So who was the guy?"

For a second she wondered what Cara meant. "What guy?"

Charlie didn't think she deserved the eye roll. "The one who helped you? Who was it? Does he live around here?"

Clearing her throat, she tried to act all casual when answering, but anticipated Cara's reaction, nonetheless. "My neighbour."

"You were so lucky he was passing—" Her big brown eyes widened. "You mean *the* neighbour?"

Grabbing the wine bottle, Charlie poured the last of it into her glass while pretending there was no big deal. "Yep. The guy that lives down the hall."

"*The* neighbour? What are you talking about?" Jas asked. Of course he would, because now Cara had a wide grin stretching from ear to ear, and both Jas and Selina were looking between the two of them.

"I cannot believe I have had to wait a week for you to tell me this."

"What do you mean?" Charlie asked, trying to stifle the desperation to blurt everything out about Jake like some excited teenager. "You didn't know, so how have you had to wait?"

"That's not the point. Now I do know that you kept it from me for seven whole days." She had now moved to the edge of her seat.

"Ok," Jason interrupted. "What the hell are you two going on about? Can we get in the conversation too?"

"A new guy moved into the flat down the hall about two months ago and Charlie has been stalking him."

"Cara!" She looked at Jas and Selina. "I haven't done anything of the sort." *Liar.* "He always seems to keep his face hidden whenever I see him and I'm just curious about what he looks like. That is all." The last part was said through her teeth while glancing back to Cara. "He lives in the same building and he was giving me strange vibes. Not even Mrs. Hughes knows who he is and she's an expert at knowing everyone's business."

"I told her to be careful because it was weirdo behaviour." Cara held her hands out like she was about to burst with impatience, her focus now back on Charlie. "And now? Come on Char. . . What does he look like?"

Try as she might, Charlie couldn't hold the smile back as an image of Jake popped into her mind. A towel had never looked so good on anyone. "Good." She looked down into her glass with a silly smirk on her face.

"What's that now?" Cara pressed.

When she looked up at her friend, Charlie knew she was grinning like an idiot. "He's really good looking."

"I knew it!" Slapping her hand on her thigh, Cara beamed.

Charlie laughed. "No you didn't."

"I had a feeling. I did. Now he's your hero." Throwing her head back, Cara's hands went to her chest and she went all dramatic. "And you're going to fall in love. . ."

"Oh God." Leaning over the table Charlie hit her friend's leg. "Stop. Just, stop that."

"Yeah, Cara. A minute ago you said he was acting like a weirdo." Jas looked across at Charlie, eyebrows low. "I'm glad he sorted those lads out, but just be wary of the guy. Sounds to me like he's hiding from something."

"You don't know that," Selina chimed in. "He might just be shy."

Nope. Charlie never got that from him. Broody? Yes. Closed off? Definitely. Especially since last week. Granted, she'd only seen him a few times, well, she'd seen a lot more of him earlier—*Christ*. Those abs. Until their recent exchange, he'd barely acknowledged her.

"I highly doubt that. Charlie, just watch the guy, ok."

I intend to, she thought as she smiled at Jas, nodding to appease him.

Thankfully, a change in topic of conversation meant the rest of the evening went by in a flash after they'd got back to having some fun. Another bottle of wine and a few games of Cards Against Humanity and Charlie's face was aching she'd laughed so hard.

At the door, they were hugging and saying goodbye when Cara suddenly grabbed Charlie's arm and leaned in, putting her face right in front of hers. "Hot guy alert," she said through the side of her mouth. And then everyone went quiet. When she followed Cara's gaze down the hall, Jake was just reaching his door, hood up, helmet in hand, and he stopped and looked up for a second. There was no movement in those rigid features, no hint of a smile like he'd given her earlier. It was like they weren't even there. He unlocked his door and went inside. The slam that followed made her blink. Honestly, you would think there would be a head nod or some kind of smile between them, an acknowledgement that they did know each other by name now as opposed to complete strangers. Nope. It was like everything in the past week hadn't happened, which was fine by her. If he wanted to keep to himself that was his choice. She was the one that owed him something not the other way around. He certainly didn't owe her any conversation and she accepted that. Now he was back to not even acknowledging her.

It was Jas that was scowling now. "Stay away from that one, Char."

Cara also had a look of concern for a moment until the side of her mouth went up. "You were right. He is gorgeous. All that brooding and mystery I could get on board with." She leaned in and kissed Charlie's cheek. "See you tomorrow. Sweet dreams." That last part was said with a wink.

Charlie nudged her friend.

"Goodnight," Selina said. "It was fun."

"It was. Thank you for coming."

As her friends wandered down the hall, failing to keep the noise down, Charlie hesitated, glancing at Jake's and wondering what the hell was up with him. She was pretty sure she hadn't done anything to upset him while she'd been in her flat all evening.

Whatever, she thought, going back inside.

Right then, Charlie was honestly too tired to care.

Chapter Ten

SHIT!
Dropping the knife, Charlie brought her bleeding thumb up to her mouth as she went to the sink and ran the cold water tap. Her stomach flipped as she shoved her hand under the water and was afraid to look. In her mind she'd chopped the end off and was about to bleed to death on her kitchen floor. Reality: on proper inspection, a small slice about half a centimetre across the pad of her thumb. Silly cow. That'll teach her to have the TV on while she was cooking.

Why did she think this was a good idea again?

It was late Saturday afternoon and instead of being out there in the world enjoying her time off—maybe a bit of shopping, a lunch date with Cara—Charlie was covered in potato with pots everywhere, and to top it all off she'd nearly chopped her thumb in half.

She stayed there holding the wound under the cold water until it went numb and appeared to stop bleeding. Now she could see the extent of the damage proper and cursed herself for being such a baby. Wasn't even bad enough for a stitch, for crying out loud. Rummaging through the drawer under the crime scene where the half chopped onion was, she found a box of plasters and wrapped one around the wound so that if it did start bleeding again, she wouldn't get any blood in the food.

Leaving the rest of the onion where it was, she scraped what she'd chopped into the pan on the cooker and lit the ring. Cooking wasn't something she did very often, but she wasn't that bad at it. Growing up, her mum had always let her help in the kitchen so she did know a thing or two, but it was her first attempt at a shepherd's pie—a bit ambitious considering microwave meals and instant noodles were regular dietary additions since she'd become a student. Not just because money was limited, but so was her time and she could never be bothered. Today she was fed up with eating crap food. Something had come over her in the supermarket and before she'd realised, Charlie had filled her basket with fresh ingredients. She'd even bought some plums and a punnet of grapes, for Christ's sake.

Half an hour later and she realised she'd made enough to feed half the building. Instead of one baking dish, she'd had to fill two; both were now in the oven. There was going to be a lot of potato and minced beef for dinner in her future.

Unless. . .

Nope. Bad idea.

An hour later, after the pies had turned out great, and Charlie had stuffed her face while she'd watched a couple of episodes of Friends. Her stomach was full to the brim. That's not what had given her indigestion though. Nope. It had been caused by the bright idea that she'd tried to talk herself out of umpteen times, yet was still contemplating as she stared down at the other pie that had cooled down on the counter.

Honestly, though, did she really want to eat this for dinner for the next four or five nights when she could give it to somebody else?

You see, this was why she was still staring at it: It made perfect sense in one half of her mind. The other half, though, was telling her it was a crazy idea and she was only setting herself up for another fall. Inclined to agree with the latter, she walked away, sat down on the sofa and un-paused the show she was watching. Definitely a bad idea.

Why then, was she standing outside Jake's door, shepherd's pie in hand, twenty minutes later?

Bloody hell, her heart was pounding. *Get a grip, Char*. After all, she was the one who said it didn't matter either way it went.

Her mind was on that page, but her body wanted to run back to her flat, lock herself inside and throw the key out of the window so she couldn't make the same stupid decision again.

Forcing her hand to let go of one side of the dish, Charlie sucked in a breath and held it. Just as she was about to knock she heard that lovely song again inside Jake's flat. Pausing, she closed her eyes for a moment, listening to the melancholy tune and the soulful voice that sang along with it. That song. That voice. She was going to have to ask Jake who it was so she could get the album on her phone.

Ok. Let's get this done, she thought, then knocked on the yellow door. She waited, but nothing. So she knocked again, harder this time, and the music cut off. Her ears strained to pick up any sound from inside, any indication that he was on his way, and she prepared herself to look casual.

The door opened and it caught her off guard—like as if she hadn't expected him to answer after she'd knocked on his bloody door—and she almost dropped the dish.

Jake was standing there in a form-fitting, black T-shirt and grey sweat pants holding a blond, acoustic guitar down by his side by the neck. Charlie looked at it and then at Jake as she realised the music she'd heard had come from him. That was his gorgeous voice? Oh, wow. She felt herself melt a little inside.

His brow creased, as it always did whenever he saw her. Why did she think his brooding was so sexy? Stop!

"Hey," he said looking past her a moment.

Thankfully, her brain managed to get back on board and got her mouth moving. "Hi. Sorry. Did I disturb you?" She looked down at the guitar again.

Jake did too, then back at her, brows still pulled down low. "Uh, no."

Man of many words as always, at least when he wasn't strumming the guitar. "Okay, I decided to do some cooking today and I overestimated, so I have an extra shepherd's pie. Thought you might like to have it." Her hands gripped the dish as she held it out to him.

"Why would you think that?" The sharp tone in his voice surprised her.

Seriously? *Shit.* Charlie couldn't keep the heat from her cheeks. She knocks on the guy's door, doing a friendly neighbourly thing, and he gets annoyed by it? Well, hadn't she quickly learned from her mistake. Biting back what she really wanted to say, she went with nonchalance. No way was she going to show him how embarrassed she was.

"Look, I'm just going to throw it anyway, so you might as well do what you want with it." Giving him no choice, she practically rammed it into his chest and he took it from her hands quickly like he'd known what she really wanted to do with it.

Without looking at him again, Charlie walked away, trying to seem casual but really wanting to get the hell away from there as quickly as possible. "You can keep the dish," she threw at him over her shoulder as she headed back to her place.

Well, that definitely put the top hat on her attempt to befriend her neighbour.

Arsehole.

You're a dick!

Before she got too far, Jake called after his neighbour, wanting to make the situation right. Yes, he wanted to deter her from trying to befriend him, but he wasn't a total prick.

"Hey, Charlie?"

She paused and the way her head straightened before she turned back to him, Jake knew he'd fucked up. *You are a total prick.*

When she looked at him, her gaze narrowed slightly and she gave him a smile that didn't reach her eyes. "Yeah?"

"I apologise for that just now. It was out of order." He hoped he sounded sincere, but he wasn't used to this kind of stuff. "I've had a shit day and I shouldn't have taken it out on you."

After a moment, he expected her to tell him where to go, but he saw her shoulders drop a little, the storm clearing from her expression. "Okay."

"And thanks. I appreciate the food." It wasn't a lie. Jake had been so busy with work lately that he'd been too familiar with his microwave. Not that it was such a bad thing. He'd eaten far worse food than the shitty ready meals he'd lived on for the past couple of years. He couldn't remember the last time he'd had a home-cooked meal, but he knew who would have cooked it for him. His stomach sank at the thought. Nope. Not the time to go there right now.

The smell coming from the dish in his hand made his stomach rumble.

"I have some leftover gravy too if you want to come get some." Charlie walked away and he almost told her it was okay. Then figured he might as well if she was offering. He used to drown his food in his mum's gravy. The memory made him smile, which was something he rarely did lately. Especially when he thought of her.

Going back inside, he put his guitar on the stand in the hall and took the food to the kitchen, grabbing his key from the dish he kept by the microwave. When he got to Charlie's flat, he knocked and didn't have to wait long until she opened the door, holding a jug with foil over the top.

"Here." When she passed it to him Jake noticed she seemed to be avoiding looking at him. "Put the pie in the oven for half an hour or so."

He nodded. It was the first time Jake had really looked at her. He'd been so intent on dismissing her, he'd barely glanced at her whenever their paths had crossed, and he'd been so surprised and unsure when she'd appeared at his door that his only thoughts at that time were of how to get rid of her. It was now, as she stood in front of him in her navy leggings, white baggy jumper and beige fluffy slippers, that he realised how pretty she was. Her blonde hair was tied back in a messy bun and he noticed she had a light dusting of freckles across her nose that trickled onto her cheeks. She had one single, more prominent one sitting above her top lip towards the corner.

Look at me, he urged in his mind, wanting to see the colour of her eyes. The awkward silence he'd created seemed to do the trick. She looked up at him and finally, after he'd failed at trying not to wonder about them, the colour of her eyes was revealed as they questioned him—somewhere between blue and green. Unusual.

An unwanted feeling warmed his chest and knocked him off guard. He cleared his throat, like that was the way to get rid of it. Thinking he better say something before he started to look weird just standing there staring at her, he got his mouth moving. "Thank you." Yeah, that's all he seemed to have in his vocabulary right then, and the more he tried to expand on it, the more muddled his brain got.

Shit.

"I'll bring the dish and jug back when I'm done." So he did know other words?

Charlie nodded, still barely looking at him. "No rush. Just... whenever."

Jake needed to get back to his own place. This was already too much interaction. The effort he'd put in to avoiding her, appearing unapproachable so she would give up on trying to befriend him, didn't seem to be working. This wasn't a good idea. It certainly wasn't what you called keeping her at arm's length. Christ! He wished he had longer arms.

She had to stay a stranger. No matter what.

Still, it was just some shepherd's pie.

"Have a good night then," he said backing away from her door.

"You too."

When he got back inside his flat, he stood there for a second behind the closed door. It seemed his neighbour had piqued his interest, which wasn't helping the situation at all. *Don't be stupid, Jake.* Just because she was a nice woman, pretty, clearly thoughtful, it still wasn't going to change anything. Trouble was, she wasn't easily forgotten. It was bad enough he had to see her at all; it was pretty impossible to avoid her altogether when they lived on the same floor down the hall from each other. Now they'd interacted—more than just a passing acknowledgment—he'd made the mistake of taking notice.

Swallowing down his annoyance, Jake figured there was no point letting good food go to waste. He put the jug down on the counter, got a plate from the drainer and pulled the drawer open to get a knife to cut the shepherd's pie in half. He paused and looked over at the cutlery stand in the drainer beside the sink. No knife there. Then he looked in the sink, but it was empty. In his cutlery drawer there was a section where the sharp knives slotted into the plastic drawer separator. There were only three slots and one knife was missing. Checking around the kitchen, he couldn't see the missing knife anywhere. He checked the two other drawers underneath. Nothing. It wasn't like he had a huge amount of kitchen items in the small open-plan space for anything to get lost. Pausing, Jake knew he hadn't misplaced it. He'd cut up some potatoes with it last night, put his food in the oven—baked potatoes he'd later covered with microwaved tinned steak—then had gone for a shower, leaving the mess in the kitchen until later. Glancing at the drainer again, he searched through last night's clean pots just in case it had fallen through the basket. No joy there either.

With his brain now kicking into overdrive, he walked around the living room, checking everywhere, under the sofa and chair; pulling the cushions up, even wedging his hand down the edges to see if it had somehow managed to fall down there. It wasn't anywhere. Jake stood there panting, a tight feeling started to gnaw at his chest as his mind went back to last night, seeing Charlie outside his open flat door.

Fuck!

Had someone been inside his place?

Was it irrational to think someone had come in while he'd been in the shower and stolen a fucking dirty knife from in his kitchen? It was ridiculous, wasn't it? Nothing else appeared to be missing. He had an almost new iPhone he'd left on the side table in the living room along with his wallet, next to the sofa where he always kept them. Surely some opportunist who had ducked inside his open door would have taken something valuable, not an old kitchen knife.

He had to be way off. It was going to turn up somewhere and he'd laugh about it. Right?

Simple explanation.

Why, then, was he lying in his bed later that night with sleep evading him because he couldn't stop thinking about the fucking knife? And why had his flat door been wide open when he knew for a fact he'd closed it, just like he always did?

"...*when I was passing I saw the thing open and wondered if you knew.*"

Glancing over at the digital clock on his chest of drawers confirmed it was way too late to knock on Charlie's door, and also that he'd been lying there stewing over the damn things for over two hours. Two a.m. and he was wide awake.

Throwing the quilt off, he got up out of bed and grabbed the jogging pants he'd left on the laundry basket. Half-dressed with his phone in hand, Jake went out into his hall and switched the light on. He stopped at the front door and opened his phone, scrolling the top menu down and pressing on the torch. Shining the light on the lock, Jake inspected it on the inside first. No sign of anything being tampered with. So he opened the door and did the same on the outside. Just regular scratches caused by his and the many other keys that had been used in it before him. Moving to the edge of the door, he shone the torch all the way down. Nothing that looked suspicious. So he turned to the inside of the door frame.

There... right under the keep of the night latch. There were scratches, and some of the paint had rubbed off the frame underneath. He moved his finger over the marks that felt like scrapes. Paint came off on his finger.

Bingo! So some bastard had been in his flat.

The question was, who?

Closing his eyes, he forced his breath to remain steady as dread moved through him like a snake slithering and menacing.

This wasn't happening.

But it was.

With that and the phone call to his work, a knowing feeling twisted his gut. There was no more hesitating.

Jake was going to have to move again.

Chapter Eleven

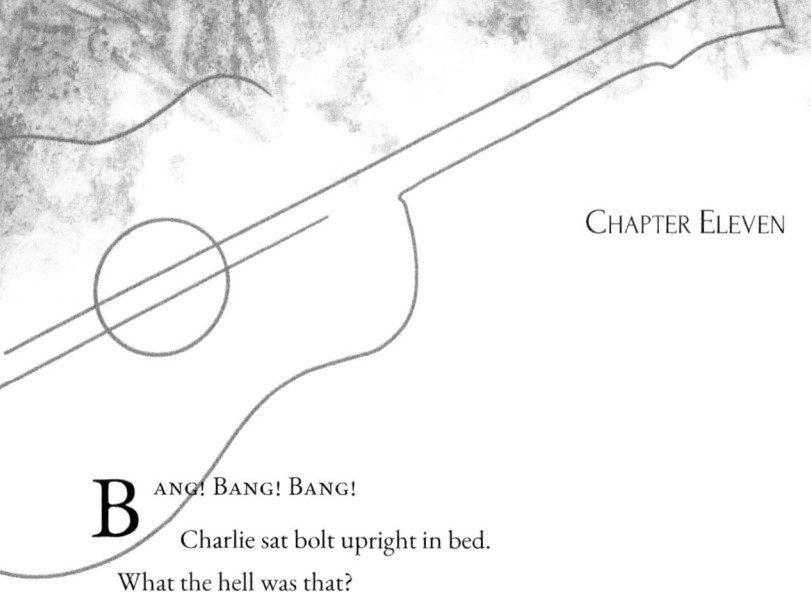

Bang! Bang! Bang!

Charlie sat bolt upright in bed.

What the hell was that?

Heart racing, her mind hadn't woken up with her body yet and she struggled to focus her vision for a second.

There it was again, only now it didn't sound so loud and was evident that someone was knocking on her front door.

Bloody hell.

What day is it? Sunday, her brain managed to somehow surmise through the fog. Yes, Sunday. After swinging her legs off the bed, Charlie tapped the screen of her phone that was on the bedside table.

Eight forty-seven. In the bloody morning. Sunday morning.

Who the hell was at her door at this time on a weekend?

"Charlie?"

It took her a second, but then she realised she knew the voice.

Jake.

Really?

With a fuzzy head, she got up and put her white fluffy dressing gown on, the one with the little cute owls all over it, and headed to the front door. A quick check in the mirror while she was passing revealed that she needed far more help than a quick hair straighten to make herself look more presentable, but with her neighbour's relentless knocking, she didn't exactly have time for a makeover.

When she opened the door, Charlie couldn't believe she was right. It was Jake, standing there with his hand on the door frame, his dark hair dishevelled, thick stubble coating his jaw. The man looked sexy as hell. And also like he hadn't had any sleep.

"What the—"

"Friday. When you found my door open. Did you see anyone hanging around the flats or anything?"

Hello to you too, she thought. Charlie was so confused for a minute; she just stared at him as her brain misfired. Then the fog cleared. Friday? What did she do—yes. Now she remembered. "Yes. There was a man."

"What man? Where?"

She made a quick glance down the hall. "Come inside."

He did, but turned to her the minute he stepped into her hallway. "What man, Charlie?"

"I don't even know where he'd come from, but just as I got to the door for our floor, it flew open and a man came rushing through. Almost knocked me over he was in such a hurry."

"Did you get a look at him? What did he look like?" His hand went in the front of his hair and it looked like he was having trouble keeping still.

Charlie thought back, trying to remember if she had seen his face, but all she could really remember was his dark clothes going past in a blur as he barged past. "He had a black cap on, so I didn't really see him properly. The prick never even looked back after he'd knocked my bag on the floor. Didn't acknowledge me at all." Then something registered. "Wait. He had grey scruff on his face." She blinked. "I don't know how I remember that. He didn't smell clean; was dressed quite scruffy."

"Anything else? Think," he snapped, looming over her in her personal space. In any other situation, Charlie would welcome the idea of him getting so close. Instead, she took a step back, annoyed by his boorish demeanour.

Eyes narrowing on him, she folded her arms. "I am thinking. You do realise I'm still half asleep, right?"

Jake stepped away, his shoulders dropping as he looked away from her, wiping his hand over his face. "Sorry. I've been awake most of the night. I waited until it was some kind of acceptable time before coming here."

"It's acceptable on a weekday." She took a breath, appeased by his apology. "What's going on anyway? I mean, you almost broke my door with your fist. Surely I get some explanation for it?"

Jake turned to her with a strange expression on his face. When those steel-blue eyes landed on her with such chagrin, his brows twisted. Then he blinked and looked away.

"Jake?"

"I need to go." Walking straight past her, he opened the door before turning halfway back around. "I'm sorry for disturbing you. If you think of anything else will you let me know?"

"Of course. But wait—"

Then he was gone, leaving her standing in her doorway completely perplexed as to what just happened.

Chapter Twelve

The following few days went by in a bit of a blur. Charlie had wrapped up most of her coursework for the term and was glad to get to Wednesday without any more drama. She hadn't seen Jake since Sunday and still felt bad that she hadn't remembered anything else about the man who had been in their building, especially as it was clearly very important to him. But she hadn't known she'd need to remember anything at the time. She'd been too pissed off with the idiot with no manners to care anyway.

On her way through the common room before she'd left, Charlie had noticed the poster for The Gifted Crow's open mic nights and it instantly sparked an idea. She'd taken it down off the notice board and had it folded in half in her hand as she approached Jake's flat. His bike was outside where he always parked it, so she knew he was home.

Here goes nothing, she thought as she knocked on his door, noticing he had a brand new, shiny lock. While she waited for an answer, Charlie prepared herself for the knock-back he was likely to give. The door opened and her heart sped up. What the hell was that about? He was just a man.

Mhmm. A man who made her stomach flutter. There was no denying it. And as he stood there in front of her in his navy work overalls, he looked pretty bloody handsome; the oil on his face only making this visit more of a treat for the eyes.

"Hey," he said looking surprised, and maybe a little irritated to see her.

"Hi. Hope I'm not disturbing your dinner or anything."

"I was just about to take a shower. What's up? Did you remember something?"

"Oh, no. Sorry." Holding the poster out to him she said, "I've heard you singing and playing your guitar a few times. It sounds great, by the way." That was playing it down a little. "So I thought you might be interested in this."

He hesitated then kept his eyes on hers when he took the poster. "You heard me?"

"Yeah, a few times when I've walked past. I liked it. You're really good." *Okay, calm it down a little Charlie.* She internally eye rolled herself.

His brows pulled down, probably at her over enthusiastic praise, which was annoying seeing as she'd paid him a compliment. People were usually happy about things like that.

"Thanks. What is this?" When he opened it up she noticed the oil on his hands too. And how strong they looked, and—*Stop it, you maniac.* As if it was appropriate to start thinking about his body parts. *For God's sake.* She really needed to get a grip. He was her neighbour. And honestly, he was a big hunk of confusion, especially when it came to their friendship. Or lack thereof. Sometimes it was like he wanted to talk to her, other times he seemed to do all he could not to. It was dizzying.

After a moment, Jake folded the poster again and handed it back to her. "It's not my scene. Thanks though."

When he backed away and started to close the door, dismissing her just like that, she reached out, stopping the door with her hand. "Wait.

How about you just come along? Get a feel for it. Then see if it's not your scene."

His hand flattened against the outside of the door and she fought hard not to look at it again—like she had some weird hand fetish all of a sudden. "Look. I appreciate you thinking of me—"

"We could go together." *Shit!* It just came out. When Charlie noticed his eyes widen slightly, she wished she could redo the moment so that she could maybe shove the poster in her mouth or something.

"It's not going to happen. Really. But thanks." The door moved slowly and his eyes narrowed a little as he looked at her. "Goodbye, Charlie."

When the door closed she stood there staring at it. Something about the way he'd said that last part didn't feel right. It wasn't said in a 'see you later' kind of way; it sounded like a permanent goodbye to her ears. And his face. . . Charlie would swear she'd seen regret in his eyes right before he disappeared from view.

Without realising, and before she could even think better of it, she found herself knocking on the door again. "Jake?"

After a few seconds, the door flew open this time and when he came into view she saw his chest expand as he closed his eyes. He breathed out steadily. "What now?" he asked more calmly than she'd expected.

"Is there something wrong?"

Dropping his head, the side of his mouth went up as he huffed out a, "Jesus."

"You can talk to me. I know we don't know each other all that well—"

"No. You're actually wrong about that." His frown was fierce. "We don't know each other *at all*. I helped you out of a tough spot. You repaid me with pie. That's the extent of our relationship." This time when he looked at her, the regret she thought she'd seen was nowhere on his face. Now he looked annoyed. "We're not friends Charlie."

"You're right. And I'm sorry if you think I was trying to interfere in your life. I just thought you could maybe use one. A friend, that is. But hey, let's just forget I came here and you can go back to ignoring me out in the hall."

Deflated, and more embarrassed than anything, Charlie started to walk away when. . .

"Someone was in my flat."

She stopped and turned to face him. He was half out the door and he tipped his head towards the inside, gesturing for her to go in by the looks of it. "You might as well come in."

Well, that was unexpected. A little nervous, Charlie went back and followed him inside, closing the door behind her. She couldn't keep her eyes from roaming around, checking the place out while she followed Jake into the living room.

"Want a tea or coffee?"

"Tea please." His flat had the same layout as hers only the opposite way around. Like she suspected all the flats in the building did, at least on their floor: A small hallway leading into the open plan living room and kitchen, separated by a breakfast bar. Another small hallway down the side of the kitchen that would have the one bedroom and bathroom, some of the flats had two bedrooms, but they were on the floors above. There would be a small storage and boiler cupboard at the end. Where her place was bright and neutral, Jake's was quite dark with one navy blue painted wall, the rest light grey. The kitchen had black cupboard doors and white countertops. Not much furniture to speak of, less than her, dark grey sofa and one matching chair, and a light wood TV unit with a decent size TV in front of the navy wall. A nest of tables had a lamp on it next to the sofa and there was a smaller lamp on the breakfast bar that separated the two rooms. Both were on, giving the room an ambient feel. She could smell something nice, a masculine scent that could be aftershave or deodorant.

"Have a seat while I make a drink."

She picked the chair; it was far enough away from him to feel comfortable. After all, he was right: they didn't know each other. This way, if he did turn psycho, like Jas already thought, she was closest to the flat door if she needed to get out of there fast.

Strange thing was, though, she didn't feel unsafe in his flat. There was something about Jake that she couldn't put her finger on. Yes, he was moody, as far as she could tell, that's all it was with him. Even when he'd clearly been annoyed that she'd knocked on his door again, he hadn't been an arse with her. She'd seen him calm down. Obviously he hadn't wanted to be one.

He seemed so conflicted whenever they interacted that it was hard for Charlie to get a proper read on him. It was almost like he was trying to be something he wasn't but the real him kept coming through. Like he wanted to keep her at arm's length and his attempts at being an arsehole weren't quite working out.

After a few awkwardly quiet minutes, Jake came in with two mugs and a bag of sugar that looked half full. "I put milk in. I should have asked."

"No, it's fine," she said as she took the hot mug. "I have it with milk."

He made quick work of getting the smaller table from the nest and putting it next to where she sat. "Here. Thought you could put your own sugar in. Or not. Whatever you want." He put the crumpled bag and a spoon down on the table.

"Thanks." She put one in.

"I didn't mean to be a dick with you out there." Taking a sip of his drink, Jake glanced over at her as he sat down on the sofa. "You can't think much of me when all I do is speak to you like that."

"I knocked again for a reason, Jake. If I thought you were a dick, I wouldn't have bothered. A moody git? Yes."

Was that a hint of a smile as he looked down into his cup? Funny how much you could learn about a person in such a small amount of time. She was beginning to think she was right and Jake wasn't what he was trying to be. Slowly, Charlie was peeling back the layers, and now she had seen a glimpse of his real self, she wanted to see more. Especially more of that smile.

"You said someone was in here? Do you think that was why your door was open?"

He nodded. "I know it is. There are marks on the door frame where someone slipped the lock."

"Did they take anything?"

"A kitchen knife. That's all that seems to be missing."

How strange? "Why would someone break into your flat and only take a knife?"

Jake shook his head before taking a sip of his drink. He leaned forward, resting his elbows on his knees. "It's something I've been asking myself since I realised it was missing."

Charlie suspected he wasn't telling her everything, but it wasn't her business, so she didn't want to press. He would tell her if he wanted to. It did unsettle her, though. Apart from the attack, she'd always felt safe here, but if someone had managed to get in the building and break into Jake's flat when he was inside, she couldn't help worrying about her own safety.

"Did you tell the police?" she asked as Jake got up and walked past her to go into the kitchen.

"Uh, no. Didn't see the point. I changed the lock on the door for a deadlock. You should maybe do the same."

He was right. She'd ask Jas to do it next time she saw him. Maybe she'd get a security camera too. When Jake finished rinsing his cup he stood facing her in the kitchen, hands leaning against the breakfast bar. When he looked at her he gave her a tight smile, but the lack of words made Charlie feel like he'd done talking.

Not one to outstay her welcome, she put her mug down and got up. "I should go. Thanks for letting me know about the break in."

"No worries." He kept his gaze down like he always did, especially when he was done interacting. So Charlie headed for the door, wanting to remove herself from the awkwardness as soon as possible. She stopped just as she reached the door and turned back to look at him as she got the poster out of her bag. "Look, I'm going to be at The Crow tomorrow night," she told him as she put the poster on his small hall table. "You should come along."

Charlie didn't give him time to tell her no; she left quickly, wondering why he'd closed off again so suddenly. And thinking she might be better off giving up trying to be Jake Sure's friend.

In the end, you get fed up with hitting your head against a brick wall, and it seemed like Jake's was also covered in a thick layer of concrete.

Chapter Thirteen

He'd never been near the university before. In fact, he hadn't been anywhere near the area, so it took him a few wrong turns before he found the street where The Gifted Crow was situated. Since Jake had left his place, there had been a few times he'd almost turned around and ridden back home again. What possessed him to accept Charlie's invitation, he didn't know. But he was here, standing a few yards away from the front entrance where two bouncers chatted and greeted those who had arrived as late as him. There were people coming in and out all the time, a few hanging around outside smoking. Jake wasn't exactly dressed for any kind of night out. Unlike the clientele in this place, with their trendy, stylish clothes, he knew the minute he went inside he'd stand out like red dye in a swimming pool in his bike gear.

Best get it over with before he changed his mind then.

Giving his bike another once over, for no other reason than to delay a little longer, Jake headed to the door, waiting behind a couple of girls who had to present their IDs. Then it was his turn. One of the doormen, the taller of the two, looked him up and down and nodded to his helmet. "You can't take that inside."

Ridiculous. Pretty sure if anyone was going to start trouble they wouldn't bother wearing a motorbike helmet to do it. "Do you have a cloakroom?"

The guy looked at him for a second. "Right inside. Make sure you check it." he warned as he opened the door.

"Will do." Jake checked his jacket in as well, and felt much better in his T-shirt. For some reason, he felt the need to straighten his hair, trying to ignore the most likely explanation for it. As if it mattered anyway. Like she hadn't seen him in a worse state, all oiled up and in his work scruffs.

What the hell was he doing?

He'd be leaving soon anyway, so what difference did it make? Just as soon as he found another place he'd be gone. Hopefully somewhere further south and as far away as he could afford to get from here.

There was a band in full swing when he got inside. They were pretty loud; it took a minute for his ears to adjust. The place was packed, and he felt uncomfortable straight away, the urge to leave riding him again as his eyes darted around the place. He couldn't see the band. The room he was in was just a bar area with a pool table that was covered over and had some people sitting on the edge of it. Following the music, he squeezed through the bodies until he entered another room. This one was pretty big and he clocked the stage at the far end. Most people were standing. Only a few sat at tables he could see around where he was, and he wondered if he was ever going to spot Charlie. Maybe she hadn't come after all, which would be better for him in the end.

Jake squeezed himself on the end of the bar, figuring he might as well get a coke. The band was pretty good actually; only three musicians; a drummer, bassist, and guitar vocalist. The music was a little heavy for his taste, but they could certainly play. After he'd listened to another song, he went walkabout again, hoping to catch a glimpse of Charlie before he gave up and left. Just as he was squeezing past a group of lads who were obviously fans of the band, singing along loudly to every word, he thought he heard his name. Looking around through the sea of heads, he couldn't see anyone. Probably wasn't even him they were calling. There could be any number of Jakes in the pub tonight. He started forward again then felt a tug on his arm.

When he turned around, Charlie was beaming at him, and for a crazy moment, Jake found himself smiling back at her just as wide.

"You came," she said, stating the obvious. Her blonde hair was tied back from her face at the top, the rest hanging down just past her shoulders in shaggy waves, the lights overhead shining off her highlights. She had dark makeup around her eyes, far more than he'd seen her wear before. He watched her mouth move, her muted brown lipstick enhancing her full lips as she spoke to him, and he found himself transfixed on them. But he couldn't hear a damn thing as the guitar on stage went crazy, belting out a crunching solo that tore at his ears.

He pointed to his ear and shook his head. Then Charlie gestured for him to follow. He took that moment to give her a quick once-over as she went off a little in front of him. She wore the tightest grey jeans that made her slim legs look like they went on for days, and a light pink, strappy top tucked into the waistband. Jake looked up, not happy with how much he appreciated the view. Instead, he kept his eyes on the back of her head as she moved away from the main thick of the crowd into a smaller room just off to the side.

It was still loud, but was much more bearable.

She stopped at a high table that had three other people around it. Jake recognised the man. He remembered the look the guy had given him outside Charlie's flat last week. There were two women, one of which—the one with the brightest coloured bandana holding her hair up—he'd seen in the hallway that night too. The blonde one he wasn't sure about.

Charlie leaned into him and he got a strong waft of her perfume, all fruity and fresh. He did not inhale deeply. Only he did; he liked it. *Really* liked it. "These are my friends, Jason, his girlfriend Selena, and this is Cara."

They all said their hellos. Jason the most reserved, giving him the side-eye while the other two smiled and introduced themselves. Charlie dragged a stool over from the next table and put it in front of him. Jake wasn't all that pleased about meeting her friends. In fact, part of him thought she might have come on her own; it was the main reason he'd forced himself to come at all. He should have known, though. It was sensible not to come to such a busy place alone, especially after what had happened the other week. Although why he was so concerned, he didn't want to think about too deeply.

Jason got up. "Gotta take a piss. Anyone want anything from the bar?"

Orders were called out to him, and Charlie looked at Jake. "Can I get you a drink?"

"No, I'm good thanks," he held up his half-empty pint of coke.

"Make sure you wash your hands before you handle my drink," Cara shouted across the table as Jason left. "So, Jake?" She leaned towards him, her chin resting on her hand. "Are you from around here?"

"Cara." Charlie rolled her eyes and looked at him as if to say *"sorry"*.

"What?" her friend asked all innocent. "It's just a normal question you ask someone when you first meet them."

"No," he replied, not elaborating any further and he saw Cara's eyes narrow, her overly long lashes almost meeting.

"Ooh, the mysterious type." And then she gave him a playful wink.

"Ignore her." Charlie smiled at him. "I promise she isn't this bad when she hasn't got alcohol inside her."

"You lie," Cara said, and laughed along with the other woman who seemed more timid.

The night went by quite quickly and wasn't too painful even though Jake was on soft drinks and he got the sense Jason wasn't all that eager for him to be there. They watched two male solo singers, and a male/female acoustic duo, and when the MC came on and thanked the artists, it looked like it wasn't only Jake's cue to leave.

"We should get out of here before the god-awful dance music starts," Charlie said close to him, filling his head with that scent again, making him dizzy from it. Jason and his girlfriend got up at the same time, and Jake and the others joined them, grabbing coats off stools and belongings from the table.

After getting his jacket and helmet from the cloakroom on the way out, he went outside where they were all waiting for him by the front entrance.

"No. It'll cost way too much," Charlie was saying as he joined them. "I'll get a separate one."

"It's no problem. We'll all chip in," her friend Jason said.

Jake was curious. "What's going on?"

"They want to share a taxi so they can drop me off first, but it's right out of their way."

Cara put her hand on Charlie's arm. "It doesn't matter, Char. There are three of us so once we split the fare it'll be hardly any different."

"I can give you a ride." Hmm. For some reason he couldn't surmise, Jake hadn't even had to think about it. Why not? It made sense seeing as they were going to the same place.

No one spoke for a minute. Instead they all looked at him. Jason's face was like a thunder cloud. Jake was starting to wonder if there'd been anything between him and Charlie with how territorial the guy seemed to be over her. Then he noticed Cara move her gaze to Charlie as she tried to bite away a smile. Yeah, he wasn't too happy her friend was already close to marrying them off. Maybe it wasn't the best idea after all.

"On your bike?" Charlie asked.

"Yeah. You okay with that?" he asked, curious as to why she'd started biting the edge of her lip. "You' never been on the back of a bike before?"

Her eyebrows went up. "No. But I'm more concerned about these heels." She lifted her foot slightly and gestured to the ankle boots that had maybe a three inch heel. "Shouldn't be an issue. They'll hook the pegs. Makes sense seeing as we're going to the same place."

"Umm, yeah, okay. Thanks." Turning to her friends who were still far too quiet, and Jason was looking at the floor, definitely unimpressed. "I'll see you all tomorrow then."

Cara was first to hug Charlie and Jake was sure she whispered something in her ear, especially when he saw Charlie's jaw tighten a little before she gently nudged her friend away. "Goodbye, Cara." Her friend giggled.

"Bye Jake. Nice to meet you," Cara said with a narrow-eyed smile.

After the goodbyes were done, and her friends had gone, Charlie looked at him briefly, her hands in the pockets of her waist-length leather jacket. Then she gave him a tight-lipped smile and looked down the street. "Where's your bike?"

So this was just as awkward for her.

He started walking. "Just down here."

As they approached where he'd parked, Jake heard her footsteps slowing behind him and he turned back to her. Going by her blank expression, he could tell she was nervous, made more obvious by the way she swallowed as if her throat had gone dry. Without thought,

Jake reached for her hand. It was too late when he realised what he'd done, so he made out like it was a natural thing to do, no big deal at all. Ignoring how he really felt. Gently, he squeezed her fingers in reassurance, just like he would if it was anyone. Yeah right.

"I'll keep you safe," he said with a slight smile before letting go of her hand.

Charlie just looked at him, and he saw her take in a breath through her nose right before she nodded.

Taking his gloves out of the helmet, he held it out to her. "Here, put this on. Might be a little loose but at least it's something."

She held it in both hands and looked up at him. "What about you?"

"I'll be fine. I'll stick to the back roads."

Shame really; the night was clear—perfect conditions for a blast out down the motorway. He'd have liked to take Charlie for a real spin, show her how exhilarating being on a bike could be. *Shit.* Now he was thinking of things he'd like to do with her? Good job there was only one helmet then. He wouldn't risk getting pulled so it was out of the question anyway.

Maybe another time, he thought, and then quickly dismissed it.

As he mounted the bike, he did worry she might not be warm enough. With the weather getting milder, she was in a waist-length jacket and it wasn't very thick. When he looked up to give her the gloves to at least keep her hands warm, he couldn't help the smile that graced his usually deadpan face. The helmet almost covered her eyes and she was struggling to tighten the strap under her chin.

He reached up and crooked his finger. "Here. Let me help."

Charlie moved closer and he tightened the strap, careful to avoid trapping her skin. When his eyes moved up to hers she was looking at him in a way he didn't want to take any notice of. But of course he did, swallowing at the sudden warm feeling in the pit of his stomach.

Blinking, he held out the gloves to her. "You should put these on too. Your hands are going to be exposed to the wind at the front of me."

Without a word, she took them and put them on.

"The only thing I need to ask you is, don't try and fight me when I lean into a bend. Just hold on and go with me, okay? I promise you won't go anywhere."

He watched her head move up and down, and could still see the uncertainty in her eyes.

"Trust me." Jake climbed on and powered up the engine, the twin exhausts growling into life. He twisted his wrist on the throttle and gave it a rev or two, then scooted as far forward as he could. The seat wasn't really equipped for a pillion passenger, but she was small enough to fit back there and luckily he had a short back rest so she wouldn't fall off.

When he felt her hand grip his shoulder, Jake braced himself as Charlie mounted the bike, trying to force his thoughts away from the warmth of her body against his. It didn't work. Then she made things worse when she wriggled a little as she made herself comfortable, placing her feet on the back pins. When he felt her hesitantly move her arms around his waist, he closed his eyes for a second. Last thing he wanted was to like the feel of them there, but, yeah... his body was on a different page with that. Ignoring it as best he could, he realised she was only holding on lightly.

He turned to speak to her above the roar of the sawn pipes. "Put your body right up against me," which wasn't going to help him at all, "and hold on as tight as you can. Lock one hand over the other."

As soon as he felt her press up against him, and after giving himself a minute to compose his damn self, he said, "You ready?"

When she nodded, he touched her hands briefly to check they were tight, and moved off slowly to give her a chance to get used to it. When he'd gone a short distance, he turned his head to the side and shouted, "You okay?"

He felt her squeeze his waist in reply. Then he pushed his body back into hers just a little for some extra security, and sped up.

The ride went without a hitch.

They didn't see any police, and thankfully, Charlie was still there on the back when he pulled into their street. Jake purposefully slowed a little, wanting to postpone their arrival just a little longer, and cursing himself for the fact. He took it easy as he approached the building where they lived. Then he pulled into his dedicated space close to the front door. When he kicked the stand down and switched off the engine, he felt Charlie rest her head on his back. She hadn't removed her arms from around him yet either and he paused, taking advantage of the moment, his shoulders relaxing for what felt like the first time in a decade.

No. *Stop.*

What are you thinking, you idiot?

Covering her hands with his he squeezed a little. "You okay?"

When she sat back and removed her arms, he felt both relieved and bereft.

"Yeah. Oh wow. Yes I'm fine." Jake stayed where he was so she could use him to get off the bike. "Um, well. I actually enjoyed it for the most part," she said in a muted, breathy voice as she dismounted.

So had he, except he enjoyed the whole of it.

Jake got off the bike. "I'll be right back." He quickly went inside to his letter box and got the chain lock out. Back outside he secured it to the ground anchor he'd put down after he'd first moved in. When he stood, Charlie had removed the gloves and was, again, struggling with the chin strap on his helmet.

"This bloody thing," she huffed, sounding frustrated with herself.

Sighing internally, he went to assist her, this time making quicker work of it. Not wanting to fall into the entrapment of her greeny-blue eyes again.

"Thanks," she said as she removed it and handed it back to him.

They faced each other for a minute and Jake suddenly didn't know what to say, but he knew he wanted to retreat and get up to his flat as soon as possible. He'd already been around the woman for too long tonight, and that ride back, with her body moulded to his as she'd clung to him, had only made things worse. He was intrigued by her—couldn't deny that he fancied her; it was the reason he'd gone to the pub tonight. Charlie was getting under his skin and it was dangerous. There was no way he could stick around after what had happened the other day. After tonight, he was even more determined to leave behind another complication. Even if she did make him feel things he hadn't expected.

"Best get inside then." The shiver in her voice brought him out of his head.

"Shit. Yeah you're freezing," he said, noticing her teeth were almost chattering as she hugged her small jacket tightly closed.

They made their way inside and even though Charlie was trying to hide it, he could see she was still shivering.

"I was okay for the first half of the trip."

He let her go up the stairs first, and made sure he kept his eyes downward of her body. Choosing to admire the grey linoleum-covered steps. "Yeah, the wind doesn't half get you on a bike. I thought my body might shield you a bit more."

Once they got to the first floor, they were quiet for the rest of the short walk down the hall. When they both stopped outside his door, Charlie faced him, her cheeks a little pink, and didn't that make her look even more attractive.

"I'm really glad you came tonight."

Although he shouldn't have gone, Jake didn't want to lie to her. "Me too. The music was great. It was busier than I expected."

"The open mic nights have really taken off." Those unusually coloured eyes widened and lit up her whole face. "Hey, you should perform."

He took a step back. "Oh, no. I'm not—"

"Jake." When she stepped closer to him, her hand landing on his forearm, he looked down at it, wanting to pull it away. This was too close for his comfort, "You have a brilliant voice, and the way you play is. . . you should let people hear it."

"It's not my thing. But thanks for the compliment." Turning away from her, needing to break the contact, he stuck his key in the lock and opened the door. When he glanced back she was moving away with a crestfallen look. Jake wished he could tell her yes. Not for any other reason than the fact he actually liked her and didn't want her to look at him like that.

For a moment, he found himself biting back words he couldn't say. *You can't do this, Jake.* As much as he'd love to play for an audience again, it wasn't his life anymore. He couldn't get any more involved with Charlie or her friends. Never mind think of living a regular life. There was a brief moment when he thought he could move on. Now, though, the only moving on he could possibly do was from this place. If that prick was back, Jake couldn't risk staying here. He had someone else to think about, and now Charlie too. The darkness had started to creep back in. At least he'd had a brief respite from it. He hated the way his life had turned out, even more so now because he had to turn away from Charlie. In a strange turn of events Jake found himself not wanting to.

"Okay. Well, thanks again for the ride." Her voice cut through Jake's unease and he realised he'd missed his chance to say something as she walked away. He watched as she reached her apartment, unable to accept what should be a simple invitation to perform at the fucking pub, which is what he'd like to do.

Looking back down the hall at him, Charlie gave him a slight smile as she paused at her door. "Goodnight Jake."

"Night Charlie."

Still he stayed there, wondering how the hell he'd allowed himself to get here.

Inside his flat, when he was stripped of his clothes, Jake sat up leaning against the headboard of his bed with a coffee on the bedside table, reading the same line of the John Grisham book over and over again whilst trying to rid his thoughts of his neighbour. Except, all he kept thinking about was her arms gripping his torso tightly, her thighs either side of his arse. He put his head back and when he closed his eyes she was there, the image of her smiling at him when he'd turned around in the pub. And again, the way she'd looked at him as he'd tightened the helmet's neck strap, her eyes unmoving. He'd been trapped by the intensity of them in that moment, and he'd felt like she was letting him know she was interested too.

Dangerously, Jake imagined what it would be like to kiss her. He knew her lips would be soft; he could tell by the fullness of them. And, of course, he already knew in a way what her body felt like wrapped around him.

Shit.

He lifted his head, expanding his lungs as he tried, again, to push her from his mind, but it was too late. His cock had enjoyed the brief fantasy and he wanted to punch the fucking thing. Punishing it for betraying him, Jake ignored the hard-on and put his book on the side.

When he was under the quilt, he reached over and turned the lamp out.

Sleep needed to happen straight away.

If it was the only thing that would stop his mind, or his hand for that matter, from wandering to things it shouldn't. *Fuck*. He'd sleep his whole damn life if he had to.

"Goodnight Jake."

Shit.

It was going to be a long night.

Chapter Fourteen

Six days had passed since the night Jake had met her at The Crow and Charlie had seen no sign of him since. It wasn't hard to guess he was doing all he could to avoid her, and if she was being completely honest it stung. They'd got on pretty well. He seemed to warm to her friends and vice versa. Or so she'd thought. Perhaps he was being polite because he'd regretted it, and had spared her the embarrassment of skipping out on her in front of her friends.

Maybe she was completely mistaken, but outside the pub, when he'd helped her with the helmet, she thought there had been a moment between them. Clearly she'd misread that, as always. Since then Charlie hadn't been able to get him out of her head. No matter how hard she'd tried.

In the pub that night, Jake had been so different to what she'd seen of him before. He'd laughed, smiled, even though she knew he'd been uncomfortable sitting there with her friends. She'd seen another little glimpse of the real him coming through. Then, when he promised to keep her safe on his bike, Charlie had believed him.

It made her even more determined to keep chipping away at him.

But he'd gone off the grid.

They usually left around the same time in the mornings, and she hadn't seen him leaving for work once since. Every time she'd left the building his bike was already gone. Charlie had started to wonder if he'd moved out. But his bike was in its parking spot tonight when she'd got home and the moment she'd spotted it a spark of joy lit up inside her. This foolishness had to end.

That was why she'd quietly shoved the poster for the open mic night under his door on her way past earlier instead of knocking.

It was ridiculous really. Why she was still hanging on to the hope of them being friends, she didn't know. Well, that wasn't entirely true. She fancied the hell out of him. That was that. Why deny it?

Still, Jake had made it pretty clear the feeling wasn't mutual.

Charlie was glad when her hair was dry so she could finish getting ready and stop moping around thinking about the man.

Twenty minutes later, she was heading out of her flat when a glance down the hall had her ducking back inside. Carefully and slowly, she leaned her head out to watch the two police officers who were leaving Jake's flat. They turned to him, one of them spoke and Jake nodded, his expression grim. They said goodbye and when they moved to walk away Charlie ducked back inside, closing her door as quietly as she could. Why would the police be at Jake's? Now her mind had started working overtime. What if something had happened and that was the reason she hadn't seen him. If that was the case she'd feel really shit for thinking he was avoiding her. Perhaps he was in trouble. But as much as she didn't know him, and unlike Cara, Charlie was reluctant to believe he was into anything dodgy.

Then she remembered about the break-in. Perhaps he'd decided to report it after all. It made her feel a little better.

Besides, what was the point in speculating when she probably would never know anyway? It was none of her business—end of story—so why the hell was she standing there doing this?

Grabbing her phone out of her bag, she texted Jas to tell him she'd be another five minutes to make sure the police had gone and that

Jake was back inside his flat. Jason and Selena were picking her up for their dinner date with Cara for her birthday, and she was already ten minutes late. But still, she waited.

Funny, before tonight, Charlie had wanted to bump into Jake and now she was making sure she didn't.

After a little while longer, she headed out, walking swiftly down the hall. When she got near Jake's door she heard the guitar and couldn't help slowing to listen to him play for a minute. There was no singing right then, just the soft, ambient sound of his acoustic, his fingers picking a slow tune.

It was lovely. And if she wasn't already late she'd stay there a little longer.

Forcing herself to move, she headed out and cursed at the rain, staying under the cover of the arched porch as she looked for Jas's grey Vauxhall Astra. When she spotted it outside the next building she ran but still got soaked. The back passenger door opened and she jumped in, surprised to see Cara was in the back already.

Shivering, Charlie wiped the rain from her face, hoping it hadn't smudged her makeup. "Could you have parked further away?" she asked Jas, flicking her hair out of her face.

"Well, it wasn't raining when we parked up but you've taken so long it's even changed seasons," he said from the driver's seat.

"Funny."

As the car pulled off Charlie was about to mention the police at Jake's when she realised no one was talking. She looked over at Cara. "I thought you were meeting us there?" Then saw her friend's eyes were all red. "What's wrong?"

Cara wiped her nose on a tissue she'd had screwed up in her hand. "My parents are splitting up."

"Oh no. I'm so sorry. I didn't know they were having problems." She reached over and took Cara's hand.

"Neither did I. I mean, they argue and stuff, but that's normal. They've been together a long time. That's how it's supposed to be." Her breath hitched. "Dad is leaving to stay with my grandparents in Barbados for a month and then they are going to talk. I just feel like my whole world is changing, you know?"

Cara looked at Charlie with such sadness in her eyes it filled her own eyes with tears. Her friend was always smiling. She never let problems deflate her bubbly personality; always looked upon the world with challenge in her eyes. If there was a problem it was in Cara's nature to defeat it. Seeing her so upset reminded Charlie that no matter who you were, life kicked you in the stomach at some point. No one could escape adversity.

"You'll get through this. All of you."

Cara nodded, her mouth drawn down as she sniffed and wiped her nose, holding her hand for the whole car ride.

The meal was great. A much needed time out that Charlie hadn't realised she needed. Time went too fast, but that's what happened when you laughed all the way through dinner and had such a great time. Cara had forgotten her woes too, which meant their night had been a success in many ways. Charlie's friends meant the world to her. Since she'd moved down from Warrington this small group of people had changed her life in a way they couldn't possibly know. Dale had really shattered her confidence and self-worth, to the point where she'd doubted herself so much she'd almost turned the university acceptances down. Charlie could have gone to a few different places, but she'd chosen Hatfield because it was the furthest away, figuring the further away she got from her so called ex-fiancé, the harder it would be for Dale to get to her.

He wasn't the main reason she was glad to have chosen to come here; now it was more about the friends she'd made than how much safer she felt.

Had felt, she should say. Past tense.

Her stomach sank for a moment at the thought of that arsehole trying to get in touch with her after all this time. Pushing it aside, she was determined not to let that man in her head again, especially not when she'd had such a good time. It was Cara who needed the attention tonight. Thankfully, she was her usual sunny self by the time they left the restaurant.

Jas and Selena walked arm in arm in front of Charlie and Cara as they made their way over to Jas's car. It was a typical spring evening with a slight breeze in the air. The temperature had changed over the last week meaning the days were getting warmer but the nights still remained a little chilly. There was a familiar smell in the air reminding Charlie that summer was on its way.

"I feel so much better after spending time with you guys. Thank you for cheering me up," Cara said as she linked her arm through Charlie's. Her friend sighed. "It's a shame to waste this lovely night, though. It's still early." Stopping abruptly, she squeezed Charlie's arm. "Hey. How about we be spontaneous and go to a club."

"It's Wednesday." And it wasn't like Charlie's feet could take anymore torture from her strappy shoes. The bloody things weren't made for standing in never mind clubbing.

"So, it's a school night. We're adults though, in case you didn't notice, which means we get to make our own decisions and won't get told off for them."

"What's going on?" Jas asked as he and Selena went to their respective sides of the car.

Cara looked at Charlie with that beaming smile she always wore whenever an idea had taken route. She skipped over to Jas, pulling Charlie along with her. "How do you fancy making a night of it?"

Jason's eyes narrowed on Cara. "Like how?"

"We're going clubbing. Are you two coming?"

"Hey. I haven't said I was going anywhere," Charlie said as her friend's eyes pinned her again.

"But you were going to." The woman turned away before Charlie could protest. "Come with us. Let's have some fun."

When Jas looked at Charlie she pulled a *help me* face behind Cara's back.

"No thanks. We're going to my place. You two enjoy yourselves though." Jas, who had just become Charlie's ex-friend, didn't hide his smirk as he quickly got into the car. Selena gave them a sorry smile right before she got in her side.

"How rude," Cara said, keeping hold of Charlie's arm. "We don't need those love birds tagging along anyway, fawning over each other."

"Cara." Charlie held strong when her friend went to walk. "We really shouldn't be going clubbing tonight."

Then her friend's eyes dropped along with her shoulders. "I suppose I could just go home and get depressed again. Yeah. You're right. Let's just go home."

Oh, she was good. Even though she knew Cara was being sly, especially when her friend's eyes flicked up to see if her ruse was working before looking back down at the ground again with her mock sadness, Charlie couldn't help feeling guilty about leaving her. It was probably the truth; Cara would go home and get all depressed about her parents again.

"Come on." Charlie started walking the other way. "But I mean it, Car, I'm home by midnight."

"Okay, Cinderella."

As her friend bounced along, Charlie knew she was going to regret this in the morning.

Chapter Fifteen

Rubbing his dry eyes, Jake rested his head on the back of the sofa. He'd scrolled through enough web pages he was getting dizzy from it and his eyes couldn't focus properly anymore. Closing them to rest them for a minute, he got instantly irritated with himself when a certain blonde woman's face popped into his head.

Shit. He needed to get a head check.

He'd have thought by now, after doing all he could to avoid Charlie since last week, that he'd be over these thoughts by now. No such luck, it seemed. She'd been on his mind almost constantly; the harder he'd tried to forget her, the more persistent his thoughts got. It was like his own brain was mocking him.

It was making him irritable.

When he was done powering down his laptop, he reached over and turned the lamp off before he got up from the sofa, grabbing his phone on the way out of the living room. He might as well go to bed, even though he knew he'd have trouble sleeping. Seemed a waste to dirty the sheets when he wasn't getting proper use out of them, but he'd been on the couch searching through places to rent for hours and his neck and lower back were stiff as hell. Might as well be more comfortable.

He'd just turned the light out in the kitchen when he heard a noise out in the hall. He knew it was pretty late, but he looked at the time on his phone. Almost one a.m.. Pausing for a minute to see if he heard it again, he glanced down at his tool bag under the hall table. When there was a muted bang, he reached down and quietly got out his wrench before walking on light feet to the door. Slowly unlocking the deadlock he pulled the lever down, opened the door as quietly as possible, and looked through the gap as he made it bigger. Right outside was all clear. Then he heard a soft giggle as he leaned around the door frame to check down the hall.

When he stuck his head out, he was surprised to see Charlie was up the hall about halfway between his door and hers. She was bent over trying, and failing, to retrieve one of her shoes from the floor. He noticed the other one was under her arm.

Jake put the wrench down just inside his doorway and noticed a piece of folded paper on the floor. He ignored it and went out. "Charlie?"

She spun around and wobbled as she put her finger to her mouth. "Shh. You'll wake them up."

"Who?" He started to walk towards her, guessing she'd just come in from the pub or somewhere. She was wearing blue skinny jeans and her black shoes were dainty things with big heels.

"The neighbours."

"What are you doing?" Jake couldn't fight his amusement as he approached her and she looked up at him from her bent over position. She started laughing quietly; her mouth was open, and her face was amused, but there was barely any sound coming out. She dropped her shoe and clutched her belly.

"I. . .," more laughter. Louder this time, "tripped over my shoe and I wasn't even wearing it." Her laugh grew louder, and as she closed her eyes, she almost went down.

Jake grabbed the top of her arms, and her eyes widened as she tried to focus on him. "Oops. I'm a little tipsy."

Yeah, no... Definitely more than tipsy.

"We were in the club and Cara kept buying the shots, and there was Prosecco, and...," frowning, her hand came up and she pointed at him with a wobbly finger, "I told her to stop buying shots."

"I don't think she listened. Come on." He held her gently and guided her around to face the right way, picking up her shoe. "I think you need to get some sleep."

"Why?" she asked as she tried to turn back around, but he kept her walking. "Is it morning?"

"Not yet." They stopped at her door. "Where's your key? Is it in your bag?"

Practically lifting the small black handbag to her chin, Charlie struggled to open the zip.

"Is this mine?" She held it out to him and started laughing again, falling forward this time against his chest.

When his arms went around her, he got cloaked in the same perfume scent that had almost knocked him out in the pub last week. He enjoyed it for a moment before helping her stand on her own again. When her laughter died down, Jake got her handbag in his chest and he caught it just before it fell.

"Oh, Jake. I can't do it."

"They're in here?" Opening the zip, he felt awkward as hell putting his hand inside a woman's handbag, but if he didn't they'd be here all night. He peeked inside just as his fingers hit a bunch of keys.

Charlie had hold of his forearm and while he held it in place for her to balance on, he juggled the keys in his other hand and recognised one of them. It was the same make as the one he'd had before he changed the lock. As he tried that one in the lock, Charlie leaned into his arm and he glanced at her, smiling like an idiot as he took in her lazy expression. Her cheeks were flushed and it looked good on her.

"Jake?"

"Yeah?"

Bingo. The door opened, and not before time because the next thing she said was, "I don't feel too good. I think I'm going to puke."

Oh, shit.

"Whoa. Okay." He guided her in front of him, keeping hold of her arms. "Don't do it yet." Luckily, her flat was a mirror image of his so he guided her straight to the bathroom, lifting the lid of the toilet and getting out of the way just in time. She let out a moan and. . . out it came.

Holding her steady with one hand while she emptied her stomach, he pulled her hair back, noticing how soft it felt in his calloused hand. "You okay?" he asked when it stopped.

It took her a minute to answer. "Oh God. I'm so sorry, Jake."

Leaning over, he broke some toilet roll off the roll in the holder on the wall and handed it to her. "Here."

She stood up and her shoulders slumped when she took it and wiped her mouth before throwing it into the basin and flushing the chain.

"Feel better now?"

When she turned to him she just nodded, looking up at him with black, mascara-smudged, puppy dog eyes that told him how awful she felt. And it must have made her dizzy because she fell forward and he caught her—again.

Except this time when he went to right her, her arms went around him, pulling him forward and he froze when she placed her head on his chest, holding his arms out of the way, wide enough not to touch her, Jake closed his eyes and tried not to inhale that intoxicating scent deep into his lungs. He failed. *Damn*, she smelled good. Christ, now he could also smell her fruit-scented hair, and her closeness was driving him up the wall.

"I know this is probably wrong," she said, still holding him, "but can I just stay here for a second?"

Probably wrong? How about definitely wrong. For all the reasons Jake had spent the last few days convincing himself of. "I don't think it's a good idea, Charlie."

"Okay. I know sober me would agree with you, but. . ."

She made a little noise when she sighed and his eyes went up to the ceiling as he tried not to take any notice of how good it felt to have her so close. "I haven't had a hug for ages, and you're warm."

Fucking hell. So was she. Jake took a deep breath, fighting his flight mode as her mixture of scents washed over him, doing stuff to his insides and almost knocking all the sense out of him. She's drunk, he reminded himself. That's all this is. Nothing more. He wished she hadn't tripped outside in the hall; he would have been lying in his bed right now, not sleeping as usual, imagining her body pressed up against his from a safe distance, instead of standing in Charlie's flat with her actual body pressed up against his.

Shit. It was nice.

Before he could stop it happening, his arms slowly closed around her, keeping his touch light as his hands rested on her back. As much as he had the urge to explore, he made sure he didn't move them. Then he felt her arms tighten a little, and he tried desperately to ignore the feel of her breasts pressing into him. But he couldn't. Neither could his dick all of a sudden. *Shit.* He needed to put space between them—to breathe.

"Okay." His hands moved to her arms, gently prizing them from around his body. "I need to go." When he was free, he backed away, his heart beating faster than it should be. She wobbled a little but managed to find her balance herself this time.

"Yes, you should leave so I can go lie down and try and sleep this dizziness away." she said, waving that finger at him again. "Oh, and thanks for, you know. . ."

"It's no problem." Actually, it was a big fucking problem. "Will you be okay?"

Her eyebrows shot up when she looked at him. Then she squinted and waved her hand in the air. "Of course." Turning away, Charlie threw him a wave over her shoulder as she walked towards her bedroom. "You're a good hugger, by the way. You should hug more people."

Charlie's voice drifted away as Jake headed out of her flat.

Maybe she was drunk enough to forget this happened. With any luck she won't remember a thing in the morning.

Jake wished he could be so lucky.

As he headed back to his own flat, he felt no relief even though he was away from the situation—away from her. Instead, he dreaded going to bed because it was time alone with his thoughts, and they'd caused him enough grief after she'd been on the back of his bike. Now, having had her wrapped around his front this time, Jake knew he was doomed.

Chapter Sixteen

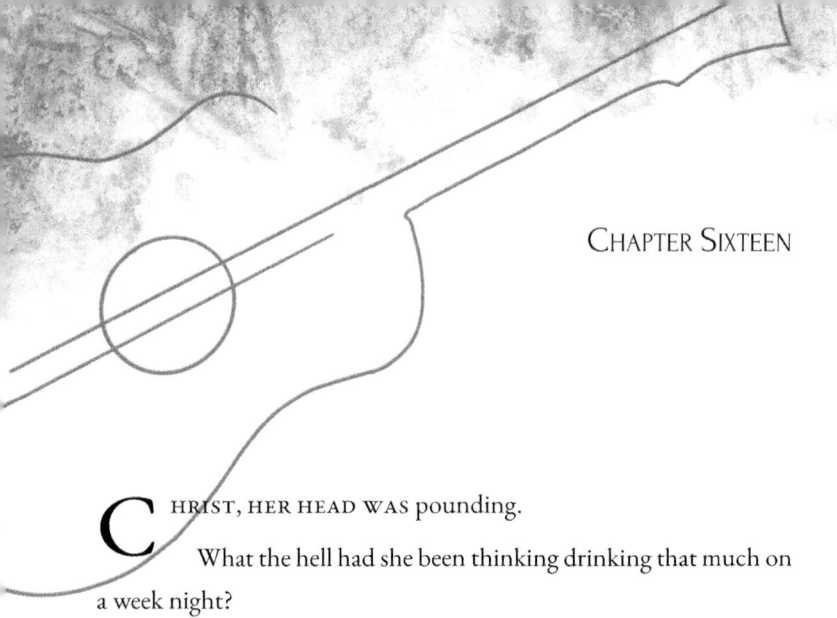

Christ, her head was pounding.

What the hell had she been thinking drinking that much on a week night?

It wasn't going to be a fun day and she only had herself to blame. Not true. Cara was totally and completely to blame. Her friend had been so upset about the news of her parents. Charlie had only agreed to go to Full Circle because she'd felt sorry for her. A couple of drinks turned into many, mostly led by Cara, of course. Going to a club on a Wednesday night wasn't the best of ideas, which was evident in the way Charlie couldn't even wait until she got to the kitchen for a glass of water. She needed hydration sooner than that.

Going straight in the bathroom, she grabbed the glass off the side and filled it with water, drinking it down quickly and instantly needed another. When she was satisfied, she leaned against the sink and looked at her sorry state in the mirror. Panda eyes. Another sign she'd drank too much. Her make-up was still mostly there and she had an angry crease down the side of her left cheek, which she wouldn't be able to cover with fresh make up and would no doubt be there for half the bloody day. Wasn't like ironing her face was an option. Or wearing a balaclava.

Getting a tissue out of the box on the little shelf above the sink, Charlie blew her nose and when she crumpled it up and threw it into the toilet, that was when she remembered. *Oh!* She groaned.

Memory was a brutal thing sometimes, especially when it came back to you in a rush, bringing with it the most embarrassing thing to come from the bad decision she'd made to go clubbing last night: Jake had seen her in all her drunken glory. Covering her face with her hands, she groaned again. He'd seen her throw up. How mortifying.

She had to move. It was the only way to escape the humiliation.

Holding the side of her head, she left the bathroom and when she walked into the main hall, she saw a piece of paper folded in half on her mat and her heart sank a little. The poster from The Gifted Crow.

Shit! There was no chance of that happening now.

Charlie groaned as the pressure in her head amplified when she bent down to pick it up. When her eyes focused on it she saw the indent of some writing from the underside.

Nervously she opened it up and turned it over. *Nice try,* was all that was written. And even though Charlie was disappointed, she couldn't help smiling as she looked at Jake's scruffy handwriting. Ok, so the poster was an obvious hint and he'd point blank turned her down. But he hadn't ignored it and thrown it in the bin like she'd expected, even after she'd embarrassed herself.

This gave her hope.

Maybe she didn't have to move after all. Just avoid him for as long as possible until he maybe forgot all about last night's mishap.

Still wearing her smile like some love sick idiot, Charlie went to the kitchen where she got a pen from the middle drawer and scribbled something on the poster right under his message, leaving it on the counter so she didn't forget to grab it when she left.

Her *happy* was short lived. When she got the box of cornflakes from the cupboard, Charlie almost gagged thinking about eating a bowl of them.

Too much. No way would her stomach handle it.

Dry toast it was then.

Today needed to be over already.

Yes, Charlie did feel a bit of an idiot in the sunglasses when it was pissing down with rain outside and there'd been no sign of the sun all day. Had to be done though. She was rocking Hangover Hayley in the uni canteen and the glasses had been the only thing to get her through her lectures so far.

But it wasn't her delicate condition that was chafing her nerves at that moment; the look of sympathy on Cara's face, crossed with the it's-your-own-fault eyebrows, made Charlie want to run away. Or throw a piece of bread at her. As if she didn't know already. Shit, she'd already spent the day admonishing herself for it.

"I honestly haven't seen you like this for a long time," her friend said, smiling as she tucked into the lunch that Charlie couldn't stand the smell of. Some sort of pie and gravy. Charlie put her hand over her mouth and squeezed her nose shut between her thumb and finger. "Shit. You really are still suffering aren't you?"

Dunking some dry bread into her vegetable soup, which was the only thing she could stomach, Charlie looked across the table at her friend through the tops of her glasses. She had bright pink, wavy earrings and matching lipstick, with a navy, pink, and yellow neck scarf. Charlie bet they looked a right pair sat across from each other. Cara with her bouncy, black curls and colourful everything, while Charlie imagined herself as grey. Grey clothes, grey skin, sitting under a grey cloud of sorrow. "You don't say. And, how are you not?"

"What can I say? I'm obviously made of tougher stuff."

"Or it could be that you're always out clubbing so you're more used to it than me."

"Yes." Cara pointed her fork at Charlie. "See, you need to get out more. Then this wouldn't happen."

"No, I really don't." Not if she was going to feel like this every time. She was never drinking again as far as she was concerned. Ever. At all.

"We did have fun though didn't we?" Tilting her head to the side, Cara got a strange look on her face, like she'd drifted into a memory. And going by the sparkle in her eyes it was a good one.

"Cara? Are those dreamy eyes?"

They landed on Charlie and a huge wide grin appeared on her friend's face.

"What are you not telling me?" Her memory was a little hazy from the alcohol, so there were gaps in their evening; unfortunately not where she wanted them to be: Jake.

Cara pushed her empty plate to the side. "Guess who I snogged last night." she said, resting her elbow on the table, chin on her hand.

"You didn't. Nathan?"

"Yep."

"How did that happen? You finally got the balls to tell him?"

She sat up straight. "No actually. He was the one who came on to me. Told me he'd fancied me for ages but didn't know if I'd be interested. He didn't give me chance to respond; he just started kissing me, and OMG, Char... It was so much better than I imagined."

Charlie couldn't help the wide smile as she looked at how happy Cara was. She needed a distraction and she'd been vying for this particular one for long enough. "I'm happy for you. Really. Did you...?" The unspoken question warranted shrugged eyebrows.

Her friend's eyes widened. "No! I wasn't that drunk. No. The guy can take me out a few times first." She laughed and it made Charlie feel a little better to see Cara smile today. With what her best friend was dealing with at home and how upset she'd been, Charlie could at least feel that last night was a success. Was the hangover worth it? Yes. *No.* Yes. Of course it was. Because she'd gone against her usual weeknight rules and agreed to go last night, Cara had finally kissed Nathan. Mission complete for her friend.

If only the night had turned out better for herself.

Her stomach sank for like the hundredth time again today when Charlie thought about it. God, she wished she'd been drunk enough to not remember anything this morning. She was so embarrassed by her behaviour that she hadn't even told Cara yet and didn't know if she was going to. Until...

"What aren't you telling me?" When Cara got that narrow-eyed look on her face there was no escaping it. Sun glasses or no sun glasses, the bloody woman's eyes caught you in their trap until you confessed.

Never mind studying to be a surveyor; she'd make a great interrogator.

Cara didn't press with words, but her face said it all.

"Okay. But you promise not to tell anyone else."

"Ooh." Sitting bolt upright, Cara actually rubbed her hands together. "Juicy goss. I promise. Tell me."

"I was pretty drunk last night, Cara. This is the reason you should have insisted I stay at yours." Taking a deep breath, Charlie led with, "I saw Jake when I got home. I was a little worse for wear falling over my shoes, trying, but failing miserably, to get in my flat without waking the whole bloody building up. Well, of course Jake was going to hear me. He came out of his place and helped me to mine."

"You are joking?"

Groaning into her hand, she wished she bloody was. "No Cara, I'm not. And that's not the most embarrassing part."

"Oh no." Her voice sounded concerned, but the woman was twitching as she tried to hold in her joy. "What happened?"

"Seriously, Car! I'm suffering here."

"Okay. I'm sorry. Go on." But the smirk still remained.

"I almost threw up on him."

Now the laugh burst out of her and Charlie was on the verge of leaving the table. Except then she laughed herself. "Stop it. It's hard enough as it is and I haven't finished yet."

"You said 'almost' threw up on him."

"I did. Because luckily I managed to hold it in until I got to the toilet. And I only managed that because Jake helped me bloody walk there." She took her glasses off and scrubbed her face. Reliving it only made her head pound more.

Her friend looked perplexed. Charlie got that. It wasn't like her to get so wasted. She wouldn't be doing it again in a hurry that was a fact.

"After I was done, somehow I must have fallen into him and..." Oh God. She couldn't even say it.

"And? Come on Char. What?"

"I hugged him." Her own eyes widened along with Cara's. "Then I asked him if I could keep hugging him."

Slapping her hand over her mouth, Cara spoke a barely audible, "Charlie!" behind it. "It would have been commendable if you'd have kissed the guy."

"I know." Her shoulders slumped. "I also sniffed him."

More laughter. "Oh God. You need to move. Or get laid. I would choose the latter."

"Cara!"

Another laugh. Charlie was glad it was her misfortune that gave her best friend so much cheer.

"There is no way you're going to live that down. How are you going to face him? Wait," she reached over and grabbed Charlie's hand, "what did he smell like?"

Like that was the most important thing right now. It was the first time she'd allowed her mind to go back to last night as she thought of Jake's aftershave. It had smelled like a mix of watermelon and spice, with an undertone of his own manly smell. Charlie's mouth watered before she set it tight. Looking across the table at Cara's eager expression, she wasn't getting sucked into it. But then again she couldn't help herself. "Nice, Car. Too bloody nice."

They laughed so hard the rest of the canteen looked over at them, but she didn't care. In fact, the whole conversation had taken her mind off her head and she noticed her headache had almost gone.

Oh well. Charlie couldn't turn back time. What was done was done. And it wasn't as if Jake liked her all that much anyway. In fact, he'd probably be happy when *she* avoided *him* from now on.

"Do you need a place to stay for a bit? You can sleep on my couch until you find another place to live," Cara said between the laughter.

Charlie broke a small piece of her left-over bread and threw it across the table at her friend. "No. Thank you though."

"Hey. Maybe you should go home early seeing as you're not feeling too good. You don't have much work left today do you? You definitely won't bump into Jake that way."

It was tempting. But Charlie was so close to the end of her studies she figured it was worth pushing through till the end of the day.

"He gets in from work just before six. I just won't go home before seven o'clock ever again."

"Well you better call in at the retail park and get yourself a change of clothes for tonight then," her friend said as she assessed her attire disapprovingly, "because we'll be leaving at half past."

"What are you talking about?"

"It's Thursday. When we were at Nando's last night we arranged for Jas to pick us up to go to The Crow. Seven thirty."

Oh God. She'd completely forgotten. Her stomach lurched. Charlie didn't think she could even be near any alcohol after last night. Just the thought was bad enough. She went to protest until Cara's hand went up like the police directing traffic.

"I'm not listening. You're coming." Cara got up and grabbed her bag by the strap from the back of the chair. There was that smile she wore when she was being smug. "See you at seven thirty."

Surely I'm being punished for something I did in a past life.

Chapter Seventeen

Charlie's heart was galloping in her chest as she walked on light feet past Jake's flat door. She'd left it as late as she could to get home, giving her just enough time to get in, have a quick shower, and get back out again to meet Jas and Selena downstairs. Her further attempts to get out of going, including the boxed slice of red velvet cake she'd picked up to bribe Cara with from the canteen when she'd left, hadn't worked. Luckily, with all the water she'd put away throughout the day, Charlie felt more like herself by the time she left uni.

All she needed now was to get to her flat without Jake seeing her, and she was halfway there.

Her ears sharpened as she went past his door. Not a sound from inside.

When she was safely past, she noticed there was something on the floor outside her flat door and quickened her steps. There was a small brown paper bag folded over at the top. Next to it was the folded poster from The Crow that she'd carefully put back under Jake's door that morning after she'd waited for him to leave for work. She picked them both up, too curious about the package to care about being seen anymore. Opening the bag, She peeked inside first, and then reached in and pulled out a small bottle of Pepto Bismal. Smiling, she opened the poster out and looked on the back where there was more writing underneath where she'd written: *You should think about it some more.*

She read his words:

Thought the pink stuff might help today.

Oh, and the answer is still no.

Relief washed over Charlie as she put the stuff under her arm so she could open the door. She glanced back down the hall before going inside, grinning from ear to ear. He hadn't been scared off after all, which was a miracle in itself. He'd even thought about her wellbeing. Shame he hadn't dropped it off this morning when she really needed it, she thought as she huffed out a little noise of excitement.

Bloody hell, woman.

What was happening?

She'd never felt so giddy in her life before. Why though? It wasn't like he'd shown any real interest in her. And let's be honest, the gift was a joke—something to remind her how much she'd embarrassed herself.

That being said, Jake didn't have to put those things outside for her.

Charlie was taking it as a positive anyway.

Even so, the thought of running into him was still a problem she couldn't bare thinking about.

After all, could a guy really fancy someone who almost threw up on him?

Mortifying!

The Gifted Crow was a funny kind of place. On Mondays, Tuesdays, and Wednesdays, it was more like your local cosy pub that served light meals and had a whole side behind the bar that was dedicated to gin.

Thursdays, however, were the complete opposite end of the scale.

Bursting with students, drinks were served in plastic glasses, most of the tables got removed or repositioned in the more snug areas of the place, and the management hired in security and a loud speaker system for the bands and artists who gave their time for free just for the fun of it.

Charlie had managed to persuade the gang to sit somewhere out of the way again. Although she felt much better, her head was still not quite right and she didn't want to sit in the main room and risk it getting worse.

Which was how she'd bribed Cara: If her head got worse she was going home. No arguments.

So they were tucked in a cosy corner with an assortment of drinks on the table; absolutely no alcohol for Charlie. Instead, she had a couple of J2Os that would probably last her the night if she sipped them.

"So how's your head, Char?" Jas asked, having to raise his voice above the female singer that was currently doing her bit on stage.

"Better. Thanks."

"That's good." He had a strange expression as he looked at her across the table. "So there's no danger of you throwing up on anyone tonight then?"

Of course she did!

"Cara!" Charlie kicked her friend's leg under the table.

"Ouch," she groaned through a laugh.

"I can't believe you blabbed straight away."

"As soon as she got in the car," Selena said as she rejoined them from having a cigarette outside. It really shouldn't be a surprise. Cara had always been a gossip. Selena gave her a sympathetic look as she sat down. "Have you seen him since?"

Charlie's shoulders slumped. "No." She didn't want to mention the gift he'd left, so she joked. "He's probably moved out. Left the area. Maybe the country. I wouldn't blame him. I'd want to get as far away from me as possible after that."

"'You kidding me?" Jas said. "You hugged the guy. He's probably thinking you're fair game. I'm surprised he hasn't asked you out already."

"Jas!" Selena shoved him in the arm and said something else that Charlie couldn't hear due to the applause that erupted at the end of the woman's set.

"Joking." He looked across at her. Then when he looked at Cara his eyes went wide and he gave a subtle shake of the head.

This might have been a worse humiliation. "Piss off, Jas. As if I don't feel bad enough."

Selena went to say something then paused as the MC announced the next act.

"*Please welcome to the stage for the first time, Jack.*"

She tried again when the clapping died down and an acoustic guitar began to play. "He's not meeting you here tonight then?" Selena asked, her brow creasing.

"Definitely no. Probably won't ever speak to me again."

"Oh." Selena got a quizzical look on her face. "I thought I saw his motorbike outside just now."

Charlie's stomach knotted. "What?"

"I might have got it wrong. . ."

In an instant Selena's voice drifted into the background along with everything else when all Charlie heard was the warm husk of the voice singing a familiar song through the speakers. Was that. . . *Jake?* She froze, time standing still as she listened to the soft, jagged tone of his voice accompanying the familiar guitar riffs. She'd listened enough to know who was on the stage right now, and before she even had to think about it, her body shot up from the chair.

"Charlie? What the hell's wrong. . ."

Her friend's voice drifted away. Nothing else mattered in that moment, and when she pushed and squeezed through enough people to get a view of the stage. . .

Her lungs expelled all of her breath.

There he was.

Jake. Not *Jack,* as the MC had introduced him.

Strumming and plucking away on his blonde acoustic guitar, singing in that sensual tone into the microphone. Charlie could barely see his face under the camouflaged, trucker-style cap he wore, but even without a full visual she absolutely knew it was him. His blue and white plaid shirt was bunched up as he hunched over a little on the stool he was sitting on. One of his bike boots tapping to the beat.

Without realising, Charlie had moved closer and was now standing on the top of the three stairs that led to where most of the crowd were standing in a semicircle in front of the stage. Now she could see him uninhibited and she watched, eyes fixated, heart racing, as Jake performed his song beautifully. His eyes closed sometimes as he appeared to get lost in the words he sang. Like they meant a lot to him. Charlie could feel that they did through the emotion he poured into his performance.

Suddenly, when Jake's eyes opened again they found hers and his head lifted ever so slightly. Charlie smiled nervously as she tried to breathe, warmth filling her chest. His eyes stayed fixed on her, and right then it was as if he was singing those beautiful words directly to her. Heat spread through her cheeks, and she was instantly caught up in him; locked in his gaze. So overcome in the moment that part of her wanted to look away just to catch her breath. But she didn't. Couldn't.

As the song continued into the chorus, they could have been anywhere. Right then there was no bar, no people.

Only the two of them.

Quietness surrounded her. Then Charlie realised it wasn't only because she'd zoned the crowd out, so focused on Jake that she couldn't possibly hear or feel anything else, but also because everyone in the place was listening.

Using it as an excuse to look away, her eyes moved around the crowd to see people smiling as they watched, listening to the same stunning song, the same voice that was melting her into a puddle.

A hand went on her arm, pulling her out of the spell.

"Charlie?" She turned at the low sound of Cara's voice. Her friend leaned in. "You didn't tell me he could sing."

No. She hadn't. And she didn't quite know why. Maybe it was because she wanted it to be something only she knew about him.

The crowd went crazy. Charlie clapped too, grinning widely when she realised it was all for him. He'd finished the song and had stood up.

"Thanks," Jake said into the mic as he adjusted the stand higher, but she barely heard him for the noise, especially with Cara wolf whistling down her ear.

It was the best response she'd heard anyone get at The Crow, and it made her chest fill with pride, which was weird because she barely knew him really. Charlie knew Jake had something special though. It was why she'd dropped enough hints for him to perform here. When he caught her eye again, he gave her a hint of a smile and she inhaled deeply, a glow spreading right through her. You could see he wasn't used to the response by the way he held himself as the crowd called for more. His shoulders were hunched a little, and he reached up to brush his hand on the back of his neck.

"Yeah, okay. If you're sure." His voice was louder this time, sounding more confident.

A collective "YEAH" rang out through the room.

"You can play all night if you want to," someone called from behind her, and people laughed.

Jake gave a soft laugh with a smile that lit up his face like she'd never seen before "Uh, thanks. I probably won't, but I can do another one." The crowd noise died down and Jake sat on the stool again, adjusting the stand and putting his guitar in position. He leaned forward to the mic. "This one is a song I did from a poem I wrote a couple of years back for my mum."

There was some whooping. And then Jake started to play a soft, ambient tune, the fingers of his left hand picking the notes in an almost classical way while his other hand softly plucked at the strings.

Then his voice filled the room, the soft husk sailing out of the speakers and singing more beautiful words:

"And when the colours of your rainbow dripped into each other,
I still saw your colours as they were. . ."

A prickling sensation travelled over her skin, goosebumps washing over her and causing her to shiver as her eyes began to sting at his beautiful words. She listened for what felt like hours when it was merely minutes, until the music slowed and Jake struck his last chord.

If possible, the response from the crowd was even louder this time. But as Jake said his thank yous, unplugging the lead from his guitar and nodding his head in acknowledgment while the MC eagerly made a fuss of him, his expression had changed as he backed away slowly to the edge of the stage. Charlie caught a pained look on his face right before he disappeared from view. It was like he wanted to get off there quickly.

"Shit, Charlie. . ." She'd forgotten Cara was standing there. "He's brilliant."

Nodding, her smile was wide as she almost giggled like a teenager. "He is, isn't he."

Selena and Jason joined them with their drinks. Selena passed Charlie her handbag. "Thanks."

"You kept that quiet," Jas said before he took a sip from his stupidly undersized bottle of coke that you could barely see in his big hand. He must have seen the way Charlie looked at it. "What? They've run out of post mix."

Selena said, "I knew that was his bike outside. He has a great voice. I really enjoyed it."

"Omg, I could listen to him for hours," Cara said something else too, but Charlie was only half listening as her friends continued to compliment Jake. Glancing back towards the stage, she zoned everything out when she saw that he'd gone. She looked around, her eyes scanning the room frantically as the MC introduced another singer, but she couldn't see Jake anywhere.

"Um. . . Earth to Charlie." Cara pulled on her arm. "I said do you think he'll come back next week? If he does we should definitely come. Maybe we can go for some food somewhere first. Charlie?"

Still no sign of him. "Yeah. Sounds good. Listen. I'll be back in a minute, okay?"

Not that she gave her friend chance to answer. Making her way through the crowd, she kept looking around for Jake as she headed towards the door, but in her gut, Charlie knew he'd gone before she even got outside, and wondered why he hadn't come over to her, at least to say hi.

Why, though? Surely it wouldn't be because of last night? Had that one stupid moment really messed up the chances of his friendship? And why would he have performed tonight if that was the case? Charlie couldn't think of a reason, especially after the way he'd looked at her during his performance, the way he'd sang to her... God, she was so confused.

There was no sign of his bike outside. Even though he would have parked it close for Selena to have spotted it, Charlie went to the edge of the pavement and glanced both ways down the street anyway, on the off chance he'd moved it further down for some reason. Nope. It didn't matter how much she looked for it, Jake had gone.

Disappointment had her lowering her head and the moment she did she saw something catch the light by the drain. She bent down to pick it up. It was a brown leather wallet. It had only caught her notice because of the small, rectangular, metal label which was stuck to the outside that had reflected the light back at her. Charlie contemplated taking it inside and handing it in to a member of staff, but something stopped her. It wouldn't hurt to have a look inside. Maybe she knew whose it was and could just give it back to them herself. She never trusted the lost and found in places like this.

When she unfolded it, she took one of the cards out, a bank card, tilting it in the light so she could read the name. She gasped when she read Jake Andrew Sure in the embossed silver letters. What were the chances that he'd drop his wallet outside the busy pub and she would be the one to find it? Perhaps she shouldn't have, but she nosied at a few more of the cards: a gym membership, she knew he worked out; another debit card this time from a different bank. In the last slot was a piece of cardboard. As she slid it out, a piece of paper fell to the floor. When she picked it up and unfolded it her heart stopped for a minute.

No. It couldn't be. Suddenly the memory of the man in the hallway who'd almost knocked her over came into her head. Charlie had seen more of his face than she'd remembered because right then, she was looking at a newspaper clipping with that man's face on it—knew it one hundred percent. She read the headline above:

Hunt for suspected murderer still underway.

But if Jake knew him, why wouldn't he have known the man was in their apartment building? Was this who'd been in his apartment without him knowing?

Her heart began to race as she got her phone out of her bag and opened up the Uber app. There was a car two minutes away. She booked it, sent a quick text to Cara telling her she'd had to go home, and went back to staring at the clipping while she waited. It was the one word that caused her stomach to knot tightly:

Murderer.

Bloody hell.

What was Jake involved in?

A bad feeling went through her. She was so thrown by it that she didn't realise the Uber guy had pulled up in front of her and was talking to her through his open window.

"Charlie?"

"Oh, yes. Sorry." When she got in the taxi, she put the newspaper clipping back in Jake's wallet exactly where she found it, and then stared out of the side window thinking of that man in her building over and over again for the whole journey home.

When she realised they'd pulled up outside, she gave the driver a couple of quid tip and got out, looking at the empty space where Jake's bike should be.

Shit. He wasn't home yet.

Charlie wished she had his phone number.

Frustrated, she went inside.

When she got to her flat, she left the door wide open. She was on the opposite side of the building to the car park, but she was sure she'd hear Jake's bike when he came back. It was loud as hell. Placing his wallet on the side, she went and made herself a cuppa, then paced the floor while she drank it. There was no way she could settle. Not until she'd spoken to him.

Twenty minutes later, while she was perched on the arm of her sofa looking through all the Jake Sure's on Facebook, just in case she could leave him a message that way, her ears picked up on a distant rumble. Charlie stood up, closing her phone, listening to the roar of a motorbike getting louder until it was abruptly cut.

Heart racing, she grabbed the wallet and headed towards her flat door. Then she paused. Best not to jump at him the moment he came up the stairs or anything, even though that's what her body was urging her to do. She didn't want him to know she'd been anxiously waiting.

So she hung around in her hallway for a few minutes. Jake would have to secure his bike before coming in, so she tried to time it right to make it look like she was just coming out of her flat to try his door again, like it was purely coincidental.

After what felt like forever, Charlie's keen ears heard the door to their floor open. Preparing herself, she tried to look casual as she left her flat, closing the door behind her. He looked up just as she started to walk down the hall towards him. When he gave her a smile like he actually was pleased to see her it caused a warm feeling in her chest.

"I was just coming to see if you were back yet," she said, trying to mask her nerves. "I knocked when I got home." Charlie noticed he didn't have his guitar.

Jake had his keys in his hand as he waited for her. "I noticed my wallet was missing when I got back. I've obviously dropped it somewhere. Been out looking for it, but no luck."

"Well," she said with a smile, "you're going to love me."

As his eyes narrowed, she realised what she'd said and felt her cheeks heat, wishing she could take it back. Moving on, she held up the wallet to divert his attention from yet another embarrassing moment. "I found it. That's why I knocked."

"Shit." He reached for it. "Where was it?"

"Outside The Crow. In the gutter."

"Must have fallen out my pocket when I got on the bike." When he looked at her his face was serious, eyes intense. He was tall anyway, but he looked so much bigger with the motorbike jacket and the black and red face cowl he had around his neck. "Thank you. You've no idea how much you've saved my arse."

"It's okay. I'm just glad I saw it before anyone else." How to approach it? She figured she might as well just say it. "Jake, I, uh. . . I looked inside, obviously to see whose it was. And a newspaper clipping fell out. I honestly didn't mean to pry, but I saw it and. . ."

Charlie saw his nostrils flare a little and his jaw had gone tense. Warily, she continued. After all, he had to know. "That man, the one in the picture—"

"What about him?"

She was surprised at his sharp tone and for a second she hesitated. "I saw him."

"Yeah, well. You said that." He turned and unlocked his door, turning halfway back to face her. "Listen, thanks for bringing my wallet—"

"No Jake, I mean I saw him here."

He visibly froze, eyes widening with what she could only describe as horror. "What the hell do you mean?"

"The day I stopped outside your wide-open door. The man who almost ploughed me down? It was him."

Without another word, Jake went inside, but he left the door open so she followed him in. He threw his keys on the side table and put his helmet on the shelf underneath. "You must be mistaken."

"I'm not. It was him, Jake."

He spun around. "You told me you didn't see the guy properly."

Charlie gestured to the wallet he was still holding. "As soon as I saw that picture I remembered his face. I don't know how, but I just did. It's like the picture triggered the memory." He was staring at her with that same expression. "It was him. Definitely."

"Fuck!" he said, running his hand down his face. He turned away. "Fuck!"

"What is it, Jake? Do you know him?" Stupid question really. Surely he wouldn't have a newspaper clipping of the guy in his wallet if he didn't.

"What?" He turned back around, but kept his eyes lowered. "Yeah. I mean, I did. He's someone from my past, that's all. Haven't seen him for a long time."

"So what was he doing in your apartment?"

Now when he looked at her he had a strange expression she couldn't make out. "I don't know. Coincidence. Maybe?"

What? How was that possible? Charlie knew it had to be a lie. Now she knew he was hiding something from her. "But, Jake... That newspaper clipping says he is a murder suspect." Then she remembered. "Shit. You said whoever had been in here had taken a knife—"

"Charlie, just stop." Jake closed his eyes. "I'd just rather not get into it right now." She was taken aback a little by his tone and he must have seen it. "I'm sorry. I'm just tired."

He turned away, walking to the breakfast counter that separated the two rooms. Feeling awkward in the following silence, and also a little annoyed, she decided she wasn't doing this hot and cold with him anymore. Whatever the issue was it was nothing to do with her and he obviously didn't want her there. She turned away from him and walked back towards the door. "I've done my bit," she said under her breath. "I'll leave you to it. I'm glad you got your wallet back. Oh, and I also wanted to say you were brilliant tonight." Lowering her voice again she mumbled as she got to the door, "Which I would have said earlier if you hadn't run out like you did."

Then she left before he could say anything to her.

Why the hell did she even bother?

Slamming her door closed, she paced up the hall and into the kitchen, swallowing down her annoyance. If Jake didn't like her she wished he'd just say it. It was infuriating that one minute he acted like he didn't want to know her, and then the next—a vision of him looking at her from the stage popped into her mind—he looked at her like that.

Five minutes later there was a knock at her door.

Charlie closed her eyes and took a moment to breathe before she went to open it. Jake was standing there. He'd taken his jacket off and she absolutely did not notice how tight his T-shirt was. That was a lie. Ignoring the bumps of his pecks, looking at his face not his muscled arms, she went to say hi, but he spoke first.

"So I'm going to apologise again." One of his eyebrows went up. "I shouldn't have got all pissy just now."

This man, Charlie thought as all the indignation seeped out of her. He confused her so much she should just forget him. Yet as he stood in front of her looking the way he did with his dark brown hair all dishevelled from his helmet, and his blue eyes looking at her as he eagerly awaited a response, Charlie's ire melted away. She couldn't seem to fight the pull he had.

"Do you want to come in?" Her breath paused as she waited for his knock back. Stupid really, to expect he wouldn't be done with her again now he'd said his peace. It hadn't escaped Charlie's notice that he didn't seem to care at the time he was snapping at her, and then all was well again as long as he apologised. Still, that was something she could put him straight on if there was a reason to later on.

A quick glance down the hall, and the way his body had already turned as if he was going to leave, pretty much confirmed his answer. Charlie was preparing to accept it when he surprised her.

"Yeah, sure."

Quietly, after Jake had closed the door behind him, they walked into her small living room and she saw Jake take a quick look around as if trying not to look nosy.

"Can I get you a drink?" Why the hell was she so nervous all of a sudden? Because Jake Sure was in her flat, that's why. It felt different to when she'd been in his. For some reason, more personal. Stupid really.

"Yeah. Thanks."

"Tea or coffee? Or a beer?"

"Beer would be good."

He stood by her breakfast bar as she opened the fridge, his hands shoved in his jeans pockets. Charlie tried not to notice how wide his shoulders were when she glanced at him on the way to get the bottle opener from the drawer next to him. The whiff of aftershave didn't help her nerves. It was so manly, did things to her insides, and she absolutely wasn't quietly inhaling it deeply as she pulled the top off the bottle.

Glancing up at him as she passed him the beer, she was so glad Jake couldn't read her mind.

"Thanks," he said, thankfully unaware of the mental torture she was giving her own self right then. If he only knew how crazy she actually was. They wouldn't have this hot and cold problem at all. He'd have run a mile ages ago.

Getting a glass from the drainer, Charlie got some water, then turned back to him, leaning against the counter. "I was surprised to see you there tonight. You seemed pretty adamant you weren't going to play there." While he looked down at his bottle, she smiled to herself briefly, remembering how great he was, and feeling a little smug that she'd coaxed him there.

"Yeah." He looked up at her and leaned his hip against the breakfast counter. I don't know why I did to be honest." His brows lowered harshly. "I shouldn't have."

"I'm glad you did."

He glanced up at her, his face softening a little. "Thanks. I was a little rusty. I haven't played properly for a long time."

"It sounded perfect to me." And everyone else in the pub.

"Well, the owner seemed to like it. He asked me to play a gig there tomorrow night. The duo who was meant to be there had cancelled on him."

Joy lit up inside her, and she was aware that her smile spread right across her face. "That's fantastic. I'll have to tell the gang you're playing. They'll definitely come." Charlie guessed by his wary eyes that he wasn't as enthusiastic about it as she was. "Wait. You did say yes, right?"

"I did."

"You'll be brilliant. I just know it."

His attempt at a smile wasn't fooling her. Ever since meeting him for the first time Charlie had noticed that Jake always seemed to have something gnawing at him. Whatever it was gave him that permanent frown, and she suspected the mood swings were connected also. She wondered what he was dealing with. What kept that sorrow in his eyes?

"It's thanks to your annoying persistence. So you can be pleased with yourself." Taking another drink of beer his eyes narrowed on her.

Charlie smiled, only slightly though; she didn't want to gloat too much. "I am. But I know you're pleased too."

Another drink. "I guess so."

Jake looked at her, his nostrils flaring a little, his eyes so intense that she held her breath for a moment. The silence grew louder as they stood in her kitchen. Should she say something else? Why was he looking at her like that?

Then his face straightened. "I should go actually." He closed his eyes and shook his head like he was clearing away what had captured his mind just then. He put his half empty bottle on the counter, and when he walked away, she followed him. "Thanks for the drink," he said as he went down her hall. Recognising the tone he always seemed to have when he was annoyed with her, Charlie wondered what she could have possibly done now.

"Jake? Is there something wrong?"

He slowed as he got to the door.

"You can be honest with me. I know we're not exactly friends, but if you want to tell me to stay out of your life, you should just say it."

"You're right. I should say that to you."

Charlie huffed out a laugh. "Then say it. Most of the time you act like you don't like me very much, and then sometimes you do. I can't keep up with you. What's the problem?"

"You." He turned around swiftly. "You're my problem, Charlie."

God. If she could fall through the floor right now it would be great. Her heart dropped into her stomach at his directness. So it was worse than she'd even thought.

"It's because of what happened last night isn't it? I'm mortified, Jake. I was out of line pushing myself on you when I," she was so embarrassed to say it her cheeks burned, "hugged you like that. I don't get drunk very often. It's not me. Cara had had some bad news and I wanted to take her mind off it and. . . Shit. I should have made the effort to say it before now. I'm sorry—"

"Don't."

Pausing, Charlie watched his head drop, his shoulders rise then fall. When he looked at her again she was surprised to see his expression had softened. "You don't need to apologise for that. Like you said, you were drunk. I helped you home. That was it. You didn't do anything to offend me. In fact, you made me smile and I haven't done that all that much lately."

"Oh," was all she could say. It was a far cry from what she'd expected him to say. She'd been convinced it had caused a problem. Maybe she had got it all wrong. But why was he being weird again? Whatever it was, Charlie couldn't get past what he'd said. If none of this was about last night, what did he mean?

She didn't want to ask. How could she? It wasn't like he was easy to talk to. Still, she couldn't let it go.

Looking at him with narrowed eyes, Charlie spoke in a quiet voice. "You said I'm your problem. I thought the drunk thing was why."

She watched him as he seemed to struggle with words. His lips tightened and as he stepped closer to her, she inhaled deeply.

"I like you, Charlie, and I guess I'm worried that you'll get caught up in. . ."

"In what? What's going on? Jake, you can tell me."

His eyes scanned her face and she saw desperation in them. "I wish I could, but it's my problem." Then he surprised her when he put his hand on her arm. The crease had gone from between his brows. "Look, I don't want you to worry about that guy. I'll go to the police in the morning and tell them what's happened. It's an old grudge from college. Nothing serious. He's probably messing with me. It's something you don't have to worry about okay? I promise."

So that wasn't the reason the police were at his apartment. Charlie looked at him for a moment, trying to see some sign that he was lying to her and she hated that she felt that way. She guessed she had no choice right now than to take his word for it. Besides, there was a chance that it was true.

If so, why could she not shake the doubt that was suddenly eager for her to push away from him?

Chapter Eighteen

Standing in the manager's office somewhere behind the main bar at The Gifted Crow, Jake straightened his collar in the mirror. The last time he'd worn a shirt and dressed smart it had been a very different day. One he didn't care to remember, especially five minutes before he went on stage to perform his first gig in four years, which, up until recently, he never thought he'd ever do again. He'd neatened his hair a little, even had a shave, unsure whether it was to impress the punters, or a certain woman who lived down the hall who he knew would be in the audience with her friends tonight. Who was he kidding? He might have been more nervous about her than anything else, although he was supposed to be working on getting a grip of that.

The place was pretty full by the time he'd arrived. A lot of them regulars apparently, most had come again tonight after the MC had announced last night that he'd be playing here. Simon, the guy who'd booked him, had told Jake it was busier than usual for a Friday night. There was a lot of expectation from him then. Nice to have the added pressure when you were nervous anyway.

As he looked at his reflection, Jake was sick of his past following him around. He hadn't deserved any of it, his mum hadn't deserved any of it. It had been so long yet it still wasn't over.

He closed his eyes for a moment as an image of his mum popped into his head. This time he allowed it. Just for a minute. He saw her smiling at him on the evening before his first day of high school. After lots of persuading, Jake had tried his new uniform on and she'd looked so proud. *"Look at you, my handsome boy,"* she'd said. And at the time he'd pulled a face, squirming at the silly compliment and the way she'd straightened his hair. Now, though, even at twenty six, he'd give anything to hear her say those words to him again. She'd been so happy in that moment he would never forget it. It had been the first time since his dad had died that she'd really smiled.

Too much, he thought, squeezing his eyes shut. Jake inhaled an unsteady breath as he stopped his mind from reminiscing. It was dangerous; the bad always followed the good. Right now, he was in a good place and he wanted to keep his mind peaceful so he could deliver a decent performance.

He couldn't let the bad anywhere near his head right now. Not when he was about to go on stage. Tonight he'd sing for his mum. That's what will get him through.

There was a knock at the door. "Jake?"

"Yeah."

It opened and one of the lads who worked behind the bar popped his head in. "Hi. There's a woman here, wants to see you."

"Uh, yeah. It's cool." He wondered who it was for a moment and then Charlie walked in with a smile that lit up her whole face and sent a feeling through his chest that took him aback. *Shit*. What was it about this woman? Straight away his dark cloud lifted a little; it wasn't the first time her presence had done that.

"Hi," she said, looking a little unsure. "I hope it was okay to come back here." She closed the door.

"Yeah, of course." Jake was very aware he was looking at her through different eyes now and it was unsettling. The feelings she always brought out with her presence alone were getting harder and harder to ignore. But he had to keep fighting it. There was no way he could start something with her. Not now.

Allowing himself a minute, he took her in, liking what he saw. Tight black jeans and a casual, grey top that fell off one shoulder. It was a nice shoulder. Unbidden, he imagined his lips there, his tongue tasting her silky smooth skin.

For fuck's sake, get a grip, Jake.

"Nervous?"

Of you? Yes. "No, actually. Well, maybe a little."

"You'll be brilliant. I know it."

Words didn't come, no matter how much he tried to respond to her good faith in him, his mind shorted out. Damn, the woman had a way of doing that.

"Anyway. I just wanted to come and wish you luck." A glance behind her told him she was obviously casing where the door was so she could make a quick getaway due to the awkwardness he'd thrown out in the small room. Man, he was a right dick.

"Thanks." See... you *can* say words. What the fuck was happening right now?

Whatever, he had to put this right before she went out the door. When she turned he reached out and touched her arm. "Hey." She faced him again, those blue-green eyes with their black spidery lashes capturing his. "I really do appreciate what you did. I tried to tell you that the other night." A frown appeared. "If it wasn't for you I wouldn't be here tonight doing this. So, thanks."

Charlie didn't say anything for a minute and he wondered if he'd actually said all that out loud. Then she surprised him when she stepped into him and stretched up like she was going to say something in his ear. Jake bent a little, then froze when she kissed his cheek. Instinctively, he pressed his face towards her when she lingered, and thank God he was consumed by that lovely perfume. It was something to focus on instead of turning into her kiss and devouring her mouth like he wanted to. The fresh familiar scent filled his head and he closed his eyes briefly while he enjoyed it.

When she pulled away, her cheeks were flushed. "For luck." Then she turned away with a smile and Jake couldn't say a single word as she left the office. For a moment he stood staring at the door. The kiss had been unexpected, and now he didn't know how to deal with it. It might have been just a peck on the cheek. But the way his body had reacted, he knew it was much more than that.

As he repositioned himself in his jeans he figured he'd better get to thinking of other things before he was forced to walk out on stage with an obvious bulge in his pants.

Shit.

An hour and a half later, while he was singing the song he'd written for his mum, Jake felt more content than ever before. The nerves had left him quickly, and the audience seemed like they loved his set. He'd mixed it up a little, singing his own songs mixed in with covers of Ed Sheeran, Coldplay, and a few more, trying to cater for everyone. He'd even done a couple of requests. As he was reaching the end of his set, he'd wound it down a little. It was harder than he realised to sing the lyrics he'd written so long ago. This song had been the first he'd penned as soon as he was capable, and the poignancy was making him a little shaky.

His eyes sought Charlie out, and he fixed his gaze on hers as she sat at the table a little to the right with her friends. Holding his gaze, she smiled, her head falling to the side as he sang to her and it wasn't long until those feelings of sadness turned into something else. He knew damn well he was falling for her. It was crazy, but he couldn't ignore how she made him feel. Of course, there was a chance he could be mistaking his feelings. Perhaps it was the friendship he was grabbing hold of. He'd been alone for long enough. And from what he knew already, Charlie was a warm and kind woman. And hot. Sexy. He definitely fancied her. There was no doubt about that.

No. The way his chest warmed and his body responded when he thought of her at night in his bed. . . Jake wasn't dumb enough to dismiss it as friendship. Charlie had mentioned the word friend, but he was pretty sure she was into him too. Her eyes in that moment as she watched him told him that.

But he could only allow her to get close to him in his thoughts.

As much as he wanted her he couldn't act on it, not only because he couldn't risk caring for somebody, but after knowing what he did now and who might be back, he wasn't willing to risk her safety.

Jake focused on the last words of the song, the ones that meant the most to him:

"I am me because of you. Your love will live on inside my heart."

Then, after he struck the last chord and the applause filled the room, he stood from the stool and smiled, directing it at Charlie and then the crowd who had welcomed him.

Maybe he shouldn't have accepted the gig. It was a risk, after all. The police had no leads on Arsehole and things had been quiet. Jake had laid low for the last couple of years, doing his own research, conducting his own enquiries, trying to find the bastard who seemed to have disappeared off the face of the earth. He'd had the same kind of luck as the investigators.

He'd spent so much of his life looking back that hiding away came naturally to him—was used to isolation. Refusing to think about anything else other than revenge, it had dominated his life for so long he hadn't realised how deep he'd fallen—how much of himself he'd lost.

Then he'd met her.

It was only since Charlie had come into his life, not that she was in his life as such, that Jake had started to feel like he could take a step forward. He'd finally glanced outside of the darkness that had consumed him for so long, and he liked what he saw.

So now he was here, doing something he'd abandoned long ago. Playing gigs was how he'd managed to climb out of his first well of darkness. It had helped him to breathe, to live some kind of life while he'd been in college. Little did he know that it would all come crashing down. Playing music had since been associated with tragedy. The thing he'd once loved had become something he'd despised. Until recently, he hadn't even taken his guitar out of the case for God knows how long.

Since then, Jake had slowly learned to love playing again.

It wasn't like he didn't know what, or who, had driven him to do the open mic night last night. He was glad he had though. And had done tonight's gig for that same reason.

Jake was playing with fire even thinking about letting her in.

He gave one last glance over at the table Charlie was sitting at as he exited the stage. Still clapping as she watched him leave, the proud smile caught him off guard, something he hadn't felt before lightening his chest.

Was it possible to leave such trauma in the past and move forward?

Jake wasn't all that convinced. What he did know, though, was that for some reason, there was a hand pulling him closer to the light and for the first time since he could remember, he wanted it.

Chapter Nineteen

Charlie had to force herself to make a conscious effort not to stare at Jake as he coyly chatted with her friends. He'd joined them not long after he'd finished playing, and was sitting next to Charlie, sipping on a glass of coke, looking more relaxed than she'd ever seen him. It was hard to keep her eyes off him. The frown he'd constantly worn since they'd met hadn't completely gone, but it wasn't so harsh and she was struck by how handsome he was. She wasn't the only one. Ever since he'd sat down he'd almost had a constant stream of people—mainly of the female variety—coming over and complimenting him, some clearly flirting. Although, when that happened, she noticed Jake would close off. The women did too, but still, they poured compliments over him and he accepted them gracefully, even though Charlie guessed he probably wanted to duck under the table and hide.

It was endearing.

Thinking back to how closed off he'd been, how intimidating he'd seemed when Charlie had first met him, she wouldn't have imagined being here with him now, socialising, watching his gig, watching him.

She couldn't deny what she felt for him.

It hadn't taken long for her to start looking at him with more interest. It was confusing at first. There were times when she'd catch him looking at her with a quizzical look on his face, like he was trying to figure her out. More often than not the tension between them brought forth a feeling of unease. All this time Charlie had mistaken those feelings for wariness, warning signs that she shouldn't get close. Now she realised it wasn't that at all. She'd been afraid of losing her heart to someone who didn't want it. Now, on top of those feelings there was excitement, anticipation. Hope.

He also seemed to be warming to her. Though in what way that was she didn't know. When she'd had a moment of bravery and kissed him on the cheek in the office, Charlie had felt him go ramrod stiff, and when she'd pulled away he'd had a strange look on his face; not one she could decipher. If she was to guess, he'd probably been annoyed by her audacity.

Since then, though, Jake hadn't run a mile, so that was a good thing. The kiss hadn't scared him off.

A voice she didn't recognise brought Charlie back out of her head. There was a man standing at their table.

"Jake?" He offered his hand. "My name's Tommy Dickson. I'm an agent in the music industry."

Unsure, Jake reached over and shook the guy's hand. He was dressed smart in a navy two-piece suit and white shirt. No tie. His greying hair neatly styled to the side. Charlie noticed the gold watch and even in the brief appearance she could see it looked expensive.

"Hi," was all Jake said, his face stoic.

"I just wanted to congratulate you on a great show."

"Thanks."

The smile the man gave him was a confident one and he didn't seem put off by Jake's passive tone. "You write your own songs?"

"I do. Yes." No change in Jake's demeanour and Charlie wanted to give him a bloody nudge as she looked between the two men.

The guy already had a card in his hand and he passed it to Jake, giving him a nod as if to take the hint that Jake wasn't up to talking. "Give me a call. I'd like us to chat."

After giving him a tight-lipped smile, Jake picked up his coke and acted like the interaction hadn't taken place. Meanwhile, after looking at the card Jake had put down on the table, Charlie was all joyful about the fact an agent had shown interest in him at his first gig. "Isn't that great?"

"Oh, yeah. The guy's probably a chancer."

The come down she felt right then doubled when he turned to her friends who'd been oblivious to the exchange. "Listen, guys? I appreciate you coming. It was good chatting with you, but I think I'm gonna take off."

Charlie straightened, a pang of disappointment flashing through her as Jake moved to get up. Then he looked at her and seemed to hesitate. "Do you want a ride home?"

What disappointment? Joy had come along and kicked its arse. Trying not to appear too eager, like one of the unpopular girls who couldn't believe the hottest guy in school had asked her to dance at prom, she blinked and tightened her jaw.

"Umm," looking around at her friends, she saw Cara's eyes flare wide for a split second, silently urging her to say yes. "Yeah, okay."

Grabbing her bag from the floor by her feet, thankfully her hair fell down and hid the heat that had exploded to her cheeks. When she got up, she ignored the smirk on Cara's face as her friend glanced over to share a knowing look with Selena. Jason saw it too, his eyes going from one to the other, a crease appearing between his brows.

"I'll see you guys on Monday then?" Charlie said, her nonchalance not fooling them at all.

"Yeah, sure." Jas wasn't as enthusiastic as the other two, by the sound of it. But he could go stick his disapproval somewhere dark as far as she was concerned. She appreciated that he cared, but Jake hadn't given him a reason to be weird.

"Goodnight." Selena practically sighed as she leaned against her hand with a smile.

"Night guys," Jake said, glancing at Charlie before walking away from the table, hopefully oblivious to the not-so-subtle exchanges going on between her interfering friends.

"Have fun," Cara called in that sing-songy way of hers as Charlie followed Jake, resisting the urge to look back and glare at her friends. Staying close to Jake as they made their way through the pub, Charlie smiled while people stopped him to pay complements, a few asking for selfies. She felt her chest swell with pride, but she suspected Jake wasn't really into all the attention; his head bowing lower the closer they got to the exit.

When they eventually got outside, no matter how hard she tried, Charlie couldn't get the smile from her face. The bouncers smiled and nodded at Jake as he descended the three steps to the pavement, then he turned to her, taking in a breath like he was glad to be out of there.

"What's that for?" he asked, his eyes narrowing.

Of course he'd noticed. "What?"

"Why are you smiling like that?"

"Oh, you know... I'm pleased it went so well for you."

Giving her tight smile, he nodded. "Bike's this way," he said, gesturing down the street.

They walked side by side, and the lack of talking made Charlie scramble her brain for something to say to fill the silence. "I know I keep saying it, but you were great tonight. I enjoyed it so much."

Glancing down at her, Jake smiled in that same tight-lipped way he always did, and she guessed that even a compliment from her made him uncomfortable. "Thanks. It was okay. Forgot some words, but I think I covered it well enough."

"Really? I didn't notice." She was too busy internally swooning at him to hear actual words. Except for the ones he'd seemed to sing to her, especially during the song towards the end of his show. "That song you said was for your mum, you really wrote it for her?"

"Yeah."

"It's a beautiful song."

"She was a beautiful person."

Charlie heard his voice falter and she felt an ache in the middle of her chest. "Was?"

When he glanced at her she saw pain in his eyes. "Yeah. She died a few years back."

"I'm sorry. Must have been hard."

"Yeah. It was." Clearing his throat Jake stopped next to his bike. That's when Charlie realised he'd forgotten something. He was only carrying his helmet. "Where's your guitar?"

"Can't get the case and you on the back. Simon let me leave it in the office. I'll swing by and pick it up tomorrow sometime."

Going to the back of the bike, he unlocked the metal storage box she didn't remember seeing last time. He took out a helmet similar to the black one he wore, only this one had a white stripe going around the middle. Holding it out to her he said, "Brought a spare with me this time. It's a little smaller than my main one. Ordered the wrong size so it's tight for me."

As she took it, warmth ignited through her chest at the thought of him planning to ask her if she wanted a ride home. More of that wall was coming down. Small pieces, but they made a big impact. Grabbing hold of the neck strap either side, Charlie pulled the helmet over her head. It sat much more comfortable than the one she put on last time, but it was still a little loose.

As she went to mess with the strap, Jake was already reaching up. "Here, I got it," he said, clearly anticipating the same struggle she had last time. Their eyes met as he fastened it and she felt him pause with his hands still there. Then he let go, getting his own helmet, putting it on, and straddling the bike.

When Charlie stepped closer, she couldn't quite believe she was doing this again. In that moment she was torn in two halves: one part of her was nervous, the other excited as she flung her leg over the seat. This time she didn't hesitate to put her arms around him, feeling more confident with her body wrapped around his this time. Since she was less nervous, she could enjoy the feel of him even though she shouldn't. Even through his bike jacket she could feel the strength of him. His hard physique felt good in her arms.

When he turned the engine over, the deep vibration soared through her body as he twisted the throttle a couple of times. This time, for reasons she'd have to question later, the excitement of being on the back of his bike outweighed Charlie's nerves. Maybe it was the cider, but she suddenly got the overwhelming need for some speed. Last time, with it being her first time, she'd gripped onto Jake so hard, keeping her eyes closed for a lot of the ride, not really wanting to think about the journey.

This time, whether adrenaline or booze had a part to play in it, she wanted to experience it properly. Tapping Jakes shoulder, he turned his head to her.

"Everything okay?"

Forgetting she had a much bigger head than usual, Charlie nodded and cracked her helmet against his. "Sorry."

Jake laughed and she smiled even though she felt like an idiot.

"I'm okay. Listen," she said, her voice raised to get over the deep sound of the motorbike ticking over, "we don't have to go through the backstreets this time. Why don't you take the faster way home?"

His body twisted around more, and she could see a glint in his eyes behind the Perspex visor of his helmet. "Yeah?"

"Yeah."

"You sure?"

It was so hard not to nod, especially as it was an easier way to answer over the noise of the bike. Instead she held her thumb up, tapping her fingers on his shoulder.

The bike revved, a loud groan, like an almighty beast roaring, waiting to be let out of its cage. She felt his arm press against hers at the front of him for a second, and then he pulled away, the force this time pushing her back against the backrest.

Shit. She gripped onto him hard with her arms and her thighs. *You can do this*, she told herself, taking a deep breath and hoping she could hold on tight to the adrenaline that had spurred her on as he weaved through the streets.

It was crazy; something Charlie never imagined herself doing.

For some reason she trusted Jake implicitly. Felt completely safe on the back of his bike.

He leaned quite sharply into a bend and she couldn't help the nervous "whoa" she let out. When he was straight again, she saw his head turn back a little while his hand covered hers over his stomach, and she knew he was asking if she was okay.

Charlie answered by squeezing him, and he immediately increased speed. Nerves kicked in the moment she realised they'd entered a slip road for a faster road. The force wanted to push her body back, but she held on tight. Then as quick as she could blink, they were racing up the motorway in the fast lane, and, God, it felt fantastic. With a grin as wide as her face, Charlie held on to the leather-clad torso of the man who had already put a kink in her mundane life.

A while later she noticed their surroundings were no longer familiar. They'd been riding down quiet country roads for some time now, Jake proving he was a hell of rider as he navigated the winding turns with ease. Charlie never once felt unsafe. She did wonder where they were. Nowhere near home, that was for sure. The roads were dark, hadn't been a streetlight for miles, only the bike's headlights illuminating the road out in front.

After what felt like forever, they turned into an even narrower, tree-lined road, this one a little bumpy, which made Charlie hold Jake tighter. After another few minutes, the bike slowed right down and turned again, and from what she could see—which was very little—the space around them had opened up into a car park.

The bike came to a stop in front of a wooden fence with dense trees behind it. When he kicked the stand down, Charlie dismounted the bike as Jake removed his helmet. Taking hers off, she looked around, her eyes trying to decipher where they were through the darkness. When they adjusted, she realised there was more light than she'd first thought and saw the small car park was surrounded by huge trees. The moon illuminated the open space while the woods surrounding them were swallowed by darkness, the canopy too dense for the light to break through. She could just about make out a wooden cabin across the way.

"Hope you didn't mind coming here," Jake said as he got off the bike. He took the helmet from her and put it back in the trunk-type box on the back.

As long as you're not going to kill me and bury me next to one of those trees, I'm good. "Where are we?"

It was a wooded area that seemed to be in the middle of nowhere. There wasn't a sound. No passing traffic, no anything, except for the sound of hers and Jake's boots on the gravel ground. The musk of the trees was heavy in the air.

"Symondshide wood." She'd never heard of it. Didn't even know she lived anywhere near somewhere like this. Proof she needed to get out and explore. "I found it out on a ride about a month back. It was in the day. I went for a walk on one of the trails. Not far. Just to see what it was like in the woods. Last time I came was a couple of weeks ago. I couldn't sleep one night so I went out on the bike and ended up here."

Moving to stand close to her, he said in a low voice, "Look up."

She did, and immediately gasped. Now that she lived in a large town outside of the capitol, it was the first time in years that Charlie had seen a dark sky. Living in Hatfield, the town's many streetlights and lit buildings polluted the night sky enough that the stars where she lived were few enough to even notice. She'd never seen anything like this though. Through the canopy of the trees that surrounded them, the inky-black sky was awash with a million lucid stars, like sparkling glitter dust, each one so bright and glistening. Beyond them were a million more. Charlie's eyes watered as she tried to take in the wondrous sight. This, there were no words for. She didn't think she'd ever seen such a clear, untainted sky.

"It's beautiful," she said when she could finally speak.

"It is, isn't it."

Charlie sensed Jake looking at her, and when she lowered her head to look at him, his eyes glistened in the moonlight as they stared back at her. Then he looked down, and she was surprised when he took her hand in his.

"Come over here."

Walking with him, Charlie liked the feel of her hand in his, strong and warm, skin a little rough. His hold was surprisingly gentle as he pulled her over to the wood cabin. She wondered what he was doing, noticing the spring in his step while he pulled her along as eager as a kid in his favourite toy shop.

"Where are we going?"

"You'll see." Walking down the side of the small cabin, he stopped at a recycling point, a wooden structure housing several bins inside, about waist high. Without warning, Jake jumped up on it, standing there looking down at her while offering his hand.

"You're joking?" Yeah, she really had the right footwear for climbing on things. If she'd have known she'd been going on an adventure she'd have worn hiking boots instead of three inch heels.

"Come on. I'll help you." You'll be glad you did."

After a few seconds of thinking about it, the light expression on his face was hard to ignore. So she took his hand, pressing her foot on the wooden frame and using it as an anchor as he pulled her up. He hadn't finished though. Bending down, he linked his hands suggesting he wanted her to step into them.

Charlie's eyes widened, looking up at the roof and back to Jake who was wearing a smile. "Up there?"

"Yep. It's easy. Come on."

For him maybe. Not for someone who only just managed to navigate stairs without tripping herself over and was likely to break her neck. Preparing herself for the impending embarrassment, she put the toe of her boot in his hands, and with one hand on his shoulder, she reached up with the other. When Jake hitched her up, she grabbed hold of the roof's edge, lifting her knee and climbing up. Thank God he couldn't see how she'd practically face planted onto the roof. Without any effort, Jake pulled himself up and over before walking to the middle where it was more level. When he sat down, Charlie joined him.

"It's so peaceful here." All they had for company was the trees that surrounded them and whatever nocturnal wildlife lived in the woods. Charlie could see why he liked it. It was a shame she didn't have a car; she'd like to come here again. She'd love to see what this place looked like in the daylight.

Jake lay back and she wondered if she should too. After all, they were only enjoying the stars and it was easier to see them lying down. As soon as she did, Charlie couldn't help feeling the intimacy of the moment.

"It's hard to believe it's real," she said, staring up at the sky, feeling a profound sense of peace.

"When I was young, before my parents died," Jake said, "we used to go to Wales on holiday quite regularly. My dad used to always take me into the mountains to look at the stars. He loved astrology. Taught me all the names of the constellations, always bought me books for Christmas. So when I found this place and saw how clear the sky was here, I didn't want to leave. It brought back memories of my dad, stuff I hadn't thought about for a long time. I felt like I could almost reach him up there, you know."

No longer looking at the stars, Charlie's eyes traced the silhouette of Jake's face as he continued to look up to the sky. Lying back with his hands behind his head, knees up, the frown that was usually constant no longer marred his face. Just like her, he was at peace here. Charlie couldn't help wondering what he'd been through to make him so closed off—so solitary. He always looked like something was troubling him; like he had the weight of the whole world on his shoulders and wasn't happy about it. To think that he could find solace in something as simple as this, it made her more curious about his past.

Charlie hadn't realised how long she'd quietly watched him, until Jake turned his head to look at her. A blush hit her cheeks that she was glad he wouldn't be able to see. She smiled coyly before looking back up to the diamond encrusted ceiling.

In her peripheral, she knew he hadn't turned away, awareness kicking her pulse up a notch. "Thank you," she said, needing to break the silence.

"For what?"

"For bringing me here." She looked at him again. "I'm glad you did."

Jake removed his hands from behind his head. "Me too." Then he turned back to their stunning view. A quick glance and Charlie saw one hand resting on his chest while the other went down by his side, and she felt his fingers brush hers. For a split second she contemplated moving, but she left it there. Then the movement of Jake's finger as it brushed the back of her hand caught her breath.

Nudging hers against his, before she knew it their hands were joined, his warm and big around hers, their fingers interlocking. When he moved his thumb over hers, softly stroking her skin, her stomach buzzed with nerves as warmth seeped through her chest and made her inhale sharply. She didn't know how long they lay there, but she felt like she could stay there all night, just the two of them, peaceful, enjoying being at one with nature. Close to each other.

A shooting star shot across the sky right past her eyes, and she gasped.

"I only just caught that," Jake said, their hands breaking contact as he got up onto his elbow, turning towards her.

"I don't remember seeing one since I was little." Sure she'd seen one or two back home, but not for a long time. It was exciting.

He looked at her. "Really? My dad and I used to do this thing where we'd see who spotted the most. This is the place to see them. I saw quite a few when I was here last time. I didn't leave until around five in the morning."

"You stayed here all night?"

"No better place to sleep than under the stars."

When he looked up again, Charlie couldn't take her eyes off him, unable to fathom the change in him since they'd got here. It was like all the baggage he constantly carried around hadn't entered the woods with them.

When he turned his head it was too late to look away so she smiled, not really knowing what to say in that moment. Then she noticed his expression change. The smile disappeared and is gaze became intense. When he moved towards her, leaning in closer, her heart took off in a gallop and she tried to look calm when in reality she was close to hyperventilating. Charlie's eyes never left his as he leaned in. Then he stopped, his face only a hair's breadth away, as if he was waiting to see if she pulled back. Or maybe he was about to change his mind.

The trees illuminated a little, the sound of tyres moving over gravel ruining the moment. Jake looked up, shadows moving around him as they ran from the headlights of the car that was pulling into the car park. Glancing down at her, he cleared his throat and when he moved to sit up, Charlie quietly huffed out her disappointment.

Funny how you could feel the loss of something you never had.

"We should head back," he said, getting to his feet and holding his hand down to help her up. Moving quickly, Jake jumped from the cabin roof onto the bins down below, his haste a little unsettling. She couldn't help feeling that if he could run away and leave her there he would. When Charlie sat on the edge of the roof, he reached up his hands, and she lowered herself into them, trying to ignore his proximity and the strong feel of his hands holding her waist as he helped her down. Barely saying two words, they got on the bike, ignoring the car that had pulled into the car park even though Charlie felt like letting the tyres down or something for ruining the moment.

Talk about shit timing.

This time Jake left her to fasten her own helmet. Before she could blink, they were out on the road, and she was wrapped around him again, filled with a mix of emotions as he navigated the bends of the country roads.

Charlie decided to file what had almost happened away until later, not wanting anything to sour their evening even though she knew he'd already retreated again. She'd have enough time to dwell on the almost kiss tonight when she was in bed no doubt struggling to sleep while her brain spun it around and around in her head.

The ride back was as exhilarating. Charlie suspected Jake liked having her on the back of his bike. Showing off his speed the moment they hit the motorway. It was exciting. Charlie was sure she actually laughed with joy at one point, Jake acknowledging her by tipping his head. This was something she could get used to; impromptu rides at midnight, lying under the stars with a gorgeous man.

The journey was over too soon. When Jake pulled into his parking spot outside their building her stomach sank a little. It was going to be hard to get back to reality after this, but at least she felt like they'd taken a step forward. Towards what, after his quick change in direction earlier, Charlie didn't know, but she'd take the win, nonetheless.

She waited for Jake to secure his bike and, again, there was barely a word spoken as they went upstairs, a definite sign of Jake pulling away again. When they got to his door, he turned to her and the genuine smile he gave made her relax a little.

"I enjoyed tonight," he said, fishing keys out of his pocket.

"Me too." Charlie watched as he opened the door. Then he paused and turned to her.

"Thanks for coming to watch me. Made me feel better to see a familiar face out there."

It was almost like the ride out to the woods hadn't happened.

"It was a great night." That was all she could think to say. Reflecting on the almost kiss was stalling her brain. She started to back away down the hall, trying to look as casual as she could, not wanting to make things more uncomfortable than they already were. For her anyway. "Goodnight, Jake," she said, taking control of the situation.

For a moment, when he hesitated, Charlie thought he was going to say something. Then his brows pulled down and all he said was, "'Night," as he pushed his door open.

She turned around before he'd gone inside, eager to get to her place where she could flop on the floor and curl up in a ball. It was late, she was getting a headache—whether from the alcohol or all the excitement she'd felt on the back of Jake's bike, she didn't know. Maybe it was her brain protesting all the mixed signals he continued to give her. When she'd kissed him on the cheek earlier at The Crow, Charlie hadn't been mistaken when she felt him turn his face slightly towards hers like he'd wanted more.

The guy was becoming a theme park ride: so many sharp turns and drops, it was making her head spin.

Tomorrow is another day, she thought.

Then she wondered what version of Jake she would get the next time she saw him.

Chapter Twenty

Two days had passed without their paths crossing. Charlie'd had a busy weekend: lunch with her friends, and a movie date with Cara on Saturday; then she'd gone over to Cara's for the day on Sunday because her friend wanted to learn how to cook a Sunday roast to impress Nathan, who was now officially her boyfriend.

The cookery lesson had gone well, apart from the Yorkshire pudding disaster, but Charlie had never cooked them before and for a first attempt. . . Nope. She couldn't even lie. They'd been bloody awful, hard like rock cakes. There was no getting away from it.

Charlie was lacking motivation this morning, moving around her flat like she'd had no sleep when in reality she'd had too much. After going to bed early, she'd fallen asleep pretty much straight away. The long hours she'd slept, there should be a spring in her step—well rested and raring to go. But as she packed her uni bag, all Charlie wanted to do was get a blanket, curl up on the sofa, and watch all the daytime telly she used to love.

Twenty minutes later with a half-eaten piece of toast stuffed in her gob, she stepped out of her flat and her ear was immediately drawn to a door opening down the hall.

Expecting to see Jake heading out to work, Charlie paused when a woman stepped out of his flat instead. Making like Nancy Drew, she quickly ducked back inside, peeking around the doorframe. The woman turned to face his open door, an affectionate smile on her face as she nodded a couple of times, listening to whatever Jake was telling her. She wasn't old, maybe early thirties from what Charlie could see. Long brown hair hung neatly down her back. She wore a camel-coloured coat that stopped at her knees, with tailored grey trousers and black shoes that had a slight heel, and was holding a small, black handbag.

The woman nodded a couple of times, laughing and saying something back to him. Then it looked like she said goodbye before walking away.

Jake's door closed, and Charlie stood there for a minute.

Had the woman stayed the night?

Charlie's stomach sank a little. After what had almost happened on Friday night, she thought there might have been something starting to happen between them.

There could have been a reasonable explanation for a nice looking woman to be in his flat at that time in the morning, but her mind, of course, wanted to stick to the most obvious answer no matter how much she tried to convince herself otherwise.

Disappointment crushing her hope, Charlie walked down the hall, hitching her bag up higher on her shoulder and wishing she could somehow erase what she'd seen. Then Jake's door opened swiftly as she was passing. Great. Just what she needed. But she didn't stop. Glancing back at him she said, "Morning," in the most regular, not-jealous-at-all voice she could conjure up. Then she carried on walking, wanting to appear like she was in a rush.

She heard him say, "Hi," before she pushed through the door to the stairwell and descending the stairs like the place was on fire.

Phew. Thank God that awkward situation had been dodged.

In her mind, Charlie was making light of the situation. Shame the rest of her wasn't following along. She wanted to brush it off, she really did. *It is what it is*, she told herself. She was happy for him.

Why, then, did her chest feel so hollow all of a sudden?

It's for the best.

The words were in Jake's thoughts, had been for most of the day, but it didn't mean it was truly what he wanted. All day he'd been on edge. Pissed off with the way things had gone with Charlie and it was no fault on her part. He'd been the one to get scared. It was him who'd pulled back, having second thoughts about kissing her at the last minute when he'd already showed his hand. So tempted. He'd wanted to kiss her. All night at The Crow he'd barely been able to take his eyes off her. And when she'd suggested going for a ride, he knew immediately where he wanted to take her, and had planned on doing it there under the stars.

You're a fucking idiot.

Like he didn't know that anyway. For getting involved with her in the first place. For starting to feel things he'd hidden away for most of his adult life. For hoping.

Then he'd lost his bottle, panicking at the last minute; the distraction giving him a get out.

Holding back because he was too fucking set in his ways.

His life had been pretty straight forward until she'd come along. Granted, it was shit, yes. But at least he'd had a plan. And now a woman who lived on his floor had thrown it all into disarray.

What was he supposed to do?

With the shit that was hanging over his head, getting involved with someone was impossible, let alone unfair to Charlie.

And now he had another issue to deal with.

However, that issue might have just helped him. When Samantha left his flat this morning, he knew Charlie had seen her. He'd spent most of his day ignoring the urge to go and clear things up

This could be his out.

It's for the best, he told himself again, for both of them. He would leave things as they were in the hope that Charlie made her own assumptions and pulled away from him.

Why then, hours later, was he waiting outside their apartment building, leaning against his bike, waiting for Charlie to get home?

Because he'd lost his fucking mind.

And he meant in the actual cognitive sense—as in, he needed a mental health check-up.

The truth was—and he hated himself for not sticking to his plan—that he didn't want Charlie thinking he'd been with another woman, which was madness; he couldn't afford to care about what she thought of him. It wasn't like he could explore the attraction that was so blatantly obvious between them.

Shit.

His head was so fucked up it was exhausting.

Which is why he was standing here now. Jake needed a break from the battle he was constantly fighting within himself since Charlie had shown up in his life. And yes she *was* in it, there was no denying it. Albeit temporarily. Maybe if he stopped fighting, just for a brief moment, he might fare better when he left.

Not that he was leaving anytime soon.

Earlier he'd received another phone call to let him know he hadn't got one of the flats he'd enquired about. The others hadn't been back to him either. So it looked like another night in front of his laptop.

Good job he had plenty of beers in the fridge.

"Jake?"

He'd been so preoccupied with his thoughts he hadn't noticed Charlie approaching. The instant pleasure her voice alone elicited inside him took him aback, but he forced the unease away. It was something he'd think about later. Turned out, when he looked up at her and saw the smile she gave him, he forgot it all anyway.

"Problem with your bike?" she asked, hugging a large file to her chest. She had a rucksack over one shoulder too and he realised she'd have carried all that from the train station, but she didn't look tired from the walk. In fact, she looked beautiful with her reddened cheeks flushed from the wind. Honestly, that flush did things to him that he shouldn't allow himself to think about, but had done too many times. Her blonde hair was pulled back into a wavy ponytail that bounced with her steps. She wore black leggings and a jade green top under the short leather jacket she always seemed to favour. Her makeup was subtle, black eyelashes curling up like spiders around eyes that seemed to sparkle as she waited for an answer.

Jesus Christ!

He was noticing more and more things that he liked about her.

Blinking, Jake got his shit together. "Uh, no. I was waiting for you actually."

Now he was fidgety. Fucking *fidgety*. What was this woman doing to him?

"Oh?" Some of the light left her eyes and her brows pulled down. "Is something wrong?"

Smile you idiot. He did, sort of. "No. I wanted to talk to you about this morning, that's all."

Her head tipped a little to the side. "This morning?"

"Yeah. Shall we go inside?"

"Okay." Glancing at him again, because obviously it was quite clear to her that he was acting weird, she walked ahead and they made their way inside.

As he followed her up the stairs to their floor, he wondered if he should start talking, get it said and out of the way then they could part ways and go about their evenings separately. He was beginning to think he'd made a bad decision and should have let the damn thing go like he'd planned.

Seriously, he was out of his depth with all this.

Before he knew it, they were approaching his flat and he realised neither of them had said a word, which only made the situation worse. Now he'd probably made Charlie feel awkward too, which was evident in the way she looked at him when they stopped outside his flat door.

"Are you sure nothing's wrong, Jake?"

This time he didn't hesitate. "Yeah, everything's fine." He unlocked his door, trying to act casual. "I wanted to explain about Samantha."

"Who's Samantha?"

Jake looked back and hopefully gave her a reassuring smile. "Let me just put my helmet inside. Unless you want to come in for a minute."

He was glad when she followed him inside, but he left the door open so as not to make things more uncomfortable. Placing his helmet on the shelf under the sideboard in the hall, he turned back to Charlie who had swung her backpack off her shoulder and had put it down on the floor beside her, still holding onto the folder like it was a shield.

Keeping it casual, he said, "Samantha called round this morning to drop me some information about this thing I'm looking into." He wasn't going to go into too much detail. It wasn't something he was ready to discuss with her or anyone right now.

Charlie looked at him like she was expecting him to continue, or she was trying to act like she didn't know what he was talking about.

He gave her a half smile. "I saw you duck back inside this morning when she was leaving here."

As her eyes widened, he was glad to see her cheeks fill with that nice pink glow they'd lost after coming inside.

"I didn't want you to think anything of it. That's all."

"Oh, no. Of course." Holding the folder with one arm, she shoved her hand in her jacket pocket. "Um, why would you think I would even have an opinion?"

Ok, so he was quite enjoying this. "Well, I know how it must have looked. Which is probably why you tried to hide, right?" He turned away and removed his bike jacket, stepping past her to hang it on the hook by the door.

She let out a sharp laugh. "I did not try to hide." She stuttered a little. "I forgot my bag."

Stepping back, but only a little so he remained close, he lowered his voice. "Oh. I thought you might have assumed she'd stayed over."

He saw Charlie stiffen a little and her reaction sparked something in him that urged him to continue teasing.

Her eyes flicked up to his for only a second and she moved back a little. "Even if I did think that, it has nothing to do with me who you sleep with." Another glance.

Maybe it was because he'd done nothing but think of the woman for weeks, but Jake found he couldn't stop himself this time. She'd awoken something in him he thought was buried deep; it had done nothing but mess with his head ever since.

"So you wouldn't be bothered," he stepped closer and saw her shoulders straighten as she swallowed. His gaze fell to her tempting lips, "if I'd shagged someone last night?"

"No. Like I said, why would I be?"

When she stuck her chin up at him, her eyes pinned him with her defiance, which only spurred him on even more. Hit with a sudden urge to pick up where his cowardice had left off the other night, Jake was desperate to kiss her, and he had a feeling he wouldn't be able to stop himself this time.

Chapter Twenty-One

What was happening here?

And why was he looking at her like that? This conversation hadn't been expected to begin with, and now it had taken a turn she hadn't seen coming at all. The way Jake had closed off from her, again, last time they'd been together, she wasn't expecting to see that look in his eyes when she came here to talk.

After seeing that woman, Samantha, leave his place this morning, Charlie hadn't stopped thinking about it. She'd even had unwelcome visions of the two of them in bed together popping into her head at random moments throughout the day. She'd been about ready to never speak to him again after that. Yet here she was in a very different scenario. Now she knew who that woman really was, and was face to face with a very different Jake who, in that moment, looked like he wanted to devour her.

The surprise threw her off guard as his glare made her body heat.

As Jake moved in closer, Charlie tried to step back but her heels hit the wall, stopping her retreat. With her back now against it, heart hammering in her chest, she tried to gather herself in preparation for what she hoped was about to happen. Looking at his handsome face, his enticing blue eyes burrowing into her, she saw his sculptured jaw was set tight. When he spoke again, she found herself mesmerised by the fullness of his lips.

He raised his hand and placed it on the wall next to her head, tilting his head to the side a little, like an animal gauging its prey. "I think you're lying, Charlie." God, that voice. It was all deep and husky. "I think the thought of that woman being in my bed has plagued you all day."

It might have been the truth, but Charlie tried her best not to react, even though his words and the way he spoke them made her blood heat. She would play him at his little game.

"I think that's what you were hoping for," she said, trying to keep her voice steady. "But you're wrong. I couldn't give a stuff what women you sleep with."

Those taunting eyes narrowed as a sly smile lifted one side of his mouth. Bloody hell. She should just grab hold of him and crush her mouth to his, but she wasn't going to be the one to do it. If Jake wanted her then he could make the first move. Besides, this was more fun.

"Because it's none of your business," he repeated back to her, his face closer now.

"Exactly." Shit. The breathlessness in her voice betrayed her. How could she talk normally, though, when he was doing this to her: stealing her breath, all rational thoughts? Going by the look in his eyes he knew he was affecting her. She had to try harder. "Besides, why should it bother you anyway what I think?"

"Maybe I want it to bother you."

Bloody hell. Her lips felt dry and when she licked them, his eyes dropped down to her mouth and she saw his chest expand.

"Tell me the truth, Charlie. Tell me it bothered you."

Now that he was standing so close, Charlie was consumed by the heady masculine smell of his aftershave, and she inhaled it in deep, also biding herself a little extra time to get the courage to give him a smart answer. It didn't come. Oh, what the hell. It wasn't like she could hide her reaction to him any longer anyway.

"Yes. It did bother me, okay?" Her heart was pounding so hard now she was surprised he couldn't feel it.

"Why?" His eyes roamed her face before he leaned close enough to talk by her ear. "Why did the thought of me fucking someone else bother you?"

Shit. As his breath warmed her ear, sending a pleasant shiver down that same side of her body, his words sent a rush of heat to other parts of her she tried not to think about.

It was hard to answer. All of a sudden her plan to play his game had wilted and died. But she would answer him. If he was brazen enough to act this way with her, she could find the confidence to answer him truthfully.

"Because I want you." Did she just say that? Her lungs seized as she waited for his response. It came in the way of a huffed out breath over her neck, and this time she felt it right between her thighs. Then his lips grazed her ear as he moved back to look at her.

For a moment there were no words spoken as his eyes roamed her face, and she struggled to keep her composure. It was hard though, when she had a gorgeous man doing things to her insides she hadn't felt before, with barely even a touch.

Then his eyes dropped to her mouth and he moved in slowly, pausing only inches away like he was waiting for her to object. When she didn't, he pressed his lips against hers. Charlie inhaled a sharp breath through her nose, needing some air in reserve as he kissed her. Her eyes closed with the soft, warmth of his lips as they moved against hers.

At first his kiss was gentle, a tentative embrace so much better than she'd imagined, chaste, not pushing for more. But she sensed he was working hard to keep it that way. Charlie wanted more. She wanted him to lose the control he was holding onto, and it surprised her. Elation went through her as his tongue pressed against her lips seeking access. She opened to him, her tongue meeting his and inviting him in. Twisting, swirling.

When he stepped into her, she dropped the folder she'd been carrying so it wasn't in the way. Running her hands over his hard pecs to his shoulders, she moved them to the back of his neck as his hard body pressed against her.

He was everything, far more than what she'd imagined alone in her bed at night the many times she'd thought of him. What her mind had wondered was nothing compared to the reality. Their kiss deepened, and as his hands moved up her sides, her nipples hardened, her body alive and yearning for his touch. But his hands went either side of her face, caressing her cheeks softly.

His mouth slowed, tongue retreating as she felt him take a deep breath. All too soon, Jake broke away and her head moved forward as she yearned for his lips to return to hers. Then, after placing another soft kiss on her lips, he pulled back to look at her with eyes dark and hooded.

In the silence that followed, as she watched him lower his gaze to her mouth, Charlie somehow managed to regulate her breathing, wondering what he was thinking in that moment. He licked his lips and gave her a smile while he closed his eyes for a second.

Then she sensed the change.

"I'm sorry," he said when he looked at her again, pulling away. The smile had gone, replaced by that same bleak look he regularly wore. "I shouldn't have done that." Turning away, he paused, hands resting on his hips and his head low.

Charlie almost wilted as her heart sank. She had to keep him there, not the Jake she'd first met who was cold and closed off, but the Jake she was with the other night under the stars—the man who had kissed her so affectionately mere seconds ago. "Jake. Don't close off from me again. So what, we kissed. It isn't like we both haven't wanted it for a while now. Well, I know I have anyway. Why does it have to be such a big deal?"

When he turned to her he looked almost worn down. Whatever was going on in his head kept pulling him away from her. She could see in his eyes he was fighting this and it confused and frustrated her. After all the back and forth, now it was pretty bloody obvious he was into her, so—

"We should forget this happened."

Blinking, Charlie looked Jake in the eyes as she processed what he'd said and saw nothing. The stoic expression didn't fool her at all. Deflated, all she could do right then was nod. Then she picked up her things from the floor and when she straightened he was still looking at her. Fine. If that's the way he wanted it.

"Okay. I'll walk out of here and act like nothing happened. If that's what you really want. But don't expect me to forget the way you just kissed me." She couldn't even if she tried. Charlie had a feeling it would be burned into her memories for the rest of her life. Her knees were still weak from it as she turned to leave.

"Charlie—"

"It's fine, Jake." Glancing back at him, she kept her chin up, bag slung over her arm and her folder hugged tightly to her chest. "I'm getting pretty used to it now."

Charlie left without looking back.

Difference was, this time she didn't have the urge to.

Chapter Twenty-Two

Throwing the quilt off, Jake got up and sat on the edge of his bed. His mind was driving him insane, everything rushing through his thoughts on a loop, over and over.

He'd gone to sleep with Charlie in his head. The kiss they'd shared had shocked him. Not only because he'd liked it so much, but because it had changed the direction of his feelings. What was it about that woman that messed with his self-control? Jake had never even been this way about any of the women he'd been with in his past. Why then, after all this time of disinterest, was she getting under his skin?

He knew if he gave in, it would be his biggest mistake.

The woman had skewed his focus.

Then there was Terry. That bastard was still crushing him even though he'd been out of Jake's life for three years. But how long was it supposed to take to get over trauma like that? He guessed at never. Scrubbing his hand down his face he was hit with memories that threatened to destabilise him again just as they had a million times before.

He was a mess. Consumed by it all and it was getting harder to deal with.

Going into the bathroom he turned on the shower in the hope that the water spraying over his body would jerk him out of his reverie. Nope. Did it hell. Instead, thoughts went back to Charlie. He'd lost control earlier, showing a weakness he couldn't afford to have. But the way she'd looked at him, the things she'd said so candidly, Jake had seen her in that moment, *really* seen her, and she'd never looked more attractive. She'd taken all rational thought from his mind in an instant, forcing him to admit to himself that he was beginning to feel things he shouldn't.

Fuck, he was in trouble here.

Things were far simpler before he'd met her that day in the street.

Not only that, but Jake realised right then that Charlie was now taking up more of his headspace than his other problem.

When he was done in the shower he didn't feel any better. In fact, he felt worse. The way he'd closed off from her, after allowing the kiss to happen, was riding his guilt train hard. He knew he was being difficult, had wanted to be at first, hoping she'd dislike him enough to move on. But what was the point if he wasn't going to try harder?

One thing was for sure, Jake had a feeling he wasn't going to get any sleep tonight unless he apologised.

Going into the kitchen and searching through one of the drawers, he eventually found a small notepad, then a pen. So it was lame putting his apology on a piece of paper, but it was all he could do right then to ease his conscience enough to get his head down for a few hours.

Charlie,

I want to apologise for last night. When I said I shouldn't have kissed you, it wasn't because I didn't want to. But I'm dealing with stuff right now that I can't get into. I promise you haven't done anything; this is all me. I know that's a cliché, but it's the truth. I really wish things were different, because if they were, I wouldn't hesitate to kiss you again.

If you only knew how bad the timing of this is.

I just wanted to let you know why I've been behaving like a dick.

I'm sorry.

J x

P.S. Maybe we should have each other's number. Save the trees and all that.

Twenty minutes later, after staring at the note and convincing himself it was a good idea to post it, Jake was back in his bed, regretting posting it.

Fuck.

What a mess.

Standing at the breakfast counter while he hurriedly ate his bacon and eggs, Jake was still unsettled about the note to Charlie. On heavy reflection—the reason he'd only had about an hour's sleep—he should have just left things as they were. Too late.

And now so was he.

Bollocks! He had ten minutes to get to work.

Considering it took him ten minutes to get there, depending on traffic, the fact that he was still standing in his flat didn't bode well for him getting there on time.

Tipping the rest of the breakfast he didn't have time to finish in the bin, he put the plate and fork in the sink and went down the hall. When he'd put his bike jacket on, a rustling sound drew his attention over by the front door. He saw a piece of paper on the carpet, and went over to get it, recognising his own handwriting on the outside of the folded note.

Opening it, he smiled when he read the short reply.

Jake,

I accept your written apology (coward).

But I won't deny that you have been behaving like a dick. Whatever is going on with you, I'm here as your friend.

Char x

P.S. I will give you my number next time you kiss me.

Shit!

Chapter Twenty-Three

Singing the last words of his final song, Jake's eyes were closed, savouring the moment. When he opened them again the crowd was already on their feet, their applause growing louder as he struck his last chord. It humbled him. After everything, to be on stage again singing to an appreciative crowd was the last thing he expected to be doing. The last few years had almost destroyed him and he was starting to think there was no way back from the black hole he'd been in. Yet here he was, performing another gig at The Gifted Crow to a packed out crowd who had come to see him again.

It wouldn't sink in properly.

But behind the adrenaline that rushed through him right then, there was an ominous feeling that he couldn't ignore.

It wasn't going to last.

He was leaving.

Soon, his future would be lost again.

"Thanks. Goodnight," Jake said, holding his guitar up as he started to leave the stage. Then right in that moment his eyes caught on someone that froze the blood in his veins. The man had been hidden in the shadows until one of the lights in the ceiling shone right on him.

It was *him*. There was no mistaking the man staring at him from the right side of the room. Dressed in dark clothes, a dark hoodie and what looked like deep-blue jeans. He must have seen Jake notice him, which was what Jake suspected he wanted. After all, he was standing right in a place where Jake wouldn't be blinded by the stage lighting. Arsehole*'s* eyes lingered as he turned away and made his way out of there.

Jake didn't waste any time. He left the stage, barely hearing the continued applause as he ran to the office and put his bike boots on in a hurry. Putting his guitar in the case, he left it there in the room. Then he grabbed his jacket and helmet and raced out of there.

Heart racing, his body started to tremble with anger as he pushed his way through the busy pub. His mind raced, blocking out anything else. All the thoughts he'd had about this moment, the plans he'd made in his head, pushing everything else aside. This was it—this was what he'd been desperate for: retribution.

Finally, after almost three years of waiting, Jake was about to come face to face with the man who had destroyed everything he'd ever known.

Charlie couldn't wait any longer. She'd been bursting for a pee for the last four songs, but hadn't wanted to miss any of Jake's set. As soon as he'd finished singing, she told Cara where she was going and hurried to the toilets. Of course there was a queue. The place was busier than she'd ever seen it and it looked like all the women in the place had waited for Jake to finish too; now she was behind most of them, doing her best to keep the impression of a bouncing spring on the down low while trying not to think about how close she was to peeing in her jeans.

The taps in constant use did nothing to help.

Eventually she got to a cubical and her eyes literally watered when she finally sat on the loo. As she emptied her bladder, she got lost in her thoughts of Jake. He'd sung to her again and she'd got all embarrassed, much to her friends' amusement. Well, all except Jason who still didn't seem that impressed with Jake.

Again, she'd been transfixed on him as he'd sung the powerful words he'd constructed into such a beautiful song. There was something happening between them. She couldn't deny it. But despite what he'd said in his note, she was still confused by the way he was acting.

I really wish things were different, because if they were, I wouldn't hesitate to kiss you again.

Words that were bitter sweet; he would kiss her again, but something in his life was preventing him from getting any closer. It was so frustrating.

"Did you hear what Dominic said about him?"

Charlie's ears picked up on the gossiping in the next cubicle.

"No. What did he say?"

"You know his dad owns a garage? Well, he reckons one night he heard his dad telling his mum that one of the men who worked for him had been in prison. There was a whole conversation about him giving the guy a chance because he was a grafter. Anyway, it's that Jake Sure he was talking about."

Charlie's heart froze in her chest at Jake's name. Prison?

"Did he say why?"

"No. But I don't care. The guy is hot."

"Oh my God, I know..."

Their conversation fell away as Charlie started to hyperventilate. Prison? Surely it was just a rumour. How did this Dominic know it was Jake his dad was talking about? He wouldn't be the only one who worked at the garage.

Someone knocked on the door. "You done in there?"

"Yeah." Charlie got out of there as quickly as she could, a profound sinking feeling washing over her as she made her way back to the table. There had to be a mistake. She wasn't the type of person to take someone else's words as the truth, especially toilet gossip. People liked to make things up.

That's what it was. Just talk.

At least, that's what she was going with for now. She'd had a great night and Jake's show had been a huge success. There was no way she was going to let meaningless gossip ruin her night, or anything else, for that matter.

So, putting on her happy face, she joined her friends, hoping Jake was with them when she got back. Her smile slipped a little when she didn't see him there. Glancing around, he wasn't anywhere.

"Where's Jake?"

"I thought he'd probably found you. Haven't seen him," Jas said casually.

That was strange. Maybe he'd been mobbed by fans. There could be a queue of them somewhere wanting autographs. She smiled discreetly. Then recalled those girls in the toilet practically drooling over him and a pang of jealousy straightened her face.

Picking up her drink, she idly sat on the edge of her friends' conversation while keeping her eye out for Jake. Forty five minutes later and there was still no sign.

Charlie left the pub a little while after Jake had disappeared. Her friends, namely Cara, had talked her into staying for another drink and when she managed to make an excuse to get away, she got an Uber and was home by around eleven. Jake's bike hadn't been there when she got back, but she'd been too distracted, still feeling strange about what she'd overheard and the fact that Jake had run out on her to think about where he might have gone and why he'd ghosted her—again.

Then she couldn't help thinking about all the women fawning over him. Perhaps someone had caught his eye. It wasn't as if she was in any kind of relationship with him. So what they'd kissed. Charlie had felt it was more than that. It was ridiculous to even think they were heading anywhere, but Charlie had thought things were ok again after their silly note exchange.

Instead of worrying, all she wanted to do was eat ice cream and watch a bit of TV before bed. Curled up on the sofa half an hour later, that's exactly what she was doing when there was a quiet knock on the door. Shoving the last spoonful of Ben and Jerry's Baked Alaska in her mouth, she put the bowl down on the table and went to look through her peephole, the wood floor cold under her bare feet.

Jake was standing outside her door.

Crap.

Charlie checked herself over and straightened her soft nightie, which was more like a long T-shirt. He couldn't have knocked half an hour earlier when she was still dressed.

Ah, well.

Opening the door, she ignored her racing heart and the hope that his visit had ignited. Maybe there was no woman after all. "Hi," she said, trying to sound casual.

"Hey. Sorry for knocking so late." Why was he barely looking at her? Was it guilt? *Stop it Charlie!*

"It's fine. I was only watching telly."

Jake nodded and an awkward silence fell between them, so Charlie broke it. "Do you want to come in?"

He looked at her then dropped his gaze, rubbing his hand over his mouth, and she expected him to say no. "Yeah. Okay."

She took a step back and he came through the door. For some reason, he looked so big in her hallway. She couldn't afford to think about what had happened last time they'd been in each other's company. Not right then when this was the first time she'd actually spoken to him since their kiss.

There was no way she was going to bring it up.

"Do you want a drink?" Needing to get out of the small space of the hall that felt half the size with him in it, Charlie went to the kitchen and Jake hesitantly followed.

"No. Thanks."

"Sure? I'm making one."

"I'm good." He leaned against the breakfast bar counter, and she switched on the kettle to make a cup of tea for herself, mostly because she needed something to do.

"You were brilliant again tonight." When she looked over at him his eyes shot to hers but he still wore the frown. "Everyone in there thought so too." His jaw tightened, but he stayed quiet. Something was definitely off with him, more off than usual anyway.

"Thanks. But I'm wishing I hadn't taken the gigs."

Charlie wondered why, but didn't press.

"Well, I'm glad you did. You're so talented. You deserve to be heard. You deserved the response you get." When he remained quiet, she turned away to make the tea.

"I looked for you when you came off stage," she said, going with the truth seeing as she was the only one talking right then.

"That's why I came. I didn't want you to think I'd just left like that for no reason."

She paused after putting sugar in the cup, knowing she shouldn't say what was about to come out of her mouth but saying it anyway. "I thought maybe you'd left with someone." *Jeez, Charlie. How third year high school.*

"What do you mean?" Out of her peripheral, she saw him straighten.

Glancing over her shoulder, she almost faltered when she saw the confusion he was throwing off as he folded his arms. "Oh, nothing." Why was she doing this?

"Didn't sound like nothing. Who did you think I'd left with?"

Turning to face him with the teaspoon still in her hand, she still couldn't get control over her mouth. It was like she'd been taken over by some jealous bitch who had no right to say anything like she was. "No one in particular, but you've had a lot of women practically throwing themselves at you tonight, so I—"

"You assume a lot don't you, Charlie. Because some women see me, the singer guy, as a piece to link their arm through, show off to their mates, you *assumed* I'd be interested? Thought I'd revelled in the attention so much I just had to have one of them?"

Charlie tried to inhale down her embarrassment while turning back around to pick up the kettle. She squeezed her eyes shut for a second before pouring water in the cup and silently kicking her own arse. Her shoulders slumped as she put the kettle back on its base. *None of your business anyway remember?* "Look I'm—"

"No. Actually you weren't far wrong. Only there were two of them. I took them around the back of the place and we all had a fucking great time. I'm surprised you can't smell them all over me, your nose is so close to my business."

Her cheeks enflamed at the contempt in his voice and she begged the ground to swallow her whole. Only, that was impossible, so she sucked it up and turned to face him.

"Oh, wait. You like thinking about me fucking other women, don't you?"

Oh God. This wasn't how she expected things to go tonight. And what the hell? It definitely wasn't a time to get turned on by his words. *Focus Charlie.*

She'd made this happen; it was her responsibility to put it right.

"Stop. I'm sorry, okay. I was out of line. I didn't mean for this to happen. It's none of my business where you went and I didn't really think you'd gone off with someone like that. I'm just—"

Leaning back against the counter, she inhaled and the sigh that followed had her shoulders dropping. Putting her hand to the front of her head she said, "God, this is so not me."

The edgy silence that followed made her want to look up at Jake, but she was too embarrassed to move her eyes from where they were fixed on the toes of her boots. Could she have ballsed this up anymore? What a mess. If Jake walked out the door and never looked at her again she wouldn't honestly blame him.

Bloody hell, was he going to say anything? Was he still there? She could hear her own heartbeat pounding in her ears.

"When I got off stage I had an important message on my phone. I had to leave straight away and I didn't have time to find you to explain."

Relief washed over her and she closed her eyes. Deep down, even though he didn't offer any further explanation, she'd known there was a reason. Leaving without even saying goodbye didn't seem like something he would do. Never mind leaving with a woman when Charlie had gone to watch him play.

Okay, she barely knew him, and what little interaction they'd had hadn't been easy. As mysterious as the guy was, though, he'd never been downright horrible.

"It's okay. I was worried, that's all." Immediately, Charlie realised what she'd said.

"Why would you be worried?"

Her stomach knotted. And she panicked, trying to think of an acceptable reason for saying it, but all she came up with were questions for herself. Why was she so worried? Probably because she knew there were things going on with him. He was hiding from something. Someone had been in his flat.

Now she lifted her head and found his eyes on her, his intense stare making her want to drop her gaze again so she didn't have to face him when she answered. She didn't though. "I thought there was something wrong."

It was all she could say. It could mean anything really, so she wasn't lying. Charlie had worried. But her reasons weren't even clear to herself.

"The only thing wrong right now is that I can't seem to stay away from you."

His words stunned her. She fought to keep her eyes from going wide. "Jake—"

"You know what I was doing this last week? Looking for a new place to live."

What?

"That's what I should have been doing tonight as well, but instead, I was singing in a packed-out pub, pretending my life wasn't in the shitter and imagining things that are impossible."

"Why are you leaving?"

His eyes never left hers; instead they pulled her in until she was almost drowning in their steely-blue depths. "Because I have to. That's all I can tell you."

So he *was* hiding something.

As Charlie thought of him leaving, no longer living down the hall, she wanted to grab hold of him and beg him not to go. Thankfully, he couldn't read her thoughts; he'd be out of there like a shot otherwise. Caught up in her head as she tried to think of words that might make him stay, she didn't notice he'd moved closer.

"It should be easy," he continued, taking another small step that brought him right in front of her. Charlie straightened as she looked up into the handsome face that had haunted her mind since she'd first seen him properly. "If I could go back to this time a few weeks ago it would be."

He wasn't really making sense, but she didn't want to interrupt him and risk him clamming up. Instead, as she listened, she just swallowed, trying to lubricate her dry throat.

"I tried to ignore you." When he reached up and lifted a strand of her hair from where it rested on her shoulder, his eyes watched as it slipped from his fingers. Charlie's heart sped up as he moved in closer. "But since we kissed you're even harder to escape." He closed his eyes for a second. "And now I'm here wondering if. . ."

She breathed in sharply and he opened his eyes, the look in them now hungry.

He was going to kiss her again and she was so ready for it.

Suddenly he backed away. "I can't," Jake said, more to himself than to her.

Can't what?

When he looked back up at her his head shook slightly and he backed away.

"Jake?"

"I need to go. *Fuck!* I'm sorry. I can't deal with what's going on in my head right now."

He headed for the door then turned when he opened it. Her heart sank at his expression when he glanced back, pained and sorrowful.

Then he left, closing the door behind him without another word, leaving her twisted up inside. Standing in front of the door, Charlie leaned her forehead against it, wishing she could take back her stupid words and erase everything that had just happened. Why were things so complicated between them? It seemed the closer they got, the stronger the force was pushing them in opposite directions, like two magnets reaching out for each other, their poles repelling, forcing them apart.

Her mind went back to the toilets in the pub, the things those women said. Maybe there was some weight to it after all, and Charlie knew that they had no chance if he was going to keep it from her.

But he said he was leaving.

That way he wouldn't have to tell her.

A knock on the door had her jumping back and almost out of her skin. It was so unexpected and loud it frightened her half to death. Still trying to get her heart to go back down into her chest, she opened the door swiftly without even thinking to check her peephole first. But she knew it was him.

Something had changed. She knew it as she looked into the handsome face staring back at her.

"Jake?"

There was an expression on his face she hadn't seen before, but before she had time to analyse it, Jake stepped right up to her, put his hand on the back of her neck and took her in a kiss that brought her heart right back up into her throat again.

No breath. In that unexpected moment he'd taken all of it and all she could do was whimper. Her hands reached up and gripped onto the front of his T-shirt as his mouth desperately moved against hers. Sucked up in a whirlwind of emotion, Charlie had no idea what had prompted this, but she kissed him back without question.

Keeping hold of his shirt, Charlie pulled Jake inside where their kiss resumed. The door closed hard; Jake must have kicked it shut. Then when he pushed her against the wall she slid her arms around him, pulling him closer. They'd been working up to this: the moment in his flat, the argument in her kitchen. It was a result of all those pent up feelings that had been brewing and brewing. The ones she'd had to cage and that Jake had tried to deny. It was inevitable: like a barrel of gunpowder sitting on top of a naked flame. It was really only a matter of time until it exploded. But with the two of them, it could have gone one of two ways: they'd have had a huge falling out never to speak to each other again, or this.

This was welcomed.

By both of them, it seemed.

But would it end with Jake's denial again?

This time Charlie would do what she could to keep him there.

Chapter Twenty-Four

As Charlie's hands went into his hair, Jake's mouth ravaged hers. Their crossed words had heated his blood, the jealousy he'd sensed from her had confirmed her feelings, and from that moment he knew he was in trouble. Again, he'd tried to walk away, to use their argument as an excuse to get away from her, but it had backfired in a big way. Yes, he'd walked out the door, slamming it behind him, but his feet hadn't taken more than a step before he turned back around, his mind throwing up what she'd looked like standing there in her kitchen in a nightshirt that barely covered her. Seeing her like that hadn't helped at all. At her door, he'd realised he couldn't fight it any longer.

No. He didn't want to fight it.

Pressing his body into hers, a surge of electric heat soared through his veins as he thrashed his tongue against hers. Charlie met him with the same vigour and he felt the fire in her just as it burned in him. A hard kiss meant to ignite the passion that had been building between them. Mouths crushing, teeth clashing. This was nothing like the kiss they'd shared in his place. There had been precaution behind him then. He'd wanted to take it up a notch, but the fear of falling was riding him in the back of his mind.

That fear had gone now.

Replaced by desperation.

Too many nights he'd spent in his bed hard for her. She'd consumed his thoughts to the point of madness.

This time he wasn't letting fear break them apart.

Jake's hands began to explore, one sliding around to her arse and pulling her into him, while the other slid up her ribs until his hand covered her breast. A whimper into his mouth, her warm breath rushing into him as he kneaded her through her nightshirt, making him rock hard. He pressed into her, wanting her to feel what she did to him, and her head tipped back with a gasp. "Jake."

Fuck, he loved that she said his name with such need.

Moving his mouth down her neck, he tasted his way down her front, nipping and licking her smooth skin, with only one destination in mind. He bent and put his mouth on her breast, nipping at her pert nipple over the cotton fabric. When her hand went to the back of his head, letting him know she was quite happy for him to be there, he reached down and pulled the nightshirt up, exposing her almost naked body to his hungry eyes. When she held it in place, Jake looked into her hooded eyes as he brushed his hand over her bare breast causing her to gasp, her head falling back again. Then swiftly, he replaced his hand with his mouth, tongue flicking her hard nipple before he suckled it.

Moving to the other one, he cupped her with his hand before ravishing her, her nails digging into the back of his head as she held him there.

Fuck, he was so fired up. Ready to take this to the next step, but he was also mindful that if he went there, he probably wouldn't ever leave.

Straightening, his mouth clashed against hers again. And when her arms went around his neck, he lifted her up. Legs wrapping around him, their kiss never faltered while he moved them around. Stepping up to the sideboard, he placed her down on top of it.

Breaking the kiss for a moment, Jake wanted to see in her eyes if she was as hungry for him as he was her. The bright flush in her cheeks and the way her breaths panted as she looked at him through thick lashes gave him his answer.

When he looked down, her nightshirt was bunched up by his body as he stood between her thighs. Then she grabbed it by the hem and pulled it off over her head, throwing it behind him.

His eyes went to her full, round breasts, nipples that were rock hard. Fuck, she looked hot. Cupping one with his hand, he bent down and took her breast in his mouth, causing a faint cry of pleasure. He wanted more of that.

Standing up, he rested his hands on the sideboard either side of her, leaning in to kiss her again. Then he said, "I want to touch you," against her lips, feeling her warm breath rush out against his. Kissing her again, he ran his hand gently up the inside of her thigh. "Will you let me, Charlie?" His thumb found her centre and he brushed over the gusset of her knickers with the lightest touch. Teasing.

Charlie's mouth dropped open with a gasp. "Yes," she whispered, and when he touched her, she grabbed the back of his head and pulled him in for a hard kiss, moaning into his mouth as he began to rub her with his thumb in slow circles.

Fuck, he felt her wetness through the silky soft material of her knickers and wanted it on him. Her legs parted when he slid the delicate material to the side and she moaned again the moment his fingers found her, rubbing gently through her folds.

"Oh God." Her voice trembled and he liked the sound of it like that.

When her hips started to move, pushing herself against his hand, Jake groaned, his cock twitching, desperately wanting to get in on the action. But he wasn't going there. Not tonight. This was the first time he'd allowed himself to properly act on his feelings and he already knew being with her like this was going to make it harder to leave.

He wanted her so badly, but this was all he could afford to take in the hope that it would stem his craving.

Breaking their kiss, Jake moved his mouth along her jaw line, his fingers working her swollen flesh faster now, causing Charlie to get more vocal, more breathless. When he got to her ear, he licked around it then plunged his tongue inside at the same time he pushed a finger inside her wet heat. Another moan from Charlie, louder this time as her pleasure heightened from his fingers, her legs open wide as she pushed against him. Her response fired him up so much.

"Fuck, you're so wet, Charlie," he said beside her ear as he inserted another finger, moving them in and out, picking up the pace. "I want to feel you come around my fingers."

Her panting breaths grew more rapid as he worked her over. "Oh, Jake."

He sucked her lobe into his mouth. "That's it," he practically growled, curling his fingers towards the front of her and pressing rapidly against the sensitive spot inside as he rubbed her clit with his thumb.

Digging her nails in his back, Charlie tensed, crying out as she came, arching her back as her body convulsed around his fingers with her release. Jake slammed his mouth against hers, kissing her hard through the wave of pleasure he was giving her, until the pulses faded away.

When she smiled, panting against his mouth, his tongue slowed and he licked her bottom lip before pulling away to look at her. That glorious blush was in her cheeks. With lazy eyes, the look Charlie gave him was sultry, satisfied. The complete opposite of what he felt right then as his cock screamed for attention in his jeans—so hard it was painful.

Charlie hissed in a breath as he slowly removed his fingers, reluctantly leaving the warmth of her body.

Then she leaned into him and kissed him softly. When her tongue slid into his mouth firm and sure, it distracted all his thoughts for a moment until he jerked at the feel of her hand gripping him between the legs.

Groan.

Fuck, he almost came.

She sat more upright and he felt a button pop, then another, until the front of his jeans gaped open.

"Your turn," she said, those green-blue eyes so full of heat, looking at him through her lashes like she was about to devour him.

And he was happy to let her.

Licking his lips, he watched her watching him as she slid her hand inside his boxers. When her warm hand wrapped around him, he squeezed his eyes shut and cursed with the struggle to hold back.

Shit, he wasn't lasting long here.

He shoved his pants and boxers down his hips, freeing himself quickly, his hand falling against the wall to hold himself up. She began to move, her hand gripping him and sliding up and down his length in a tormenting rhythm. When he saw her look down, watching as she wanked him off, her tits wobbling to the movement of her arm, it sent a sharp electric heat right along his shaft. And when her tongue slid out right before her teeth bit into her bottom lip, his head shot back with a groan.

"Fuck." Looking down, he watched her hand bring him to release, come pulsing out of him onto her thigh, the floor. He saw fucking stars in that moment, his breath catching, and when it was over, she stood and he pulled her close, taking her face in his hands and kissing her like a mad man. He'd wanted this woman so badly even though he'd done everything he could to deny it. How he'd held back he didn't know.

The trouble was, this had done nothing to ease the want, the desire for her. If anything, he was far more desperate to be with Charlie now.

Shit. What was he going to do?

Chapter Twenty-Five

Great. Even though she still felt blissfully content, she was starting to get a headache, no doubt from the alcohol and the way Jake had just made her sweat. She needed hydration, stat.

After getting a glass of water to take to bed, Charlie turned everything off, leaving on the small lamp she'd almost knocked from the sideboard in the hall only a short time ago. Her bed was calling. It had been a strange evening—one so full of varied emotions. At least it had ended on a high after what she and Jake had done together. Though she might find it hard to sleep for different reasons now.

Jake filled her thoughts. The way he'd looked at her from the stage earlier that night. The way he'd kissed her at the door and what it had led to in her hallway. She couldn't believe she'd been so brazen. So confident.

Charlie would never be able to look at that sideboard again without thinking of him and how he'd destroyed her in such a glorious way.

Her dreams were going to be fantastic tonight.

After cleaning her teeth and rinsing out her toothbrush, she turned the water off and heard something fall, out in the hall. She froze, pausing her breath while she listened. When she moved towards the door, treading as softly as she could, a floor board creaked outside.

There was someone out there.

Putting her ear close to the door, Charlie waited, listening out for more movement. It may have gone silent but she could feel someone's presence on the other side of the door. Dread filled her, casting her mind back to the day she'd found Jake's door open. Now someone was in her flat.

Backing away slowly, heart racing, her wide eyes scanned the bathroom, looking for something she could use as a weapon.

Reaching down she grabbed the only thing that might do some damage.

She looked at it in her trembling hands. *Really though?* A toilet brush?

It was better than a toothbrush which was her only other option.

She heard a rustle of clothes and another creak. Someone was walking around out there.

Preparing for anything, Charlie held up the brush like she would a bat and waited. It was like she was in a nightmare. Or one of those psycho killer movies where she was just a side character who got brutally murdered, and not the star of the show. She never thought she'd find herself in this kind of situation. Maybe if she stayed quiet whoever it was would take what they wanted and get out of there. The noise of movement got closer and sounded like it stopped right outside the bathroom door.

Shaking, Charlie stayed as quiet as possible, barely breathing while she waited, knowing that someone was going to come through the door at any second.

When it opened slowly, she did the first thing that came to mind, her body taking over. She snapped the door open and there was a man on the other side. Fear shot through her when she saw the balaclava. Charlie had no time to process what was happening. Summoning all the strength she could muster, she flew at him, hoping the element of surprise was enough to buy her some time to get away.

She got lucky.

The intruder fell backwards with a huff, but as she pushed away from him he lashed out and she felt a burning sting across her forearm. The pain barely registered as she scrambled past him, but he grabbed her ankle and she went down. That was when she saw a trail of blood on her arm. No time. Kicking back as frantically as she could, Charlie heard a grunt. She looked back and the man had fallen backwards, holding his face.

She shot up off the floor, running to the kitchen. Leaning over the breakfast counter, she managed to open the drawer and grab a knife, even with her hands shaking as violently as they were. The man ran at her, and instinctively Charlie pointed the knife at him, but he didn't stop. Swerving to avoid it, he took her down, tackling her to the ground.

They struggled and Charlie only just saw the fist before it connected with her cheek, knocking her head sideways and stunning her for a moment. It hurt like hell, and she was glad he hadn't had enough leverage to get a full swing in.

She managed to get her arm free and went for his side just as his hand clamped down on her other arm. She felt something connect. And when the guy called out, his grip weakening, she knew she'd got him.

Suddenly, he paused and she reached for the balaclava he was wearing and pulled it just as he scrambled off her. A gasp tore up her throat when she saw his face; pitted skin, greying beard, the same as the man who'd been in Jake's flat. The newspaper clipping. Charlie watched in stunned fear as he got up to his feet, holding his side. His eyes were wide with shock as he looked from her to the hand that was bloody from holding the wound. Then rage filled his features, contorting his worn face as he looked at her.

There was a noise out in the hall and it stopped him coming for her.

"Help!" Charlie cried as the man looked behind him. He took one last look at her and backed away down her hall, gripping his side where she'd stabbed him.

Charlie was too stunned to move, watching through wide eyes as he turned and ran.

"Hey!"

It was Jake's voice.

Looking down at her arm, she saw a slash that was bleeding. He'd sliced through her arm with the knife. All of a sudden she felt sick and slumped onto her side, curling up in a ball on the floor, adrenaline leaving her quickly, her body now trembling so hard.

God, she thought as she lay there, her body shaking now she didn't have fear rushing through her veins with the fight to stay alive. That's when the nausea came.

She could have died tonight.

She might not have seen her parents again.

Never got to have sex with Jake.

All that work for the past two years in uni wasted.

Funny the things you thought about when you were in shock.

Chapter Twenty-Six

WHAT WAS HE THINKING?

Jake couldn't settle. He'd seen no sign of that prick when he'd left The Crow, and he'd started to think he'd imagined him. Surely he wasn't brazen enough to turn up at Jake's gig.

But Jake knew he was back. Charlie had sworn it was him when she'd seen the newspaper clipping so how could he not be on high alert? The asshole was fucking with him. He should go to the police, but honestly, with the stand-up job they'd done so far of finding him, Jake wanted to get to him first.

Now he paced his flat like he'd swallowed some speed—heart racing, agitated to fuck—not only because his nerves were shot, but because he was doing his best to stay put.

Since leaving Charlie's he couldn't get her out of his fucking head. As soon as he'd got back to his place he'd showered and had to cut it short because he was thinking about her. He was on his second glass of rum and she was still right there at the forefront of his mind. He'd expected to feel satisfied after what they'd done, maybe he wouldn't crave her as much. It was bollocks.

Like an arse, he'd left her flat pretty swiftly, but it was only because he wanted more, and he knew she'd have let him have it.

He rubbed his forehead then downed what was left of his drink, slumping on the arm of the chair.

Fuck!

It had only gotten worse. Now that he'd had a bite, he wanted the whole damn pie.

He could kick his own arse for doing what he'd done—for allowing himself to get so involved with her.

What did he expect was going to happen when he finally gave in? The moment he decided to do the open mic night he knew he'd be setting himself up for this shit. He was never any good at self-control. In the short time he'd known her, Charlie had gotten under his skin in a big way, and he couldn't understand it. Tonight, when he'd seen her sitting there across the room in the pub he'd been fixated on her. There'd been no audience. Everything had fallen away until there had been only the two of them in that room.

Shit. He felt like he was falling.

Life was doing a number on him again; the threat he'd waited all this time for had become very real tonight, confirming his reasons for not wanting to start something with Charlie. It was also why he'd thankfully come to his senses earlier before he'd done something he couldn't take back.

There was a reason he'd been looking for another place to live, but deep down Jake had still wanted to believe he could stay; just for a little bit he'd wanted to feel normal.

Impossible; if he stayed there he was risking too much, including Charlie and there was no way he could let that happen.

Jake's stomach sank as images entered his mind that he didn't want to deal with right now.

He was going to go mad.

On top of all the anxiety he had, he knew Charlie must think he was a complete arsehole after the way he'd argued with her and then lost control like he had. Maybe he should go and apologise.

Was he stupid? He'd done enough.

No. He had to let it go.

That's why twenty minutes later he was standing in the kitchen staring at nothing, still holding onto everything. She was like a fucking drug and he was doing everything he could to fight his addiction to her. He was losing; his will power dissolving into the alcohol he was drinking.

Next thing he knew, his feet were moving towards the flat door and he was heading down the hall before he could stop himself, ignoring the voice in his head that was telling him to turn back around and go straight back home again. He had no clue why he so desperately had to see her again this minute. Yes he did. Aside from the fact that he wanted to finish what they'd started earlier, he also wasn't going to settle until he'd spoken to her, to make sure she was okay after what happened and that she hadn't regretted what they'd done. Why her opinion of him had become so important, he didn't know.

Of course, he was lying about that too. He was falling for her. It was evident in the way she made him smile, made him feel comfortable. For the first time in a long time he wanted to get close to someone and he very probably would have allowed it if his past hadn't caught up with him tonight.

Jake thought he was seeing things when he approached her door; it was wide open. He paused, glancing back down the hall. Empty. It was too late for anyone to be about. Frowning, he approached slowly. Maybe he hadn't closed it properly when he'd left earlier.

Keeping his voice low in case she didn't know and was sleeping, he said, "Charlie?"

Then he heard her call out, ice filling his veins.

"Help." Her voice sounded frail followed by a whimper.

Jake flung the door open and just about got a glimpse of a lamp on the floor along with some other things strewn about before he was tackled by someone. It caught him off guard and the bastard slipped free of him, sprinting down the hall with a hood over his head. Jake took off after him. "Hey!"

The guy was well ahead of him as he practically flew down the stairs. Grabbing his phone from his pocket, he had a feeling the prick was going to get away so he called 999. When he got out front the man was quite far down the street. Charlie came into his head and he stopped. He needed to know if she was okay. If she was in trouble she could need him right now.

The call connected and Jake explained everything to the woman on the other end of the line as he ran back up the stairs. When he got to Charlie's flat, he paused for a second, not knowing which way to go. A gentle moan alerted him to the living room. Jake flew towards her voice and saw Charlie slumped on the floor by the coffee table, holding her forearm. He went to her, crouching down to give her a hand as she went to sit up. "Fuck, Charlie. Are you okay?" Then Jake saw the blood and his heart almost died in his chest. "You're bleeding?"

"I'm fine," she said and when she moved her hand and held her arm up to him he was relieved to see the wound wasn't as substantial as his mind had imagined. The slice was about two inches, but didn't look too deep. "He had a knife."

"You hurt anywhere else?"

Her hand went to her cheek and she stretched her mouth. "Here. He punched me."

Jake put his finger tips under her chin and lifted her head. "Let me see."

There was red all around her cheek bone and he could see a little bit of grey in the middle, the bruising already started. The rage in his chest was overwhelming. "Probably going to have a nice bruise there tomorrow. You should get it looked at when you go to the hospital."

She groaned. "I'm not going to the hospital."

"You have a slice on your arm that needs stitches. You really don't want that getting infected. I'll go with you if you want. After you've spoken to the police."

When she looked up at him he noticed her eyes were red, and she blinked quickly, still looking a little dazed. "Okay. Thanks."

"Are you going to tell me what happened?"

As she went through the events of her attack, Jake got a damp cloth from the kitchen and when he returned, he started to clean the blood from her other hand, and from close to the wound. Then he reached up and wiped the transfer from her face, the side of her nose and by her ear.

"It was the same guy, Jake. The one who had been in your apartment."

The blood turned to ice in his veins. He couldn't believe what he was hearing. "Are you sure it was him?"

"Definitely."

Jake's fury grew to explosive levels. He dropped his hand from her face and stood up, hands forming tight fists at his sides as his breathing became erratic, rage ringing in his ears. The sound of the buzzer was distant now as he tried to process what she'd told him.

Then his mind went back to that bastard standing at the back of the pub. He'd just pushed right past Jake. He'd been so close. "I saw him tonight."

"What?"

Jake explained how he'd chased him out of there. "That's why I left so suddenly. But I lost him. He was nowhere in sight by the time I got out of the pub. I spoke to the bouncers but the place was so busy, people coming in and out all the time. It was no surprise they couldn't help. I took off on the bike and rode around for ages, driving myself mad looking for him. It was pointless though. He could have been absolutely anywhere."

Looked like Jake had only needed to look around the place where they lived.

But why had he targeted Charlie?

A shiver ran through him. The bastard had to have been watching him.

Admonishing himself wasn't going to help right then, but Jake couldn't help thinking that if he hadn't given up looking he might have been able to stop the fucking asshole hurting Charlie.

Another buzzing sound.

"Jake? That'll be the police." Charlie's pained voice brought him out of his head, his anger lessening when he looked at her slumped back on the sofa, eyes closed, with a face full of distress. This wasn't the time. He needed to let the police do their job so he could make sure she was ok. Then, depending on the outcome, he would decide what he had to do next.

Chapter Twenty-Seven

"Here you go."

Charlie took the steaming hot mug from Jake, reaching for it with the arm that wasn't bandaged; she was using that one to hold the wrapped up bag of frozen sweet corn against her sensitive cheekbone. She'd only been back home briefly to get her handbag and a bag of her things so she could stay at Cara's for a few days until she could face going back to her flat.

Jake had gone with her to the hospital and had stayed with her, just like he said he would. Then after a three hour wait to be seen, they'd got a taxi back. Now she was sitting on his sofa with twelve stitches in her arm, feeling sorry for herself, but also comforted by the fact Jake had offered her to stay there for however long she needed. "Are you sure I'm not going to be in the way?" She asked before blowing over the top of her tea.

"Not at all. You've been through a traumatic time. Do you think I'm going to see you go back in that flat right now? I'll just get you a pillow and some blankets. You need to get some sleep."

Charlie looked up at him to see his handsome face wearing that rugged frown she was already so used to. "Thank you." She smiled, then winced a little.

Jake must have caught it; he paused. "You sure that's okay?"

"They said it's just bruised, thankfully. The ice is helping a little though."

He nodded then left the room.

It was strange being in his flat. He'd offered to sleep on the couch so she could have his bed, but she'd insisted she didn't want to put him out. He'd already done enough. That horrible feeling of dread that had been a persistent bother since the attack washed through her at the thought of what would have happened if Jake hadn't disturbed that psycho. Had he intended on killing her? Or did he just want to hurt her. He certainly hadn't broken in to rob the place; when she thought back, she knew he'd been looking for her. Then there was the fact the police had found the knife that had been missing from Jake's flat in her hallway.

When Jake came back in with an arm full of blankets, he put them down next to her folded up legs and passed her the pillow, which she put behind her back.

"Thanks," she said as he sat down on the chair, leaning his arms on his thighs. He looked as tired as she felt, staring down at his feet.

She wondered where his mind had gone in that moment.

"I think he was trying to set me up," he said, his voice low and husky.

"What do you mean?"

"Just think about it. You said he had gloves on. He attacked you using my knife. A knife I'd used that would have my prints all over it. If he'd have managed to. . ." She saw the tension in his jaw as he inhaled sharply. "If he'd have killed you, he'd have got away and the police would have had my prints."

"And you didn't tell them about the break in here."

He nodded. "So they wouldn't have known my knife had been stolen."

"Why would he want to do that to you?" Someone had a fierce grudge against a person to want to frame them for murder.

He glanced up at her and back down again. "I don't know."

Charlie didn't fully believe it. Jake knew that man and there was a reason he had a psychopath after him.

Then she remembered.

Prison.

Could what she'd heard from those women be true?

Maybe this game just wasn't funny anymore. Jake had been a mystery to solve. Something she'd only pursued in the beginning because it seemed harmless. At the start of all this, it had been fun trying to find out who her neighbour was, and despite what Cara had joked about, Charlie hadn't honestly believed he was a bad guy, even with his mood swings and his ever-changing signals. Now, though, even after what they'd done together and the way he'd kissed her, she was starting to doubt him.

He was hiding something big.

Charlie hated the fact that she was being made to feel this way, but she was growing wary of Jake Sure, and even though they'd gotten closer over the last few weeks, she didn't know what to do about it.

"Hey," Jake's voice brought her out of the thoughts that were persistently crowding her mind. She blinked and saw that he'd moved to crouch down by the side of her. "You sure you okay?" He reached up and brushed the backs of his fingers down her good cheek.

Hugging her mug, Charlie swallowed the uncertainty that she was desperate to shake, especially when he looked at her like that. And besides, she was too bloody tired to pursue anything right now. "I'm still a little shaken, that's all. Can't believe what actually happened. If it wasn't for the physical things, I'm sure my brain would be trying to convince me it was a nightmare."

"I can't stop thinking about what could have happened to you." Jake's hand was beside her hip, resting on the cushion. When he lowered his eyes to his hand, he moved it a little, touching her hip gently with his finger.

Her heart kicked up as he continued, that same finger making the slightest movement against the material of her cotton pyjamas. "He could have... *Fuck!*"

"He didn't. And it's because of you that I'm sitting here instead of lying in a hospital bed, or worse."

When his eyes met hers, she couldn't read them, but the silence that followed said plenty. As warmth filled her chest she inhaled deeply. Conflicted by a mixture of panic and need, she couldn't look away from those striking blue eyes as he moved onto his knees.

"Charlie."

Her name left his lips in a ragged whisper right before he leaned in. She had a split second to decide whether to back away or accept his kiss. Deep down she knew she shouldn't continue with this until she knew the truth. Knowing she was probably making a big mistake, and choosing to ignore it anyway, her heart raced as she met his mouth with hers.

Closing her eyes, she lost all her breath as his soft lips tentatively pressed against hers, a million miles away from when he'd kissed her last night. When his lips moved, she sighed against them, her shoulders relaxing as she melted into him. It wasn't possessive, it was sensual, like he was letting her know he was there for her, and it only heightened her confusion.

His tongue gently pressed against her lips and she opened for him, meeting it with hers in a slow sensual dance. All her worries left her mind. How could she think of anything else while he kissed her so gently? It was such a contradiction to the last time, but she wasn't complaining. Gentle was what she needed right now.

When he pulled away, she almost protested.

Jake looked at her for a moment, his eyes scanning her face. And then he rested his forehead against hers and closed his eyes. "Thank fuck you're okay," he said, his voice low. He pulled back. "Imagining what could have happened to you..." Inhaling a deep breath, he closed his eyes and shook his head for a moment. Then he took her hand in his, looking down as their fingers linked together. "I know it doesn't seem like it, but I care about you, Charlie."

Feeling brave while he wasn't looking at her, Charlie said, "I feel the same about you."

His eyes met hers, and when he smiled she did the same, managing to keep the unease at bay. The decision she'd made would probably jump up and bite her on the arse like a rabid dog, but she couldn't help it. Yes, she had to have a conversation with him about what she'd overheard in the pub last night, but part of her was still hoping it was a misunderstanding, or a load of bullshit this Dominic had come up with perhaps because he was jealous of Jake and all the attention he was getting.

Both things were possible; until Charlie knew otherwise, she'd reserve judgement.

Jake stood and reached for the cup she was still holding, taking the frozen peas and the damp towel from where they lay on her leg. "You need to get some sleep. I have to go into work for a few hours after I get up. You can get into my bed when I'm gone if you're uncomfortable here."

The thought made her feel strange.

"Stay as long as you want, okay?" He leaned in and tucked a strand of hair behind her ear.

She nodded. "Thanks."

They looked at each other for a minute and Jake smiled again. "Goodnight, Charlie."

"Goodnight," she said as he walked away. Well, this certainly complicated things. It probably would have been a good idea to wait until she knew whether Jake was a criminal or not before she snogged him again, but let's be honest. Why did any of it matter after what happened last night? They'd already been far more intimate. Reaching for the blankets, she covered herself and settled back on the pillow, noticing straight away that it smelled of Jake.

Bloody hell. What was she doing?

Closing her eyes, Charlie was aware of the smile that spread across her face. Right then, she was thinking of the things she'd shared with a hot guy who'd she'd fancied since they'd first met. That's all she allowed into her head as she drifted off to sleep wrapped in his scent.

Chapter Twenty-Eight

Charlie woke with a start, sitting up abruptly, clutching at her throat and gasping for breath.

Heart pounding, confused and disoriented, her eyes tried to focus on her surroundings. Unfamiliar. Panic began to set in until reality seeped through the nightmare and she remembered where she was. That bastard was choking her. She'd fought him but he'd got the better of her and this time she didn't have a knife. Neither had he, but he'd almost killed her anyway. Then his face had morphed into Dale's.

As if sleep wasn't tough enough with the nightmares she'd had for the past two years. Now she had more trauma in her head.

Trembling and clammy, she threw the blankets back and swung her legs off the couch, realising she hadn't fared as well as she thought she had from the attack last night. Muscles ached everywhere, even in places she never realised she had them. Running, yoga, even a couple of sessions at the gym a week never made her feel this sore, but her body wasn't used to fighting. Her arm was throbbing, her ankle sore—she must have twisted it in the struggle—and her throat was dry as a bone.

Giving herself a minute, she waited until she'd calmed down before attempting to stand up. How long had she slept for?

She guessed it had been a while. The curtains were closed, but light shone through the cotton material.

A vibration sounded from her handbag. Reaching over she grabbed the bag and fished inside. When she pulled the phone out to see Cara was calling, Charlie sighed. She couldn't face talking to her friend right now. There was no way she couldn't mention what happened and honestly, she didn't want to even think about it for a little bit. It was hard enough keeping a handle on her anxiety as it was. She needed a little time before dealing with Cara's fussing, which the woman was bound to do.

When the ringing stopped, Charlie opened her phone and saw that Cara had called three times already and there were two text messages from her, and one from her mum. Later. She'd return everything later when she felt better. Glancing at the clock at the top left of the screen, she couldn't believe it was half past ten. The place was quiet. Jake must be out at work.

She got up and went to the kitchen, noticing a post-it stuck on the kettle.

Pulling it off, she read the handwriting she'd become familiar with.

Hope you slept well. There's bacon in the fridge and cereal in the cupboard right in front of you. Help yourself.

Will be back home just after midday.

Hope you'll still be there.

J.

Charlie smiled. Then, remembering the reason why she needed to be there when he got back, her stomach knotted. She had to talk to him about the prison thing. With any luck he'd just laugh at the absurdity and they would kiss again and she could put all the doubts behind her.

Her shoulders slumped; somehow, she didn't think that's the way their conversation was going to go.

Thinking better of the bacon, her stomach letting her know she couldn't face anything too heavy, she got the Cornflakes and searched his other cupboards for a bowl.

Leaning against the breakfast bar as she ate, her mind took her back to last night. If Jake hadn't come back to her flat she could be dead. Then she realised she had no idea why he had. Maybe he'd heard the struggle. If she remembered, she'd ask him when he got back.

Charlie finished her food and washed up, feeling strange being in his place alone. It smelled of him. Manly. Not in a bad way. In a very good way. And she remembered how strong that scent had been when they'd kissed and done those other things. Her stomach started doing back flips as she thought about his mouth on hers. He was a great kisser. And those hands. . .

Deciding there was plenty of time to take a shower, she went over to her bag and fished inside for some clean underwear. She didn't feel all that comfortable, but there was no way she was ready to go to her flat. Not just yet. And he had told her to stay as long as she wanted.

She went to the bathroom and took the room in. Again, it was similar to hers, but his was sparser: bare white walls and a white bathroom suite. There was a small, navy wash basket in the corner with a pair of jeans and a T-shirt thrown on top of it. Still damp from when Jake must have used the shower, the musky air held the spicy scent of his shower gel or aftershave. Charlie hadn't brought much in her bag, so she decided not to wash her hair and tied it up in a knot on top of her head to keep it out of the way. Thankfully, she'd grabbed some shower gel so she didn't have to use his masculine stuff that would be far too strong smelling.

Charlie caught a glimpse of herself in the mirror in the medicine cabinet above the sink. When she paused in front of it she was shocked to see how bad her cheekbone looked. Leaning forward to get a closer look, she reached up and gently touched the sensitive skin that had now turned a horrid grey. A small area at the outside corner of her eye had turned purple. She hissed when she prodded it. God, it looked bad, like she'd had a disagreement with Tyson Fury. That's what it felt like too.

When she'd stripped her pyjamas off, she leaned into the shower that was inside the bath like hers, and turned it on, finding the right temperature. Stepping into the tub, she faced the spray, careful not to put her bandage under the water. She closed her eyes as the water washed over her skin, allowing herself a moment of peace as she concentrated on the warm sensation trailing down her body. For a moment, when she cleared her mind of everything, Charlie forgot she was in someone else's flat and managed to enjoy the shower.

What the hell had happened to her life? Since she'd moved to Hatfield to start her uni course, she'd felt like she was finally in control of it. After what she'd been through with Dale—his control, his narcissism—she'd finally moved on and had future prospects she was excited about. For the past two years, uni had been the most important thing to her, and she'd poured her soul into her work.

Since Jake had moved in, and her curiosity had taken over, the man had caused a kink in the precision of her focus. Made worse by the fact she'd found herself caught up in something Jake didn't seem to want to tell her about.

Charlie knew she should have run a mile way before now. He'd been quite off with her on a number of occasions, had avoided her, snapped at her. Clearly he was a man with issues, things to hide. Trouble was, she didn't want to run from him. Even now, knowing he could have been in prison, and that he had some crazy psycho after him who had targeted her for some reason. There was something about him. He'd been nice to her. Under all the angst, she had seen a decent man and deep down, she knew she wasn't wrong about it.

Stepping out of the shower, Charlie grabbed the towel from the closed toilet seat and wrapped it around herself. *Shit*. Her toothpaste and brush was in the bag in the front room. And she might as well grab her clothes too and get dressed in the bathroom out of the way, just in case Jake came home early.

Leaving the bathroom, she was too busy undoing the corner of her bandage patch to have a nose at her wound that she didn't see the wall of solid steel until she bumped into it. Only, it wasn't a wall, nor was it steel; it was Jake. It surprised her so much she actually let out a scream until she realised it was him who had hold of the tops of her arms, probably to stop her falling over.

"Fuck, you scared the shit out of me," he said, his eyes wide because no doubt she'd just given him a heart attack too.

"Oh God." She swallowed in attempt to lubricate her dry throat so she could talk. "I thought you were home after twelve."

A frown appeared on his face. "It's ten past."

Her hand shot to her chest. "What?" Shit. How long had she been in the shower? "I'm sorry, I lost track of time somehow."

When she saw his eyes drop to the towel she was wearing, Charlie suddenly felt like it wasn't there. Her cheeks heated and when Jake's gaze met hers again she saw him swallow. Then he cleared his throat. "It's fine. I told you there was no rush." His eyes dropped again right before he turned and walked to the kitchen.

Charlie moved quickly over to her bag.

"Do you want a drink?"

He was at the sink filling the kettle and she tiptoed back towards the small hall down the side of the kitchen. "Uh, yes. Tea please."

He turned and Charlie caught his gaze as she went to go past him, pausing when she saw his strange expression as he looked at over at her. "I'll just be a minute," she said, wondering what he wasn't amused by.

Five minutes later, she was dressed in her navy joggers and a soft pink, vest top, finished off with a white pair of sports socks. Sexy as hell. She rolled her eyes internally. Jake was placing her tea down on the side table when she walked back into the living room. He sat down on the end of the sofa closest to the window and she joined him, sitting on the other side.

"Thanks," she said as she reached for the cup. She could feel his eyes boring into her and when she sat back, he had a harsh frown.

"Your face." So that's what he was glaring at. "Looks pretty bad. How's it feel?"

"Sore." She gripped the hot cup between both hands. "I can't believe how bad it looks."

Jake scooted up towards her. "Let me see." Facing her body towards him a little, she looked at him, turning her head slightly away as he reached up. His touch was so gentle she barely felt it as his fingertips danced over her bruise. It didn't stop her pulse from racing. "At least it isn't swollen. It'll get worse before it gets better though."

"Great." It was all she needed, turning up to classes on Monday with a face full of bruises. There was no way she'd cover it with makeup as it was. "I think I'll lock myself away for the next week."

His fingers moved down her cheek, stopping at her chin. When she saw his gaze drop to her mouth, her lips parted, breaths going shallow. But just as she thought he was going to kiss her, his eyes met hers again and he removed his hand, seeming to shake himself.

Sitting back, he leaned his elbow on the back of the couch, his body still turned towards her. "I went to the police station on the way back.

Wanted to know if they had any new leads. Nothing. They only pulled my prints from the knife, which was clearly what he wanted."

Ignoring her racing heart, Charlie had to ask. "Who is he, Jake?"

Pausing with his cup near his mouth, Jake's eyes bore through her for a second. "I told you, just someone from my past."

"Someone who's really got it in for you; you must have done something pretty bad to him."

She saw his jaw tighten. "Not now, Charlie." He leaned forward and put the mug on the table before resting his forearms on his knees.

Not now? A sting of anger rose up inside her. How dare he brush her off after what she'd been through. It was because of him she had a black eye on the way and a nice big gash on her arm that had a million stitches, and he had the cheek to shut her down. She put the cup on the table and got up. There was no way she was staying there another minute. Not with the way he'd pissed her off.

"So, hey," she said as she grabbed her things, "why don't I just get out of your hair. You just be sure to come and tell me when you feel like talking. Because, you know, I wouldn't want you to be inconvenienced by actually telling me what the fuck is going on."

Her voice was harsher than she'd planned, but in order to stop herself from crying, lashing out was the better option.

Jake looked shocked as she threw her bag strap on her shoulder, bending down to grab her boots.

He stood up and went to touch her. "Charlie, I—"

Charlie shrugged his hand off her arm. "No. It's fine. I'll just keep getting broken into and stabbed while you decide when it would be a good time to start talking." Turning around, she went to leave but stopped. With the adrenaline soaring through her veins, now was as good a time as any. "And when you do make that decision, be sure to tell me about prison too." When she glanced at him right before she went to walk away, he was stock still with a look of horror on his face. His eyes were wide, mouth open. She should ignore it and go. But she stayed there anyway. "Well? Got something to tell me about that? Or is that not up for discussion either?"

Silence followed, and something about the way his face screwed up gave her pause. "Why did you say that?"

"Well, when you overhear something like that about the man you're falling for, you take notice."

Shit. She really shouldn't let words come out without thinking about them first. Thankfully, her declaration seemed to have escaped his notice. He dropped his head, eyes closing, reaching up to pinch the bridge of his nose.

Why was she still standing there? During her rant she'd got up with conviction, ready to walk out and leave all thoughts of Jake Sure behind, at least for now anyway. So why was she suddenly filled with regret at the way she'd blurted that information out? It wasn't how she'd planned to ask him about it.

Oh God. Her stomach sank. Jake hadn't laughed like she'd hoped. In fact, he hadn't said anything. Now that he wasn't even attempting to deny it, icy fingers trickled down her spine, the devastation of what she'd stumbled upon hitting her full force in the solar plexus.

He had been in prison.

Jake stared at her and pulled his hand down his face. When he turned his back, he said, "I knew I shouldn't have started going to those open mic nights."

Chapter Twenty-Nine

"So it's..." She couldn't bring herself to say it for a minute. "It's true? You've been in prison."

"No!" When he turned back around his face was telling her something else entirely. "It's not as straight forward as that."

She started to back away from him. *What the hell did that mean? How could this be happening?* She knew things had been too good. Things were finally happening between them and she was starting to feel like they were really heading somewhere.

"Don't look at me like that." he said, pain etched in his handsome features.

"Tell me the truth, Jake." God, she was shaking.

As he stood there scowling at her, his jaw tightening, Charlie felt like her heart was going to leave her chest.

"I thought I'd left it all behind," he said eventually, his voice quiet. "Shit! I should never have let you talk me into that gig."

Surprised at his anger, and his lack of answers, Charlie couldn't quite speak in that moment. Her life was about to come crashing down around her. She was learning that the man she was falling for wasn't who she thought he was, and her heart felt like it was deflating right in her chest.

"Fuck!" She jumped when he slammed his hand on the counter, leaning over with his head in his hands.

"Jake. Tell me. I deserve to know."

"Why did it have to be me who saw those lads taunting you that night? Why couldn't it have been someone else who stepped in? Then I'd still be here minding my own business, no one knowing me, me not knowing anyone that I didn't have to." His head slumped. "Never knowing you."

Her breath caught. Struggling to keep her tears at bay, Charlie's heart shattered. It was all a lie. *He* was a lie. And she needed to get the hell out of there right now.

Carefully, she kept her eyes on him as she backed away down the hall towards the front door. Then the floor creaked under her foot and she paused just as Jake spun around to face her.

"Charlie." His voice sounded hoarse. Desperate. And there was a part of her that hurt for him, as crazy as that was. She could be standing in front of a murderer, for God's sake. Something in his eyes kept her there when in reality she should get as far away from him as possible.

"What, Jake? You wish you never knew me. It's easy to make that a reality. All I have to do is leave this flat and we never have to see each other again."

"Shit. I didn't mean it that way. I'm just. . . "

"Just what? Angry that I've found out who you really are? A criminal?"

He stepped towards her with his hand out, as if he was telling her he wasn't going to hurt her. But she took another step back and he paused.

"No. I'm trying to find a way to tell you. Yes, I didn't want you to know about my past, but not for the reasons you think."

"Then what is it?" Those tears threatened again, but she managed to keep them inside. "Tell me the truth before we never see each other again."

Shoulders slumping, Jake moved to sit on the sofa near the window, putting a welcome distance between them. She waited, watching him as he seemed to break, her heart beating a frantic rhythm in the silence. Then...

"I was in prison for a time. Eight months to be exact. But I didn't kill anyone, or anything like that. I'm not a criminal."

All the breath rushed from her lungs, but she stayed exactly where she was. Jake looked up at her and the anguish in his face twisted her gut.

"Sit down, please. Hear me out before you leave. Then if you still don't want to see me ever again, I will respect that. I promise."

Walking around the single chair close by, Charlie's eyes never left his as she sat down in it, her hands going in her lap, fingers twisting. "Tell me. Everything."

With eyes that seemed to hold so much pain, he nodded. "When I was nine my father died in a road traffic accident. He was a director of an IT company, very successful. He was involved in a four car pile-up in the city where we used to live on his way to work one morning. The coma lasted for around two months, but with the extent of his brain trauma, eventually the decision was made to turn his life support off.

"My mum never really got over it. I would hear her crying for hours in her room at night and she rarely smiled. Even when she did you could see it wasn't a real smile. There was always something in her eyes that revealed her sadness. It was just the two of us from then on. My mum's parents had died, and only my dad's mum was still alive but she had Alzheimer's, didn't know who any of us were, and was in a care home. I knew, even at such a young age how lonely my mum was, so I guess I could never blame her for falling for the charms of the first man who showed her some kindness. I was eleven when she met the man who would become my stepdad. He was nice for a time. I got on well with him at first and he and my mum seemed happy, until they got married."

A hollow feeling settled in Charlie's chest. It was all too familiar. But this wasn't a time for her to think about her past.

Jake got up and went in the kitchen to the fridge. He got a bottle of lager and held it up to Charlie. "Want one?"

It was a little early, but it was the weekend so what the hell. "Okay." She had a feeling the story she was about to hear was going to be a tragic one. Maybe it would settle her nerves a little. He passed it to her.

When he returned to sit down, he looked at his bottle and swallowed hard while he picked at the corner of the label, his expression now pained. Charlie waited, taking a sip of her cold drink, aware of how difficult this conversation was for him.

"You know the expression a wolf in sheep's clothing?" he asked.

Yes she did, only too well. But instead of voicing it, Charlie just nodded.

"I think it was invented for that guy." Jake took a long drink of his lager. "He changed so quickly it was like a whirlwind knocking both me and my mum off our feet. And I mean everything changed. He started drinking all the time. He was aggressive a lot, mostly for no reason at all. I started noticing things about my mum's behaviour. She would be in her room for two or three days at a time and whenever I asked, that arsehole would give me the same old excuse that she had a migraine and for me to leave her alone. She'd never had migraines before, but they seemed to be quite frequent."

It was all too familiar for Charlie and her stomach twisted in knots at his words. An image of Dale popped into her head—one of him with his screwed up face right in front of hers—but she shut it out. This wasn't about her. And by the way Jake was getting more agitated, peeling more bits of the label from his bottle as he stared down at the rug, he needed her full attention right now.

"One day, not long after my thirteenth birthday," he continued, "when Arsehole went out to work, I knocked on my mum's room. When she told me to leave her alone I ignored her for the first time and walked straight in. She was sitting up in bed and failed to bring the quilt up over her face in time. There was a big bruise on her left cheek and it was swollen."

On instinct, Charlie lifted her hand to her cheek and when Jake saw her his nostrils flared as his jaw went tight.

"When I first saw you like that, my mum's face replaced yours for a second."

That's why he'd looked so furious, she remembered.

"Anyway, I got angry and snapped at her. I said, 'That's why you disappear? Because he's hitting you?' and immediately saw the fear in her eyes. It was that moment I knew how scared she was of him. My mum panicked and made up some story about him having a rough day and lashing out, and how sorry he was. She swore to me it was the first time, like I wasn't living in the same house. I had no choice but to listen. I was thirteen. But I made sure I told Arsehole I knew what he was doing. After that, it didn't happen again for a while.

"We lived in a nice house paid for by my dad and his job. After he died, my mum told me he'd left money in an account for me that I could access when I was eighteen. I knew my mum had been well looked after. She'd have inherited quite a lot of money from my dad's estate and sold the company before she met Arsehole, so there was also the money from that. Unfortunately it didn't take long for him to know that, and as I got older I realised exactly why he'd wooed my mum. By then she was already in too deep. She didn't want to be on her own and although I understood that, I could never accept that she'd chosen the life she had. Arsehole was bleeding her dry. He'd regularly say he was going away on business trips. I knew he had a shit job though. He made out he worked at some big marketing firm, but in reality he was in telesales. The business trips were him going on holidays at the expense of my mum—my dad.

"I was too young to do anything about it, even when he continued to hit her. I'd scream and shout at him, but then he'd hit me too. Her hospital visits got more frequent, and when he broke her eye socket, social services got involved because of my mum's hospital record. That was when we ran. I was seventeen when we left our home in Sussex."

Jake drained the rest of his bottle as Charlie's stomach began to knot. She knew he was building up to something—something that caused him a lot of pain and she wasn't sure she wanted to hear the rest.

"The three of us had lived in a poky two-bedroom house just outside Glasgow for two years when I decided we needed to move out. I begged my mum to leave him, but she was now drinking all the time too; there was no changing her mind. Arsehole was being more strategic with the beatings by then, making sure he didn't do anything too serious that might put her in hospital. There wasn't any money left; he'd developed a gambling habit too, which had practically finished it off, but he didn't know about my inheritance. My mum had kept it to herself.

"One time I came home and they were going toe-to-toe in the living room. I'd heard the shouting as I'd walked up the driveway. When I walked in, the bastard had my mum in a headlock and I saw red. I flipped. I pulled him off her and punched him in the face. Then I hauled him up against the wall—I was strong enough to fight him by then—and I threatened him. He laughed in my face, his nose busted and blood all in his teeth, and my mum got distressed and started screaming at me to get off him. It was at that point I realised I had to get out of there. I was nineteen; I had access to my inheritance and used some of it to put a deposit on a small flat I rented not too far away from my mum. I might have left that toxic environment, but I had to stay close by to make sure she was ok.

"I got on an engineering course in the local college, and had started to play some gigs around town, so I was seeing my mum less and less the busier I got."

Pausing, Jake moved forward leaning his arms on his thighs, his bottle dangling between his legs in his hand. He closed his eyes, a deep frown appearing between his brows. Then he dropped his head, and Charlie saw his chest jerking. He was fighting to keep it together. She moved to get up, a sudden urge to go to him, but then his head came up and he inhaled deeply, as if to force his anguish back.

"Jake, you don't have to—"

"Yes I do. I have to keep going." His eyes were so intense as he looked at her that her own filled with tears. This was torture for him. "I've kept all of this inside me for far too long."

Now the tears left Charlie's eyes. There was no way of holding them back while she saw Jake, a big, strong man, breaking down right in front of her. She'd begun to feel that what she'd overheard was the truth; even after all of the times they'd spent together, how safe and comfortable he'd made her feel. She'd hated thinking that he'd kept the information from her because of some smeared past that he was hiding intentionally.

Now, though, she saw a vulnerability in the man that broke her heart. In that moment, all her uncertainty, her anger towards him had turned to pain.

"I'll never forgive myself for leaving her. If I hadn't I…" Shaking his head, he looked down at the floor and breathed deeply. Then he took a long drink from his bottle and continued. "I'd had another altercation with him. This time we'd fought properly and the neighbours called the police. Arsehole did a good job convincing them I'd been the aggressor, that I'd hit my mum too, and he wanted me charged. My mum was so distraught she said nothing. I got taken into the station, spent the night there. They let me go in the morning, but told me to stay away from the house for the time being." Jake huffed out a laugh. "Arsehole was still pressing charges."

He got up and walked over to the kitchen counter that separated the two rooms, placing his hands down before hanging his head. "My mum texted me every day without fail. She always had, to tell me to have a good day in college, or to enjoy my gig. Even just a hello. Five days later and I hadn't heard from her."

Jake paused, keeping his back to her, head still low, and Charlie could see by the movement of his wide shoulders that he was breathing heavily.

"I went..." He cleared his throat. "I went round there one morning after I knew he'd have left for work. There was no answer. Something didn't feel right. I had this. . . this nervous heat in the pit of my stomach. My mum rarely left the house. I kicked the door in and that's when I found her. She was sprawled on the couch. There was. . . blood everywhere."

Charlie put her hand to her mouth to cover the gasp. The pain in Jake's voice broke her heart. She knew before he even said the words what it all meant. And as he struggled to continue, she got up and walked over to him, not knowing what to do to help. She was shocked by what he'd revealed but kept it inside.

"He'd killed her. I knew that fucker could seriously hurt her, but I never thought he'd. . ."

Placing a hand on his back, Charlie needed him to know that she was there for him, that even though she'd started out accusing him of lies, now, none of it mattered.

He turned his head a little in her direction in acknowledgement before he continued. "I was in shock, just so fucking distraught that without even thinking, I went to her. I moved her and tried to get her to breathe. Her eyes remained vacant and I couldn't deal with it. I'd stupidly picked the knife up, staring at it in my hand, covered in her blood, unable to process what had happened. So her blood was all over me, my finger prints were on the knife, and when the police came it was me they cuffed, dragging me away from her like I was the one who'd taken her life away. *Fuck!*"

Tentatively, Charlie slipped her arms around him, hoping she wasn't overstepping. When he didn't resist, she rested her cheek on his back. Then he surprised her by taking her hand and moving it up to his chest, holding it there tightly under his. "It still hurts so fucking much."

Jake sniffed up, running his other hand down his face. When he straightened, Charlie stepped back a little, and he turned to her, keeping hold of her hand. Her stomach knotted at his harrowed expression.

"After my arrest two days before, that arsehole had seen an opportunity to get away with murdering my mum. The police found a letter in the house. The envelope was dated from the day after I got arrested. It had been sent first class from a post office somewhere in Northumbria. It was from him to my mum, telling her he'd had no choice but to leave. He couldn't take the threats and the violence from her son anymore and worried for his own safety." A grim smile appeared as his eyes went past her, staring at nothing. "I was in deep shit in that moment. I expected the police, the courts, to realise they'd got the wrong guy... Didn't work out that way."

The tears in his eyes brought more of Charlie's own. He looked at her, his red-rimmed stare glistening and pained, as if he was begging her to take the pain away. She placed her hand over his forearm. "Jake."

God. When Charlie had overheard those women, she couldn't ever have imagined this would be Jake's explanation.

He swiped at his eyes with his free hand, leaning his hip against the countertop, looking down at their joined hands. His thumb stroked over the side of hers. "He almost got away with it. I was in that prison for a little over eight months, accused of murdering my own mum while he was out here somewhere. I had to grieve for her in a six by four room. The anger I felt kept me occupied. In a way it helped me through. It was like, inside my heart had broken into tiny pieces, but my mind was refusing to accept all knowledge of it. The revenge that was germinating inside almost destroyed me in that cell.

"My solicitor was working with one of the detectives who had been involved in the case. They found some new evidence. They'd followed the postmark on the letter, traced it back to the post office from where it had been sent. CCTV footage showed Arsehole hadn't gone in there that day, but they looked into everyone on the footage and found a connection with a man who had been. The guy's phone number was in Arsehole's call log. They'd been talking for years; he'd worked in a scrap yard up in Northumbria with him before he met my mum. He was a friend of Arsehole's, at least until he confessed to posting the letter for him. Arsehole had given it to him on one of his so-called business trips months before. So he'd planned it all. He'd planned to kill her." A shaky breath followed and Jake looked at her, his hand now sweaty in hers.

"I was cleared of all charges; given a full pardon. Walked out of those prison gates a free man on the seventeenth of May, almost exactly two years ago."

"And your stepdad?"

The dark clouds still filled Jake's eyes as he looked vacantly across the room. "They never found him."

Charlie gasped. "What?"

The feeling of utter dread that followed almost had Charlie gasping for air. *Suspected murderer,* the newspaper clipping had said. The man's face filled her mind, followed by the memories of him in the stairwell, the balaclava, the attack in her flat; all of it played on a twisted loop through her mind like someone had hit fast forward on a slide projector. Holding her stomach, Charlie felt sick. Knowing what this was all leading to, she could barely get the next words out.

"Jake? Did your stepdad try to kill me last night?"

Chapter Thirty

GRIEF TWISTED JAKE'S FEATURES as he walked towards her. She felt numb, stood frozen as she tried to get her head around the fact she'd been targeted by a wanted murderer. Suddenly, her stomach lurched and she threw her hand to her mouth as she ran past him, trying to get to the toilet in time. She did, thank God, and while she emptied her stomach, Charlie realised this was the second time Jake had seen her throw up.

Footsteps slowed behind her. "Are you okay?"

It was hard to answer, so she nodded as she flushed the chain, turning to the sink to rinse her mouth out with cold water. After she splashed her face, a towel came into her eye line.

Charlie took it and dried her face, then turned to him. She leaned against the sink as he stared at her with a look that was somewhere between anger and horror. She stayed there while she got the shaking under control.

"I'm so fucking sorry," he said before hard arms went around her and the moment Charlie found her face pressed up against a rock hard chest tears spilled from her eyes. Distantly, she was pretty sure her arms gripped him back, and while she was in the cocoon of Jake's body she felt him inhale a hitched breath.

"It's all my fucking fault," she heard him say, his voice ragged, thick with emotion. "When I had a visit from the police recently, they informed me they believed he was back in the country. It worried me, but I figured he'd be too busy keeping his arse out of prison." His breath hitched. "I didn't try hard enough. I knew he was out there somewhere; I should have kept you safe, just like I should have kept her safe." She heard him fight back a sob, his chest contracting.

That's why the police were here. Pulling back, Charlie reached up and put her hands either side of his face, holding him steady. "No. Don't you dare blame yourself for what that arsehole did. You are not responsible for any of this. Don't take any of the blame away from that evil man. Not one bit of it."

Filled with disgust, his eyes looked over the top of her while he clearly fought some battle inside. "I tried not to speak to you—to avoid you. I tried to make you dislike me, but I couldn't. I've been selfish."

Then his eyes lowered to hers. "I couldn't do any of it, because you. . ."

He moved out of her hold and stepped back. "You came from nowhere—completely unexpected. I thought I had everything under control. All that I've thought about since I found my mum that day was Terry. Finding him was my only purpose in life."

He dragged in a breath, looking at her with a deep longing that made her want to step back into his arms. "Then you came along, throwing me off balance, making me want to forget what my life has been over the years. You made me think about living again."

Charlie took a step towards him. "Jake—"

His hand went up, stopping her. "I should have fought harder. I had no right letting you get twisted up in this just because I liked the way you made me feel. I knew what that prick would do if he knew I'd got close to someone." Turning, he left the bathroom and she followed him into the hall, almost slamming into him when he whirled around.

She fell into the depths of his blue gaze, her jaw tightening as she saw how much he was hurting.

"That's why you have to go, Charlie."

Her chest tightened. What was he saying?

"Please don't look at me like that. You need to stay away from me. I don't want you involved in this anymore than you have been."

A sting of annoyance started to climb up the back of her anguish, standing on its shoulders and stomping it down. "Isn't it up to me what I choose to get involved in?"

Jake's eyes widened. "Not when this could mean your life. This isn't even your problem and you were almost killed. For fuck's sake Charlie, look at your face—your arm." His lip curled up and he looked like he was about to snarl. "I'm already having a hard time looking at you like that knowing that if it wasn't for my weakness, for my wanting things that are impossible, you wouldn't have had to endure that." He walked into the kitchen.

Charlie followed him. "So you're blaming yourself for wanting some happiness? After everything you've been through, Jake—"

Turning to face her, he pushed his hand through his hair. "I don't give a shit about me, Charlie. My happiness means nothing if it threatens you."

She could see his quick breaths moving his chest up and down, floored by the anguish in his gaze, and she felt confused. How had they gotten to the point where he was more concerned about her life over his own, so quickly? Charlie would never have believed she could have such strong feelings for someone she'd only known for a short time. There was no denying it to herself though. Jake meant something to her, she cared about him. And by his reaction here, it seemed like he felt the same.

"That's why I'm leaving tonight."

The breath rushed out of her, like some invisible hand had reached inside her body and squeezed her lungs. No. He couldn't leave. Not now. "What? Tonight? No, Jake. You don't have to be alone in this anymore."

"Yes I do. I have no choice." His voice was calmer. "I need to lure that fucker away from you. It's the only way to keep you safe."

"Where will you stay? What about your job? You're life here? You can't leave. Not now, when. . . When we—"

"You're not listening. This," his hand gestured between them, "can't happen, Charlie. As long as he is out there somewhere, he'll keep trying to get at me, and he clearly doesn't give a shit about using you to do it. He won't stop. He's already proved that. The guy has got nothing to lose. The police are hunting him down for already murdering someone. He knows he's going down and he clearly wants to take me with him. Like the time I've already done in prison for something he did wasn't enough.

"You need to get as far away from me as possible, Charlie. This isn't going to end until he's either dead, or in prison, and he's managed to avoid that last part for long enough already."

Dread seeped into her veins at the last part, giving her pause. He couldn't mean what she thought he did, could he? Was he planning on doing something stupid? Now she definitely had to try to convince him to stay.

She walked up to him, placing her hand on his chest. "What if I don't want to stay away from you?"

Standing there, looking like all he wanted to do was run, Jake stared at her, his face hard to read, his eyes moving over her face like he wanted to remember her when he did go. Then his brows lowered. "I can't do this, Charlie; I'm not the man you want me to be."

"Then be the man *you* want to be."

Stepping back, Jake shook his head. "It's not as easy as that. I can't be anything other than who I am as long as that arsehole is still free." He turned around, dropping his head. "*Fuck!* I have to do this. My life isn't important until that man is out of it for good."

Charlie couldn't imagine what he was going through, but she understood why he believed he couldn't move on. No matter how hard she might try, she could see the resolve every time he looked at her. The need was so strong he was already half gone. "Then stay with me today. If I only get to be with you for a few more hours. . ."

He turned back to her and stepped right up into her face, causing her back to hit the wall. "You have no idea what you are doing. I don't have much control left, for fuck's sake. Do you know how hard it is not to say 'fuck it' and kiss you right now; to act on what my heart is screaming at me and just be with you regardless of the consequences? But if I do that, I might not be able to leave and I have to. I have to."

Looming over her, the tension set his jaw tight as his eyes bore into hers. "I fucking want you so much, Charlie. I came back to your flat last night because I wanted to finish what we'd started."

"If you want to that much, then do it," she said, surprised at her directness, her pulse racing through her veins. "Right now, right here, we are together. What do we have to lose?"

The battle raged in his eyes, his jaw tightening, nostrils flaring. He dropped his head and turned it to the side, closing his eyes. After a few seconds, he looked at her, that same thunder in his gaze. She jumped when his hand smacked on the wall next to her head and he leaned in a little. Brows lowered, breath hissed through his teeth.

"Fuck it."

His mouth crashed down on hers and she sucked in a startled breath through her nose. Throwing her arms around his back, she clung on for dear life as he kissed her hard, every movement of his mouth conveying all those emotions that had been swirling around in his eyes. Charlie was assaulted by the passion soaring through her veins. If this was the last time they got to be together then she was going to make it count.

Jake's other hand came up into her hair at the back of her neck, his fist closing around it, and she pulled him closer with a need she'd never felt before, wanting his body to consume her. It did, every inch of it.

She was dizzy with the way Jake's mouth devoured hers. Her head tipped back as he gave and she took, full of want and need as his tongue penetrated her mouth, frantically duelling with hers, their teeth catching, breaths panting.

Charlie's head spun with desire. This morning when they'd kissed, it had been with care, slow, caressing. Now, there was nothing tentative or tender about the way his mouth moved against hers, his warm lips firm as they assaulted hers with a ferocity she hadn't realised she needed, the taste of him fuelling her desire.

When he broke away, she gasped for air as he kissed his way down her neck with the same fervour. He must have moved his hand from the wall because next thing she knew it was on her hip, rubbing up over her ribs, the warmth searing through her vest top. Then he covered her breast and she arched her back, gasping as he gripped her hard. Moving his mouth down, licking and kissing, Charlie glanced down as he pushed her breast up to meet his mouth, trailing hard kisses along the top of her cleavage, nipping at her flesh. He pulled on her top, taking her bra with it as he freed her for his mouth, and he hungrily latched on to her nipple.

Letting her head fall back, Charlie moaned at the glorious sensation of his wet kisses, his tongue flicking over her tight bud. He pulled the other side down and did the same to her other breast, both hands now pushing them up as he devoured them one by one.

Then he moved back up to her mouth, pressing his body into her as he leaned down to her ear and said, "In about thirty seconds from now I won't be able to stop." Teeth nipping at her lobe. "Now's the time to change your mind."

She answered him by reaching down between them and cupping the hard length behind his work pants.

A groan by her ear. "Thank fuck," he hissed, then his mouth was on hers again as he thrust into her hand, his kiss desperate, full of fervent need.

Her top came up and their mouths broke apart only while she took over and pulled it over her head. Mouths clashed again, unable to get enough of each other. Then when she pulled his T-shirt up, he made quick work of getting rid of it. Charlie's eyes drank him in as he stretched up and pulled it off, his torso thick with solid muscle that stretched beautifully under his skin. He had a light dusting of dark hair in the middle of his chest, whispering over his pecs. She ran her hands up his rippled stomach, moving up and touching those feathery hairs when she brushed over his hard pecks. Her arms went around his neck just as he reached for her, pulling her into him with a heated look in his eyes.

Charlie jumped up, her legs wrapping around his waist as he caught her under her bottom. She kissed him this time, tongue straight into his welcoming mouth and she felt his hand fiddling with her bra clasp at her back. A second later, it popped open and she moved the straps down her shoulders, wriggling herself out of it and dropping it to the floor. Then she flung her arms back around his neck and pressed her bare breasts into his chest, enthralled by the feel of their bodies meeting flesh to flesh for the first time. He carried her through to his bedroom, all the while his mouth nipped and licked at hers. Then he lowered her to the bed, his body covering hers.

Arms wrapped around him, Charlie held Jake close as his mouth met hers again, his intoxicating kiss so full of desire it overwhelmed her. No one had ever made her feel this way before. No one had kissed her like Jake did, like he couldn't get enough of her, and she felt the same way. As their mouths fused together, tongues wrestling desperately, it was like she couldn't get him close enough.

She let out a moan when Jake's hips pressed into her pelvis, grinding his hard length in exactly the right place. Her body responded to the heat of his desire. Running her nails down his muscled back, she pushed up into him as she moved her hands to grip his firm arse cheeks, feeling them tense under her touch as he ground into her again.

Jake pulled back, his cheeks flushed and his eyes heavy. "Are you sure about this?" he asked in a breathy husk. "It won't change anything."

It will, she thought as their eyes locked together. It might not stop him from leaving, but she knew it would change her. She was already in deep. Giving herself to him would leave it's mark, no matter what. "I've never been so sure about anything before."

He bent and kissed her cheek. "That's good enough for me." Another kiss to her temple as his hips pressed into her again. "Now, where were we?"

There was no going back now, so she would give him everything.

Another kiss, this time firm and unrelenting, and by the time Jake broke away, kissing her jaw, moving to her neck, Charlie had to gasp for air. Her head went back and she got lost in the sensation of his hungry mouth tasting her body as he moved further down. Warm hands covered her breasts and pushed them up to meet his mouth. His tongue laved her tight nipple before he sucked it into his mouth, and she arched her back. He worked her other between his fingers, the sensation causing her to writhe her body under him as wetness pooled between her legs.

Jake moved down, kissing under her breast, tongue licking over her stomach, her belly button. His fingers hooked the waistband of her jogging bottoms and her knickers, and he pulled them down. Charlie lifted her bottom and he moved them down her legs, getting rid of them quickly before pulling off her socks.

The moment her legs were free, she opened them for him as he looked down at her with a fierce hunger that made her body twitch. Moving into position, Charlie swallowed, her mouth going dry, heart now hammering in her chest with anticipation. Smoothing his hands up her thighs, when Jake's dark, handsome features looked up at her from between her legs, it paused her breath.

"Beautiful." His thumbs skirted the soft flesh either side of her centre. Then she watched him dip his head, flick out his tongue and lick her with one tender stroke that made her gasp. "You taste so sweet," he said before he did it again, teasing her enough that she undulated, desperate for more. "So fucking wet."

"Jake," she begged.

He gave her a lewd smile that made her cheeks heat before returning to give her what she so desperately needed.

Charlie gripped the covers in both hands as his tongue pressed firmly against her sensitive flesh. Then he moved quickly, devouring her.

"Oh God."

Her exclamation seemed to spur him on, his whole mouth covering her, tongue flicking her clit, then sucking into his mouth, his hands opening her. It was too much, and not enough. Charlie pressed her hips up, pushing into him, legs wide.

Then she felt a finger push inside. "Oh. Jake."

In and out. Then another. His fingers moving faster while his mouth lavished her, causing her body to ignite with a fierce heat. Then the rush came soaring through her like an eagle taking flight, pushing her over the edge in a glorious release, her body pulsing around his fingers as his mouth helped to ring out every last bit of pleasure.

He moved up her body as she lay there strung out and panting from the best orgasm she'd ever had in her life.

Soft lips caressed her neck, sending a wave of shivers through her. "That was just a taster," Jake said in a harsh whisper as he kissed her ear before moving his mouth to hers.

Sighing, she accepted his kiss, his hard body pressing into her, reminding her that he still had his pants on. "Aren't you wearing too many clothes?"

He smiled against her mouth, and then pushed up onto his knees between her legs. Unbuttoning his fly, his eyes never left hers, but she was too curious not to watch, knowing how big he was. Pulling them open, she forced her eyes not to widen when she saw his hard length jutting out from his tight, navy, boxers. Quick as a flash he was out of both of them, her eyes hungrily enjoying the sight of him, flushing again at the size of him. She'd had trouble getting her hand around him before, and she couldn't wait to feel him inside her. She couldn't help biting her bottom lip at the thought as her eyes roamed over his tightly muscled body, enjoying the sheer magnetism of his physique.

Gloriously naked, he crawled up her body like an animal stalking prey, those blue eyes pinning her right before he took her mouth again in a hard kiss. Still on all fours, he took one of her hands that were now exploring his torso and guided it to his cock. He hissed as her hand wrapped around him. She began to move up and down, her body heating with the feel of him in her palm again, soft silk moving over hard steel.

Moaning, Jake jutted into her hand. "Fuck." After a minute or two, when she began to move faster, his hand went over hers and stopped the movement.

He paused and stopped kissing her. "Hold on," he said as he leaned over to his bedside table.

Charlie couldn't help the smile. "I am."

His laugh lightened her heart as he pulled the top drawer open and started searching for something. "Where the fuck is it?" he said, moving a little further over and she lost grip of him.

Charlie knew what he was looking for and lay there patiently waiting while the thought of him being inside her made her skin buzz. It was crazy; she'd never felt so sexually comfortable with anyone else before. As Jake cursed again, she looked over at where he was now searching in the next drawer down.

"I was sure I had a condom in here." He looked at her, face screwing up a little then his eyebrow popped. "Don't suppose you have any?"

"No," she said, feeling a pang of disappointment.

"Shit." Moving again, Charlie couldn't help admiring his lean, muscled body as he stretched over even further to reach the bottom drawer. God, she desperately wanted this, but if it wasn't meant to be then there was plenty of other ways to enjoy each other. "I know there's one—Got it."

Joy sprang through her as he moved back over her. *Thank God.* She was beyond ready.

"Way for me to ruin the moment." He hung his head as he huffed out a laugh and she got a whiff of his hair gel.

Her hands went on either side of his face when he lifted his head. "You definitely haven't. I love that you even care about protection." When she pulled him down and crushed her mouth against his, Jake groaned, and with his body perfectly placed, he pressed his groin into her, his erection rubbing through her folds. She rubbed against him, careful not to have him penetrate her, panting with wanton need and desire

He thrust his tongue in her mouth. "Fuck," he said in a ragged voice. "I want it in there."

Charlie's core rushed with heat as her body screamed for his. "Then get that thing on you."

Answering her demand, he shot up onto his knees and the way he ripped the foil packet open with his teeth fired her up even more. It was so hot watching him hastily put the condom on himself, his big hand rolling it onto his hard length. Her pulse raced with anticipation.

Then he was over her again. She moved her legs as he settled between them, pulling them up so her knees were bent either side of him as she lifted her hips a little. His cock rubbed her again as their eyes locked together and she struggled to keep hers open.

There was a moment between them right then, as their bodies moved against each other, his eyes roamed her face, his breath hitching.

"I just want you to know before we do this, how much you've changed things for me," his voice was low and coarse with emotion. He moved his arm a little, the pad of his thumb smoothing down her jaw.

Unable to say anything in that unexpected moment, Charlie nodded, biting down the tears that suddenly threatened. This really meant something to him, to both of them. And it would make their first time more special because of that, even if it was to be their last.

Placing his mouth on hers, Jake reached down between their bodies and then she felt the head of him at her core. When he entered her, pushing all the way inside her slowly until their pelvises met, Charlie hasped and he nipped softly at her bottom lip. He stayed their unmoving, his mouth going to her ear.

"I'm going to make sure neither of us forgets this moment." His voice was a harsh whisper, making her body tingle as he started to pull out. "I'm going to fuck you until you come undone."

God, she was almost there already from his words and his tauntingly slow penetration.

"I've had plenty of time to imagine what I'm going to do to you." He sucked her earlobe into his mouth, his teeth scraping the soft flesh. Holding her breath as he stopped again, this time only the tip of him inside her, Charlie wanted him to do things to her. She'd seen this side to him in her flat last night and it had excited her then, but this felt more intense. She wanted the dominant side of Jake Sure that she'd seen a glimpse of; craved it so much she surprised herself.

"Then what are you waiting for?" Excitement lit up her veins. She'd never been this brazen before, but Jake seemed to bring something out of her that she never knew was there. Then a low chuckle sounded by her ear, and no matter how ready she thought she was, when Jake thrust into her hard, she called out, her body unprepared for the quick invasion, but wanting more.

This time, Jake didn't stop, withdrawing and thrusting, all the while he watched her with those intense eyes. Brows pulling down as his body pounded into hers.

Reaching up, Charlie held on to his arms, her hands gripping onto his tense biceps as she moved her hips to meet his thrusts. "Fuck, Charlie." He slowed a little, swallowing hard as he squeezed his eyes shut. Then he stopped thrusting, moving slowly instead as his mouth crushed hers. They were both panting, bodies slick as they rubbed against each other. Moving, Jake palmed one of her breasts as he continued to ravage her mouth with wide open-mouth kisses, his tongue invading, twisting in a frenzied dance while he slid in and out of her with small movements.

Then he pushed up on his arms, pulling out of her then wrapping his arm around her back and bringing her with him as he positioned himself on his knees. Charlie straddled him, grabbing his face in her hands and kissing him hard as he positioned his erection for her. They both moaned as she slid down onto him until he was fully seated inside her. She began to move. Jake's hand slid up her back, fingers tangling in the back of her hair. Then he held her head as she rode him, the other hand grabbing hold of her arse cheek.

It was too much for Charlie, she tipped her head back, moaning and gasping, holding him close as her body soared towards release. Electric heat pulsed through her veins as she neared the edge. He must have sensed how close she was. "Charlie, look at me."

Bringing her head back down, his tense expression told her he was almost there too.

"I want you to look me in the eyes when you come."

That's what did it.

Charlie cried out, her body contracting around his as she came, and he followed her with a groan, their eyes never leaving each other even as they were overcome with lust. Still holding her body close, Jake tipped his head up and she met his mouth with hers, panting as her body came down from the high he had just given her.

Breaking off the kiss, she saw him smile just as she rested her forehead against his. It was a thing of beauty—an expression she hadn't seen him wear before. In that moment, there was nothing weighing him down; all his problems had been left outside the bedroom door. And Charlie wished she could somehow prevent it from consuming him ever again.

Chapter Thirty-One

Warm fingers smoothed up and down her side, her skin prickling as goosebumps followed their movements, the gentle rhythm causing her to sigh with contentment. Charlie had never felt so relaxed as she lay in the crook of Jake's arm with her head against the side of his chest, her own fingers playing with the hair around his nipple, hard from her touch. She could hear the dull, rhythmic beat of his heart, slow and steady, a lullaby she'd happily listen to every night to fall asleep.

They spent all afternoon exactly where they were, more exploring, more orgasms. She had no care for the time, or the reality that was waiting for them when they left Jake's bedroom.

A knot formed in her stomach. Charlie knew that at some point, they would have to address him leaving. He'd been adamant about it before. Now, even though he'd said it wouldn't change anything, there was a part of her that wondered—no *hoped*—he'd changed his mind.

"What are you thinking?" The deep voice rumbled in her ear.

Lifting her head up, she moved a little, her leg slipping between his as she lay against him, their naked bodies so comfortable with each other. Her heart kicked up when she locked gazes with him. Afraid if she hesitated she might not say it, she just came out with it. "Stay." The moment the word left her mouth she saw his easy expression falter, only slightly, but enough that he no longer looked so relaxed, his jaw tightening. "I know you are leaving to protect me, but the truth is, I don't want you to."

"Charlie." His hand slid up her back to the nape of her neck. "I can't stay. I won't allow you to get hurt again. I couldn't deal with something else. . ."

When she saw the darkness wash over his face before his eyes closed and his lips pressed together, she bent down and placed her mouth on his, kissing away the anguish that tore at her heart. Knowing what she did now was a blessing and a curse: Jake wasn't a criminal—a huge relief—but now she knew how broken he was, her stomach sinking when she thought of all he'd been through. Being the one to find his mum in that awful state. . . It was unimaginable.

She broke the kiss, leaving their lips still touching when she said, "Please. We've only just found each other. Don't let that man take anything else away from you."

He seemed to go rigid and he turned his head away. "What's the matter, Jake? Is there something else you're not telling me?"

Guiding his head back to face her with her hand, Charlie stared into his eyes until he closed them with a sigh. "He already has taken something else." Shifting a little, he rubbed her shoulder. "I have a younger brother."

Charlie pushed up a little so she was on her elbow. "Where is he?"

"He was adopted while I was in prison. Nobody asked my opinion. It happened without my knowledge. After what happened to my mum and I was sent down, he was placed into the system and went into foster care. The family who he went to live with adopted him and of course I was the criminal in prison. Even though I was his next of kin I had no say."

His eyes lowered with a frown. "He's the reason I moved here. I don't see him very often. The couple who he is with, the Morgans, won't speak to me so it's hard for me to arrange to see him. That woman you saw leaving my apartment that morning, she is a liaison officer. She is the only reason I get to see him at all. Although the family knows I was wrongly imprisoned, they don't like me. Must be the stigma surrounding everything that happened. Maybe they assume it runs in the family. I don't know. All I know is they make every excuse under the sun for me not to see him.

"I've been let down so many times. Whenever I've arranged to see him they've always come up with an excuse."

Charlie ached at the sorrow in his voice. He'd been through so much she couldn't fathom how he felt. And now he couldn't even see his own brother. There was no reason for that. None of this was Jake's fault. "How old is he?

"Almost nine now. I don't even think I've seen him half a dozen times since I got out. And even those times were brief."

"I'm so sorry you're going through this. Can't you get access through the courts?"

"I've spoken to so many people. But they're his legal guardians now and what they say goes. I don't have right of access as his brother."

Why did the world keep shitting on this man? As if he hadn't been through enough. "There has to be something you can do. It isn't fair that you should lose out on seeing your brother. It's not fair that your brother should lose out on seeing you because of the actions of that evil man."

Jake reached up and brushed her hair behind her ear. "Let's not talk about it anymore. I don't want anything else to spoil today. I spend most of my days trying to keep that man out of my head. Not that it ever works. Most of the time he's here inside me, every minute, every hour, every second. Right now I want to be with you. I don't want him intruding on us. He's done enough already—to both of us."

"Okay." Settling back down, Charlie rested her chin on his chest, unnerved by what he'd told her. It was no wonder Jake was the way he was. How can someone go through all that and come away unscathed. It wasn't possible. The scars ran deep, she knew that now. Maybe there was something she could do to help him heal from them. "Jake? Will you promise me something?

Jake nodded. "If I can."

"Will you let me see if I can do anything? I'd like to see if I can help with your brother."

His brows pulled down and for a minute she expected him to say no. Then he looked at her, his expression lightening. "There's nothing you can do."

"I'd like to try. At least, let me do that while you're gone."

The sorrow she saw in his eyes right then cut her deep. He nodded. "Okay."

Pulling her in closer, she met him in another kiss. When he pulled away, he reached up with both hands and placed them on her cheeks. "Do you see now why I have no choice? Jonathan is in as much danger as me as long as that prick is around." She felt his chest rise with a deep inhale. "I have to go. I won't let him get the chance to hurt you or my brother. I have to make sure you're both safe."

He blinked hard and then his eyes held hers. "When it's all over, if you still want me, then we can be together without the threat of him looming over us. I can try and live my life again."

"Of course I'll still want you." Letting out a soft laugh, she eyed him coyly. "I've barely had you."

The side of his mouth rose. "I don't know. We haven't done too badly today."

His mouth captured hers and he rolled them over, moving his body on top of her.

Charlie tried to keep her mind in the moment, but the cogs were already turning. If it was the only way she could help, she would do all she could, call in all her favours, anything to help Jake get proper access to his brother.

Chapter Thirty-Two

It was funny how Charlie had to console Cara after she'd given her best friend the news about her attack, and not the other way around. The woman was almost inconsolable as they both sat on Cara's sofa. Sniffing into a tissue, her mascara had run. Eyes as black as night stared back at her, full of sorrow and concern.

"Are you sure you're okay? My God, Charlie. How are you so together after something like that?"

"I promise I'm fine." She wouldn't mention the reoccurring nightmares and waking up in hot sweats every night since. At least those nightmares had replaced the others for now. Placing her hand on Cara's knee, Charlie smiled, hoping to reassure her. It seemed to work. The hiccuping stopped and she no longer had tears streaming down her face.

"Do you want to stay here for a while? I can understand if you don't want to be in that flat right now. The couch is really comfortable and we can go into uni together in the mornings. That way you won't be alone."

One of the things she loved about Cara was that she cared fiercely for her friends, almost to the point where it was smothering. As much as Charlie appreciated it, there was no way she could be mollycoddled right now. There was too much going on in her mind to deal with that kind of comfort.

"That's okay. Thanks though, but I'm handling it." Better. Handling it *better*. Last night when she'd returned to her flat after staying at Jake's, anxiety almost knocked her off her feet as soon as she'd walked through the door. The mess had made it even worse, everything exactly how it had been after the police had left the night before. When she'd come back from the hospital to gather up some things to take to Jake's, she'd been too desperate to get out of there to notice any of it.

It had hit her pretty hard when she'd gone back there. Her broken things had still been strewn all over the floor exactly as they'd landed in the struggle. There was black powder over things where the police had dusted for prints. She'd spent the whole night cleaning up. But at least when it looked like her flat again, it hadn't felt too bad. Today, though, after struggling to feel comfortable enough to sleep last night, even with the added security of a new lock and a direct-line number to the police, Charlie had been exhausted all day, only surviving on strong coffee. Thankfully, she was currently drinking another.

"Want me to stay with you for a bit then?" The sorrow in her friend's eyes had her fighting back tears in her own.

"No honestly, I appreciate your concern, but I'm really okay. It's something I have to deal with. Since I sucked it up and went home to stay last night, it helped."

"As long as you're sure. You can ring me anytime, though. You know that. Even if you get scared in the middle of the night, I'll get a taxi straight over."

It warmed Charlie's heart to have such a good friend. "Thank you," she said, moving in for a hug. "I honestly don't know what I'd do without you, Cara."

Cara hugged her hard and Charlie sank into it, holding back the tears that she kept fighting on the regular. She hadn't come here to break down all over again.

When they pulled back, Cara's brows lowered and she looked past Charlie for a minute as if something had just come into her mind. So, if last night was the first night you stayed in your flat, where did you stay Friday?"

It was only a matter of time until Cara twigged to that, and with the way her friend was looking at her, eyes narrowed, pinched smile, her mind had already come up with an answer. Although Charlie doubted it was an accurate one.

"Jake came with me to the hospital and we didn't get back until early hours. He asked me if I wanted to stay there."

Those perfectly shaped brows jumped up into her hairline. "You stayed at Jake's place?" The cogs were turning loud enough to give Charlie a headache, and she know there was no getting out of giving Cara the information she'd stop at nothing to receive. The woman would chase it down till the death.

"Mhmm," Charlie answered casually, drawing it out on purpose.

Big brown eyes bore into hers, willing the information out of her. "*And?*"

"And what?" Charlie tried to keep the smirk from her face, but knew she hadn't hidden it well enough when Cara smiled, dropping her head for a minute. But Cara was her best friend, and she was dying to tell her what went on in Jake's flat.

"Did something happen between you two?" Her hand went on Charlie's knee, squeezing it in delight. "Oh my God, it did, didn't it?"

Charlie's eyes moved up to meet hers, but she still said nothing, mostly because she liked to see her friend's frustration.

"Char! Don't go all silent. I need details right now. What happened?"

Smiling, Charlie slumped back against the couch, warmth filling her chest, her stomach fluttering. "He kissed me." Her friend let out a squeak. "And we did some other stuff too."

"Oh, my God, Charlie. I knew it was going to happen." Her hands did tiny claps as she shifted to the edge of the sofa. "How? Tell me all the details."

Bloody hell, she couldn't believe how wide the grin was. Her cheeks actually ached. "So, first, he almost kissed me the night of his first gig." Charlie explained what had happened in the woods and then the woman she'd seen leaving his place, as Cara leaned on her hand, enthralled by the narration of Charlie's life.

"Then last Monday, when I got home, Jake was waiting for me to explain who the woman was."

"Oh, he actually cared enough to wait for you." The woman only bloody sighed.

Ignoring her, she continued. "Our conversation turned a little heated and well. . . we kissed. Cara, it was so good." Her stomach tickled just thinking about it. "But then he got a little strange, like he shouldn't have done it. He closed off, again, and we left it at that. We kind of made up in between then and Jake's gig Friday. He got back later than me that night. Then came to tell me why he'd had to run out after the gig. We talked for a bit, and then stuff kinda just happened."

Pausing on purpose, Charlie waited, watching as her friend's expression changed. "And?" Cara pressed. "What stuff just happened? Come on Charlie. I need the deets."

Laughing, Charlie relayed what she could without going all X-rated, just to give her an idea. The rest Cara could fill in herself, which she no doubt would.

"But wait. There's something I have to tell you."

Her hands still clasped in front of her chest, Cara paused in her elation, shoulders slumping. "You're going to ruin my happiness aren't you? Was he not good?"

"Cara! That's not what. . . I am not going *there* with you. You've had enough details. But no, he was *really* good."

They laughed until her friend's curiosity got the better of her. "So what do you have to tell me?"

"Friday night, at the gig, when I went to the toilet I heard some girls talking about Jake in the next cubical. There were rumours he'd been in prison." She watched her friend's eyes widen. Charlie continued. "I asked him."

"I knew it. You're about to crush the fairy tale. He is a criminal, just like I said. I warned—"

"Cara." Rolling her eyes, Charlie needed to stop her friend's mind from racing ahead of their conversation. "He isn't a criminal."

"Oh, then why?"

"Well, if you'll let me finish. . ."

Pressing her lips together, Cara mimicked zipping her mouth shut.

"Yes, he did go to prison, but he was wrongly convicted of murder."

Her friend's mouth dropped open. "Murder?" It came out in a whisper.

"Yes." Charlie went on to explain everything that had happened to Jake, leading to his stepdad and telling her that it was him who'd attacked her. The whole time Cara had a profound look of horror on her face. "He has a little brother who he barely sees because while he was in prison, the foster family who had taken him in adopted him. Now, even though Jake was cleared of all charges, they are being difficult about contact."

"Can they even stop him from seeing his own brother?"

"Legally, it's the family's decision. They allowed contact, but they are making it difficult. Every time they arrange something, the family moves the goal post. It's always last minute; excuses that Jake said he knows are just that."

Cara shook her head, looking as disgusted as Charlie felt. It wasn't fair on Jake or his brother. Torn away from each other in the most horrific circumstances, they shouldn't have to go through this after everything that's happened. They needed each other.

It broke Charlie's heart to think about it.

Chapter Thirty-Three

The library at UH was extensive. In fact, the Learning Resources Centre at the University of Hertfordshire was one of the reasons Charlie had chosen to come here. There were books amongst the shelves that were hundreds of years old, books you would never have access to in a public library. It wasn't one of those old fashioned places; it was sleek and modern with several floors, light and bright with a zen-like feel. She loved the smell of the place. Despite its modern feel, it was so much better to sit in a room so steeped in history and knowledge than to sit at a laptop searching the internet without the peaceful atmosphere. Charlie liked to come here often to do her work. It was like the words and knowledge of the millions of pages that surrounded her seeped into her blood and helped her work much better than if she was anywhere else.

It was as if being in here cleansed her soul.

She needed that today more than any other.

Jake was leaving tonight. Charlie had persuaded him to wait a little longer until she could give him something to hold onto while he was away. Her stomach sank with worry at the thought of him out there setting a trap for his stepdad. What if it didn't go to plan? What if he got hurt? Or worse, what if she never saw him again? Sucking the anxiety down into her lungs with a deep breath, she closed the door on those thoughts for now.

There would be plenty of time to worry after Jake had gone. Right now she needed to focus, for him, for his little brother.

As well as doing her own work, Charlie had found some textbooks relating to social care. Grabbing the next book from the pile, she looked through the index, running her finger gently down the list. A few pages later, she found what she was looking for: *Siblings, contact and the law: an overlooked relationship?*

Flicking to the page, she began to scan through the text, her stomach sinking the more she read. Then she took notes when she found something that might be worth looking into.

Almost an hour later, the alarm she'd set so she didn't miss her next class buzzed her phone. *Shit*. She wasn't done. With things not looking too promising, she found herself leaving the LRC on her campus completely lacking the motivation she had when she went in.

Before she put her phone away, she thought about texting Jake. They'd finally exchanged numbers last night so they could stay in touch, so Charlie sent him a brief message to let him know she had some information to discuss with him. He was at work, but figured he'd pick it up at some point.

Grabbing her bag off the back of the chair, she made her way downstairs and to the main entrance where she spotted Jason strolling in looking as much worse for wear as she'd ever seen him. His eyes were down, looking at his phone, so he didn't see her at first. She snuck up to him.

"Did you sleep in a hedge last night," she said, stepping in front of him and drawing him up short.

"Shit, Sommers!"

"Shh!" the woman on the front desk spat as Charlie suppressed her laugh into her hand while Jas clutched his chest.

Pulling him outside, she was still laughing when he playfully punched her in the arm. "I'm too sensitive today for a shock like that."

"I can see that. You look like shit. What gives?"

Her friend leaned against the wall, placing the sole of his vans shoe on it, his hands in his dark blue, denim jeans pockets.

"Stayed out too late last night. I knew I'd regret it, but my drunken arse didn't give a shit."

"Good night though, I take it?"

"Yeah, it was. You know my mate who works at East Street, that MMA club in the city?"

"The fight club?"

"Yeah. He got me a ticket for one of their fight nights. Man, that guy who won—he trains at East Street, right? Ryder Cruz—he can't half fight. Finished his opponent in the second round. They had to carry him off. Brutal."

"That's his actual name?"

Jas popped one of his dark eyebrows. "He could call himself Sarah Jane and I doubt anyone would dare say anything about it. Man's a machine." When he shook his head he winced. "Anyway, we stayed at the club afterwards and played some poker. I won a pretty big hand. Then somehow, we ended up drinking with the boss. Don't remember much after that. I haven't been home yet."

Eyes widening, Charlie laughed. "Jason."

Wincing again, he held his hand up. "Too loud," he said, his eyes barely open. "I know. And yes Selena is proper pissed off. I spoke to her on my way here and she ended up hanging up on me."

That's when he looked at her, eyes full of guilt and seeking her sympathy, silently asking for her help.

"Oh no. You are on your own there." She wagged a finger at him. "That girl is the best thing that's happened to you; you need to grovel like you've never done before."

"I know." Eyes widened on her. "I won quite a bit of money; maybe I'll get her something nice."

"Presents aren't the way to go with this, Jas."

A grumble preceded a shoulder slump. "Yeah. I'll figure something. Well, enough about me and my woes. How's you?" His brown eyes narrowed as he reached for her hand. "Heard anything more from the police?"

Shaking her head, Charlie blinked at the flash of memory that hit her. It was the same one she always had, of opening the bathroom door and seeing that balaclava. It was imprinted on her mind, and she suspected it would be for a long time. "Nothing yet." She'd only told Cara the full story. Jas thought she'd had an intruder and that was as far as his knowledge went for now. Cara only knew everything because when Charlie had begun to explain things, thinking she was side stepping the whole stepdad thing, Cara had picked up on something, prompting Charlie to tell all. Ears like a bat that one.

"I hope they get the bastard. How many other people has he done that to? Some scum live their lives breaking into places. Probably some junkie needing to fund their next fix. He'll trip himself up. He almost did with you. At least you got a good look at him. Did they get prints off the knife?"

"No." Only, Jake's, but she kept that information to herself too.

Jas cursed. "I still can't believe it happened. You need to have a word with whoever owns the place. That building needs better security."

"I've requested a call back from the office."

Chapter Thirty-Four

Armed with the information from the library—though she was disappointed that it was no more than he already knew—Charlie had raced home, eager to see Jake. She'd missed him these last couple of days, which didn't bode well for her; soon she wouldn't see him at all. Stopping at his door, she tried to ignore the sinking feeling in her gut and knocked on, waiting with nervous anticipation for him to answer. All sounded quiet inside. Usually, she could hear his TV when she passed, or his guitar, but there was no sound at all. As she stood there with disappointment seeping into her chest, Charlie realised that she'd been so eager to see him, she hadn't noticed if his bike had been parked outside. When she knocked again there was still no answer.

The sound of a door opening down the hall turned her head to see Mrs. Hughes stepping out of her flat, curlers in her hair, wearing a deep pink skirt and blouse with matching slippers. When she started to make her way up the hall, her age showing in the way she was hunched over, she began to wave a white envelope in her hand. Charlie rushed to her so she didn't have to walk far.

"Oh, I'm afraid I'm a little stiff in my bones today," the nice old lady said as Charlie took her arm. "Hello, my dear. I've been listening out for you."

For her? Why would Mrs. Hughes be waiting for her? "You have?"

"Yes. I have something for you." When she held up the envelope, Charlie took it with a frown. "He said to make sure you got it as soon as you got home. So I've been sitting at my telephone table by the door listening out for you."

"Oh, thank you, Mrs. Hughes. Here, let me help you back to your flat."

Gripping the envelope, Charlie offered her arm, helping to steady her kind neighbour before she saw her inside. Then she guided her to her living room and helped her sit down in a worn, red, chintz chair that faced the TV.

"There now. Thank you, dear. I wish I had your young legs."

"Can I make you a cup of tea before I go?"

"Oh, that'll be very kind. No milk, one sugar, if you will."

Her mind ticking over, wondering what was in the envelope, Charlie made quick work of the tea, spotting a pack of biscuits by the bread bin and putting a few on a plate. She had a gnawing ache in her gut. Jake was most likely the *he,* and there was perhaps only one reason he would leave her a note.

Taking the tea and biscuits to Mrs. Hughes, Charlie was eager to leave, trying not to appear rude. After finding a space, she placed the things down in front of a framed picture of a jolly looking man on the little table next to the old lady's chair, and waited for a minute. "You okay now?" Charlie felt sorry for the woman, wondering if the man was her husband. It must have been so lonely here for her, and she wondered why the lady didn't live in one of the assisted living flatlets over in the next street.

"Oh yes, very kind of you," she said reaching for a biscuit. "You get yourself home. And don't you worry about him. He's a strong man just like my Henry here." Her frail hand gestured towards the picture.

That was enough to get Charlie's feet moving. "Okay then. Thanks Mrs. Hughes. Bye."

Charlie heard the lady's voice in the distance saying goodbye, as she hurried out of the flat. When she was halfway down the hall, she couldn't wait any longer and opened the blank envelope. There was a folded piece of paper inside that she could see the imprint of the message on. Opening it, her heart began to race as she read Jake's handwriting:

Charlie,

I didn't want to just send you a text. I'm not great when it comes to phones. Anyway, I know you probably think I'm an arsehole for leaving without seeing you first," her heart dropped into her stomach then, *"but I have a pretty good excuse for it. If I saw you, I know I'd probably change my mind and stay. I can't do that goodbye. Meeting you has made me realise how lost I've been. I've been existing only for revenge. You have made me want to start living again. I've been thinking about the future, which is something I haven't done in a long time. So I have to put an end to this.*

Please don't worry. I'm not planning on doing anything stupid. I've experienced enough of prison and don't wish to go back there. I'm going to try to find him, and if he won't turn himself in, I'll do it for him.

Everything will work out. I promise.

The flat is still mine for at least the next three months.

I hope you'll still be there when I get back.

I like you Charlie, a lot.

Jake x

Holding the note against her chest, Charlie fought back tears as a sickly feeling gnawed at the pit of her stomach. Though the sting in her eyes told her she wasn't doing a great job of it.

"You have made me want to start living again."

But he'd gone. Searching for a psychopath who wanted revenge, and so she feared he might not get the chance at a future at all.

The man was risking his life; he could be doing exactly what that murderer wanted him to do. It was clear his stepdad had been watching him. What if he walked into a trap? What if something happened and she hadn't even had chance to tell him how much she cared about him?

Overwhelmed with panic, Charlie didn't hear her phone at first, too caught up in her head as she wandered idly to her flat. It was when she fished in her bag for her keys that she realised it was ringing. Frantically fighting to find the phone, her pulse was racing. It could be Jake. Maybe he needed to talk to her as much as she needed to talk to him.

The moment she found it and pulled it out of her bag, the bloody thing stopped ringing. Pulling up the number gave her pause. It wasn't listed in her phone. Wouldn't be Jake then. She'd saved his number under his name. The only people who called were in her contacts.

Then, when a message box popped up in the middle of the screen, Charlie froze, another kind of dread taking over.

All she saw in the preview box was: *Charlie, it's Dale. Please call me back on this...*

A battle began to ensue inside her. Part of her didn't want to open it to read the rest, but the other part needed to see why the arsehole had used the word "*please*" in a sentence. Closing the phone down, she dropped it inside her bag and went inside her flat. Refusing to let him get to her, she took her coat off and left her bag on the floor near the door with her phone still in it.

She found herself still pacing up and down the hallway ten minutes later, everything swirling around in her head. Pausing, she looked down at her bag and after a minute, grabbed it off the floor, removed the phone and swiped the message away to delete it.

What a nightmare.

He was not doing this to her right now, no matter what game he was playing. She had far more important issues to concern herself with some arsehole who was irrelevant in her life, who was trying to taunt her from nearly two hundred miles away.

Jake. Right now, she needed him and he was gone.

Leaning against the wall, she closed her eyes, seeing his face. The two men couldn't be any different. Dale, a narcissistic mummy's boy who had never struggled a day in his life, had anger issues, liked to emotionally and physically abuse women. Granted, he'd only actually been physical with Charlie once, but that was enough on top of everything else. And then there was Jake, a man who had literally been to hell and back, and had treated her better in the short time she'd known him, than the other arsehole had in their whole relationship.

Gut twisting, Charlie hated that she'd met Jake under such difficult circumstances.

"If I saw you, I know I'd probably change my mind and stay."

Damn him for being so strong.

Chapter Thirty-Five

"I hope they look as bad as you." Jake looked up at the bartender as his drink was placed on a napkin in front of him. "Rough night?"

Lifting the bottle to his lips, the side of Jake's mouth quirked up. "You could say that." Taking a swig from his lager, he wasn't surprised by the guy's inquiry; the cut on his eyebrow and thick lip were bound to draw attention as he nursed his bruised ego at the bar. Turns out, his loving stepdad, Terry, had a long line of people he'd pissed off over the years, including the three men who'd jumped Jake last night, thinking he was something to do with the guy and that through him they'd get the money *Arsehole* owed them. Luckily, Jake had managed to talk them off, explaining that he was also on the hunt for Terry and they'd backed off. Still, the wankers had left him with a bruised body and some new facial aesthetics that were clearly a topic for conversation.

Thankfully, Bartender Guy got the hint that he wasn't in the mood for small talk and moved on to someone else, leaving Jake to wallow in his shit luck at the end of the bar on his own.

This was taking too long.

Funny how your whole life could change so quickly.

Full of loathing, the hate that had manifested inside of him had been the sole focus in his life. He hadn't thought of anything else since the day he'd found his mum's body.

Until her.

Charlie had made him recognise himself again.

There hadn't been a time in his adult life that he'd needed someone. He'd been a loner for long enough now, had even gone through prison time, so was used to his own company. Now, though, it had only been just over a week since he'd left Hatfield, but he felt like something was missing.

Charlie.

Jake had known he was beginning to feel something for her, but only now, while he was away from her, did he realise how much he'd started to care. She'd gotten under his skin in a big way, and he hated that circumstances involving that prick were disrupting his life—again.

Eight days he'd been searching for him. It had only taken Jake a few days to get a couple of leads that he'd been hopeful about, but the man who Terry had supposedly been bunking with for a few months had made him leave a couple of weeks ago, and was adamant he didn't know where Terry had gone. He did tell him about this place, though. Apparently Terry had come to this bar quite frequently while he'd been in town.

Jake was chancing his arm; he had a feeling he wasn't going to get lucky tonight. Going by the disdain in Terry's former friend's voice he'd probably skipped town now that he'd lost one of his allies. His stepdad had clearly done something to piss the guy off, so there was a chance Arsehole would worry he'd rattle on him.

An hour later and Jake decided to head back to the hotel. It was walkable from the pub. Thankfully, the rain had stopped a little while ago, but he kept his hood pulled up, keeping himself inconspicuous as he always did.

Disappointment reeled through him. Another night gone and Terry was nowhere to be seen. Jake feared he was never going to track him down. He'd hoped it would be an easy task. It wasn't as if the guy was a criminal mastermind. Far from it. He'd emotionally and physically abused, and then murdered a woman, had clearly felt that targeting Charlie would be easier than facing Jake, and he was a waster with a gambling habit. How was the arsehole so elusive?

Terry had clearly moved on from here. No doubt he had more so-called friends he could use.

Maybe it was time for Jake to move on as well.

Taking a short cut, he turned down a narrow street that cut through some tall buildings. He'd taken this route a few times while he'd been in the town, but tonight was the only time someone else had walked that way too. Slowing a little, he heard the echoing steps from the person behind stop. A hand wrapped around Jake's gut, telling him to turn around. There was no doubt someone had followed him down the alley. His increased heart rate letting him know what to expect, Jake turned around and finally came face to face with the man who had dominated his thoughts—his life—since he could remember.

It was a shock. Jake wasn't sure how he'd react to seeing Terry again, but as Arsehole stood there all dishevelled and scrawny—a far cry from the man he'd once pretended to be—it was hard to deal with the onslaught of emotions that took hold of him. Rage burned so fiercely, the hurt, the devastation at what this monster had done. Confronting him brought all the grief to the surface that Jake had pushed away for so long.

"Today is a good day," Arsehole said, the familiar gravel in his voice was harsher now. "I wasn't expecting you to come to me."

The smirk that followed grated on Jake, but he held firm where he stood for the time being. The distance was needed for now.

"Well, you're clearly too much of a coward to come straight to me. So, here I am."

"Thought I'd have a little fun. Would have been far more satisfying seeing you go down for murder and stay there this time. How is your girlfriend by the way?"

Biting down the burning anger that threatened to ignite, Jake managed to keep it together, playing the game, waiting for his moment. "Stronger than you thought. How's your side?"

"Flesh wound. She got lucky."

When Jake took a step forward, Terry's head tipped to the side, eyes narrowing as he watched Jake cautiously.

Finally, Jake had the opportunity to ask the question that had been plaguing him for almost three years. "Why did you do it? What did my mum do to you to deserve you taking her life?" It was a struggle, but Jake managed to keep his voice level. He tried to prepare himself for the answer, expecting the smug attitude, but he knew that what came out of Arsehole's mouth next was going to snap his control.

While Terry stood there silent, his mouth curving into a sordid grin, Jake's deep, rapid breaths were the only thing keeping him where he was. "Answer the fucking question."

Eyebrows rose. "Are you sure? You might not like the answer.

Was he kidding? "Yes I'm fucking sure."

"You don't know what it was like. You'd left as soon as you were able, so you didn't see everything." His gaze moved past Jake's shoulder, but he appeared to be staring at nothing as he continued, like he'd gone into his head. "She was always sobbing, telling me how bad her life was. Well, let me tell you, I was the one who needed rescuing. . . from her."

Unbidden, Jake ran at him, and before he even realised what was happening, the bastard pulled a gun on him, pausing Jake's advance, shocking him into silence for a minute. But the rage came back just as quickly. "You murdered her, took her fucking life away." The tears came then as his heart shattered for the thousandth time. "Why? Why did you have to kill her?"

Then the world seemed to fall away, no street sounds, nothing on the breeze, just the sound of Terry's next words as his eyes moved to Jake's.

"I couldn't stand the sound of her voice anymore."

The distraction was probably what saved Jake's life in that moment. A sound from behind had him twisting around to see another man had come to join their little gathering. It wasn't some random passer-by, not with the way he walked up with a cocky swagger and stood there grinning. Terry hadn't been thinking when he'd looked over Jake's shoulder; he'd been waiting for this guy.

"So what? You think you're going to keep getting away with this shit," Jake said. And just as he turned back to face Terry, there was a loud bang that bounced off the walls and echoed all around the narrow space, causing Jake to duck on instinct.

He noticed the distain on Terry's face as he said, "No. I just wanted you to join her, you little shit. At this point, what have I got to lose by ending your life as well?"

It was then that Jake felt a burning pain rip through his stomach. Gripping the area with his hand, he looked down and saw the blood dripping over his fingers, deep crimson seeping through his grey T-shirt, right before he fell to his knees.

No! It couldn't end like this. After everything, that bastard was still going to win.

A ringing in his ears drowned out any other sound as black pulsed at the edge of his vision. He hit the ground still clutching his stomach, fighting to drag air into his lungs.

Scuffed up boots came into his view as he squinted, trying to focus his eyes.

"Goodbye, Jake. You little brat."

The words that *Arsehole* had said to him so many times when he was younger, were the last thing Jake heard as he watched Terry retreating into the dark. Then his vision went black. Still, it was nice to see Charlie so clearly in his mind's eye—her beautiful face with those blue-green eyes and the soft, silky blonde hair that he'd liked the smell of—right before he left consciousness.

Chapter Thirty-Six

It didn't matter what she did, Charlie couldn't stop thinking about Jake, wondering where he was, how he was. Of course, she had his number, but she didn't feel it was right to contact him. He'd have messaged her if he'd wanted to.

But he hadn't.

No matter how often she'd looked at her phone—nothing.

It had been over a week since he'd gone and she was sick with worry.

Cara had noticed straight away that something was off when she'd seen her friend the next day after Jake had left. Charlie had lost her appetite, only eating when she had to, and her friend had pulled her up about the leftovers she was pushing around her plate at lunch. Eventually, after Cara had practically followed her around asking the same question over and over again, Charlie told her about Jake leaving. Now the woman was smothering her, constantly going on at her about looking after herself, threatening to sleep on her couch if she didn't, always trying to get her to spend more time with her friends.

Which was why she was sitting in the back of Jason's car, Selena sat next to him up front, on the way to games night at Cara's place. Cara insisted as Cara always does, until you got so sick of her voice you either screamed or agreed. Charlie knew by experience the latter was always the best option.

The loved up couple in the front did their best to talk about everything and anything that didn't involve Jake on the drive over, and Charlie was thankful for that. She wasn't sure if she'd be any kind of company. Still, it had to do her some good, right? *"Spending every day wallowing in worry isn't healthy for anyone,"* Cara had said during her latest pep talk. Charlie couldn't deny she was right. It was miserable.

All she could do now was hope that a couple of rounds of Trivial Pursuit would give her some much needed respite from all the anxiety that had been surging through her for the last nine days.

"So, you two are talking again?" Charlie caught the daggers Jas gave her through his rear-view mirror and tightened her lips around her smile. Jason had been in a foul mood for most of the week because of the cold shoulder Selena had given him. It would do him good. He was learning how a proper relationship worked, and Charlie was enjoying watching from the sidelines.

Selena glanced at her boyfriend. "I let him sweat for a little while, didn't I?" Jas *mhmm*ed in reluctant agreement then gave Charlie more narrow-eyed daggers before looking ahead at the road. Selena reached over and placed her hand on his knee. "Then he came to mine one night with the biggest bunch of roses and this..." She reached up and put the interior light on, turning in her seat and pulling the end of a gold necklace from inside her jumper for Charlie to see. The small heart pendant she was holding between her fingers had a single stone that looked like a diamond in the top left corner.

Leaning forward to get a better look, Charlie gave Jas a quick what-did-I-tell-you look in the mirror.

"So how could I not forgive him?"

Ok. So her advice was clearly well wrong and the shady smirk Jas gave her as if to say "What do you know" confirmed it. She stifled a laugh, pleased that they'd worked it out. "It's beautiful. I'm glad he was made to grovel."

As the evening went on, Charlie was glad of the distraction. Being with her friends had definitely extinguished some of the tension, albeit temporarily. Her sleeping pattern had messed up, causing even more stress because of uni. Every time she went to bed, she lay there with thoughts of Jake, wondering where he was, if he was safe. Due to lack of sleep, she'd found herself dozing in some of her classes, seeming to sleep uncontrollably early evening in front of the TV, which then made bed time even worse.

It was a vicious circle, one she couldn't get out of no matter how hard she tried.

"You cannot have that." Jas grabbed the little round yellow tray from the brown space on the board, tipping the brown triangle piece back out of it.

Everyone else laughed, especially Cara who'd totally cheated. "What are you the Trivial Pursuit police? My answer was so much better."

"It doesn't work like that. If you can't play this without having to cheat I'm sure I have a Guess Who in the cupboard at home. I could bring it next time. Maybe that's more your level."

"I love Guess Who!" she replied with too much delight to even be joking, her eyes wide and watery. Tonight her mountain of curls was tied up in a colourful headscarf.

Jas grumbled and rolled his eyes, picking up the dice for his turn.

Charlie's cheeks ached from laughing so much. She wasn't used to it, and it felt great. It was the most relaxed she'd been for ages and she was grateful for Cara using her relentless powers of persuasion to get her here.

When everyone quietened down while Selena took her go, Charlie heard a buzzing coming from her bag. Reaching down, she grabbed it off the floor and pulled out her phone. Staring at the unknown number for a moment, she worried about answering because of the whole ex-trying-to-get-hold-of-her thing.

"'You going to answer or just stare at it?" Cara asked, shaming her into it.

"Yeah. I'll be back in a sec." She got up from the table and walked out into the hallway. Her friends didn't need to hear her arguing with Dale. Connecting the call, Charlie held her breath and waited in silence to hear the voice she despised on the other end.

"Hello? Is that Charlie?" A woman's voice and not one she recognised.

"Yes?"

"Oh, hi. My name's Janet, I'm a nurse at Scunthorpe General Hospital. We have a patient here and you were the first in his contacts list of only four people in his phone." Immediately, Charlie's heart dropped to her toes as she listened to the woman continue. "We have no other contacts for him, and no way of obtaining that information at the moment until the police can trace down a family member. I hope you don't mind me calling you."

Police? "N—No." Her throat almost closed up as an icy chill straightened her spine. "It's Jake, isn't it?"

"Are you a friend of his?"

There was an obvious tone in the woman's voice that sent a sting of dread right through Charlie. "Yes."

"I'm sorry to tell you this, but yes, Jake is in a critical condition and is currently in the ICU. He's stable right now, but it's a waiting game at the moment."

Heart galloping in her chest, Charlie tried to comprehend what the woman was saying. "What—What happened?" The tremble in her voice was parallel to what she felt in every part of her body.

The woman hesitated; like she didn't want to tell her or perhaps she couldn't because of patient confidentiality. "He's been the victim of an attack. That's all I can tell you right now. The police are conducting an investigation. I hope you understand."

"Yes, I..." she swallowed past the lump in her throat, "I understand. Can I come to the hospital? He doesn't have anybody else." As she thought of what had happened to his mum and the attack in her flat by his stepdad, her stomach knotted, acid burning up her throat. That bastard was going through the family. Anger seeped through her veins, competing with the grief she was overcome with.

"Of course." Her voice lowered a little, the sorrow Charlie heard in it stinging her chest. "He needs someone with him."

"Thank you. Thank you for phoning me."

"It's no problem. Are you okay?"

No, she thought, pulling air into her shaky lungs. "Yes. I'll try to get there as soon as I can." Her mind was frantic, already planning her trip.

"You can come to the ICU anytime. Just ring the buzzer outside of the ward. I will leave your name on the visitor's list."

"Where abouts are you? Can I have the address?" Heart racing, she went back in the living room and mimicked writing with a pen to Cara. One was passed to her quickly and she scribbled down the address the nurse gave her.

"Oh, one more thing, Jake was able to give his first name to the paramedics when they picked him up. Do you know his surname?"

"Yes. It's Sure."

"Thank you. Well, I'll no doubt see you when you get here. You take care."

Part of her registered saying goodbye, but the rest of her was numb. Holding her phone against her chest, she stood there, staring into nothing, Jake's rare smile filling her mind, almost like he was standing there right in front of her.

"Charlie?" Suddenly, Cara's face replaced Jake's and Charlie blinked. "Hey, what's going on? Why have you gone so pale?"

Looking her friend in the eyes, she was finding it hard to get her words out without bursting into tears, breathing rapidly past the anguish in her chest.

"Charlie?" Her friend's voice had softened. "What's wrong? Who was on the phone?"

Swallowing down her anguish, Charlie said, "It's Jake. He's in a hospital in Scunthorpe. He's critical." There was nothing she could do to stop the tears. But she held it together while they fell down her cheeks. She had to. *Please let him pull through*. She had to go there now.

"Oh my God, Charlie, what happened?" Cara guided her back to her seat and she noticed Jas and Selena looked worried.

"I don't really know. She said he'd been attacked."

"Shit," Jas said across the table. "Is he going to be okay?"

Cara answered. "It's serious."

Rolling her hands in her lap, Charlie looked at Cara who was next to her. "What time is it?"

"Just gone nine. Why?"

"I have to go to the hospital. He's all alone there." An image of him lying in a bed on his own in a strange hospital in a strange town brought nausea gnawing at her stomach.

"Charlie, Scunthorpe is a long way from here."

Ignoring her friend, she felt determination riding through her. "Do you think there's a late train I could catch?"

Taking her hand, Cara held it in hers, interlocking their fingers. "I don't think so. Not at this time. Why don't you let Jas take you home and we'll look at the train times for tomorrow morning. I could go with you."

"I'll take you," Jas said, and Charlie saw that Selina had her hand on his arm.

Charlie's heart jumped in her chest. "You will?"

"Yeah, sure. He held up his phone, screen side facing her. "Google maps says it's two hours and forty-two minutes from here. If we leave now, we could be there before midnight."

"Now?"

"Now?"

Both Cara and Charlie spoke at the same time.

"I'll come too," Selena said by his side.

Jason smiled at his girlfriend. "Yeah, we'll go now. I only have a couple of short classes tomorrow but they're nothing important. I can do the work at home."

"Can you move work around?" Cara asked her.

Charlie shook her head, trying to think as her brain went into overdrive. "Uh, yeah. I can call Professor Randall tomorrow and tell him there's been a family emergency. I'm sure he'll be fine with me having some time off. I don't have much left to do."

"Well that's it then. Do you need to go to yours to get some things?" Jas asked.

"Yeah. Just a small bag of stuff." Her heart was galloping wildly in her chest.

Jas and Selena were already up and heading for the door.

Cara shot up, following Charlie. "Well, don't think I'm staying here." She grabbed her handbag and her phone and caught Charlie up, linking their arms together, giving Charlie an I've-got-your-back smile. And she always did. "Besides, I could do with a distraction from all the parent stress."

An hour later and they were on the motorway. Selena was dosing in the front seat and Charlie was sat looking out of the rain-streaked side window, her heart had been non-stop racing since the phone call from the hospital, her mind swimming, trying to figure out what might have happened. It had to be his stepdad. Jake had said he was only going to find him and talk—get him to turn himself in. Deep down Charlie had known that wasn't how it would go. She'd seen that psycho in action. There was no reasoning with someone like that, and it was clear he'd wanted to get at Jake. Or maybe Jake had seen him and snapped, all that pent-up rage taking over and making him do something he couldn't take back. He'd gone to confront a murderer, all on his own, full of hate and anger.

Charlie should have tried harder to persuade him not to go. Or she should have insisted she go with him.

Then perhaps they'd both be in the hospital.

The anxiety she felt from it all was too much. The gnawing sickness rolling through her stomach, the twisting torment in her chest of not knowing what had happened, it was too much.

What if he doesn't pull through?

What if she didn't make it in time and that one perfect day they'd shared together was the last time she'd ever see him alive?

The warmth of a hand pressing down on her leg soothed her and when she turned to face Cara, her friend's brows were pinched in the middle and she gave her a sympathetic smile that Charlie could just make out in the low light of the late evening. "He'll make it. I just know he will."

If only Charlie could feel the same. Jake had been in her life for a small amount of time but she couldn't deny the impact he'd already had. It wasn't long enough. Charlie knew there was more. There had to be more to them. Life surely couldn't be so cruel to one person.

Aside from what she wanted between them, she was supposed to help him get visiting access to his little brother. *Oh, God.* His poor little brother. He couldn't lose someone else.

Jake had to survive.

Oh, God. Please pull through.

Chapter Thirty-Seven

The journey to Scunthorpe had been agony. Jason had managed to get them there in a little less time than expected, but still, for two and a half hours Charlie had barely said a word, unable to think of anything other than Jake and the future he might never get to have.

Having the life squeezed out of her wasn't really helping, so she was relieved to be able to breathe again when Cara pulled back from the hug she gave her in the small reception area of the hospital. "Are you sure you'll be okay on your own?"

Standing there in the stark white foyer, Charlie looked at the three friends who had come all this way to support her, even Jason who hadn't really taken to Jake, or so she thought. She swallowed past the lump in her throat. None of them had known Jake for long, so the fact they'd done this for her made her all emotional.

Nodding to her friend, she inhaled those emotions down as deep as she could. "Yes. I'll be fine. Why don't you guys go and see if there's a Maccies nearby. I'll call or text if I need you."

Cara nodded, taking her hand and giving it a quick squeeze. "We'll be back here in a heartbeat. Okay?"

Smiling, Charlie left them. As she followed the signs and the markings on the floor to the ICU, the sparse walls of the quiet corridors began to close in on her. Thankfully, she didn't get lost. Stopping at the intercom outside the main door, she inhaled deeply, letting out her breath slowly to try and calm her nerves as she pressed the buzzer. All she was aware of whilst waiting for an answer was the sound of her heart pounding in her chest in the eerie silence of the hospital. This late at night most patients would be sleeping, nursing staff settled in for the night shift. No visitors.

A clicking sound came from the little metal box on the wall at the side of the double doors. A voice crackled through the speaker. "Hello?"

"Hi. My name's Charlie. I was told I could come and visit Jake Sure."

"Just one moment."

Closing her eyes, she tried to breathe away the anxiety that was stinging her chest, putting a trembling hand over it. The loud buzz that followed did nothing to help. Figuring that was her cue, Charlie pushed the door and it opened. When she walked inside, there was a nurse coming down the corridor with a smile ready to greet her.

"Charlie?" she said as she approached. "I'm Janet who called you earlier."

Oh, thank God. "Hi." At least she didn't have to explain herself again.

"Come this way," she said walking back the way she'd come from and into a small waiting room that had a hot drinks machine just inside the door. "You must be tired after the trip here. Do you want a tea or coffee, chocolate?"

Her stomach was in knots, but maybe some caffeine would help a bit. "Coffee, please."

"Take a seat."

Picking the chair closest, she sat down, putting her bag on the floor next to her as the nurse set to making a drink. The room was a typical waiting room, but felt warmer because of the lamplight in the corner opposite. Chairs lined the whole edge and there was a wood coffee table in the middle with piles of magazines and leaflets.

"How was the journey here?" the nurse asked, passing her a hot paper cup. "I didn't know if we'd see you tonight."

"It was fine, the roads were pretty quiet. I didn't want to wait; couldn't stand to think of him on his own. I mean, I know he's not alone, but—"

"We're strangers," she said as she carried her drink over to the chair opposite. "It's completely understandable. Are you his girlfriend?"

She wasn't sure if it was disrespectful to put that label on their relationship when they'd barely had one, but it might make things easier while she was there. "Yes. We haven't known each other all that long."

In the silence that followed, she blew over the top of her cup and took a gentle sip of coffee. "What happened to him? I know you can only say so much, but—"

"He was shot."

Ice froze in Charlie's veins, a cold shiver running over her skin. It was the last thing she'd expected to hear. Thought maybe he'd been beaten up, or even stabbed seeing as that bastard liked knives. "Shot?" In shock, she could barely manage a whisper.

"I can tell you what I know since he was brought to the hospital. We operated straight away. The surgeons managed to stem the bleeding pretty quickly and remove the bullet from his abdomen. The man is very lucky it did no other damage in there. He did lose quite a lot of blood and has since had another transfusion. It was very close when they brought him in. Whoever called 999 saved his life, there's no question. He also has some bruising to the ribs and back, but those wounds look a little older. I think they were inflicted before he got shot.

It was hard not to ask the next question; she feared the answer. "Is he going to pull through?"

"His vitals have improved. The transfusions have done their job and his blood pressure, although still a little low, has improved over the last few hours. We're quite confident at this point."

The sting of tears had her blinking quickly, a glimmer of hope pushing through and taking the lead, although the worry was still there, it was definitely better news than she expected.

"What about the person who did this to him?"

A slight shrug. "The police were here earlier. I spoke to them briefly to explain Jake's condition. All they said was they were searching for the perpetrator."

Which meant that bastard was still out there. Nausea hit the pit of her stomach.

"Would you like to see him? He's sleeping, and will most likely be out of it for some time. His body has been through a lot. He needs the rest."

Charlie nodded and the nurse got up, putting her cup in the bin at the side of the drinks trolley. "I'll take you to him."

When they got to the ICU, they walked past a nurses' station that was at the centre of the room overlooking a semicircle of beds separated by half closed privacy curtains. Charlie's eyes moved around quickly, taking everything in as the sounds of machines beeping took precedence over everything else, the clinical smell burning the back of her nose. They passed the open beds to another area that had individual rooms, each with windows that spanned the whole length of the walls. When they got to the second one along, Charlie peered in as they walked past to the door.

There he was.

Her heart sank.

The man who had become so familiar to her in a crazy short space of time was lying propped up a little on a bed with wires coming out of him from various places. The lighting was low, coming from a small wall light behind the bed. Her eyes never left him as she followed the nurse inside. Charlie choked back a sob, an invisible hand squeezing her oesophagus as sorrow pinched her heart to see him that way.

"You're welcome to stay as long as you want to. It will be good for him to see a familiar face when he wakes up."

"Thank you," Charlie somehow managed to say as she approached Jake's bedside, taking everything in with blurry eyes until she wiped them swiftly. Standing there looking down at him, her stomach twisted at his pallid complexion. His cheeks looked a little hollow, highlighted by the dark stubble he'd grown in. Still so handsome. There was a chair at the side of the bed that she scooted closer. When she sat down, she rested her hand beside his arm on the mattress.

It was crazy to think what had happened. Her brain couldn't comprehend that he'd been shot. When she'd worried for his safety, she'd honestly thought Jake would have been okay; that maybe worst case scenario was him arguing with his stepdad, maybe even fighting each other, and the police doing the rest.

Now she wondered what had happened to the man she knew had done this. Had he got away again? Did he think he'd won and that Jake had died? Anger swirled like a tornado in the pit of her stomach, increasing to a category five as her mind was hit with flashes of memories from the night that man had attacked her. He'd intended on killing her and framing Jake for her murder that night. When it didn't work, he'd obviously changed his plans and got hold of a gun.

That evil prick had meant to kill Jake, there was no question. And he'd almost succeeded.

Where was he now?

After sitting there looking at Jake, silently willing him to open his eyes for God only knew how long, a nurse came in to check things over, doing something to the drip that was in his arm, and logging something on his chart. There was a tube up his nose, taped at the end, but she noticed he was breathing steadily, his strong chest moving up and down in a reassuring rhythm. He was breathing. He was stable. He was alive.

She felt sure he was going to pull through.

Charlie took the time to message Cara to let her know she was with him and that Jake was sleeping, and she smiled when Cara text back to say they'd stuffed themselves, and had brought her back an apple pie. She told Charlie they weren't going anywhere and were currently sitting in the car.

Jas is trying to sleep, but keeps grumping at the two of us for keeping him awake while we're playing Heads Up. Love ya girl.

xxx

Smiling, she put her phone back in her bag and shot back up in her seat when she heard a faint grumble, hoping to see Jake awake. But his eyes were closed and he was lying still, although she was sure his arm had moved a little.

Again, Charlie sat looking at him lying so peaceful under her gaze. She couldn't imagine how different things would have been last night when the paramedics had brought him in, bleeding, crashing, the chaotic conditions as the emergency team battled to save his life.

Stomach twisting again, Charlie couldn't think about what might have happened if the person who'd called the ambulance hadn't found him.

Jake had a guardian angel, for sure.

Sometime later, Janet, the nice nurse, came back in to the room holding a steaming cup. "I brought you a coffee. Milk, two sugars, wasn't it?" When she handed it over, Charlie could have jumped up and hugged her. Too worried about leaving Jake's side in case he woke up alone, she hadn't moved for at least a couple of hours, so the coffee was very welcome and appreciated.

"Your friend brought this up for you." The nurse handed her a carrier bag. "Asked me to tell you to eat all of it even if you don't want to."

"Thank you." Opening the bag, Charlie peered inside to see the Maccies apple pie, a packet of crisps, and a cheese and ham sandwich in a bubble pack. Her stomach rumbled so she took out the sandwich. "Oh, I definitely want to."

The nurse smiled at her before checking the screen of the monitor next to Jake's bed. When her eyebrows popped a little, Charlie worried for a minute, but the woman looked over at her with the same smile. "Another slight improvement in his blood pressure. It's looking very good."

Relief caused a sharp exhale and Charlie sat forward in the chair, all of a sudden wanting to get closer to him. "Did you hear that, Jake?" she said in a low whisper. "You're going to be okay. You got this."

The nurse nodded and gave her one last smile as she went to leave. "If you need the toilet, or want to take a break, get a drink from the trolley, just come and let one of us know and someone will sit with him until you come back."

"I will. Thank you." When she'd left the room, Charlie reached up and put her hand on the bed next to his arm again, watching him sleep for another few minutes. Then she stroked her finger over the side of his forearm, the first time she'd touched him since getting here. The soft dusting of hairs tickled her finger. His skin was so warm. Then she glanced at him before sitting back to eat her sandwich, silently thanking Cara for the food, and whoever was looking out for Jake.

Her heart felt a little lighter.

He was going to make it.

Chapter Thirty-Eight

The kiss was firm, his lips warm and soft against hers. Arms wrapped themselves around her, pulling her close, making her feel safe. Warm. Protected.

Their lips separated too suddenly. Arms pulled away from her body, no longer holding her close. Someone was taking Jake away from her. A look of horror darkened his handsome features as he held his arms out to her; she tried to reach for them, her heart pounding, stomach twisting.

A gloved hand rose from the shadows, gun pointed at Jake. She couldn't see who held it, but she knew.

"No!" she cried, pleading with his attacker.

A loud bang filled the air, consuming her, then Jake was gone, no longer standing there facing her. Her gaze went to the body lying on the floor. "No!" She ran to him, dropping down to her knees at his side as he struggled to keep hold of his life.

Blood pooled, seeping out from under his body. She yelped. "Jake, no! Don't you die on me."

But she knew deep down he was. The gunshot was fatal.

His lovely blue eyes met hers, shock and desperation filling them as he fought to stay. He lost the battle, eyes going vacant, chest stilling. No breath. No life.

She broke down. "No, Jake!" This couldn't be happening. Not to him. He needed to live.

Dropping her head down to his still chest, she sobbed uncontrollably, despair racking her so much that she didn't register the feeling at first. Then she felt it again, something touching her head, moving her hair. Lying still, she focused on the feeling, reaching out to it in her mind, pulling it close.

Charlie woke slowly to a strange sound that she quickly recognised as the beeps from monitoring equipment. She smelled the familiar clinical smell that reminded her of where she was. The base of her back ached. She was hunched over. Then she froze, aware of the tickling sensation in her hair, exactly like she'd felt in her dream. Someone was touching her head.

Jake.

Overriding the urge to sit up quickly, she lifted her head slowly instead, realising she'd fallen asleep with her head on Jake's hospital bed. Then her eyes met his beautiful blue ones and her hand covered her mouth to hold in her cry.

"Charlie?" he struggled to say through a raspy voice.

Placing her hand on his warm arm, she smiled, tears blurring her vision until she swiped them away with the back of her other hand. "Yes. You're awake."

Blinking slowly, he nodded his head. "Just about." When he spoke this time he swallowed with a grimace.

"Do you need some water?" she asked, getting up from the chair and glancing out of the windows that looked out into the corridor. She was reluctant to leave him, but he was obviously uncomfortable. "I'll be right back."

Almost sprinting to the nurses' station, she told them he was awake and that he needed some water. The nurse there told her she'd be right in, and Charlie rushed back to his room. When she returned to his bedside, her heart was racing as she looked at him, suddenly overcome with emotion.

He looked a little more awake and gave her a smile that she was sure she was going to remember for the rest of her life. "You're here."

"Yes. I'm here." Her hand went on top of his and when he looked down at them, he raised his finger to stroke the side of hers.

Then his eyes closed and his head went back a little and she saw his chest rise as his lungs filled. "I'm alive," he said as if he couldn't believe he'd survived. Tired eyes met hers again and she bit back more tears. "I feel like shit, but I'm alive. Somehow."

"Yes." Charlie was too choked to say anything else right then, but she was saved when a nurse came in carrying a paper cup. The man smiled as he approached Jake's bedside, glancing up at the machine. "Welcome back, Jake. How are you feeling?" Passing the cup to Charlie, he raised the back of the bed slightly so Jake was sitting up a bit more.

"Like someone shot me in the stomach," he said, reaching up and taking the cup that she was lifting to his mouth. Charlie's stomach sank like a stone falling to the bottom of a well when he said it so matter-of-factly. As if there was any way he wasn't going to remember it.

The nurse's mouth tightened. "Yes, well thankfully, they were a bad shot," he said in jest, straightening the edge of the covers. "You're lucky to be alive. And you're lucky to have such a wonderful girlfriend who has sat by your bedside all night."

Charlie felt her cheeks heat, even more so when Jake looked at her. She didn't know if he'd appreciate the girlfriend label. Maybe he'd be unhappy about it, after all, they'd slept together, but they hadn't talked about a relationship. Still, it was the only thing she could think to say when they'd asked; better for them to think they were in a relationship so they'd treat her the same as a family member.

When she felt his hand move under hers, she expected him to pull it out from underneath in disgust. So it surprised her when he turned his palm up and laced his fingers through hers. "Yeah, I am lucky to have her."

Warmth shot through her as those blue eyes locked on hers intensely, capturing her, holding her prisoner. In that moment the room fell away. All the noises, the smells, were far away in the distance. It was just the two of them, an undeniable moment passing between them, one that filled her heart.

Was this the start of the future Jake had begun to see? Was she a part of it now?

She wanted to be.

Excitement filled her veins at the thought of it.

It was more than she could hope for.

Later, though. Now wasn't the time to get ahead of herself. Jake needed to get better first before they could think about anything else.

Left alone, neither of them spoke. Jake was still looking at her, an expression she wasn't sure of on his face. Charlie wished she could get a glimpse of what he was thinking right then. Maybe he was wondering why someone who barely knew him would rush to a hospital hours away in the middle of the night. There hadn't even been a second thought for Charlie. As soon as she'd disconnected the call from the hospital, her mind had gone into planning mode thinking of all the possibilities of how to get to him.

"Do you want—"

"How did you—"

They both paused at the same time too, and Charlie wondered how he could smile so easily given how he must feel.

"I was just going to ask how you got here?" he said, his voice a little less hoarse.

Passing him the cup of water again, she explained that Jas, Selena, and Cara were all downstairs and he seemed surprised that they'd all stayed the night.

"They didn't hesitate to bring me. You must have made an impression on them."

A brow popped up. "Really? Even Jason? I'm pretty sure he doesn't like me very much."

She smiled. "He's just a little protective of me knowing what I went through before I moved to Hatfield."

When Jake's brow creased, Charlie realised what she'd said. He didn't know about her ex, Dale. When had she even had any real time to bring it up with him? Cara and Jas were the only other two people in the world apart from her parents that knew.

"What did you go through?"

Well, now was as good a time as any. The room was private, quiet, and maybe speaking about it again would help a little more.

"Five years ago I met someone, Dale. We dated for about a year and everything was great. I thought he was going to be the one, you know. Then he asked me to marry him. It was quick, but we were happy. My parents were happy." Faltering, she tried to disguise the anxiety that talking about it all again brought up. "It all changed as soon as we moved in together. I should have known something wasn't right when he was adamant we move to a town thirty miles away. He said it was because it was easier for him to commute to his work, but that was a lie, just as his work was. I was living the fairy tale, or so I thought, so I didn't question it at the time. He changed into a completely different person in the blink of an eye. The man who I'd laughed with, been so happy with, wasn't there anymore. He started to drink, which made him aggressive, controlling. While the whole time he made out it was me who was causing his drink problem."

Biting back tears, she looked up at the ceiling. It was hard to admit what she let Dale do to her. That she was too weak to see what he was doing. She was such a different person than she was now.

"I was so alone. He'd got me away from my family, and I was trapped. At least I thought I was. For the nine months that I stayed with him in that house, he tormented me, emotionally abused me, and eventually things got violent. It was the one and only time. He broke my arm and something just snapped in me. When I was at the hospital getting a cast put on, I phoned my dad and told him to come get me. I never saw Dale again. Not that he didn't try. I left everything I had at the house we'd shared. I didn't want any of it." There was no way she wanted to keep anything that was associated with him. His money had paid for a lot of it and anything else she wasn't interested in.

"I never looked back. He was out of my life, but didn't leave my head for quite some time. I fell into depression. I was so unhappy. Mainly at myself for letting it happen. Then one day I realised he was still ruining my life even though he wasn't in it. He still had a hold on me. Moving to Hatfield and going to university, which was something he wouldn't have allowed, was the best decision I've ever made." She looked at Jake and caught his chagrined expression before he blinked. Then his eyes settled softly on hers, making her feel warm. Comfortable. "For more reasons than I could have imagined."

The warm, strong hand that was laced with hers, keeping her grounded, squeezed a little. "Fucking hell, Charlie." His brow furrowed and he looked away, his eyes moving down. "And I was an arse with you at first." When his eyes met hers again, they looked unsure. "I'm sorry I acted like a dick. I was just. . . I was in such a precarious place. I'd been so used to things how they were, just me and my revenge." Huffing out a laugh, he shook his head. "Look where that fucking got me."

"I don't blame you for keeping hold of that hate, Jake. You had a right to those feelings after what he did. I can't imagine what hell you've been through." Leaning forward, she felt the need to be closer to him. "I'm just... I'm glad you're still alive. When the hospital called, they only gave me a little information, told me you were in ICU in a critical, but stable condition. I had no idea if—"

"That's how you knew I was here?"

"Yes. The nurse said I was one of the contacts in your phone and my name was first alphabetically."

Jake's head tilted back on the pillow and he closed his eyes. For a moment Charlie thought he was unhappy about them phoning her.

Then he huffed out a breath. "I almost deleted your number." His gaze turned to her again. "I figured if everything went south and Terry got hold of my phone, it was better for him not to find your number in there. Didn't want him to think I was still in contact with you. But I couldn't seem to do it. Fuck. Thank God I didn't."

His thumb stroked the side of her hand. "I wasn't sure who you were when I woke up. I couldn't see your face. Then I smelled your perfume and there was no doubt in my mind it was you. I couldn't believe you were here."

He knew her by scent?

Jake's eyes closed and she figured he needed more rest. "Get some rest. I'll go down and see the gang while you're sleeping. Okay?"

A gentle nod. Then as she went to move he squeezed her hand. "I'm glad it was you," he said in a slurred voice, and when he drifted off to sleep, his hand loosened around hers.

Chapter Thirty-Nine

When Charlie walked out of Jake's hospital room, she felt strange. Standing in the quiet lift while waiting to get to the ground floor, the only thing she could attribute the strange feeling to was elation. It wasn't like she was an expert in that field. When she'd first met Dale, she'd been happy, even though it was hard to remember after what she went through with him.

This, though, the feeling she had now? It had to be elation; she'd never felt anything like it before. Her heart felt like it was floating on a cloud and singing songs in her chest. The warmth she felt—it was nice. Exciting. Now that she didn't have to worry as much, Charlie could think of all those things. She was pretty sure Jake was glad to have her there. The way he'd held her hand. There was no denying they had a connection. And even though they'd only really known each other for mere months, there were definitely feelings on both sides.

She felt it even more so now.

Her phone vibrated in her jeans back pocket. Pulling it out, she saw Cara had replied to her text, telling her they were sleeping in the car. Suddenly she felt bad about them being in the car park all night, but they'd insisted on waiting until the morning to see what the situation was.

There was no way Charlie was leaving Jake at the moment, though. No doubt he would still have a fair bit of healing to do and until they had more information on his condition and where he was at, she felt he needed someone close by.

It was how she felt anyway. Maybe Jake would be fine on his own, after all, he'd managed perfectly fine before they met, but still. It was no hardship on Charlie's part to keep him company.

When she got to her friend's car, there was no movement. The windows were mostly steamed up, but she glanced through a gap at the top of the passenger one and saw everyone asleep. They'd switched places. Jason and Selena were on the back seat, Selena curled up with her head on Jas's knee while he slept with his head back against the headrest. Cara was in the front with the seat pushed back over Selena's legs. She'd obviously gone back to sleep.

Pausing, Charlie thought about leaving them to sleep, but the walk from ICU was quite far and she'd rather avoid doing it again for a while. Besides, it was just gone six in the morning so the country was waking up. Maybe Jas would want to avoid most of the morning traffic, and she knew they'd want to know how Jake was.

Smiling, because she was going to enjoy what happened next, Charlie reached up and knocked hard on the window. "Get up! Get up you lazy lot!"

All she could make out was shadows moving quickly inside and she laughed, knocking again. "It's me. Are you awake?"

"Shit, Char," she heard Jas mumble.

"My heart is in my bloody mouth," Cara snapped as she opened the front passenger side door. She looked at her with one eye half closed, her brown, dishevelled hair all frizzy and sticking up at the back of her head. "Are you trying to kill me? Honestly, I've had shit nerves as it is from sleeping in a car park all night, expecting security or police to bang on the car at any time."

"I told you we'd be alright," she heard Jas say from the back.

Charlie felt so bad. It straightened her face. "I'm sorry you've spent the night out here."

"Don't be silly." Cara got out of the car, flinging her arms in the air while she stretched and yawned. "We're not going to let you guilt yourself for something we decided to do." Bending to look inside, she said, "Not that I'd do it again with turbo snorer over there. Honestly, Selena, how do you not stuff things in his mouth when he's sleeping to shut him up?"

"How do you know she doesn't?" Jas called back in a tone, and Charlie heard Selena laugh.

Cara straightened. "Jeez. Too much information for this time of the morning, Jas."

In a flash, the others were out of the car, Jas lighting up a cigarette and putting his arm around Selena as she shivered and rubbed her hands.

The air was exceptionally bitter for a May morning. There was dew everywhere and a light fog covered the hospital car park, blanketing the tops of the trees that lined the edge.

"How's he doing?" Cara asked in her serious voice.

"Better." Charlie had caught them up by text so they knew Jake had woken up earlier. "I left him sleeping. He was exhausted. The nurse seems positive so hopefully he's out of danger. We'll know more later, I suppose, when the doctor does the rounds."

"What are you planning to do?" Jas asked, a cloud of smoke following his words.

"I'm going to stay, at least for today. I'll get a train back home. If I end up staying overnight I'll get a hotel room." It wasn't something she even needed to think about. As soon as she'd made the decision to travel up to the hospital, she'd put a change of clothes and toiletries in her bag. Staying had been her plan all along. Now Jake was awake it didn't change anything.

When she looked at Cara, she was surprised to see her looking back with watery eyes, her lips in a tight smile. It seemed Jas and Selena were wondering what was going on with her too.

"Why are you looking at me like that?"

Cara stepped closer and put her arms around her. When Charlie glanced at Jas he shrugged. "Cara? What's going on?"

It was a minute before she pulled back, keeping her hands on the sides of Charlie's waist. Her best friend smiled in a way that confused Charlie even more. "I'm so happy for you." Again with another hug.

Charlie laughed as she grabbed her friend's arms and moved her back to where she could see her. "What are you talking about? Are you delirious from lack of sleep?" Another glance at Jason and he shook his head.

"She's always been a little. . ." He tapped his temple. "You know that."

Cara's head turned to him. "Shut up you." Then she looked a little more serious. "Charlie, you jumped in the back of Jas's car and travelled all this way out of concern for a very handsome man who I know you've kissed more than once, and done other stuff with." That last part she mumbled.

Charlie's eyes went wide. "Bloody hell, Cara!"

"Oh stop. As if we haven't all talked about it behind your back."

Going to reply, Charlie snapped her mouth shut. There really was no point.

"Don't think I don't know what's happening here," Cara continued. "I'm not stupid."

"Debatable."

She threw a glare over her shoulder at Jas, then looked back at Charlie, brown, steely eyes locking onto hers. "Charlie, are you in love with Jake?"

The laugh burst out of Charlie so suddenly that Cara had to wipe her face as it screwed up in disgust.

"Sorry. Cara, how can I possibly be in love with someone I've known for a few weeks?" God. Was that what the feeling was? No. It couldn't be possible. Right? "I like him, yes. Obviously I was really concerned for him. That's why I came straight away. Plus, he hasn't got anyone else."

"But you must really like him." Jas this time, with a cheeky smile. Selena hit his stomach playfully.

The expression on Cara's face didn't change and Charlie knew she was having none of it. In fact, the denial sounded stupid coming out of her own mouth. Charlie knew her feelings were more than superficial; it was something she'd address later. Right now the main concern was Jake getting better and getting out of hospital. And she would stay for however long she needed.

A quick change of subject was in order. "I think the canteen is open at seven if you want to go and grab some breakfast."

"Yes, I'm starving." Cara linked Charlie's arm as they headed for the hospital building. "And don't think I'm going to finish with the subject just because I'll be eating bacon and eggs. I can talk with my mouth full."

"We all know that."

Cara shot Jas fierce daggers.

"It's totally true," Jas teased. "Someone could sew your mouth shut and you'd still find a way to chew my ear."

Both Charlie and Selena laughed while Cara's mouth dropped open. "Rude!"

This time it was Cara's turn to slap Jas.

Chapter Forty

Another day passed by. Charlie found a hotel that was only a fifteen minute walk from the hospital. It was basic, but last night was the first time in ages that she'd slept right through without all the worry that had been preventing such a thing since Jake had left. When her phone alarm had woken her up, she'd gone to turn it off with groggy eyes, then immediately sat up when she saw the notification for a text message from Jake:

Morning. Hope you slept well. J x

It was short, but perfect. Charlie shot out of bed, got dressed quickly, and almost sprinted out of the hotel like it was much later than just gone seven in the morning.

She was so familiar with the hospital by now, that she was almost on first name terms with the staff in the canteen where she'd just been for breakfast. Up on the third floor, Charlie had a full stomach and a spring in her step as she headed down the corridor, eager to see Jake this morning. She was just about to press the buzzer to gain access to the ICU when a nurse came through the door and held it open for her.

"Thanks." Smiling all the way down the corridor, filled with optimism about Jake and his health, she wasn't prepared for what she saw when she got back to his room.

The bed was stripped bare and for a moment she thought she'd gone into the wrong room so she walked back out again and looked around to make sure she hadn't. No. It was the right room. Where the hell was Jake? Panic pulled at her insides as dread filled the pit of her stomach. Rushing out of the door she almost ploughed the nurse down.

"Whoa, hey. Charlie, right? I was coming to see if you were back yet."

A nurse Charlie hadn't seen before held on to her arms with a smile "Everything's okay. We moved Mr. Sure to another ward. The ward sister was happy for him to go onto a general ward because of his improvement."

Almost sagging with relief Charlie let out a nervous laugh. "Oh. I thought that... I didn't know." Like she needed to trip over her tongue right then.

"It's understandable that you panicked. I didn't know what time you'd be here today so I've been looking out for you to catch you before you got to his room and saw he wasn't there. Save you the worry."

"Thank you. I did think the worst for a minute."

"Well, it's the complete opposite to that. He's doing well considering what he went through. He may even be able to go home in a few days. Come this way. I'll get someone to take you to him."

Ten minutes later and she was met with a sight that made her breathe much easier than she had since first coming to the hospital. Yesterday, Jake had slept for a lot of the day, his body needing the rest so that he could heal properly. Charlie had read through half of her book, and had familiarised herself with the cafe on the ground floor. In between, he'd been in some pain, needing to press his button for morphine, which then made him groggy.

In the evening, the nurses had suggested she go and have a break and they'd call her if there was any change, but Charlie had refused. She hadn't wanted to be anywhere else until she could barely keep her eyes open. At that point, after Jake had been awake for a couple of hours, he'd ordered her to go to the hotel.

Now, Jake's bed was more upright and the table had been pulled across him as he sat wide awake eating breakfast. Charlie waited by the door for a minute, watching him as he winced a little reaching for his drink. Thick stubble had grown in, softening his strong jaw line a little. The longer facial fur didn't hamper his good looks at all. If anything, he was even more handsome. He had so much more colour in his face, and the circles weren't as dark under the ocean blue eyes that glanced up and caught her staring.

"Hey," she said in response to his smile, walking over to his bedside as he rested his head back on the pillow. "You're own room again, huh? I think there's a bit of favouritism going on in here." She sat down on the chair that was the same type her arse was already well familiar with, leaning her forearms on the bed by the side of him.

"Yeah? If only the food reflected that. Sure someone's trying to poison me with this." Reaching for his sandwich, he lifted the top slice off one of the halves and yeah, the bacon looked like plastic, like it had been sat under a heat lamp all night. "Not easy to get my teeth through."

"At least you're trying to eat it. Good that you have an appetite."

"My stomach's asking questions at the moment though."

Right then, a pleasant feeling washed through Charlie. With Jake sounding and looking better, she could let go of the anxiety that had been so prevalent over the last week and that had risen in its intensity after that call from the hospital a couple of nights ago. She didn't know why she felt so connected to Jake, but she wasn't going to turn away from it. There hadn't really been anyone serious since Dale. Charlie had shied away from most men who had shown any interest, except maybe one or two, but they'd never really been anything. Truth was, she'd been nervous about dating. Dale had been so different when they'd first started going out and the change in him had been quick and unexpected, knocking her feet out from under her and caging her in—her confidence completely shot.

In the back of her mind, she'd always worried that she'd pick the wrong guy again.

It didn't feel the same with Jake. Instead of shying away—even when he'd been off with her, which would have been multiple red flags to most people—she'd only felt more drawn in by him. Her heart was telling her that he wasn't another Dale, that this man was everything she'd wanted, even more. And luckily her head seemed to be on the same page.

"What?"

When he spoke, her gaze focused on his, realising she'd stopped talking and was staring at him again. Forcing her mind to come up with something, Charlie quickly said, "It's just good to see you looking so well this morning. It's a relief."

She watched as creases appeared in his forehead, something clouding his expression. "I haven't said thank you." Looking down, he took hold of her hand. His gorgeous blue eyes gazed up through thick, black lashes, the intensity of them in that moment catching her breath. "I'm glad you were here when I woke up. I can't really describe what my head has gone through over the last forty-eight hours. I can only remember bits of things since I was in the ambulance, and even that stuff is strangely distant, like it happened to someone else, you know?" When she felt his thumb stroking her skin, Charlie looked down at their joined hands, a strange kind of emotion washing through her.

"When I woke up, when the first thing that registered was your perfume, I remember catching a sniff of it, the fresh, fruity smell I'd become so familiar with without even realising. Straight away I inhaled it right in, gripping onto it like it was the only way I could pull myself out of the dark hole I was in.

"I saw you. Before consciousness your face was in my mind. When I came to, I was surprised to see someone here. Didn't realise who you were for a minute. Until the scent registered. I looked down again at your head on my bed, but it confused me. I felt like I'd dreamed you into being there—questioned my reality. Then I touched your hair and knew you were real. The darkness disappeared instantly. Like your light chased it away."

Oh, wow! Blinking to try and prevent the tears that were insisting on making an appearance, Charlie looked at him, her nose flaring, jaw tightened as she tried to keep them at bay. None of it worked. They fell just as he looked away.

"I wanted to tell you what you being here means to me."

She saw his chest rise sharply. When Charlie let go of his hand, he looked over and his eyes followed her as she got up from the chair. Moving his table out of the way, she sat down next to him, careful not to squash his arm, which he moved out of the way, lifting and placing it behind his head as he watched her. Reaching up to touch his face, the stubble that lined his jaw was harsh against her hand. Charlie leaned in but paused before moving closer, her eyes never leaving his, but nerves had her wondering if she should do what she was about to.

Would he want her to? Her instincts told her he would. In any case, she decided, what the hell. After that speech, yeah, she needed to kiss him.

As she got closer, she saw his lips part and his eyes widen a little. Placing her hand on his shoulder, she closed the gap between them, leaning into him as careful as she could. Then when she placed her mouth on his, he closed his eyes. Hers followed as she enjoyed the softness of his lips through the roughness of his stubble.

Not wanting to go overboard, she went to pull away, but he moved his arm and caught the back of her head, pulling her back to his mouth. All the breath left her lungs right before he kissed her. Holding her there, Jake's lips moved against hers, his tongue sliding across her lips before pushing at them, seeking access that she willingly granted. It was a kiss she hadn't expected, soft and meaningful, like he was telling her how he felt without words.

When their mouths parted, he kissed her softly once more. Her eyes opened lazily, fixing on his, her face only inches away. She felt him sigh as he smiled.

"Now I'm very happy to have my own room," he said, his voice low.

Charlie huffed out a laugh and closed her eyes, resting her forehead against his. "Me too."

God, he was so lucky to be alive, and touching him, kissing the lips she'd craved since he'd left, made her realise how fortunate they both were. It could have so easily gone the other way. Her heart hurt at the thought of never seeing him again, never feeling his kiss again.

But, with her face so close to his, his warm breath brushing over her skin, Charlie felt the connection between them growing stronger. He was meant to move in down the hall from her. They were meant to meet that day. She just knew that fate had a huge part to play in their lives, looking down on them and positioning all the pieces to fall right into place.

After all this, as soon as Jake got better, they had one more piece on the board to play, and she would do all that she could to make damn sure that he got to see his brother regularly again.

His stepdad was still out there somewhere, but it was something she couldn't think about right then.

When Charlie sat back down on the chair, she threaded her fingers through his and notice him wince a little, a crease appearing between his brows. "Are you in pain?"

"A little. It comes and goes. When it comes, I press this." With his other hand, the one with the cannula in it, he lifted a white plastic cone-shaped device with a button on the end that was connected to a wire for his morphine. He didn't realise she knew about it already, and how it had helped keep him out of it for most of yesterday. "Then it goes and I feel kinda nice for a bit."

"And you're only pressing it when you're in pain of course."

His eyes met hers and his mouth lifted at one side. "Mostly."

"Jake. It's morphine, not your own personal supply of cocaine."

"Well, I don't take drugs, so I'm making the most of it while I can."

Shaking her head, Charlie was eased by their comfortable conversation. Even when he'd been broody Jake, they seemed to be able to talk to each other quite naturally.

Charlie didn't want to broach the subject while their conversation was light and casual. Maybe now wasn't the time, but she needed to know why he was lying in that hospital bed with a zip in his stomach from where a bullet had almost killed him. Bracing herself, she looked at him, trying not to appear too serious. "What happened, Jake?"

He looked at her for a moment, his face expressionless. Then his eyes lowered to where their hands were joined. "I probably could do with going over it all again now my heads clearer. Might help me remember some stuff."

He seemed to brace himself, taking a sharp breath before continuing.

"I had a couple of ideas about where to look for Terry. He always knew some dodgy people, and I guessed that the only way he'd managed to evade the authorities for so long was with help, at least from somebody. I figured that if I went to some of the places I remembered he'd mentioned when he used to lie and say he was working, and asked questions of the right people, somehow he'd eventually get wind of it. It wasn't as easy as I thought though. Not long after I arrived here, I got some hostility from some men who Terry had owed a lot of money to from gambling debts. I was jumped one night by three fellas who thought I had a link to him and that maybe they'd get their money through me."

"What happened?"

"I got a couple of punches to the face and a kick or two when I was down, but it could have been worse."

Charlie's chest tightened. "That was why the nurse mentioned you had some older bruising."

"I guess so. But I gave them some good ones too." When Jake shifted uncomfortably, Charlie reached up and placed her hand on his arm. "You okay? Need me to get a nurse?"

Shaking his head, he moved a touch and seemed to settle a little better. "I don't want to press my button because I need to be alert for this conversation. That's all it is."

"It can wait. You're more important."

A smile that caught her breath. "I'm fine, honestly. Just a little uncomfortable. Nothing I can't handle."

"Okay. Just let me know if it gets too much. We can talk about it when you're feeling better."

"I will. Where was I up to? Right." He rested his head back on the pillow. "I took a short cut through to the street where my hotel was. I wanted to face the prick and I got my wish."

Charlie sat back in her chair listening as Jake continued to explain what he could remember, her heart aching at the pain on his face as he ran through his account of what happened.

"Things got heated and he pulled a gun on me. I can remember asking the question I'd been desperate to ask since the night he killed my mum. Why did he do it? Only, I wasn't prepared for his answer to cut so deep. I thought I was ready to hear it. I thought if I knew *why* he'd done it, it would ease things somehow—give me some closure. It did the exact opposite."

"What did he say?"

"He told me he did it because he couldn't stand the sound of her voice anymore. That was it. He murdered my mum, took her life away from her, because he didn't like her voice." Pausing, he closed his eyes for a second and she moved her chair closer, leaning her elbows on the bed and touching his arm. Wanting to be there for him, to show him he had all her support. She would help him get through it, even though she had to force herself to hold it together.

"I didn't think he had the guts to shoot, and the fury I felt in that moment I didn't care anyway. Someone came into the alley from behind me. He had someone with him. It distracted me. I don't think he ever intended to let me walk out of the alley, which is why he had extra muscle.

"That's when the gun went off. It was so loud, so unexpected, that I didn't even feel the bullet hit. But, *shit*, the white-hot pain that followed let me know I'd been hit. So did the blood staining my shirt. I watched him leave, looking at me for as long as he could before he ran. I don't remember much after that."

"God, Jake." Her words came out in a whisper. And she'd barely even managed that, her throat was so tight with emotion. To think how close he'd been to the end of his life. She couldn't bear the thought. But this wasn't about her anguish. Jake needed her to be there for him. It couldn't be easy going over it all so soon.

"I must have come to at some point, but everything's muddled. There are only snippets of things like staring up at the ceiling in the ambulance. I remember that because I wondered why there was a poster of a map up there. I don't even know if that was real." His brow creased. "I don't think it was. There's more missing than remembered. That's mostly all I've got right now. And there were a few crazy nightmares. Then I just remember waking up with your scent all around me. It was nice to wake up to."

Swallowing down the bile that threatened to come up with the images her mind had displayed, Charlie couldn't think past the part where he was left to die on the ground in an alleyway. It made her feel sick to think of what would have happened if the stranger hadn't come along and called the ambulance. All the anguish she felt right then must have been clear on her face; Jake squeezed her hand.

"I survived, Charlie." But she could hear in his voice that he was freaked out by it too.

Nodding, she gave him the best smile she could. "Yeah. You did." Then saw his face go grave as he looked across the room.

"Shit," he said under his breath.

When Charlie looked around, two police officers were passing in the corridor, trailing the nurse she'd spoken to earlier when she'd first got to the ward. Jake shifted on the bed, sitting up a little as they came in the room.

The nurse smiled and stood back out of the way as they entered, letting the police pass. After giving Jake a tight smile, the taller one with the shaved head spoke first.

"Hi, Mr. Sure? I'm Sergeant Caldwell, this is PC Brown."

"Hi. It's Jake." His voice was low and guarded.

The man's eyes flicked to Charlie and back to Jake. "Can we talk in private?"

Just as Charlie was getting up from the chair, Jake held onto her hand, stopping her. "This is my girlfriend, Charlie. She can stay."

A warmth spread through her as she sat back down, biting down on her lip while she watched the two police officers look at each other.

"We'd like to talk to you about the incident that took place on the evening of the 13th May. But before we ask you some questions, we want to inform you that last night we arrested a man who we believed to be involved in your attack. Fortunately, the man cooperated with our enquiries. This allowed us to find a Mr. Terry Jeffreys. It is to our understanding that you had told the emergency medical team that he was the man who shot you. Your stepdad?"

"Yeah. That's him." A darkness had settled over Jake's expression as he listened intently to what the Sergeant was saying, and Charlie knew he would be anxious over what they were here to tell him.

"There was an altercation between Mr. Jeffreys and the armed officers involved in the operation, at which point your stepdad was armed and perceived to be a threat, and was shot by one of the officers on scene."

Jake sat up a little, and Charlie grabbed his hand, giving him the support he needed right then.

"Mr. Jeffreys was brought into this hospital a couple of hours ago, but was pronounced dead soon after."

Charlie failed to hold in her gasp, and when Jake looked at her, his jaw was set tight, nostrils flared, and instead of seeming relieved, there was a ferocity in his eyes that confused her. The officers remained quiet, giving Jake time to process the news.

Keeping hold of his hand, Charlie moved a little closer, concerned about him. "Jake?"

His hand formed a fist under hers. "And he gets away again." Closing his eyes, his chest inflated and he let out a long breath. "He confronted you with the gun on purpose, didn't he? So you'd shoot him and he'd escape prison."

The sergeant nodded, but it was the shorter man with brown hair who answered. "We think so. He had enough warning to drop the weapon. The officer opened fire on him when he pointed the gun and charged at them."

Eyes still closed, Jake nodded. "Suicide by police. That fucking coward."

Stroking his hand, Charlie tried to reassure him. "He's gone, Jake. It's all over." Leaning forward she smoothed her hand down his cheek and he turned his head towards her.

"I wanted him to rot, Charlie. After everything he's done, I needed that."

"Jake. You need to move on. And now you have closure, you can. He's no longer able to affect you. You can start living your life—start planning your future, just like you wanted."

Reaching up with his other hand, he brushed it down his face and when he glanced at her again, she gave him a smile and nodded her head, urging him to let it go. Opening his fist, he turned his hand up and threaded his fingers through hers. "Yeah. You're right. It's over."

"Do you feel up to giving us a statement?" The sergeant asked, the formality gone from his voice.

Taking a moment, Jake closed his eyes. Then he said, "Now's as good a time as any."

Charlie didn't want to be in the way, so she got up and Jake looked at her, brow creasing. "I'm going to the canteen to get a drink. Leave you to it. Want a coffee or tea?"

"I'm good thanks."

"I'll be back in a bit."

When Charlie got out into the corridor and out of view of Jake's room, she took a moment. Standing with her back against the wall, she inhaled a few deep breaths to help calm her nerves. If she was feeling how she was right then at the news that Jake's stepdad was dead, she couldn't imagine what he was going through emotionally. Yes, she had a right to feel relieved after the man had attacked her, but he'd done so much to Jake.

It was over.

Thank God, she thought. Now, the focus could be on Jake getting better and out of here. He had a future to look forward to. And Charlie hoped that she would be a part of it.

Chapter Forty-One

"I can't believe you talked me into this. I feel disabled."

Moving through the corridor with both of their bags resting on the handlebars of the wheelchair, Charlie smiled. "You *are* disabled for the time being. You've been ordered to stay off your feet for the next week or so while you continue to heal. You agreed, and that's why they let you leave a little earlier."

"I only agreed so I could get out of here."

"Oh, so you thought I was going to let you renege on it? Yeah, I forgot you actually don't know me that well yet. I can see why you might think that was going to happen."

Jake tipped his head back and strained to look up at her. "So you're a bossy one, huh? What am I getting myself into?" The side of his mouth went up, and even upside down he took her breath away. Pulling them to a stop, she leaned over, squashing the bags to put her face by his. "You just wait. I'll be taking care of you and making sure you don't try to do too much. You're going to love me." She saw his face straighten, eyes narrowing on hers right before she kissed him quickly.

"You might be right." Then he dropped his head.

Her chest inflating, she was glad he couldn't see the wide grin that spread across her face. Wow. They'd really bonded during his time at the hospital, she'd fallen pretty bloody hard for him. There was a part of her that was worried. What if it was all because of the situation? He was elated because he'd survived. What if, when they were back in their normal environment, things weren't quite the same.

Swallowing it down, she pushed the chair, not allowing those thoughts to spoil the day. It was his *life day*, that's what he kept calling it. The day he started to live again. Even so, when they got back home, Charlie was going to make sure he didn't overdo it like she expected he would try to.

The sun was shining when they got outside. Finally, May had brought some warm weather. Only a few wisps of cloud streaked along the welcome blue sky, and the air had that fresh summer smell. Charlie saw Jake inhale the fresh air deep into his lungs, eyes closed, tipping his head back. "Shit. I wasn't sure I was going to feel that ever again."

Reaching over, Charlie placed her hand on his shoulder and he moved his head towards it, pressing his cheek on her fingers. Enjoying the moment, she closed her eyes too. Bliss. At least, it was until a horn blared, startling her from the peaceful moment. She was about to curse at whoever it was until she saw Cara springing out of Jason's car, bouncing towards her with a wide grin in her pink shorts and orange and white striped T-shirt that was knotted at the front, and matching headscarf. Smothered by her best friend as she consumed her in a tight hug, Charlie laughed and realised she could barely take air into her lungs Cara was hugging her so hard. "Can't breathe."

Pulling back like she hadn't just almost asphyxiated her, Cara moved to look at Jake. "Wow, you look tired. Anyone would think you'd just survived a gunshot wound or something." While Charlie gasped, Jake laughed.

"That? Oh, that was nothing. It was the food in there that threatened to finish me off."

Grabbing the bags from the back of the wheelchair, Cara laughed, and Charlie couldn't help laughing too. Over the last few days, Charlie had seen a big change in Jake, not only with his health, but his whole self. It was like someone had lifted a layer off him, the layer that had covered him in darkness since his mum's murder. He smiled more, that pained expression that had been constant hadn't shown up except for the time he'd received the news about his stepdad.

This was the real him. The man she knew was trying to get out of the blackness he'd been consumed by for so long.

"Bit lazy aren't you?" With a smirk, Jas was resting his arse against the back end of the car, boot open ready for their bags. He too looked all summery in light, navy joggers and a white vest top that showed off his muscled arms.

"Got to save all my energy for when I get my woman home."

Jas shrugged a shoulder and nodded as if to say "fair play" like he approved of Jake's answer. "I've got no come back for that." The two men fist bumped as Jas got up to grab the bags and put them in the boot. The reservations Jas had towards Jake were gone, thankfully. During their time at the hospital, Charlie had video called her friends, together and individually. She'd even spoke to Cara with Nathan, pleased things were going so well for her best friend. Everyone had been concerned for Jake and the banter they'd shared together had really made a difference to the way Jason, in particular, viewed Jake. It was a huge relief that they all now got on well.

"Lucky bitch," Cara muttered, softly bumping Charlie's shoulder as she walked past to go to the other side of the car.

Shaking her head, Charlie wheeled Jake to the open door of the back seat, driver's side. "Don't think for a minute you'll be doing anything strenuous for at least a week."

When Jake had transferred to the car, he pushed the chair out of the way and grabbed Charlie's hand, pulling her to him and crooking his finger for her to get down closer. "I only need to lie on my back," he said quietly in her ear while her friends were out of earshot. Warm breath tickled her skin, a shiver creeping slowly down her side. Then he kissed her lobe.

Heat rushed through Charlie from her cheeks to her toes and everywhere in between. It was hard to ignore. The man could turn her into mush in an instant, either with a look, tone of voice. Hell, she only had to be in his company and she wanted to jump his bones. She pulled back to a wolfish grin, his steely-blue eyes gleaming.

Charlie tapped the end of his nose. "Like I said, I'll take good care of you." Throwing him a wink, she moved away, still smiling at him as she grabbed the wheelchair to return it to reception.

"Shit," she heard him huff out. "Jas! How fast can you get us home?"

It was only now he was halfway up the stairs on the way to their floor that Jake realised how delicate he still was. There'd barely been any pain on the way back home in the car, not enough for him to notice anyway. Now that he'd moved more than a few feet his stomach was angry with him, pain moving right across the front, worse where his wound was. Nevertheless, he wasn't about to let Charlie see he was struggling. She'd probably get all stern with him—have him tucked up in bed the minute they got back demanding he get some rest.

Not what his plans were.

He'd had a hard-on for the first part of the journey after his mind had stayed in the gutter he'd put it in with Charlie before they'd left. Truth was, he'd been thinking about all those things the whole time he'd been in that hospital bed. The first seconds alone with her and his libido had ramped up into overdrive. Eventually, he'd managed to take his mind off it, joining in with the conversations with her friends. Now it was back, and Charlie being in such close proximity as she helped him up the stairs wasn't doing anything to cool his cockstand.

"You okay," she asked, hand on his side, her other arm around his waist, as he rested his arm over her shoulder.

No. For a number of reasons. "Yeah." It was a good job she was busy watching where they were going. One glance down and she'd know what one of the problems was.

It was still unusual, the feelings he'd been overrun with, especially lately. Jake hadn't had anyone steady in his life, not even when he was in college. There had been a few women he'd had short relationships with, if you could call it that. And a fair few one night stands. He enjoyed sex, but had never even thought of settling with someone. After prison, even less so. It wasn't in his future plans when he got out.

So it had been a shock to his system when he'd started to think about Charlie. At first, when she'd sparked an interest inside him, he'd put it down to the fact she was attractive, which he'd never denied, and his *dry spell*.

He was human, so a nice woman comes along and seems like she's showing an interest, you can't help your mind going there. Then it went there more often, to the point where she'd kept him awake at night, and it had freaked him out. Jake still felt bad about the way he'd been with her at first. It was a mixture of confusion and fear. At least now she understood his reasoning. There were times he'd wanted to tell her he liked her, but he'd fought with everything he'd had in him to keep his mind on the path he'd been on.

She'd worked her way inside of him. Without even realising, she'd undone him in a way no one ever had. Not even close. Initially, he'd only had the sole intention of getting her out of his system. But when he'd kissed her, it had changed everything. And he'd enjoyed it far too much to deny.

Jake had realised then that he liked her. A lot. She wasn't just a temptation.

Now, he couldn't seem to get enough of her.

It was like nothing he'd ever experienced before.

When they got to his door, he moved away from her body a little. "Keys are in my jacket." The pain had subsided now that he was done with the stairs.

Inside, a familiar smell hit him and he looked around like he hadn't seen the place in years. A feeling washed over him as he looked at all of his things, a sense of solace that was unfamiliar, but welcome. Sometime, amongst all the grey of his fight for survival, Jake had realised he wasn't coming back here. He'd been convinced his life was over there and then. No flat. No things. No Charlie.

"Jake? Everything okay?"

He hadn't realised he'd sat down on the sofa facing his big TV, staring ahead at the black screen. Blinking, he looked at Charlie, her blonde hair straight down over her shoulders, those beautiful green-blue eyes looking at him with concern. In that moment, Jake knew. He'd fallen in love with this woman in a big way.

Yes. Everything was more than okay.

Reaching out he grabbed Charlie's hips and pulled her to sit on his lap.

"Jake!" When she laughed it filled his chest with warmth. "What are you doing? Your stitches."

"They're fine." He reached up and put his hand on the back of her neck, already imagining those beautiful lips all over him, those hands. "I've waited long enough to have your hands on me," he said, surprised at the desperation in his voice as he pulled her, still laughing, to his mouth.

Chapter Forty-Two

Standing in front of the mirror in her bedroom, Charlie couldn't wipe the smile from her face. In the two weeks that had passed since Jake had come home from the hospital, he'd improved so much. Their relationship was now official and Charlie had honestly never felt so happy.

Tonight was so important to Jake, which was why she'd forgone her usual casual smart for a pretty little floral dress that stopped halfway down her thighs, and a pair of beige strappy sandals with a two inch heel. The music agent, who had left his card last time Jake had been at The Crow, was coming to meet with him at his gig later. A lot was riding on the whole evening. It had taken a ton of persuading, most of it without clothes, to get Jake to call the guy, but eventually he gave in. The fact that the man didn't hesitate to arrange to meet him said a lot about how keen he must be to work with Jake.

It was hardly a surprise. Charlie could be accused of being biased, but she knew Jake had the talent to take him far. If only from the response he'd already got at The Crow, the audience there was proof of it.

Charlie was probably more nervous than he was. It wasn't only his first gig since the attack; tonight he could be performing for his future. If the agent took him on, who knows what opportunities would come his way.

No one deserved it more than him.

Washing her lips in muted coral lipstick, she straightened her dress and checked herself over once more, eager to get to Jake's. Jason and Selena were picking them up in a little over an hour, so she was ready far too early; it would give her a little time with him before they left for the gig.

A knock at the door surprised her. Must be Jake. Maybe he was as keen as her. It was crazy how the butterflies multiplied in that moment. She'd only seen him an hour and a half ago when she'd called in briefly after uni.

Almost sprinting to the front door, she felt stupidly giddy when she opened it, ready to pounce on him and drag him inside.

Her blood turned to ice the moment she saw who was standing there instead of Jake.

"Hi, Char."

It would be normal to question her eyes and ears in that moment. The mousy hair was the same, but the face was smoother, clean shaven. And the clothes he wore were very different to what she'd been used to seeing him in: Dark denim jeans that were smart and looked expensive, a soft, beige woollen jumper under a grey, knee-length tailored coat. For a moment, Charlie struggled to take air in after the wind had been knocked from her lungs.

As difficult as it was, she hardened her voice. "What are you doing here, Dale?"

Honestly, she inwardly cringed at the smile he gave her. "I've been trying to get hold of you—"

"How did you get my number? My address?" The shock was wearing off now, a mix of anger and unease taking over. "Why are you even here?"

"Char, I haven't come to cause any—"

"Don't call me that." She hated that he was shortening her name, like he was familiar enough that he felt he could do that.

When he took a step forward, she put her hand up to stop him getting any closer, her heart picking up pace. It was strange to feel what she did in that moment. The last time she'd seen Dale she'd been frightened of him, cowering to his aggression. It wasn't the same anymore. It seemed she'd underestimated her strength; as she stood before him now, all she felt was contempt.

"Charlie, I'm trying to explain here." When he reached out for her she couldn't help raising her voice.

"No. Dale. I don't want you to explain anything. You need to leave."

"For God's sake Charlie. I'm trying to—"

It happened so fast that all Charlie saw was a blur before Dale was spun around. Next thing she knew, he was being held up against the wall with a pissed off Jake gripping hold of his coat with both hands.

"She told you to leave," he spat, his expression thunderous.

"Jake." Oh God. Holding his arm she tried to get him to loosen his grip on Dale. "He's not worth it."

"Who the fuck are you?" Dale snarled, struggling to move Jake's hands.

"Someone who's putting you in your place, which is long overdue from what I've heard."

The way he was manhandling Dale, Jake was at risk of doing damage to his stomach. It wasn't like she didn't appreciate his knight in shining armour act, and she definitely wasn't thinking about how hot he was right now, but he wasn't Superman. He'd been advised to take it easy for the next couple of months. Any other time, Charlie would have left him to it—it wasn't like Dale didn't deserve it—but instead she tried harder, pulling on Jake's arm and getting up into his face. "Jake. Don't. He's not worth it."

It seemed to work. Jake threw a quick glance at her and she hoped her eyes said what she didn't want to say out loud, which would expose his weakness in front of Dale. *You're going to hurt yourself.*

Loosening his hold on Dale's coat, Charlie sighed with relief as Jake took a step back. Until Dale's bruised ego got his mouth moving.

"Yeah." Straightening his coat as Jake let go, Dale's face was full of scorn. "You put your hands on me again and—"

Well, there was nothing she could do to stop the punch Jake threw his way, except for putting her arms in the air in defeat. She didn't even see where it landed, but from the *umff* Dale let out as he fell back against the wall, throwing his arm out to stop himself falling, it must have hurt.

He wiped at his lip as he righted himself. "You're a dick," he said to Jake.

Charlie grabbed hold of Jake's arm to stop him going for him again. "No. Leave it."

"I didn't come here to hurt her." Wiping his split lip again, Dale looked at the blood on the back of his hand. "I came here to apologise."

Well, that was unexpected, and for a second she was taken aback.

"What makes you think she wants to hear it?"

"Jake." Doing her best to move him back a little, Charlie looked at Dale who hadn't attempted to retaliate, which was out of character for him. It piqued her interest. "Why would you come all the way here to apologise to me? And why now? It's been a long time, Dale."

"I didn't come here especially to see you. I'm working about twenty minutes away, and seeing as you kept ignoring my calls, I thought I'd come and see you face to face."

"And how did you get my address?" First her number, now this.

"From a friend."

"What friend?" she demanded, trying to keep hold of her cool even though she also wanted to punch him in the face.

"It isn't important. If you just let me explain why I'm here, then you'll see I'm not trying to be a creep." Dale glanced at Jake as if to push that point home to him too, which again, was not like Dale. He wasn't a reasonable person. Not the Dale she'd known anyway.

Glancing at Jake, she was glad he'd stepped away, but she could see in the way he stood—arms folded, jaw tense, and nostrils twitching—that one wrong word and he would pounce. "So, what is it you do want?"

Dale ignored Jake, addressing Charlie. "Like I said. I wanted to apologise for everything I did to you. When you left, I went right off the rails with the drink. I was out of control, and I ended up in the hospital. I got a place in rehab." His rueful brown eyes looked at her, ignoring the big, towering man who was looming behind her. And as she tried to work out what his angle was, she couldn't seem to find one.

"I've sorted myself out. I did an anger management group, but it was the alcohol that was responsible for most of it. I met someone and we're getting married. I have a good life and I know now how much I ruined yours. You were the only thing I had left to fix and that's why I'm here."

Closing his eyes for a second, he frowned. When he looked at her again, he said, "I'm sorry, Charlie, for everything that I put you through. I know you won't be able to forgive me, and I honestly don't blame you. But that's not why I'm here. I just wanted to make things right, at least in some way."

Stunned by his declaration, Charlie eyed Dale suspiciously. It was strange to see him this way. It was a glimpse of who he had been when she'd first met him. And although it was unexpected, it was hard for Charlie to deny that she'd never seen him look remorseful like he did now. He appeared to be genuine. No, she would never be able to forgive him for what he did. But she could accept this from him, for her own sake, not his.

This way she could finally close the door on that part of her life.

"I accept your apology. And I do hope you'll be happy." That was it. She honestly couldn't say anything more. Thankfully, Dale didn't expect anything. He nodded, already backing away. She saw his eyes close for a moment, as if he was relieved. "Take care, Charlie." Then he turned and walked away.

As she watched him go down the hall, she edged closer to Jake and was glad when his arm went around her. Placing her hand over his stomach, she nestled into him, needing his closeness in that completely bizarre and unexpected moment.

Jake also watched Dale leave. "Suppose I gotta hand it to him. He might be a prick, but not many would do that."

Turning into him, Charlie took the sight of her gorgeous man in, looking up into his eyes, before wrapping her arms around him. He was dressed in a suit tonight, deep navy with narrow trousers and a very sexy fitted jacket that looked tailor made. He'd dressed it down a little with a black, V-neck T-shirt and some dark brown boots. She wasn't going to lie, he looked really hot. Her body close to his, she leaned her head back to look at his handsome face again; unable to believe that he was hers. "Yeah. Even the big strong boyfriend didn't put him off." She smiled at him, warmth enveloping her heart. "My hero."

"Always." He lowered his head and she met his mouth with hers, sinking into him as his arms held her close. Dale had caught her completely off guard, but in a way she was glad he'd found her. It was strange to think of him in any other way than the man who had ruined her life—trampled on her confidence. Only, she didn't feel the hate for him anymore. His admittance, the apology she never expected to receive, had given her the closure she didn't realise she needed.

Now, with Jake's stepdad gone, there was nothing in their way.

Holding onto the man who she no doubt was falling in love with, Charlie was excited for the future. She wanted Jake to be a part of it. Especially with the way he liked to kiss her.

As the kiss heated up, she couldn't help the breathy laugh she let out right then, and Jake smiled against her mouth before he pulled back to look at her.

"I didn't know you found my kisses so amusing."

"Far from it. I was just thinking, you keep that up and we'll never make it to your gig tonight."

Suddenly, she was being walked backwards. Jake kissed her nose. "Who needs a singing career anyway?" Another kiss, this time a more sensual one under her jaw that sent a shiver of arousal through her body.

Then she found herself in her hallway, recognising his roguish smile and the wicked spark in his eyes. "How much time do we have?" He kicked the flat door closed behind him.

She glanced at the clock on the wall. "Thirty six minutes."

"Plenty of time." Scooping her up into his arms caused her to laugh as she wrapped her legs around him. Thank God for the dress. With warm hands on her arse, he quickly walked to the bedroom. Then he cut her laugh off with his mouth in a hard kiss. Suddenly there was a desperation in him. After lowering her on the bed, he got up, eyes pinning her with alluring heat as he got rid of his jacket.

Licking her lips, Charlie's eyes lowered to the large bulge in his pants and she was suddenly desperate for him too.

He reached behind and produced his brown leather wallet from his back pocket. Opening it, he took out a foil packet and threw the wallet down on the floor. There was no messing about. After biting the packet open, he undid his trousers and pulled them with his boxers down his hips, the hard length of him jutting out causing Charlie to bite down on her lip. Rubbing her thighs together, she watched, her pleasure heightening at the erotic sight of him putting the condom on.

Then as he climbed on the bed, she parted her legs ready for him. He reached up her dress, his hooded eyes watching as he hooked his fingers in the waistband of her knickers, pulling them down her legs.

"I need to be inside you." His voice was thick with a need she suddenly felt as he lay on top of her. "Seeing that prick near you drove me mad." His mouth clashed with hers as he reached down between her legs. Charlie gasped into his mouth when his fingers found her. The glorious circular movement filling her with fire as she moved her hips against him.

"You're so wet already." A harsh whisper against her mouth as he slipped a finger inside her, then added another.

"That's what you do to me. Oh, *God!*"

Then his fingers were back on her swollen flesh and her head tipped back at the delicious sensation.

He moved his mouth to her ear, licking inside. "You want me inside you?" Moving his hand away, he ground his hips against her, his hard length rubbing over her, firing up all her nerve endings. God, this man did things to her, made her feel things she never realised were possible. And she was desperate for him, her body filling with heat, craving his, needing him to give her what she knew he could.

Charlie looked into his intense blue eyes. "Yes."

"You want me to fuck you?"

"Yes." *Oh God. Yes.* But it wasn't *want*. It was need. Desperate, yearning need.

She felt him reach between their bodies and then he pushed all the way into her, the sudden fullness causing her to cry out. His mouth covered hers, capturing her moan as he moved with harsh desperation. And she clung to him, holding on to him tightly, his firm body pressed up against hers, as he continued with his hard thrusts. It was everything she needed right now.

Slamming into her over and over, firing all her nerve endings, he groaned. Another thrust, then he stayed there, their hips pressed tightly together, her legs wide as she panted with need and gyrated against him.

His mouth went to her ear. "When I saw that prick at your door, I thought he was going to hurt you." His voice was ragged, trembling. His tongue licked around the shell of her ear, and he gave another hard thrust, their hips locking tight and she cried out, her body tightening with veracious need. "I will never fucking hurt you, Charlie. I'll make sure no one else will ever hurt you."

Their sex had never really been slow and sensual. There had always been an intensity to their love making; always full of passion—tension.

This time it felt like more.

It was a claiming.

"You are mine." He looked at her. "I want you to always be mine."

Then his mouth was on hers, tongue slipping inside and moving frantically with hers as he resumed those punishing thrusts, every one of them making her moan, him groan, his increasing rhythm bringing her to the edge.

"Oh, yes, *Jake*." She flew right over, her orgasm slamming into her, shattering her apart. A glorious rush of sensation soaring through her as her body contracted around his.

"*Umff*. . Shit." His head fell into the hollow of her neck as he pumped hard. Then, with a loud groan, he came, his hips jerking against hers, his body rigid under her touch. As they both came down, panting and exhausted. They held each other, hearts still racing, their bodies twitching with the tiniest movements.

Soft kisses at her neck, then moving under her jaw. Then his lips pressed against hers. "Mine," he said again against her mouth. Unmoving, he looked at her, his penetrating stare catching her breath. There was something behind his eyes that she couldn't quite decipher right then. Until. . .

"I'm in love with you, Charlie."

Pulling in a breath, Charlie's eyes blurred with tears she desperately tried to hold onto. They fell anyway, and Jake reached up, wiping them with his fingers

"I knew it in the hospital." A crease between his brows. "But I needed to make sure it was real, you know? I've never been in love before. It's been. . . confusing. I know it now with every fibre of my being."

When he smiled, Charlie's heart wanted to burst from her chest. She'd known for some time too that her feelings for him had shifted. Although she'd hoped, she never realised he felt the same way.

Moving his hand, his finger stroked her bottom lip. "How could I not fall for you? Because of you, I have worth again. You have helped me find myself again, Charlie. It's only natural I give you my heart in return."

For a moment, she was too choked up to talk, but she couldn't allow him to speak so candidly and not profess her feelings. "I love you too, Jake." More tears stinging her eyes. God, she was going to need to work miracles with her make up after this. Nerves and elation made her laugh. "I'm sorry. I just. . . I'm happy."

The smile Jake gave her was everything, his eyes lighting up. "Shit. Well. . . What a moment, huh?"

The minute he kissed her again, Charlie's phone started ringing over on the chest of drawers. She drew away from him, looking over at the little old-fashioned bell clock on her bedside table. "Shit. We're late."

Ten minutes later, and they both looked somewhat presentable.

"It's a good job I curled my hair. At least it looks like it's supposed to be this. I'm going with shaggy chic," she said, pulling her dress down over her fresh underwear.

Pausing as he walked past, Jake turned and took her face in his hands. "You look beautiful." Then his kiss was soft and slow, a contradiction to the ones he'd punished her mouth with not so long ago. "You ready?"

One last look in the mirror, even though she felt sure her lips were still swollen, and that she had "We just had mind blowing sex" written on her face somewhere, Charlie nodded and grabbed her handbag.

"We can leave as soon as you've finished, right?"

Jake gave her a beguiling smile. "Absolutely."

Epilogue

Nerves curdled Charlie's stomach as they approached The Beanery, a small cafe in the town where she lived. She'd never been here before. Most of the time she travelled into London on her days off, and in all the time she'd been in Hatfield, she'd never spent any time in the town.

Her hand was in Jake's and she couldn't tell if the sweat between their palms was from her or him. Although, she knew how nervous Jake had been about today. After all, he had every right to be. Her nerves were only for him. Still, they were very real, and had increased tenfold since they'd got out of the Audi Q2 that Jake had bought and picked up yesterday. He'd insured Charlie on the car, insisting she use it; he wanted to know she was safe travelling to and from uni. She'd reluctantly agreed. Mainly because spending the money was a big deal to Jake. The car and the new Triumph motorbike were the only things he wanted to buy with his inheritance, and he'd said he'd only bought those because they were essential. Charlie suspected that in time he'd be at peace with all the money he'd received both from his parents and the compensation he'd been awarded from the government.

Today was another step towards that inner peace.

This would be the first time Jake had spent any time with the Morgans, his little brother Jonathan's adoptive parents, other than on the doorstep of their home. They'd made things difficult for him, so he'd only seen his brother a handful of times since he'd got out of prison.

At first, they wouldn't take Jake's call. Every time he got the answering machine and they hadn't called back. Without telling Jake, Charlie had called pretending to be from an insurance company, and when they'd called back, she'd surprisingly managed to say quite a bit to the woman before she ended the call. It seemed to work. Charlie's words must have seeped through because the next time Jake called and left a message, they did call back. He'd been on the phone for almost an hour, talking to both of the Morgans on speakerphone. He'd told them about what had happened to his stepdad, and even what Terry had done to Charlie. There was even laughter on a couple of occasions. At the end of the call, Jake had asked if they could meet up with him—well, both him and Charlie—just for a talk. Surprisingly, they'd agreed.

And now they were here.

Jake pulled her to a stop right before they got to the cafe, facing her and taking her other hand in his. "I know I've told you this already, but I want to say it again." He placed his hand on her cheek as she looked into his stunning blue eyes. He'd shaved for the occasion. Charlie had only seen him a couple of times before without the stubble she loved so much, but either way he was super handsome. "I love you."

Her heart instantly melted, warmth rushing through her chest and making her inhale sharply. He'd said those words to her a number of times since the first, and she still wasn't used to it. To think she had bagged this gorgeous, caring man who was sexy as hell... It still hadn't properly sunk in.

Smiling, she stretched up to kiss him. "I love you too, Jake."

She saw his chest expand, like he was just as overwhelmed as she was.

He lightly pinched her chin. "And thank you for stalking me, even though I didn't want you to at the time."

Grin widening, Charlie felt kind of badass in that moment. To begin with. It had all been about finding out who he was. That was her mission. She never dreamed that this would be the outcome. That she'd fall in love with the stranger down the hall, and he'd love her back as fiercely.

"You're welcome."

"And thank you for going on and on about me playing at open mic night. And pushing me to arrange to meet with Tommy." Jake kissed the end of her nose this time.

"Also welcome. I know good talent when I hear it." There was another huge reason why Jake was thankful to her for pushing him, so he kept saying since the night of his last gig. The agent had been really impressed with Jake last week. So much so he'd taken him on as a client, wanted to promote him to all the top producers in and around London. Turns out Tommy Dickson is a well-known music agent, even representing some really famous and current artists.

"You just keep writing those songs. And I'll start sending them to the right people," Tommy had told Jake after they'd shaken hands on the deal.

Charlie couldn't be prouder.

"Mhmm." Jake kissed her forehead. "I'm starting to think you need a change in career."

Pausing, Charlie thought she might as well tell him her good news, seeing as it was the day for it. "Funny you should say that. So, I've discussed with my professor about changing my studies in uni. I've decided that after I finish this year, I'd like to go into social care."

His eyes narrowed, and Charlie could see he was confused.

"Because of you, Jake. I want to help people—children like your brother."

The penny dropped and Jake's eyes widened. "What about all the work you've already done? You've worked hard, and have another year to go for your psychology degree."

"It won't go anywhere. I'll always have those two years of work. If I decided social work isn't for me, I can always continue where I left off with it and sit the final year." Taking his hand again, she smiled, feeling the excitement for the future. "I know this is for me. I can feel it."

Reaching up Jake put his hands on her face, his fingers sliding under her hair. Then he bent down and kissed her. "I'm amazed by you."

Emotions so strong inflated her lungs. Pride, elation, love, there were so many she felt right then, it was overwhelming.

"You're such a charmer," she said, her head still swimming. "Come on. We're going to be late."

Turning to face the cafe, Jake straightened, his shoulders lifting like he was gearing himself up. Inhaling deeply then blowing out slowly. "Right. I'm ready."

Taking his hand, Charlie squeezed it gently, letting him know she was right there supporting him, and they headed inside.

The place was cosy: exposed brick walls, wooden beams on the ceiling, and industrial lighting. A strong smell of coffee hit you as soon as you walked in. A mix of wooden and metal tables and chairs filled the space and as they wandered through them to the counter, Charlie glanced at all the customers, looking for a couple with a young boy. As Jake ordered their drinks, she was sure she spotted them on a table towards the back. The boy had the same brown hair colour as Jake, and there was definitely a resemblance.

"I think they're over there," she told Jake quietly. When he glanced over, the grave look that quickly appeared on his face told her she'd guessed right. "Hey... It's going to be fine." The couple hadn't noticed them, but when Jake and Charlie had got their drinks and were making their way over, Jonathan glanced up and caught sight of them. The smile the boy had from something his dad had said faltered for a second. Then he shot out of his seat with the brightest expression, the widest grin Charlie had ever seen, as he ran to his brother.

"Jake!"

Tears crept into Charlie's eyes when the boy hugged Jake. They fell down her cheeks when she saw Jake's eyes close for a minute as he hugged Jonathan back. "Hey, buddy."

It moved her to see the relief on Jake's face right then and she was a little overcome herself in the moment. As an only child, she'd never got to experience that bond between siblings. She could only imagine how hard it must have been for Jake and Jonathan to have lost each other in the way they had.

Jonathan's parents looked a little uneasy, his mum more so than his dad who was the first to smile over at them.

When Jake's brother let him go, he went back to the table, eagerly telling his parents about Jake.

Stepping close to Jake, Charlie took his hand, lacing her fingers through his, using that moment to reassure him again before they reached the Morgans. "See? It's all going to work out, Jake. This is the start of your future."

Jake smiled, his handsome face never failing to make her heart skip. "*Our* future. My future started the day I met you." Leaning down, he kissed her temple and squeezed her hand. "I want you to be a part of it," he muttered, giving her a knowing look that she read clearly.

Her heart sang right then, beating hard as Charlie understood the subtext and could only just about manage a quick nod, her smile tight so she didn't get all teary again.

There was no doubt in Charlie's mind; Jake was her future too.

The door on both of their pasts had closed firmly.

Now they could look forward to that future together.

DEAR READER,

Thank you so much for reading Paper Cuts. I hope you enjoyed it. As we leave Jake and Charlie to live their happy ever after, we move on to Ryder and Frankie in Paper Chains, the second book in the Paper Cuts Trilogy. Coming soon.

Reviews really help authors, so please consider leaving a review wherever you can.

Want to know more about future releases? Sign up to my newsletter to receive news and exclusive content.

Come join my reader group on Facebook:

L.J. Sealey's Divine Hunters
Visit: www.ljsealey.com

MORE BOOKS BY L.J. SEALEY

Paranormal Romance:
THE DIVINE HUNTER SERIES:
Awaken
Dark Deliverance
Evo - A Divine Hunter World Novel
Kindred Salvation
Mortal Heart
Raziel - A Divine Hunter World Novel

STANDALONE BOOKS:
One Fated Night - Short Shifter story
Part of the Sanctuary *anthology put together by Sherrilyn Kenyon*

COMING SOON:
Daughter of Fire and Destiny
A fantasy romance

ABOUT THE AUTHOR

L.J. Sealey was born and raised in a little Welsh town by the sea. It rains a lot, so she often has a great excuse to sit at her writing desk and while away the hours at her laptop.

She still lives in N.Wales and when she's not travelling around the country working with her husband - who is a professional singer - or singing backup vocals herself, she likes to drive around the beautiful Welsh countryside. Some think it's because she enjoys the scenery; others suspect she's hunting dragons. L.J also likes to read and watch her favourite TV shows which normally include plenty of fantasy and supernatural beings. Being addicted to reading about vampires, demons, shifters and angels, she has always had a thing for all things paranormal and fantasy, and is a big sucker for impossible love stories. So it was inevitable that when she started writing herself she would mix the two together.

Official Website: www.ljsealey.com

Printed in Great Britain
by Amazon